CLEOPATRA'S VENDETTA

Born a goddess, Cleopatra died a prisoner. But the cobra's deadly kiss was just the beginning . . .

Bari, Italy, present day. Think tank Special Ops leader Timothy Stryker and his wife Angie, a self-made CEO, haven't exactly been seeing eye-to-eye. They take a much-needed Italian holiday, but it comes to a shocking end when Angie and their daughter are kidnapped.

Still raw from the death of their infant son, Stryker is desperate to rescue Angie and reconcile their differences. As he works to locate the captors' lair, he discovers the kidnappers are behind a string of recent assassinations and attempting another high-profile hit in only seven days. But when he learns their plans for his only remaining child, the scab on his heart tears open and blood begins to spill.

Working from inside her brutal captors' high-security compound, Angie realizes the cabal is hiding an ancient secret using modern propaganda techniques. And as Stryker races hitmen across India, Egypt, and Greece to thwart the next assassination and save his family, he has to connect a series of deadly dots tracing all the way back to the time of Cleopatra. Ultimately, the estranged pair must shake the deeply buried pillars of western civilization to save their four-year-old daughter from an unspeakable fate.

Fascinating, provocative, original, and timely, Cleopatra's Vendetta *is a sizzling novel that paints a disturbing picture of some of the most intricate issues that have plagued humanity's past...challenges that color our days and provide the blueprint for our future.*

ALSO BY AVANTI CENTRAE

The VanOps Series:

The Lost Power – VanOps #1
Solstice Shadows – VanOps #2
The Doomsday Medallion – VanOps #3

PRAISE FOR *CLEOPATRA'S VENDETTA*

Global Thriller First Place Winner — Chanticleer International Book Awards

Runner Up — Paris Book Festival

"Action, adventure, and suspense! A juicy thriller." —Robert Dugoni, *New York Times* & international bestselling author of the Tracy Crosswhite series

"A fascinating look at the 2000-year culture clash between male and female power systems, and the brilliant propaganda strategies that have been deployed, from ancient Rome and Egypt to modern times." —Katherine Neville, *New York Times, USA Today*, and #1 internationally bestselling author

"Race-against-time, action-packed adventure. This is a thriller that will captivate its audience from the first page." — *Manhattan Book Review*

"An adventure that will appeal to fans of Dan Brown. It's one of those rare birds: a thriller that will have you turning the pages and leave you thinking." —Debbi Mack, *New York Times* bestselling author of the Sam McRae and Erica Jensen mysteries

"If you like your modern global threats to have a dash of ancient mystery and mysticism, you're going to find yourself with some sleepless nights while reading *Cleopatra's Vendetta*." —Kevin Tumlinson, bestselling and award-winning author of *The Coelho Medallion*

"Dangerous and intoxicating." —Audrey Wilson, screenwriter, producer, and award-winning author of *Wrong Girl Gone*

"A high-stakes race that will keep the pages turning late into the night." —Sheila Lowe, author of the Claudia Rose Forensic Handwriting mystery novels

TIMELESS PRAISE FOR THE VANOPS SERIES

Critical Praise for The Lost Power:

**Genre Grand-Prize Winner
— Chanticleer International Book Awards**

Honorable Mention — Hollywood Book Festival

Bronze Medal — Wishing Shelf Book Awards

"Written with a dynamic, cinematic style and full of action and suspense, here's a book that defines page-turner. Don't miss this riveting debut!" —James Rollins, #1 *New York Times* bestselling author of *Crucible*

"A good ole' fashioned rip-roaring adventure from start to finish. Enjoy the ride." —Steve Berry, *New York Times* bestselling author

"*The Lost Power* takes readers on a fast-paced roller coaster of a ride across the globe in a top-notch thriller with high-stakes and plenty of edge-of-seat action." —Robin Burcell, *New York Times* bestselling author of *The Last Good Place* and (cowritten with Clive Cussler) *The Oracle*

"This one's a nailbiter for sure!" —*Seattle Book Review*

"This is one of the best action/thrillers I have ever read and I can't wait for the next novel in the series." —*Midwest Book Review*

Critical Praise for The Doomsday Medallion:

Honorable Mention — Southern California Book Festival

Global Thriller Finalist — Chanticleer International Book Awards

Thriller Finalist — Book Excellence Awards

"With a jaw-dropping, rewarding twist at the end, every mystery, crime, and thriller fan should read *The Doomsday Medallion*." —*San Francisco Book Review*

"An epic and bewitching mashup of historical suspense and political thriller. Perfect for fans of Steve Berry and James Rollins." —BestThrillers.com

"Masterful. A perfect blend of roller-coaster thrill ride and historical revelation." —David S. Brody, bestselling author of *Cabal of the Westford Knight*

"An action-packed, high-stakes journey." —Al Pessin, multi-award-winning author of the Task Force Epsilon thrillers

"Centrae is a master of the page-turner. It wouldn't surprise me if Nostradamus himself predicted *The Doomsday Medallion* would be a bestseller." —Rob Samborn, author of *The Prisoner of Paradise*

"One of the best thrillers of the year." —Rick Treon, author of *Divided States*, a 2021 Best Thriller Book Awards finalist

"Sizzles with suspense!" —Elena Taylor, award-winning, bestselling author of *All We Buried*

CLEOPATRA'S VENDETTA

A STRYKER THRILLER

AVANTI CENTRAE

For Dad
USMC Corporal Don L. Baker
1940–1995

And to the gamut of heroes and heroines who save us from skinned knees, burning buildings, and the potential hell of a nuclear World War.

"The victor will not be asked whether he told the truth."

—Adolf Hitler

PROLOGUE

Alexandria, Egypt
The 10th day of Mesori, the fourth month of
the Season of the Harvest
(August 10, 30 BC)

Born a goddess, she would die a prisoner. On the frankincense-imbued balcony, Cleopatra VII Philopator smiled ruefully at the irony as she paced back and forth, watching for her faithful spy. The man was tasked with bringing her what she needed to end her life and exact her revenge. The weight of her legacy rested on his narrow shoulders now.

She stopped pacing. Her hands clenched the railing until she thought the stout wood might break. Neither immortality nor freedom was to be hers any longer. Night was falling on the day, her reign, and her life. It was time to die.

An emotional pain unlike any she'd ever known ripped through her. As if punctuating her distress, guards marched below her balcony, their leather boots slapping the paving stones with a noise like palms striking her proud cheeks.

She doubled over and put her hands to her knees.

It was all Octavian's fault. She wished she could have him impaled, as she'd had other treasonous villains.

Octavian. Julius Caesar's heir. Her nemesis.

Last fall, he'd defeated her and Marcus Antonius, her lover, in a horrid naval battle at Actium. Afterward, she and her love had fled here to Alexandria. Back in her palace, it soon became clear that no allies were coming to their aid. She'd had nearly a year to prepare for Octavian's inevitable invasion, and now it was upon her.

This elaborate two-story building attached to her balcony had been designed as a last holdout on a spit of sandy beach near the palace, but as soon as troops entered the city, she and her two loyal maids, Iras and Charmion, were put under house arrest inside. The space still held the subtle scent of the cedar and cinnamon oils she'd used to prepare her lover's body for burial. A single tear dropped from the corner of her black-rimmed eye, causing the dust between her feet to explode upward in a violent puff.

She straightened and stared out beyond the balcony, into the vermillion sunset, imagining different places in the imperial city where she could gut Octavian with her own knife. She knew the layout of the streets well, as the city had been hers for twenty-two years. With its fragrant spice stands, baths, synagogues, libraries, gymnasium, and famed lighthouse, it was the most magnificent metropolis in the world. Within the limestone city walls were two Isis temples, including one she'd commissioned herself. *Ambushing and killing him there would be appropriate*, she mused. The rectangular Serapeum, another splendid temple, was outfitted with gold-leaf, silver, and bronze, and looked over the shadowed city from its artificial hill in the Greek quarter.

This sultry city put the bastard's rat-infested town to shame.

Except the people of Rome had fallen for Octavian's propaganda. And it had cost her the war.

Despite succeeding at so much, she'd failed to keep her children and country safe from the insatiable Romans. The red-tiled homes and businesses were no longer hers, and although she'd tried to bargain for her children's right to rule, she doubted they would live to see another summer, especially Caesarion, her firstborn, who'd been dispatched up the Nile with chests full of gold.

An insistent knock came at the door to her bed chamber. A guard announced that a farmer had brought figs.

She turned and left the balcony, moving to the candlelit foyer where her best spy stood on the tiled mosaic. The clever man had passed by her window unnoticed and managed to talk his way past the guards. Slightly less than standard height and weight, he had a way of blending in, no matter the situation. Today he wore a commoner's tunic. She glanced at him and he nodded imperceptibly. Satisfaction spiked through her veins.

Yesterday evening, she'd received word from a young aristocrat that Octavian was going to head back to Rome with her in three days. If she allowed him to return her to the city she'd enjoyed with Julius Caesar, she'd be paraded through the streets wearing golden shackles and nothing else. After years of fighting Octavian's lies, she would not give her enemy the final satisfaction of humiliating her, so this last, desperate plan had been set in motion.

After the guard closed the door, the spy handed his basket to Iras, who began removing the false bottom. Inside was a young asp, which Charmion pushed to the side so Iras could extract the other, special item. The asp hissed in annoyance.

As far back as Egyptian history recorded, the rearing cobra was a sign of royalty and divine authority, perhaps because Isis had used a snake to win the throne for her husband, Osiris. The creatures also rid the storehouses of the mice that fed on precious grain. Cleopatra's grandmother had kept asps to terrify her enemies. Royal tombs were protected by cobras, who would spit poison at robbers. The snake in the basket would serve a similar purpose.

She huffed out a breath in irritation that the Romans had turned the snake into a symbol of evil.

Her spy prostrated himself before her. "My queen," he whispered.

"My final journey must begin," she said, also in a hushed tone. "Stand and tell me news before I depart. What about the pamphlets in Rome?"

The leaflets Octavian and his cursed minions, the Sons of Adam, had distributed in that backward town defamed her. She—Queen of Kings, Mother of Kings, the Youngest Goddess—had been accused of having power from Hades, of being a living pestilence and a bloodthirsty harlot who desired to rule Rome.

The spy sprung to his feet, his face struggling not to betray the deep loyalty she knew he felt for her, his queen. He said, "The false stories continue. And a sculpture of Marcus Antonius oozes blood."

"In Greece?"

"I'm sorry to report the enemy has toppled the statues of you and Antonius in the Acropolis and replaced them with two-headed serpents."

Those lies, false signs, and underhanded machinations had caused many to defect from Antonius to the younger Octavian, and had altered the balance of the fighting.

In reality, she knew the conflict she and Octavian waged was the continuation of a two-thousand-year-old war, but that didn't lessen the sting of defeat. A pulse in her temple throbbed. Anger. Frustration. No. It was *rage* she felt. She'd hoped her ascent to power would turn the tide. But it hadn't.

Even with her Roman friends and lovers she'd been unable to stem the flow. The Sons of Adam and their ideas had flooded the land like the waters of the Nile. Slow but inexorable. She'd been impotent in the face of their movement and the thought of their victory nearly blew the striped cloth off her head.

She looked into the spy's amber eyes. "And what of your most sacred mission?"

A smile lit his features. "I finally found their stronghold!"

Wanting to cut the head off Octavian's vile insect, she'd had spies seeking the location of his cult for years. Every bit of information she'd collected had gone into her gold journal, already consigned to its own hiding place thanks to this worthy man.

"Is it an island?" she asked.

"Yes, but not where we thought."

"Where then?"

He told her.

She closed her eyes, savoring the long-sought victory. Octavian's supporters had showed themselves to be well-trained, even if the morose little man wore lifts in his shoes.

"My queen?" he asked.

She opened her eyes and graced him with a full smile. When he looked away, embarrassed by her favor, she tugged on his chin so he would focus. "Evade any followers, no matter the time or cost, and go to where you hid the cache for me. Make a map of their location on an onyx writing tablet and put it on the dais. Seal the location as we discussed."

He stood up straighter. "I promise."

She hoped his pledge and skills would be enough. "Then travel to a distant city to buy your coffin before you join me in the afterlife. Maybe Tripoli or Cyrene."

A light filled his eyes. "I may join you?"

"Yes. You've served me well. Give these to your family beforehand." She handed him two gold coins made in her image that she'd secreted away, along with a heart scarab amulet to ease his journey through the underworld. "Now go."

He bowed a final time before leaving.

Motioning for the guards to wait, she took a deep breath and moved to a desk of Lebanese cedar inlaid with mother-of-pearl. Setting her royal seal to a pre-written letter, she handed the missive to one of the sentries. It was addressed to Octavian. He would read it and know she was dead. Things must move quickly now.

The guards bolted the door. The rough sound acted like an alarm, causing her maids to spring into action. The women dressed her a final time.

As the clothing ritual wore on, Cleopatra considered the good news from her spy. This last stratagem had the potential to rewrite her legacy. Revealing the island location of the Sons of Adam would cost them dearly. Her other possible revenge would be found in the Vault of Sacred Objects, where he would hide the onyx map among the treasure she'd accumulated in response to hundreds of years of propaganda and destruction by the cult. During her reign, she'd used love and tenderness to fill the vault, and it was a sight to behold.

The maids administered their last rites, and then used her makeup and hairpins to add the requested sign on her forearm. She thought of a favorite quote from Homer, "She was smiling through her tears" and wished she *could* find humor at outwitting Octavian in the end. Instead, she laid back upon the golden lion-pawed couch, holding her pharaonic blue-copper-banded ivory crook and flail in a death grip.

Within minutes, she'd join her love, Marcus Antonius, in a solar bark on the journey to the underworld and everlasting life. She wished her children safety and joy.

The solid-gold lion heads at the corners of the couch sheltered her as the poison painlessly crept through her senses. Soon, ecstasy filled her spine and she began to let go by focusing on the top of her head, as she'd been taught by the priests. Memories of her time came and went. Her last vision was of her gold journal.

Hidden from even the most determined grave robbers, she hoped her heirs would appreciate what she'd stashed, but worried that Octavian and his men would find a way to thwart even this last campaign.

Would the Sons of Adam, and their evil, finally be destroyed?

CHAPTER 1

Jeddah, Saudi Arabia
Present Day
Day One

As he stepped behind a palm frond to disguise his movements, Timothy Stryker wondered why world leaders were being picked off like tin cans atop a fence at a hillbilly family reunion. Raising his Futures Command special-issue mini-binocs to his eyes, he scanned the royal palace grounds for any threat to the Saudi crown prince, who was currently neck-deep in a seaside hot tub.

Stryker's wife, back in Bari, was probably soaking too, in their less-luxurious hotel spa. A muscle in his jaw flexed. He'd been fantasizing about a sensual holiday with Angie for months, and was irritated that their time together in Italy had been interrupted by the encrypted phone call last night.

Five feet away, looking the part of a local landscaper in loose-fitting gray and blue clothes, Jerónimo Guerrero Reyes, Stryker's best friend and a member of his M2 team, raked fallen palm fronds like a pro under a leaden sky.

"Anything?" his friend murmured.

Stryker replaced the binocs inside his own loose-fitting shirt and stepped out from underneath the leaves. An itchy but realistic silicone mask concealed his entire head and most of his chest. His ginger hair appeared black. They both wore body armor and colored contact lenses. Knowing there was no need to disguise his Chicago-area accent in this coded conversation, he replied softly into his custom-fit molar microphone, "Nope. The crown prince is relaxing in the spa by pool number two."

The prince's two lapis-lazuli pools, like the eighty-five acres that surrounded the palace, oozed modern sensibility and elegant design. The swimming area abutted the Red Sea and a private harbor, which held the family's sleek, low-slung yacht. Numerous helipads dotted the landscape, handy for a quick escape. Groups of women in head-to-toe black burqas moved like flocks of starlings through the grounds, passing knots of security guards surreptitiously stationed throughout. One guard had a Belgian Malinois, which made Stryker miss the family German shepherd back home.

Still, it all seemed oppressively quiet. No birds chittered in the trees, and in the distance, there was only the throaty growl of a lone motorboat. A low blanket of gunmetal-gray clouds made the air feel dense and heavy.

Reyes, who went by Rey when he didn't have an operational call sign, picked up some of the dead palm branches and deposited them into the short bed of an all-terrain vehicle. "Think an assassin will really take a shot at the prince?"

"Someone in Saudi Arabia is the next target," Stryker replied. "Director Wolff said it was a solid signals intelligence hit."

"That SIGINT must have been good to pull you off your fancy Italian holiday."

"Agreed. I was surprised to get the assignment last night. Sounds like the director is doing a favor for some friends in the beltway. At least Sam got to stay back in Bari." His sister-in-law, Samantha Coin, was still in Italy with his wife and daughter. Apparently, there had been enough resources to cover the other Saudi hot spots, like Riyadh, where the king was today.

Their team did deniable black ops field work for the US Futures Command, a forward-looking Army think tank that took a problem-solving approach rather than a guns-first style. A hidden hand within a hidden game, on paper they were part of the Army's Budget and Finance department. Although they had plenty of paramilitary training, they were the team that was called into delicate situations where the government needed more brains than brawn. Like now.

"Weird that our mission is just to provide eyes and ears for the Saudis, though," Rey said.

"Not really. Leadership wants to interrogate anyone who fires on the prince so they can figure out why those other world leaders have been knocked off."

Rey nabbed the water bottle from the ATV and drank. The bottle was fitted with a long-range surveillance microphone built on acoustic radar technology. "Why target the crown prince?" He wiped water off his fake beard with the back of his hand. Under the mask he had a more lustrous black mustache.

Stryker took the bottle and pretended to take a swig while he focused on the lush, out-of-place-in-the-desert gardens. He listened to the conversation about soccer happening between two guards near the ostentatiously jeweled fountain, easily translating the Arabic. Languages were one of his strengths. Thanks to his younger sister, who had been born deaf, he was grateful that he could also read lips.

"Why *not* target the prince?" Stryker asked. "Dead men don't bite. And besides, he's ticked off some religious leaders, right?"

"Yeah. He was instrumental in allowing female drivers, and isn't against things like film and pop music. Or alcohol. He thinks it should be part of the kingdom's new tourism push."

"That's probably your answer then."

"Maybe. Could be a cousin who's under the gun, though. Royals are always killing each other." Rey touched the lucky St. Christopher medallion inside his shirt.

Stryker's friend was into lucky charms, astrology, and palm readers. He preferred the special energy drinks made by the think tank and the magic of meditation. Too bad those enchantments hadn't been helping him relate to his wife of late.

"I think cousin-killing has been out of fashion for a few centuries," Stryker said. "More likely, this is related to all the high-profile assassinations. Britain's PM, a US senator, and the German chancellor. All killed in the last three months with no one claiming responsibility."

Rey picked up his rake and began attacking the palm fronds again. "Then I hope we can capture one of the assassins and learn the truth about their motives. It's probably a worldwide conspiracy."

"You always say that. Maybe it's just a loner with a grudge." Stryker paused. "Could be they go after a different royal. My money is on the king over in Riyadh."

"Bet on it?"

"Nah, that's your thing with Sam." Sam loved to gamble, and she and Rey bet on everything. On their last mission, they'd wagered on who would get the first wound, and Sam had won, getting a slash to her thigh as the prize. It hadn't stopped her from getting the USB data stick they'd needed, though. She'd done well, while he'd felt rusty. Actually, he hadn't felt on top of his game for months.

As they continued their landscaping ruse, Stryker wondered how the wedding party was getting along. Some of the women had been going to take a day trip to Bari. For once, he'd been bummed to get called up on a mission as he and Angie hadn't had a chance to make up from last night's humdinger of a fight, and he'd been enjoying the vacation with his young daughter. Harper was at that really fun four-year-old stage when the whole world seemed full of wonder and discovery. Today was to have been a father–daughter trip to an old castle. He huffed and raked the sand into Zen garden patterns.

Across the dark sea, a gust of cool wind rustled the leaves of nearby plants. The sound reminded him of visiting the barren cemetery where his father, mother, and sister were buried. On cold November days when he and his aunt would commemorate his mom's birthday, dry maple leaves the color of blood would blow around his small tennis shoes as he stared at the three granite headstones and held back tears.

Trying to forget that morbid memory, Stryker returned to the cover of the tree. They'd chosen this spot for its good view of the pools, where security had said the prince would be for the afternoon. The royal liked to conduct business on the phone under the shade of an awning. Assistant Director St. James and the prince's security detail had tried to get their big shot to stay inside, but the man refused to modify his routine. Although Stryker loved order more than the next guy, routines worried him because they made targets easier to kill. What was it about powerful people that made them feel immortal?

Pulling the mini-binocs out of his tunic, he studied the crown prince. The muscled royal had emerged from the hot tub, but kept his legs dangling in the water. Stryker scanned the area again for obvious sniper nests. The palace roof had a few hiding spots. That yacht had a lower profile than many luxury models, but would present good line of sight if the killer managed to get past security. The prince stood, and another man handed him a towel, which the prince used to dry off while gazing out to sea. Through lip-reading, Stryker gathered they were discussing the early January weather. A low-pressure system on the way from Europe was due to bring a week of cold rain. Maybe even sleet and ice. He glanced at the dark sky. No moisture yet.

He returned his focus to the prince in time to see a black dot form on the man's forehead. Without waiting to see the corresponding spray of blood that announced the royal's demise, Stryker swore as he scanned the area. Nothing on the yacht. No movement on the roof of the palace. But in the middle of the harbor, a large buoy moved, and the black tip of a rifle muzzle disappeared straight down into the water like a modern incarnation of Excalibur. Small ripples appeared on the sea's glassy surface.

Stryker took off at a dead run toward the harbor, Rey not far behind him.

Sprinting through the gardens, Stryker flew past the gurgling fountain and one of the vacant helipads to his far right. No other ripples or bubbles came off the harbor buoy. Legs burning with the effort, Stryker bolted past where men had gathered around the fallen prince and raced down the long dock, breathing hard, his footsteps echoing off the wood. Without breaking stride, he executed a perfect dive into the water's black depths.

CHAPTER 2

Bari, Italy
Day One

Ignoring the catcalls from the young men zipping by on Vespa motorbikes, Angie Stryker entered the dark Italian pub, pushed by an icy wind at her back. Sea wind always felt colder. She shivered in her expensive black down jacket, adjusted her silk scarf, and turned to her two friends. "I thought Italy was supposed to be warm."

"Me too," Zoe said. "Let's get a drink and warm up."

"Pronto!" Reno said playfully.

As her friends headed to the bar, Angie worked on getting the kids situated at a nearby booth with coloring books, grateful there was no age limit at watering holes in Italy. Reno had brought her daughter, Layla, and Angie's four-year-old daughter, Harper, was there as well. Harper had been quiet the last year and Angie had hoped this vacation would help bring her daughter out of her shell. The girls giggled and talked together as they settled in, which Angie took as a good sign. Layla was two years older than Harper and the girls had become fast friends, just like their moms had in college.

Once the kids were happily coloring, Angie joined the adults sitting at the far-right end of the long wooden bar, glad they'd gone along with her idea to grab a drink after lunch.

As an undercover agent for the CIA, Angie had been trained to keep her eyes open. The place had much in common with bars she'd visited around the world while doing business and gathering intelligence. Dimly lit interior? Check. Polished bar with handsome barkeep? Check. Red leather booths filled with jovial locals? She checked that box as well. The bar's only unique aspect was the sophisticated black-and-white vineyard photographs on the wood-paneled walls. Smoke from the patrons' cigarettes drifted around their heads, moved more than removed by the Casablanca-style fan that swirled overhead.

She noted several men giving her group a once-over. The particularly good-looking male specimens of the Italian variety sat at a table at the other end of the bar. Wide smiles. Bright teeth. Roman noses. But why wouldn't they look? She and her single friends had gussied up for the day trip to Bari.

With long dark hair, prominent cheekbones and deep-set brown eyes, Zoe looked like a tall Italian model, while Reno had the fair complexion of a maiden from the British Isles with the reddish hair to match. And although her friends often kidded her that she looked like the elves in *The Hobbit* movie due to her blonde hair and petite frame, Angie knew she could still turn heads.

Angie pushed her expensive GPS-enhanced tortoiseshell sunglasses—a gift from her currently annoying husband, Tim—onto her head and turned her attention to the menu the bartender had placed in front of them.

"*Buona giornata, signora.* How may I help your day?"

"We had lunch earlier," Zoe replied. "What do you suggest to warm up?"

He grinned at her. "Our Amaretto hot toddy is world famous."

Zoe nodded. "I'm in."

The bartender looked at Angie and Reno.

"Sounds good to me," Angie said. She preferred high-end whisky and fine wine, but decided to branch out. They were on vacation.

"Me too," Reno agreed.

Zoe put her arms on the counter and looked at her friends. "I'm so glad we were all able to come on this trip."

"Work has been insane. Happy to get a break," Angie said. It wasn't a lie, but she was tempted to sneak onto email to see the latest offer from one of the big oil boys. Not that she wanted to sell, but it was fun to see what they thought her biofuel company was worth. The last offer had been twenty-five million.

For a time, they talked about Peter and Casey's beautiful beachside wedding. They'd all known Peter in college. While they chattered, Angie kept a close eye on the girls. Harper seemed happy to be enjoying some adult-free time. Her head was bent and focused on coloring. She wore her favorite jeans today, the ones with the adorable cat faces on the knees.

During a break in the conversation, Angie walked over to see what Harper was working on. The color scheme was a surprise. "Where's all the yellow?"

"I'm not into yellow, Mom."

"But yellow's your favorite color."

"Not anymore. Now I like blue."

Angie put her hands on her hips and cocked an eyebrow, wondering how she'd missed this change. "Okay, honey, have fun. Let me know if you get bored and want to watch our favorite movie." Knowing the attention span of young children, she'd downloaded the flick on a tablet in case the girls got bored.

Returning to the bar, warmth spread through Angie's chest. She'd do anything for that little girl.

The bartender brought their drinks, pointing to indicate the handsome men she'd noticed earlier had paid the tab. She and her friends waved their thanks and got smiles in return. Angie took a whiff of the lemon-garnished beverage. It had a nice, sweet almond scent, like a fortune cookie. God, she was ready for a drink. When the alcohol hit her stomach, she relaxed into the warm flush.

When the conversation turned to family, Angie dutifully brought out her phone and showed pictures of her house in Key West and her mom's recent birthday party. As was typical, her sister, Sam, was a loud presence in the party pics, photo-bombing their mother with bunny ears and even flashing a delicately placed tattoo at one point. Her sis, who had blown off the day trip to find a poker game, had Halle Berry-ish features from their dad, and a white streak in her dark hair, whereas Angie's skunk streak was barely perceptible in the light blonde hair she'd inherited from their mom. Angie was glad Harper had her father's ginger tint instead. Angie recalled the reddish hair color of the baby she'd recently lost to brain cancer. He'd been home for only three hundred and sixty-three days.

"Angie?" Reno asked.

Angie shook off that train-wreck of a thought. "Yeah?"

Reno put her hand on Angie's forearm. "You okay?"

"Sure. Just … yeah, I'm fine." She heard the southern accent in her voice. It got more pronounced when she was upset.

Tapping her foot on the barstool, she took another drink. The creamy hint of almond made her feel like she was drinking a rich dessert. That must be why the drink was a little cloudier than she remembered.

She started to feel the familiar flush of alcohol. After the wedding reception last night, she'd stumbled on a stair on the way back to their room. Tim had berated her for drinking and lying about it. They'd gotten into a full-on fight. He'd even threatened her with divorce.

Screw him. She could handle her drink.

The guys across the bar also bought the next round. It seemed the tallest of the bunch, his smile wide and on the toothy side, was their leader, while a broad-shouldered man with a ponytail seemed more serious. Angie wondered when the men would come over and say hello to see if their time-worn mating ritual had borne fruit.

Zoe was currently sharing pictures of her dog, a German shepherd like Angie's Sierra von Skye. Reno countered with a picture of her black cat drinking water from a faucet.

"Hey, want to do a Facebook live session for our friends back home?" Zoe asked.

Angie and Reno nodded.

Zoe brought up the app and started filming. She swept the dimly lit bar, narrating the events of the wedding and giving a virtual tour like a roving reporter. The girls looked up long enough from their coloring to stick out their tongues.

"Tell everyone hi!" Zoe said.

Angie and Reno laughed and waved.

Zoe ended the transmission and sent it whirling into the Facebook-sphere.

There were fresh drinks on the bar. Angie decided to take this one slow, to prove that she could pace herself.

Twenty-five minutes later, Reno said, "I think I've had enough. Let's use the ladies' room and head back."

Zoe nodded. "Yeah, I'm feeling a little bit sick. Probably that spicy fish we had for lunch."

Angie hadn't had the fish, but felt rather lightheaded herself. The three of them got unsteadily to their feet and had the kids join them.

"Mom, do we have to leave?"

Angie reached down to hold Harper's hand. "Yes. It's time to go, honey."

Angie noticed that the men who'd bought the drinks also stood. As she and her friends headed down the hall to the restroom, Zoe used the wall for balance and Reno tottered.

Inside the lavatory, Reno and Zoe both rushed to a stall and threw up. Harper and Layla went into a stall, too.

Angie's world began to spin. She leaned against the wall next to the sink for support. Alcohol hadn't given her the spins in years. Had they been drugged?

"Hey, do you guys think . . ."

Her words trailed off as she slid to the floor and passed out.

When she came to, she was in an alley, near a black van, its rear door flung open. Night was coming on and the cold wind from earlier cut through her foggy brain. Where was Harper? Layla? Reno's leg was visible in the back of the van, unmoving as an Italian marble statue. Were the girls in there too?

Panic gripped Angie's chest and her heart began to beat wildly. Harper! She couldn't let anything happen to her baby girl.

She tried to move toward the van, but her limbs felt like they were encased in concrete and her mouth was desert dry.

They'd definitely been drugged. And were getting kidnapped, too. Could she stop it somehow?

Short Ponytail Man had a strong grip on Angie's upper arm. About six feet away, a man was pounding a sledgehammer onto a bulging cloth bag. The sound of crunching electronics filled the air. God, was he destroying their phones? Nearby, his buddy was scanning Zoe, with what—a biometrics tracker? Who were these guys?

She swore—somehow her sunglasses were still on her head. If they used their wand on them, she might be made as CIA. Couldn't let that happen.

Angie tried to yell, but the scarf she'd worn earlier was stuffed in her mouth. She'd had some Krav Maga training but was only a G3 blue belt. Besides, her hands were zip-tied behind her back and she had trouble controlling her muscles enough to stand. She tried to wiggle out of her assailant's grip, but he held her tight. She needed to get to Harper.

Zoe suddenly kicked out at one of the assailants, setting off a flurried struggle between her and her two guards.

Angie used the distraction to gather her strength and headbutt the broad-shouldered man holding her. Mercifully, the sunglasses dropped off her head and onto the street. When he slapped her across the face, she managed to knee him and bring her boot heel down on the sunglasses. The shades broke into dozens of tiny brown and black pieces.

A flash of silver metal flew across Zoe's neck. She crumpled to the pavement.

Before Angie could attempt to scream, a strike to her temple caused the world to again fade to black.

CHAPTER 3

Jeddah, Saudi Arabia
Day One

After using a metal ladder to climb out of the water onto the deserted back deck of the deceased crown prince's yacht, Stryker and Rey stripped off their wetsuits and dumped the dripping scuba gear to the floor. Stryker carefully dried off the silicone mask that still hid his true features, toweled his back more roughly, and then looked out to the dark sea. After an unsuccessful first dive, he and Rey had come back with suits and waterproof flashlights, but still no luck. Night had fallen while they'd searched the depths of the harbor and the cool wind gave him goosebumps.

He threw on his clothes and turned to Rey. "Didn't leave a trace."

"Nope. I was hoping he'd have dropped the dry bag at least."

Stryker bent over and grabbed his wetsuit, wondering if he could hang it somewhere to drain. "How do you figure he did it?"

"Probably had a team member on a submersible nearby. Swam in with a short rifle bundled up in a dry bag. Maybe had a drone in the sky to tell him when the prince got out of the pool. Used the buoy as a shelf. And pop."

"Agreed. The moss on the buoy chain was the only thing disturbed." Stryker settled for folding the wetsuit over the back of a chair. "He could have tied the dry sack to it while he fired. Still, tough shot."

Rey's currently brown eyes crinkled. "It was definitely a three-point shot from downtown."

Rey loved gathering intel so much that it was sometimes hard to remember that he'd once been a college basketball star. He'd grown up a middle-class Hispanic in Minnesota, and did both distinctive accents well. He held dual degrees in mechanical engineering and information technology. When overlooked in the NBA draft because he was only a scrawny six-footer, he'd chosen the Air Force over his father's lucrative medical supplies company. Still, between his ocular albinism, and a sensitivity to smells and noise made worse by PTSD, he'd never felt like he fit in, or so he had confessed to Stryker one night over a beer.

Stryker also loved their work, and, like Rey, he too had scars. When he was seven, his father had killed his sister and mother, nearly taking him out in the process. He ended up with a missing fingertip and a personality that leaned toward being brutally honest, which had gotten him kicked out of the military after a contentious whistle-blowing incident.

While temporarily deployed overseas on a desert mission, some of the guys in his unit had taken to harassing the team's handful of women 'two-stripers.' It began with butt slapping at the dinner table and worsened until one of the women came to breakfast with a shiner and fear in her green eyes. When he'd finally gotten her to open up, he'd discovered she'd been raped the night before by three airmen. Stryker confronted the men, who denied it while winking at each other. He'd gotten ticked off, and a sand fight had ensued. Given the three-to-one odds, it hadn't gone well for him; he'd earned a busted lip and his eye had been swollen shut for a week. He'd taken the issue to the commander, who was old friends with one of the airmen's father, and ignored the charge. Haunted by the look in the young woman's eyes, Stryker had escalated it up the chain of command until it, and his Air Force career, were finished.

He'd do it again in a heartbeat. Even though the military had made strides with their zero-tolerance policies toward sexual misconduct, until the old guard passed on, he was better off with the Army think tank. Which brought his attention back to the mission at hand.

Stryker said, "With a drone, he could have limited his time above water to, say, fifteen seconds."

"They were good."

"Yeah, but who are 'they'?"

"The question of the hour, my friend."

Footsteps echoed in the interior of the vessel. Probably a guard who was left behind. Most of the royal security detail had flown out of the harbor in speedboats to search nearby motorboats while Stryker and Rey did the underwater detective work.

Stryker's encrypted phone buzzed. "Want to debrief the locals while I take this call?"

"Sure."

Stryker headed toward the shadows of the bow, where the ship had a helipad and he could speak in private. He looked at the screen. Sam's name flashed.

He hoped his wife, Angie, and her sister, Sam, were still having fun at the wedding. Until yesterday, the holiday had been a nice break between missions, though he was never truly off work.

Angie, CEO of the world's first successful algae-fuel renewables company, was an agent for the CIA's National

Resources division. Like other recruited executives, she was trained to gather information while traveling on business, and her global intel had been amazing. When you were in covert ops, it was easier if your family was, too. Easier, but not easy—the proof of that was in the disagreement they'd had last night. His lovely wife hadn't had a vacation in years and they'd ruined it with a blowout.

As he'd been trained, he quickly blocked that train of thought. Too distracting.

He authenticated through voice recognition before answering. "Hey, Sam, what's up?"

He and Sam had been raw Air Force recruits together over a decade ago, when she'd quickly won him over with her infectious sense of humor. She'd been there laughing when he got a crossbow tattoo on his shoulder, and later she'd introduced him to her younger sister. Angie had been everything he'd ever wanted in a woman . . . at least until they'd lost the baby.

"Been trying to reach you."

Her smooth-as-honey southern voice was lower than her sister's. More of a contralto. Tight now with worry.

"Been underwater. Didn't HQ tell you the Crown Prince was assassinated?"

"Angie and Harper are missing."

The breath left his lungs in a rush. His feet stopped moving in the dead center of the helipad and he doubled over, one hand on a knee, like he'd taken a punch to the sternum. When he could speak, he said, "Talk to me. What do you know?"

"Not much. She, Zoe, and Reno went into Bari for lunch with the kids. I wanted some playtime, found a back-room poker game. They never came back."

Maybe they were okay. More information was necessary. He straightened up. "When were they due?"

"Late afternoon. Before dark. We were going to have a sunset drink."

He started to pace the broad upper deck, glad he was alone. "And no answer on her phone?"

"Right."

"Texts?"

"They enjoyed lunch and were going to get a drink before heading back."

"Maybe they just tied one on." Angie loved her whisky too much these days. But he held his tongue about the drinking issue. It was none of Sam's business and he wanted to find out if Angie was truly missing.

"Maybe. But not one of the three is answering." Sam paused. "I know you guys had a doozy of a fight last night."

Stryker ground his teeth together. Why did Angie have to blab about that? "We had a disagreement, that's true."

"I hate to ask this . . . but do you think she might have taken off somewhere?"

"What? No!"

"She said you threatened divorce if she didn't stop drinking."

He regretted using the D word, but had felt at the end of his rope. "She said I didn't care about Malachi's death. And there's two sides to every story." He clenched his fists. "She needs help, Sam."

"She's grieving."

Heat began to rise into his face. "Not in a good way."

"Be that as it may, right now she's missing. So could she have run off?"

A mixture of sweat, fueled by fear and anger, dampened his temples. "You know your sister better than I do. Angie's not a runner. She's a CEO, for God's sake. She's used to conflict."

"She just doesn't like it at home," Sam snapped.

He did his best to keep his tone level but his words still came out as a growl. "You have no idea the impact her drinking has on me, or Harper."

Sam took an audible breath. "Look. I'm just worried."

"Me too." He made a conscious effort to calm down with a deep breath of his own. "Why don't we call in the posse? Have you reached out to Assistant Director St. James and Ace back at HQ?"

Ace Majeski, former Navy pilot turned intelligence officer, had recently become St. James's right hand at headquarters. Her position was well-deserved, as the intel she'd dug out of the dark recesses of the world wide web on their last mission had been crucial to their success.

"They're already sniffing around. Don't you have an app that can check on Angie's sunglasses?"

His shoulder ached and he stretched his neck. "Yes. I was just going to look at that. Hold on."

"I have a call coming in from Ace. Let me call you back."

"Okay."

He hung up and made his feet move to the bow of the ship. Although his body usually ran hot, the whipping wind chilled him to the bone. He knew in his gut that Angie hadn't run away. Was she kidnapped by an oil baron who felt threatened by her new biofuel tech? Perhaps an enemy of the state who wanted the secrets she had in her head from the work her company did undercover for the think tank? Or did the disappearance relate to Angie's CIA work? He'd gotten her involved in that in the first place. She had been given some training in Israeli martial arts as soon as he'd hooked her up with the agency, but she was only a level-three blue belt. She didn't have his full black ops background.

And even more—what if something had happened to Harper?

His heart began to race, like a small caged animal clawing at the glass wall of its enclosure to break free.

As fast as he could, he swiped through apps on his phone until he found the one associated with the GPS sunglasses he'd given Angie last year. The glasses were new tech from Futures Command. Clicking on the screen with a trembling finger, he searched for her current location.

He struck out. No red GPS dot on the map.

The breath left his lungs in a rush.

The app, when it worked, was precise within yards, but it wasn't designed to store a user's history. Now Stryker wished it did. He'd have to give them that feedback.

Where was she?

Crushing the phone in his grip, he was tempted to smash it to the deck. Then it buzzed.

Frozen, he stared at the incoming call from Sam, afraid to answer.

CHAPTER 4

Bari, Italy
Day One

While Sam waited for Stryker to pick up the phone, she sat on the uncomfortable hotel-room couch and berated herself for finding a poker game instead of going to lunch with Angie and her friends. Truth was, she didn't feel like she belonged with the three sorority sisters, but with them missing, she wished she'd swallowed her insecurity and tagged along.

While she was daydreaming, she sure as hell wished her sister and Stryker would figure out how to get along.

Stryker finally answered. "Well?"

Ignoring his question, Sam asked, "Any luck with the sunglasses?"

"No," Stryker replied.

His tone sounded as tense as she felt. Her shoulder muscles were tied in knots.

She said, "Ace hacked the locals and found a report in their system." The next words stuck in her throat. "The Italians found a body with a fingerprint match to Zoe. She is—was— a realtor, with prints on file."

For a minute, it seemed Stryker also couldn't speak. "Did Director Wolff say if I can come investigate?"

"He did. You're to catch the next flight. Rey can wrap things up there."

"Send me any communication you had with Angie today. I'll be there ASAP."

With a quivering hand, she hung up and forwarded Angie's last texts to Stryker. Then she set the phone down on the wicker nightstand and pulled her Snoopy pajamas over her knees, wishing for something sweet and tangy to drink. Lemonade would be good. It always reminded her of home.

Zoe was dead. That ominous fact roiled Sam's guts. Plus, she knew Stryker was right—it wasn't Angie's style to cut and run, even if there was trouble in paradise. Single and glad of it, Sam didn't get commitment, but until they'd lost little Malachi, Stryker and Angie had seemed to have a good thing going.

Now Sam's baby sister was missing, maybe dead, along with her bright-eyed niece.

She looked out the hotel patio door to the dark, wind-whipped sea and recalled one of her favorite memories. She and Angie were visiting their grandparents, who lived farther north in the Keys, and had been snorkeling all afternoon in shallow water. When the waves grew choppy and the sky in the distance turned gray, Sam had insisted they get out of the water and Angie agreed, scampering up the slippery rock stairs and removing her life vest. Salty and wearing damp bathing suits under their beach towels, they sat on an old picnic table under a *palapa* made from palm fronds and watched tornado-like water spouts terrorize the sea. The danger was far enough away that they'd laughed about it, and had carved their initials into the table's wood. Sam had always felt responsible for Angie. Now that smiling, blonde-haired imp with whom she'd shared so much of her life was missing.

She stroked the lucky coin in her pocket, praying to all her gambling gods for a way out of this mess. At least she'd been here, instead of in Saudi with the guys. Thank God Wolff hadn't cut her vacation short too.

Looking around the room for a distraction from her gut-wrenching emotions, she wondered if she could be doing some sort of research.

Picking her phone back up, she reviewed the texts from Angie again. There was no mention of where they'd been going to get the after-lunch drink, nor any SOS. But these days, people also communicated in other ways. Sam decided to pull up the three women's social media accounts to see if they'd posted anything while they'd been out and about. There was nothing on her sis's—too private—and Reno hadn't posted anything either. But Sam hit pay dirt with Zoe's Facebook account.

Earlier that afternoon, the dead woman had posted a live video from the inside of a nondescript Italian bar. Sam could see the strawberry-blonde braid of her sweet little niece, Harper, as she played in a booth with Reno's daughter. The girls made a face at the camera. Then Angie and Reno were arm in arm, toasting Zoe and giving a little wave. They all smiled and laughed, having a grand time.

Sad. Zoe's last hurrah.

The bar had few identifying features, but Sam noted them all the same; it might take a while, but she would find out the name of the place.

What happened after the friends had their drinks? How had Zoe died?

With a pounding heart, Sam replayed the video over and over again, focusing on her sister and niece. A lump formed in her throat.

What if Angie and Harper were dead, too?

CHAPTER 5

Eden
Day One

The *comandante* ordered, "Dispose of the body."

On the island that had been called Eden for more generations than he could count, the leader of the Sons of Adam stood at the end of a small jetty not far from the colorful faux-fishing village that was his home. His fingers clenched tighter around the disposable phone at his ear.

"She was an American," the Bari captain of police replied. "You know they'll come sniffing around."

The *comandante*'s hackles rose at the pushback and he took a deep drag from his cigar. He was still new in the leadership role, but watching his weak grandfather and weaker father try to tread water against the recent flood of change had motivated him toward aggressive measures once his old man was gone. Some of the group's long-standing partners, like this police captain, were still learning that his fist was heavier than his father's had ever been.

He exhaled the sweet cigar smoke and deepened his baritone. "Let them sniff."

"One of the men entered the description and prints of the girl into the computer already."

Feeling a stone under his boot, he ground it into dust with his heel. "That is unfortunate. I told you before how to deal with this type of situation."

"There was a delay. We didn't know this was one of yours."

A vein in the *comandante*'s temple throbbed. His men had killed the tall jezebel when she fought them in the alley behind the bar. They knew not to slay the women they caught, and fearing his wrath at the loss of income, the team had argued. Panicking, they'd dumped her body in the harbor before loading up the rest of the catch and heading for the island. Only then had his most loyal man radioed about the situation.

The *comandante* looked out to sea and took another drag from his cigar. All was black sky and dark, violent, wind-tossed sea. It would be hours yet before the boat arrived—*without* the hothead who let his knife out of its scabbard. He would be dumped overboard alive, shackled to a heavy rock, to send a clear message to the other fishermen.

"Who made the mistake?"

The captain hesitated.

The *comandante* stroked the twin points of his beard. "How old is your daughter, Captain?"

"Sixteen." The word came out in a forced whisper.

The *comandante* let the stony silence build. The captain was painfully aware that he and his men ran the most profitable sex-trafficking ring on the planet. They were untouchable on Italian soil, as they used all of the Mafia families for distribution and had been raising unwanted Vatican babies for generations.

The captain cleared his throat. "It was Esposito. He has two small boys."

The *comandante* remained silent. Hard lessons generally left the longest-lasting impressions.

"The woman will be on my personal boat within an hour," the captain said, his voice cracking. "And by dawn Esposito and her body will be at the bottom of the Midnight Shelf."

The Midnight Shelf was the nickname for the point in the ocean floor off Bari's coast where shallow waters gave way to a deep ravine. Discovered by ancient Greeks, it had been a burial site for thousands of years.

The *comandante* thought for just a moment about another body that had been dumped into the Midnight Shelf years ago.

Not bothering with a farewell, he hung up, and threw the phone with a quarterback's grace away from the pier and into the water. It landed with a satisfying splash.

Each of his telephones was used exactly once.

He had similar high-security precautions on his vessels and on this island. The boats were outfitted with a custom GPS-enabled app, radar-jamming equipment, and portable machine guns. The island was designed to look like a fishing village from above, with only a well-hidden small-signature custom cell tower and radar unit above ground. What's more, the sea around the island had been fortified with a combination of World War II naval mines and newer models he could activate remotely.

He stared at the red embers of his cigar, took a final drag, and dropped the butt to the pier, extinguishing it with his heel before kicking it into the sea. Pulling his peacoat tight against the wind, he began to walk uphill to his blue-walled home, reflexively fingering the studded handle of the short, braided whip he always wore on his belt. His family had spearheaded the Sons of Adam for almost four thousand years, and had done their best to make the world into the vision their forefather had laid out in *il canone*, a book so old it was originally carved into stone. The medieval centuries were a particular success. But the last hundred years had seen a lack of leadership from his soft-hearted grandfather and father, which had led to a decline in membership and funding.

Six months ago, his father had gone to heaven. Or maybe the inept old man was rotting in hell. Although there had been some growing pains, the *comandante* was pleased with the changes his leadership had brought. Most notably his son, Antonio, finally a worthy lieutenant after a rebellious youth, was making progress on a special project.

The *comandante* had learned from documents handed down leader to leader that a spy in Cleopatra's court had alerted Octavian, head of the Sons of Adam at the time, that the Egyptian queen was secreting away box after box of treasure. In the years following her reign, Octavian had tried to find the golden journal rumored to hold the key to the cache. After his passing, it seemed the hunt for her journal had fallen like dust into the sands of Egypt. Only two other leaders had undertaken the quest. His father had never even mentioned it. The *comandante*, however, wanted to use the gift of modern technology to unlock the old queen's secrets. He feared the hoard might fall into the wrong hands. Thanks to Antonio's new computers, they now had several good leads, but the location of her storeroom remained a frustrating mystery.

As he entered his home, the *comandante* felt light on his feet, more optimistic about his other plans. There were several bits of good news. His best assassin, a man with heavy facial stubble who went by the call sign Cobra, had struck a warning blow to the Saudis today. Secondly, his team of social media experts was gaining a large following. And, best of all, the *comandante* had a solid plan to eliminate an important US government official, and people placed throughout North America to capitalize on the assassination.

He smiled like a hungry jackal about to feed on the fresh catch the ship would soon deliver.

CHAPTER 6

The Mediterranean Sea
Day One

Angie fought to regain her sense of time and place.

Memory returned. Harper. Harper was missing. *And, oh God, was Zoe dead?* Angie remembered seeing that flash of silver near Zoe's throat before the alley had gone dark. Dread roiled her stomach. *Dear God. Undone by a roofie.*

Without opening her eyes, she took stock of the situation. Her temple throbbed, her mouth felt like she'd been chewing sand, and she heard the loud rumble of an engine. Whatever she was lying on was moving and the smell of the sea was strong, as was the acrid odor of fear mixed with machine oil. Was she tucked away in the bottom of a ship's hull?

She prayed not. Water was not her friend. Never had been. Well, at least not since she was six. What a horrid time, and one she didn't want to think about now. She'd never learned to swim. If the boat capsized, she'd drown.

Cracking open her eyes, she took in her surroundings. Dim light from a stairwell ten feet back filtered down from another deck. The sides of the space slanted up to a low ceiling. She was on a bunk. Someone was breathing behind her. Reno's red locks were visible three women over, but Angie couldn't see

Zoe or Harper. Women were stacked next to each other like crayons in a box. *Harper!* Angie screamed for her daughter but no words came out.

Alarmed, she tried to jump up, fight, wiggle, anything, but she found she couldn't move. Her rebellious toes would not obey her mind's order to move, and she swore every curse word she could recall. Her painted fingernails couldn't dig into her palms, which were still tied behind her back. Her breathing quickened. Mind and emotions went into overdrive.

Who had kidnapped them? For what purpose?

Again, swearwords rolled around inside her head, forming new variations on the same panicked theme. She was going to die.

She hyperventilated, got dizzy, and lost track of herself.

When she woke again in the full dark, she could move her toes. That helped ease the knot of tension in her gut. Tim had tried to prepare her for situations like this, but she was a CIA agent, designed for gathering international intelligence from businessmen and -women. She wasn't an operative like Tim, or her sister, Sam. Neither talked about their Armed Forces training, but those two had probably gone for weeks without sleep, in caskets, eating only rats while undergoing waterboarding or some other "enhanced interrogation technique."

On the other hand, that also meant they would come after her. Too bad she'd had to smash those GPS sunglasses. Would've made good breadcrumbs.

She was also grateful about her other safeguard, that she traveled with false identification. If the kidnappers didn't know who she was, they wouldn't be able to trace her back to Tim, which might give him an advantage. They also wouldn't know she was worth a small fortune and held state secrets in her head. At this point, she was happy to find even one thing to be grateful about.

Then she realized that perhaps she'd been kidnapped because they already knew who she was. She closed her eyes tight, fighting back tears.

There was a splash, off her side of the boat. Probably the electronic remains of their phones, headed to Davy Jones's locker.

At least the gag was gone. She spit out a last piece of scarf—silk didn't taste nearly as fine as it looked. When sensation came back to her mouth, she chewed at her lower lip. As good as the M2 team was, they didn't have much to go on. Would she be raped in the meantime? Killed?

She prayed that Harper had been left behind, but even that was a terrifying prospect.

Her legs came back online, and she could move her wrists, though they were caught painfully in the embrace of the zip tie. All the other women remained still as corpses. Angie hoped they were breathing. It was hard to tell in the filtered light of a moving boat.

Maybe nursing that last drink had helped. Less drug in her system. She could explore while the men above expected her to be zonked out.

With the utmost caution, she sat up . . . only for her head to spin and her stomach to lurch as the boat moved up and down in the swells. She swung her feet to the floor and tried to stand. *Thump!* She landed back on the bunk.

She took a deep breath, trying to channel her sister. What would Sam do? Probably take it even slower. Even though they'd had some challenges in school due to their different skin tones, her sister had always taken care of her, and had been there when their dad died. Angie had always felt guilty that she'd been born with pale skin tone, while Sam had to deal with the social complications of looking Black. Their parents were biracial. When they were in their teens, they'd both wondered if their mom had an affair, but her mother insisted it was just an odd genetic quirk that had resulted in one White-looking child and one Black. Perhaps as a result, their lives had taken divergent paths, and in this situation, Angie wished she had more of her sister's covert know-how.

Angie's second attempt at standing worked and she spread her feet for balance. What could she use to cut the zip tie to get her hands free? Nothing even remotely sharp grabbed her attention and she hung her head in despair.

Biting her lip and giving herself a pep talk, she raised her head and looked around again. No Zoe. But there, near the front, was Harper's trademark braid and one blue cat-faced knee. Relief flooded through her and she fell back again to the bunk, closing her eyes and fighting back tears of relief. At least Harper was alive. Then she realized that having her child along would complicate any sort of escape plan, and might damage her daughter's tender psyche. Plus, who knew what the kidnappers had planned for them.

Her brief elation turned to despair and she pounded her head once on the cold berth.

A thousand unpleasant potential outcomes for Harper burrowed through her mind. She bit the inside of her cheek to pull herself together.

Eventually, she sat up again and tallied who was in the hull. Fifteen women, counting herself, and the two girls. She shook her head. *What a situation.* Certainly different than all the board meetings she attended.

Focus.

Wishing for the use of her arms, she stumbled across the floor until she could bend over her daughter's still form. Harper's breathing was rhythmic, which was a comfort. Angie closed her eyes, savoring the sweet breath on her cheek. She considered waking Harper up, but there would be no way to keep the child quiet. No. Instead, Angie kissed her firstborn on the forehead and stood.

After what had happened to Malachi, the thought of a risk to her daughter's life made her skin crawl. But there wasn't much she could do now except figure out how to get them home.

Nearby were a bathroom and a tall white cupboard. She paused by the former, tempted, her bladder more awake than the rest of her, but instead went to yank open the cupboard with her teeth. Inside were bags of white pills, some still bundled up in the manufacturer's bubble wrap.

The sound of men speaking excited Italian floated down the stairwell.

Angie swallowed hard, unsure if she'd be able to make it back to her bunk in time. Would they kill her if they saw her standing there?

Shouting came from overhead. Chains rattled. There was a yell and a huge splash.

Silence descended. Angie broke out in a sweat.

Footsteps moved toward the stairs.

CHAPTER 7

Eden
Day Two

As he sat in the command center staring blankly at his computer, Antonio imagined the limp body of the man sinking to the bottom of the sea wearing iron chains as ankle bracelets. It was too bad about the loss of the fisherman, but the men knew the rules. His father, the group's leader, had woken him in the middle of the night and told him about the knifing incident, and the fiasco with the paperwork. Three of their men would be heading back to Bari soon to clean up the mess at the police station.

Even though the dead fisherman had been only an acquaintance, Antonio couldn't help but think of Christian's recent death. They had grown up together as children, catching fish off the boats to feed the island and later sharing hopes and plans while drinking wine by nighttime beach fires. But Christian's dreams had come to an abrupt halt on a sunny day in Egypt a few months ago, at a place thought to be Cleopatra's lost tomb.

Now, even though he considered his father's goal of finding the old queen's journal an exercise in futility and worse, the cause of his friend's death, Antonio was reluctantly setting a new plan in place to pick up where Christian had left off. There was no escaping the demands of his father, who had the overwhelming presence of a cyclone.

Antonio pulled the stolen, faded picture of his mother out of his wallet. It was a palm-sized photograph that featured her large blue eyes mischievously smiling up at the camera. His father had forbidden her images, probably because the resemblance between him and his mom was uncanny, but Antonio had found the snapshot in one of his father's books as a child and had pilfered it, keeping it safe in the intervening years. The memories of his mother were a soothing balm to the wounds caused by his father's bullying nature. She had killed herself when Antonio was five, and he missed her every day since.

It was still a few hours before dawn, but he had work to do. He put the photo and memories back into his wallet and picked up a hot espresso. He was in a room full of new computers, monitors, and racks of server equipment that they had dubbed the command center. A few men already sat at workstations, monitoring the internet for mentions of Cleopatra. His obsessed father had eagerly funded the venture, and now several fresh-faced university graduates were back home on the island and using the latest Big Data techniques twenty-four-seven to find any mention of the empress, her tomb, treasure, or journal.

One of the grads had suggested bringing in a few super-techies to use the latest artificial intelligence in their propaganda war. Despite seeing their early work, Antonio still shook his head in amazement that computer-generated pictures and video could look so lifelike. They'd used deepfake technology to create entire personas of journalists, and a few stories from those fake reporters had even been printed in well-known news outlets. The ability to easily create hundreds of thousands of social media accounts made his head spin, but his father was pleased, which was the important thing.

All in all, Antonio liked this side of the business better than kidnapping women. That turned his stomach.

Paolo walked into the room and Antonio motioned for the archeologist to join him in a side office. With thinning brown hair, basset-hound eyes, and an unruly beard, Paolo looked perfect for the part he was about to play.

Antonio closed the conference room door. "Congratulations on your new post. Are you ready?"

The man's voice was thin and fast. "Of course. I'm excited. What if it is Cleopatra's tomb?"

"Then you'll follow the plan. You need to see if her journal, or any mention of it, is there."

"I know, I know. Seek clues to her treasure."

Antonio sipped his espresso. "Without getting killed like Christian."

"He was a tomb raider, not an archeologist."

Antonio's eyes narrowed. "He was a friend."

"I'm sorry, but his skills came from the brawny aisle."

Antonio's fists tightened and it took an effort to control his tone. "You're right. That's why we're sending you. What do you know about the dig at Taposiris Magna so far?"

"It's near the sea, thirty kilometers west of Alexandria. It was a city and a temple, and became known for its religious festivals after Alexander the Great founded Alexandria, which was actually called Alexandro—"

Antonio held up his hand. "I don't need the entire history briefing. Why do they think it's her tomb?"

Paolo sighed loudly. "So far, they've found twenty-seven tombs, including ten mummies." He waved a couple of fingers. "Two of the ten are stunning, gilded specimens. And there's an Isis temple, a fave of Cleo. Twenty-two coins bearing her crooked nose and otherwise lovely face have been found, along with a mask that looks like her lovebug, Mark Antony, with the cleft chin. It has all the hallmarks of a royal burying ground."

"What about the shafts?"

"Why ask me if you know so much?"

"I just want the latest."

"Three deep ones are confirmed as having been used for burials, and they just discovered a new one. Team leaders are cautiously optimistic that Cleo and Marky-poo are buried down there."

"Marky-poo?"

"Where's your sense of humor?"

"I seem to have misplaced it when Christian died." It was true. He'd been affected deeply.

"Fine, I'll be serious. I understand my orders and have a burner packed if I need to phone home. How'd I get this job anyway?"

"You'll be replacing a junior archeologist who fell down one of those deep shafts."

Paolo's face blanched. "An accident?"

Antonio just raised an eyebrow and pointed to the door. Paolo left without another word.

On a live video feed, Antonio watched as the boat docked. Even minus the dead fisherman, his father would be pleased with the catch.

CHAPTER 8

Eden
Day Two

Angie woke, feeling the ship bump softly into something she guessed was a dock. The sounds of women and children groaning surrounded her. Her heart rate accelerated. Where was Harper? What was going on?

As she stretched and tried to sit up, she briefly recalled her brave, or foolhardy, antics of the night before. Before sleeping, she had discovered that cupboard full of drugs. When she'd heard voices, she used her head to close the white door of the drug cabinet as quietly as possible before backing into the bathroom. She left the door open a crack. A stocky shadow fell over the floor, but the broad-shouldered man descended only a few steps before returning to his fellows. After her breathing returned to normal, she worked her way back to her bunk and eventually cried herself into oblivion.

She chafed against her bonds and wondered if it was morning. All her concerns from the night before came back to her in a flash, and a heavy cloud fell over her heart. Zoe was probably dead.

Women around her stirred and tried to stand despite their wrists being tied. The ship was no longer moving, and scuffling above had replaced the sound of the loud motor. A man appeared in the stairwell and began yelling in Italian. By his wild "come on" arm gestures, Angie guessed he was trying to get them up the stairs and off the boat. Fine by her.

Harper's voice cried above the din. "Momma? Mommy?"

"I'm here, baby."

Harper scrambled over to her, nimble as a billy goat. Angie kissed the top of her daughter's head, happy to see the girl appeared unharmed.

Harper's blue eyes were full of worry. "Mommy, I'm scared."

"Shh, everything's going to be fine," Angie said, hoping it was true.

"Why are we tied up?"

Angie thought quickly. What kind of jerks bound a child? She needed to stay calm and make this a game. "Don't worry, honey. This is the surprise part of our vacation."

Harper's expression held doubt. "I want to go home."

"Do what the men say, okay?"

Harper ignored the directive and turned to whisper something to Layla.

Angie stood and made eye contact with Reno, who mouthed "Zoe?" Angie just shook her head and made a subtle frown, sure Reno would get the dire message.

They all stumbled toward the stairs. Angie heading up first, Harper close to her thigh, Reno and Layla behind them. The boat stank of dead fish.

Angie had expected to see a harbor of some sort; instead they were in a deep cave the size of a city block. Only one light attempted to brighten the space, creating a ghostly gloom reminiscent of abandoned warehouses and vacant highway rest stops. Two other fishing vessels were moored nearby, shorter and more rusted than the one she was leaving. The dark sea beckoned from just outside the mouth of the cave. She yearned for it. Longed for the normalcy of dinner with Tim, reading to Harper on the couch, throwing the ball for Sierra, her corner office. Her vision misted. She wanted to go home, too.

She considered an escape attempt, a mutiny. Could she kick the guard next to her overboard? Before she could take any action, however, the women were marched down a short gangplank toward the mouth of a tunnel. Reno and the girls had been shoved to the back of the line, which made Angie's body tense.

Harper yelled, "Mom!"

"Shush, honey. This is like the theme park we went to for your birthday."

The long-haired brunette in front of her said something to a guard. It was Short Ponytail Man, the broad-shouldered ass who had knocked her out in Bari. The man spat on the ground before slamming the butt of his rifle into the brunette's kidney. The woman cried out, her back arching in pain. No one else spoke. Angie hoped Harper would stay quiet.

Since they were outgunned and without the use of their arms, Angie decided now was *not* the time to make a move.

As they entered the tunnel, she worried that the six kidnappers made no attempt to hide their identities. That did not bode well for their prospects. Who were these men? Mafia? Bare light bulbs had been strung along the upper right-hand part of the corridor. Stark shadows marched next to the line of women, reminding Angie of hand puppets from a horror show.

She and Harper sometimes played more benign wall puppet games before bed. Turning, Angie locked eyes with her daughter, wondering if her child was watching the shadows as well. Angie tried to communicate calmness and well-being through her facial expression before turning and gritting her jaw to hold back tears.

She played that shadow game with Harper because she and Sam used to play hand puppets before walking the palm-lined route to school. A memory surfaced. Their route took them by the house of a student in Sam's grade. He was only three years older than Angie, but tall for his age, and seemed a giant. A day when Sam had been home sick, the tall boy had shoved Angie to the ground and scattered the contents of her backpack to the wind. Angie hadn't told her parents but had told Sam, who'd kicked the wall, furious. When Sam spied the bully in his driveway the next morning, she had walked over and poked him in the chest with a single finger. "Don't ever mess with my little sister again."

"Or what, Skunk Girl?"

"Or you'll be sorry."

The bully pushed Sam in the chest with two hands and she fell, landing on her backside on the lawn. He moved in to gloat, towering over her. Fast as a viper, Sam kicked him between his legs. He howled, grabbed his crotch, staggered a few feet, and fell over sideways.

Sam stood and moved next to him. "Tell her you're sorry."

"I can't!" he wailed.

She kicked him in the ribs, but not too hard. "Tell her."

"I'm sorry!"

Fresh blubbering followed the sisters as they walked to the bus hand in hand.

The bully glared at Angie many times in the years that followed, but never again attacked her.

Angie wished for her big sis as the tunnel took a hard left, ending in a row of barred cells. Guards opened doors with electronic keycards and Angie was hustled into a cage with the rifle-in-the-kidney brunette. Harper and Layla were shuffled past the cell.

That wasn't what Angie expected. Her breath grew rapid and she fought down the terror that was rising into her throat like acid. She'd hoped to share a cell with her daughter or have her close by.

Harper stopped, her eyes huge. "Mom, I want to be in there with you."

Angie rushed to the side of the cell and put her face through the bars, thinking fast. "It's okay, honey. Go with Layla."

A mean-eyed guard shoved Angie back further into her cage.

Harper wailed.

"Shush, Harper. She'll keep you company." God, she hoped the two children would be together.

The guard ushered Harper out of sight. Angie's fingernails dug into her palms and drew blood. Where were they taking her daughter?

Heart racing, Angie glanced around. Their prison was cut into limestone, bars on the front only, and held no window. A few grimy bricks filled the floor where the stone had been uneven. Two metal beds, bunkbed-style, were bolted to the wall and hung by a chain. At least each held a thin mattress and blanket. She was glad she still wore her black down jacket, as the air was chilly. A round hole in the right rear corner gave off a ghastly smell, advertising its purpose.

The guard cut the zip ties on Angie's wrists, and then duplicated his effort on her cellmate before locking the door behind him.

The eerie sound of slamming doors echoed down the chamber. Angie and the brunette looked at each other, eyes wide with dismay.

How were they going to get out of here?

CHAPTER 9

Bari, Italy
Day Two

Bari's overcast sky matched Stryker's bleak morning mood. His shoulder had ached the entire flight from Jeddah, and he finally gave in and took an anti-inflammatory when the journey had proven bumpy due to weather. During the trip, he kept seeing Harper trying to ride her pink bike on the sidewalk in front of their house the night before they'd left for the wedding holiday in Italy. The training wheels were all that kept her upright, but she laughed with glee as he gave her a gentle push. White and pink tassels bounced from the handles in time with her strawberry-blonde braid and once she'd honked the little horn, scaring a neighbor's cat off the porch and into a side yard. No matter how much he'd tried to meditate in the airplane seat, he couldn't shake the memory.

Normally his stomach could handle any sort of turbulence, but he'd reached for the vomit bag twice. While he managed to keep his meager breakfast down, the experience put him in a vile frame of mind.

Departing the twin-engine jet, he grabbed an energy drink from a kiosk, hoping the caffeine would help his demeanor. Then he nabbed his duffle bag from baggage check, used the men's room to strap a knife from his luggage to his ankle, and holstered his semi-automatic. Last, he checked his mask and hair. Today, to match his CIA-engineered passport, he was Señor Rodríguez from Barcelona. These days it was easy to look like someone else for a little while, but if your legend, or backstory, wasn't complete, it was even easier for counterintelligence to see through your disguise. All think tank field operatives were given completely new identities—new addresses, parents, place of birth—that they used in conjunction with their body armor, weapons, and masks. There was even an entire industry involved in creating false social media profiles, which made him grimace. He had a stash of other disguises in the luggage.

His sister-in-law met him in a little midnight-black Fiat with the toss of her chin. They'd worked together so long that she probably recognized him from the way he walked. He threw his single duffle in the compact's trunk and sat in the passenger seat, glad to get out of the bitter wind. As Sam accelerated away from the airport, sipping coffee non-stop, her mouth was set in a grim line. Her full-head mask also gave her a Spanish look.

"Thanks for sending me Angie's texts last night after we hung up," Stryker said.

"No problem."

It was hard to see her eyes. She wore her sunglasses in spite of the gloomy weather.

Reflexively, he glanced behind them. "Did you see the note from Ace that the Italian police report disappeared from their computers?"

"I did."

As she drove, the roped muscle of her forearm stood out below her crimson short-sleeved blouse, and she held onto the steering wheel with a grip usually reserved for a combat-pistol. Sam had become a falconer during their time in the Air Force.

He recalled seeing her at the base with a leather band on that forearm, releasing a proud kestrel to the sky.

"You okay?" he asked.

She slammed her free hand on the steering wheel. "Of course I'm not okay! My baby sister is missing and the odds of getting her back alive are a million to one."

Expecting the outburst, he didn't jump. After years of dealing with Sam through stressful missions, Stryker knew to let her vent. Anything he said at this point could and would be used against him. He climbed out of his emotional hole and made a soothing noise.

"Don't try that crap on me, mister."

"What crap?"

"That 'silent so she'll vent' crap."

"Okay. What do you want me to say?"

"Maybe 'We'll get her back.' Or 'I understand how you feel.' Or swear and get mad at me and punch something. You're always so bloody calm."

Stryker inhaled slowly. "Sam. You know my past. I don't do anger well."

"This is your wife, for God's sake. Lose a little control."

He rolled his shoulders, recalling a time in high school when he'd lost his temper and beat the crap out of a poor kid who'd just been teasing him. "Can't."

"Or won't? Maybe with the divorce you don't care anymore."

"That's a low blow, Sam. There is no plan for a divorce." He counted to three. "Me getting pissed off right now would only color my judgment."

"Oh. I see. You think I can't see straight?"

Stryker clenched his jaw. "I didn't say that."

"Implied."

"Take this exit."

"What?"

He dropped his voice. "I said, pull over."

Sam brought the Fiat to a screeching halt in a parking lot for the Lama Balice Regional Park. Then she made a point of looking out the window.

Stryker reached over and turned the vehicle off, noting the parking job was crooked.

"Sam."

She ignored him.

He softened his tone and put a hand on her shoulder. "I'm just as upset as you are. I just process my feelings differently."

Her head whipped around. "Do you? Actually process?"

He instinctively tightened his stomach and chest. "I meditated on the plane." *Or tried to.* "You vent and get it out in your workouts."

She nodded slightly.

"Look. We need to tackle the day with clear heads. I want you to go inside that park and run for at least fifteen minutes. Take your time. Cry if you need to. It's okay."

"All right," she mumbled.

"I'll be here taking another look at Angie's last texts."

She grabbed a fleece jacket, exited the car, slamming the door for effect, and briskly walked to the green space before taking off at a dead sprint.

Stryker exhaled. He exited the car, got into the driver's seat, straightened the parking job, returned to his seat, and turned the car key enough to engage the radio. He found a classical music station. They both needed to channel their emotions into being productive. Still no ransom demand, so his first step was to figure out the bar the women had visited right before disappearing.

He took out his phone, pulling up a map. Bari sat on the Achilles heel of the Italian peninsula. An ancient port town with modern big-box shops, it also had a romantic section of older city with narrow streets and crowded houses. There were a lot of bars. Where would they have gone for a drink? He studied the map and reread Angie's texts until Sam returned and plopped into the seat behind the wheel.

Sweat dusted her brow and her breath was still ragged. She removed the sunglasses. Her brown eyes were red but held determination. "Thanks."

"Any time." He gave her a small smile. "I still love her, you know."

She searched his eyes. Finally nodded.

Feeling a little lighter now, too, he motioned toward the road with his head. "Ready to track her down?"

"Yes, as long as we can listen to something else." She changed the radio to Italian pop.

He cringed but didn't protest. "Okay. Jump back on the road. Looks like the restaurant where they ate is nearby."

"I scouted it on the way to the airport," Sam said once they were back on their way. "Any thoughts on motive?"

"She mentioned getting another offer on the business. That's all I've come up with."

"Think a competitor might be trying to do a different kind of negotiating?"

Stryker checked his side mirror. No company. "Could be. Since her engineers found a way to produce the biogas and green diesel cheaply, there's been a lot of interest. What have they had, three offers already?"

Sam ran her fingers along the steering wheel. "Yeah, and they keep getting better. She has no intention of selling, though."

"Angie's a smart one."

"I suspect she'll run the company until she's a hundred, especially now that they're engineering and manufacturing equipment for Futures Command, too."

"Could be a bad actor who wants think tank secrets."

She winced. "I hadn't considered that. Given we haven't seen a ransom demand yet, it fits."

Five minutes later, she pulled into a parking spot in front of La Terrazza, where the women had eaten lunch, at least according to the appreciative texts sent after.

"Let's check out the patio and see if the pics line up," Stryker said.

They walked around the left side of the restaurant, which was closed, as lunch wouldn't be served for a few hours. Wind slapped Stryker in the face and he tugged his leather jacket tight. The establishment overlooked the water and the patio held a dozen wrought-iron tables. To the right, two ferries bobbed at a pier.

Stryker checked the view against the picture of the three women. A group selfie. A lump formed in his throat.

Sam looked over his shoulder. "Match."

He swallowed the emotion. "Next text says they're heading for an after-lunch drink. My guess is they wouldn't walk far."

"They took a ride-hailing service here, so that's logical. And it's cold out." Sam shivered. "Most of the bars are close to the central part of town, just south of here. Shall we head that way on foot?"

Why did they have to go get drinks after eating? It ticked him off. "Let's."

They left the patio and walked toward town.

Sam touched his arm. "I may have a clue."

"What's that?"

"Last night, after talking with Ace, I couldn't sleep and checked out their social media profiles."

"And?"

"Zoe had posted a live video from the bar."

Although he was annoyed Sam was just now mentioning the vid, it was the first ray of hope since she'd called last night. "Definitely sounds like a lead. Why are you just now telling me about it?"

She grimaced. "It was super late by the time I figured it out."

He halted and turned to face her. "That's never stopped you before."

"Fine," she snapped. "I was too upset."

He nodded. "Thanks for being honest, and good work finding the lead. But next time let me know ASAP, okay?"

She sighed. "I will."

"Thanks. Are the shots of the bar exterior or interior?"

Sam brought up the video. "Inside only."

It wasn't very long, just a quick sweep of the dimly lit bar, Zoe narrating a summary of their vacation, some footage of the bartender mixing drinks, and his wife and her friends waving at the camera. Harper sat at a booth with Layla, probably coloring. The whole thing was sixty seconds, tops. "Did you try to match the interior with online pictures?"

"I did and came up short. The Italians aren't big on interior bar photos."

His heart sank. "At least we'll know it when we find it. Wood paneling and black-and-white photos on the walls. Looks old-school."

"We could show the video to some locals and see if they recognize it."

"Good idea."

They finished the ten-minute walk into town and decided to start left, near the churches, and work away from the water. The three-story city buildings were pale from too much sun.

Some were dirty yellow, some ghost white, some sandy tan, but all began right at the cobblestoned street. There were no front yards in this part of town.

Soon, a method arose: one of them would enter a drinking establishment, while the other stayed on lookout. The first seven bars didn't match and the bartenders didn't recognize the destination from Zoe's video. At the eighth venue, Sam closed the door behind her and did a little skip as she headed across the street and joined him in the shadow of a meat market.

"It's called Vittoria."

"Where is it?"

"Three blocks away on Via Don Bosco. Follow me."

It took no time at all to find it. Angie and her friends must've taken a right instead of the left he and Sam had taken at the entrance to town. This would've been the first place the women would have seen, looking for all the world like a traditional Italian bar with its festive stucco exterior, flower-boxed casement windows, and Italian flag. A vineyard mural was painted on the side of the building. He held the door for Sam and she sailed through.

Smoke assaulted his nose as soon as he followed. He hated the smell and knew it was illegal in Italy to light up indoors. Apparently, local law enforcement turned a blind eye.

It matched the video, though, no doubt about it—there were the red leather booths and the lazy Casablanca-era ceiling fan. The wall photographs were unique, too, and cinched the deal. A few locals were having an early lunch of soup, bread, and beer, but mostly the place had the hollow feel of an off-hours pub. Its action would be after working hours.

The gap-toothed bartender was not the same man who'd been in the video. Sam showed him the recorded moments anyway.

In passable Italian, Stryker asked about the missing women. The barkeep shrugged, admitting nothing except that the other bartender would be back tomorrow.

Even though the potential crime scene had endured an entire evening's worth of drinkers, Stryker gave the end of the bar where the women had sat a once-over. Nothing.

After checking the bathrooms, they met in the hall and both shook their heads.

"Think that leads to an alley?" Stryker said, nodding at a nearby door crowned by an exit sign.

"Only one way to find out."

The door opened into a narrow alleyway full of dumpsters. Spreading out, he and Sam circled like hawks.

Sam walked a few feet and pointed down. "This spot has been cleaned recently."

A three-foot-wide square of concrete was paler than the surrounding pavement. Freshly scrubbed. Stryker got down on one knee to examine the area. "No blood. Let's keep looking."

While Sam scrutinized the dumpster, he walked past the restaurant fifteen paces, turned around at the end of the backstreet, and examined the pavement near the opposite wall.

He bent down again, taking a knife from his ankle holster to poke at a pile of debris. Chunks of tortoiseshell. Pieces of Angie's GPS-enabled sunglasses.

They had found the crime scene and nothing else.

He stood and turned away from Sam so she couldn't see him. Throwing his head back to the wind, he balled his hands into fists and tightly closed his eyes. For an instant, raw pain threatened to rip him in half.

His wife and daughter had been taken from here. Where were they now?

CHAPTER 10

**Jeddah, Saudi Arabia
Day Two**

Rey's sleep had been full of bad dreams about Angie and little Harper, who sometimes called him uncle and always made him smile. Not that his sleep was ever good, what with the PTSD-induced nightmares, but it was going to take all he had to get through the day.

After dressing in his standard-issue body armor and silicone mask, and strapping on his personal knee brace, he took the plain-looking elevator downstairs. While it dropped, he reflected on Stryker's latest update: they had found the remains of Angie's glasses, but nothing else. How could Rey be there for his buddy? This must be tearing his old friend to pieces.

He was so caught up in his own thoughts that at first, he didn't realize he'd walked into a protest happening right outside the hotel on the busy Jeddah street.

Women filled the avenue. He assumed they were female, but it was hard to tell with the black head-to-toe religious gear. The crowd was silent, but many of the protesters carried signs.

"Divorce is a human right."

"Get over guardianship!"

"Lift the veil on women's rights!"

The quiet was odd, but he was grateful for it. He'd been born with a sensitivity to smells and sounds. Great for certain assignments, but the downside was that a loud crowd could put him on edge for an entire day, especially after his time in the service, where he'd developed a clinical case of PTSD. His therapist had recommended a less dangerous line of work, but Rey loved his job, and the PTSD was manageable. Usually. The smells today weren't bad, although he picked up the feral scent of fear underneath a subtle mélange of perfumes. These women were putting their lives at risk, and knew it.

Feeling the stress, he patted the tin in his pocket, wanting to chew but knowing he couldn't on the street. It was a bad habit he'd picked up as a teen. Besides, he was supposed to be at the embassy in ten minutes to debrief the station chief about the prince's assassination.

It had to be another Saudi behind the killing. The dead prince had been too open-minded. Rumor had it that he had even been considering allowing the country's Christians to worship in churches. Rey's intel said there was a seventh-century monastery tucked in the dunes and date palms out near the eastern oil fields. He fingered the St. Christopher medallion under his shirt. Rey would love to see that old church.

Moving slowly through the crowd, he wondered at the sudden street protest given that women's rights had come a long way in the kingdom. As he did before every mission, he'd done his research about the country. With the prince's backing, forced marriages were now illegal, and domestic abuse had been a crime since 2013. But even with the changes, Saudi women had to obtain a male guardian's approval to get married or leave prison, and while the driving ban had been eliminated in 2018, women still couldn't ride bicycles and scooters without wearing full body covering. He'd also been surprised to learn women could obtain divorces only in exceedingly rare cases—such as with a husband's consent, or if it could be proved he'd harmed her. Yeah, good luck with that.

It made sense now. They'd lost their champion.

Inside the embassy, Rey sat in a soundproof booth on an office computer dialing an operative from England. A few minutes ago, St. James had briefed him on a new threat, telling him to call Jane Parish via a secure video link. Jane, a member of British intelligence and psychological operations expert, had been lent to them by a PSYOPS group from Hermitage in Berkshire because of the recent assassination of the British PM, Sir Henry Wallace. Since Jane was to join their team, Rey had been instructed to make plans with her on where to meet.

Jane joined the video call and he sat up straighter. Framed by long dark hair, her striking face took his breath away.

Her dark eyes wrinkled at the corners before she reined in her amusement. Was he that transparent?

"You must be Jane." God, he sounded stupid.

She didn't look British, but the accent that left her full lips was certainly English. "Yes, and I understand you're called Stingray. Did I get that right?"

"I am. At least for this mission."

"I see." Her demeanor became all business. "I understand we're both heading to India."

"That's correct. We misplayed the threat here in Jeddah—I hope we do better next time."

"I'm heading to Bikaner. You?"

"Not far from there. Guarding a guru."

"I'll see you there." They made plans to meet and she closed the connection.

He was looking forward to seeing her in person.

Exiting the embassy, he looked left and right. As far as he could see, the street was filled with dark burqas in both directions.

CHAPTER 11

Bari, Italy
Day Two

Bumping into an Italian woman dressed in a black burqa, Samantha hustled down the block to the police station. She'd left a rattled Stryker in the Magpie Café, sipping an espresso. Her mission was to figure out why Zoe's death report had gone missing and see the body.

Because of the absent report, she was going in undercover. Besides, odds were always with the house. Pulling lip gloss out of her eggplant-colored fleece pocket, she dabbed it on her dry lips as she settled into her legend as a Spanish woman named Maria Donnetella. Sam rolled her r's a few times for practice. Having grown up in Florida, she could do passable Spanish. Not like Stryker, who was a walking Tower of Babel.

Three crows pecked at a fallen bag of Doritos near a trash bin, reminding her of Poe, her raven back in Key West. She'd been fifteen when the baby bundle of feathers had fallen out of his nest and she'd nursed him back to health before setting him free. Whenever she was home, he brought shiny gifts to her windowsill, even tracking her down when she'd purchased a new house across town. She longed to get another falcon but traveled far too much. She contented herself with a promise that she would set up an aviary when she retired someday.

Built from white limestone blocks, the police station had twin columns spearing the first two of its six stories. She rushed through the carved wooden doors as if she'd just lost her best friend. It wasn't a tough act. Stryker, perhaps a questionable husband but a good leader, had been right that she needed to blow off steam. It helped, but she still felt like she'd taken a gut punch. Where on earth were Angie and Harper? And how had Angie and Stryker's relationship gone so sour?

Her sister had given her the lowdown on "The Fight" before leaving the hotel yesterday. It sounded ugly. Of course, there would have been no violence, but words could be more painful than fists. Aware Angie was struggling since the loss of baby Malachi, Sam had seen the drinks at lunch, and the slight slurring at dinners and barbeques. But she also knew her sister was hurting. After Malachi died, she and Stryker physically carried a hysterical Angie home, where she'd eventually been sedated. Psychiatrists had put Angie on antidepressants, but clearly alcohol was her preferred therapy.

Maybe Sam should cut Stryker some slack. He was probably more a concerned husband than a questionable one. She could see that Angie's drinking was not a tenable solution, but also didn't see how threatening divorce was going to help.

Then again, what the hell did she know about relationships? Generally, she dated for a few months, then grew bored and moved on.

Inside the police station, she found an empty waiting room and a uniformed officer behind a plexiglass shield. She ran to the window and raised her voice several octaves. "My friends are missing."

He asked if she spoke Italian and she said no. When he gestured to a seat, she took it, allowing a few real tears to fall for effect.

Reaching into the pocket of her black slacks, she pulled her favorite coin out and rubbed it like a worry stone. When her father died, he'd left her his collection, knowing she loved the joke about coins for a Coin as much as he did. Her metal "pet" was an ancient Greek piece encased in durable plastic that she carried everywhere. The silver held an image of a caped and helmeted horseman on one side and a bull on the other. History was her passion and often the perspective of years gave her hope. She'd considered archeology as a career but found she needed more action than taking a week to brush a speck of sand from an artifact. Now she was glad for the covert skills that might help find her little sister.

No matter how much she rubbed the old Greek money, however, she was terrified. For her sister, niece, and two friends to have gone missing in the middle of the day without witnesses made her blood run to ice. Southern Italy was the birthplace of the Mafia, after all.

A man called her name. Young, with cold eyes, a thin mustache, and prominent ears, he bore a name tag that identified him as Lieutenant Caruso. She put the coin back in her pocket and followed him into a noisy bullpen with messy metal desks littered around the room. The only clean desk belonged to a Lieutenant Alessandro Esposito. She noted boxes piled on his chair, as though he was moving to another floor.

Lieutenant Caruso's workspace was located in a back corner. In cold, formal Spanish, he interviewed her, typing notes into a laptop. She dabbed at tears with a handkerchief as she told him about the wedding, her friends, and how they had disappeared late yesterday.

"Thank you," Caruso said. "We will begin an investigation immediately."

"Do you have any leads? Any reports?" She sobbed. "Any bodies?"

At that last bit, he finally thawed. "No. I'm so sorry," he said with genuine sympathy. "We have nothing."

The man was a good liar. She was used to reading faces from playing cards and his didn't give away a glimmer of what Ace had found in the police servers.

Ally made, she thanked him and stood. It was time to cash in her chips. There was nothing else she could do while undercover. Clearly, they were not releasing information to the public. She was dying to know why.

On the way out, she pointed at the empty desk. "Promoted?"

"Died."

"Oh no. What happened?"

"He slipped off the captain's boat last night in the rough seas." Caruso's face fell. "He was my friend. We trained together."

What are the odds of that being an accident? Sam thought.

Even though he had lied to her about Angie and what was probably Zoe's body, she stopped and touched his arm in sympathy before leaving the building.

She'd gathered some intel, but the big questions remained unanswered.

CHAPTER 12

Bari, Italy
Day Two

Stryker sat in the rear corner of the Magpie Café. The back of his chair rested against the wall to enable him to watch the door and his laptop was open to Zoe's video. Sam had sent the vid to him before she headed out to see what she could learn at the police station.

They had still received no ransom demand, and nothing from a competitor. And yet, if it was a foreign power, why would they have taken the other women and the children? None of it made sense. Top it off with the fact that Ace was unable to find a home location for the bartender who had served Angie, and Stryker was about ready to jump out of his skin with worry.

He pressed play and watched the video again. Harper was wearing her favorite jeans, the ones with the embroidered cat faces on the knees, and the sight of her bouncing leg caused his throat to go raw. Angie's smile and brief wave likewise made him feel like he was being burned at the stake. Slowly.

For fifteen minutes, he did nothing but replay the scene, a deep ache in his heart, until on what seemed like the millionth viewing, something new caught his eye. One of the men in the background was talking.

He cocked his head and played the video again.

Bells jingled on the front door, signaling someone's entry. It was Sam. The bounce was back in her step, which meant she must've found something. As she walked past the creepy black-and-white wall paintings of the long-tailed birds that gave the café its name, her head swiveled to the outside patio, where a few hungry feathered friends pecked at tray feeders in the gray afternoon. After ordering a lemonade and a ham-and-cheese panini at the counter, she joined him at the table. No other patrons were nearby, but they spoke in low tones, a habit from years in the field.

"You look happy," he said.

She cleared her throat. "Yes and no. Do you have a copy of the paperwork on the dead body that Ace sent last night?"

He navigated through his secure email. "Here."

"Scroll down. Who signed it?"

"A Lieutenant Esposito."

She gave a flat smile. "I knew it. He's dead. Esposito supposedly fell off the captain's boat last night. I'm betting he didn't fall."

Stryker hit the reply button and started typing. It wasn't always easy with his missing fingertip, but he'd long ago come up with a system that worked for him. "I'm asking Ace to see if she can find out who deleted the report. Feels like a cover-up to me."

A server brought Sam's lunch and Stryker asked for a similar sandwich, only vegetarian.

"Good idea," Sam said and took a bite. "But you're missing out on the ham."

He ignored the jibe. "I think I found something in the vid."

"What?"

"After studying it, I realized there's a couple of times you can see these men speaking." Pulling the video back up, he pointed to the table at the other end of the bar where three Italians sat with their heads close together, as if in a hushed conversation. One briefly faced the camera. Stryker zoomed in and hit play. "What caught my attention was the word 'president.' See? Right there."

"Looks to me like he said, 'Make it al dente.'" She smiled. "That's why you're paid the big bucks. What else?"

"I'd like HQ to use their enhancement technology and experts to validate, but I think I caught three tidbits all together."

She took another bite of the panini. "Stop. The suspense is killing me."

He put one finger in the air. "Cleopatra."

Sam's face scrunched in confusion. The reference puzzled Stryker, too.

He raised a second digit. "Deepfake."

She put the food down on her plate and moved her eyes skyward, clearly thinking. He'd heard the term about artificial intelligence that could be used to make false videos that looked true-to-life, but couldn't imagine where they fit into the rest of the situation.

A third finger joined the others in the air. "And they plan to kill the US president."

CHAPTER 13

Austin, Texas
Day Two

Why was someone planning to kill the president?

Assistant Director St. James sailed through the white metal door whose opaque window was labeled "Finance" in boring block font. Her team's headquarters were buried in the basement recesses of the Futures Command office building in Austin, Texas. Not that she wanted the limelight. She'd grown up gay in a time before it was hip, and had learned how to hide in plain sight decades ago.

Her new right hand, Ace, sat at a desk, typing.

"Please come inside my office," St. James said. "We need to call Stryker."

An excellent linguist, Stryker was one of her best officers. Like the entire team, he was whip-smart. After escaping the nightmare that had been his murderous father, he had grown up with an aunt, hunting deer on an Illinois farm. St. James always thought of him stalking prey with a crossbow. He could disguise himself as anyone, and had an unusual sense of integrity, important in a field like this. She trusted him completely—but then again, he'd never before been confronted with such a personal mission.

She yanked the wire-rims off her face, unsure if what she was about to tell Stryker would help him deal with the situation or not. Since his infant son had died, he'd been a tick slower to react, and in this business that could mean the difference between a bullet in the wall or one to the heart. She sat at her desk and grabbed a cherry-flavored zinc lozenge from the tin next to her monitor and popped it in her mouth. Ace wheeled in and parked her wheelchair on the other side of the broad desk.

A former fighter pilot from Boston, Ace hadn't been with the team long but was proving to be a fantastic recruit. Short and spunky, she wore thick purple-rimmed glasses and almost always sported some kind of pearl jewelry. Today it was a necklace, bright against her dark skin. She'd been the fat kid with buck teeth who'd grown up in a household where her parents allowed her no privacy. Braces and boot camp had transformed her outward appearance, but like the rest of the team, she still had scars on the inside. She was a loner who loved all things purple and had a gift for research.

The pearls reminded St. James that although all the members of the M2 team had issues, time and the stress of missions had polished them into something better.

Ace had lost both her legs, but was a wunderkind with a computer.

Stryker was so brutally honest he'd been kicked out of the military as a whistleblower, but would always tell the truth as he saw it.

Rey's PTSD gave him nightmares, but he also had a heightened sense of smell and hearing.

A serious gambler, Samantha had trouble committing—to men *or* women—but she was empathic and could charm her way into any heart, a talent in their line of work.

Before 9/11, all of them would have been ostracized with red stars. Back then, special ops teams had been known as boneheaded knuckle draggers. But after the terrorist attacks, Congress wanted a handful of *intelligent* teams to gather intel. In response, the military created a special unit of recruits that previously wouldn't have made it through psych testing. All members of the new unit were off-the-charts smart, but had varying degrees of social challenges. Her boss, Director Wolff, had originally called them Deep Red, but they called themselves "Military Misfits," and he eventually relented, renaming them M2.

The team was the field arm of one of the Army's cutting-edge think tanks, the US Futures Command. St. James and her group worked on missions that involved understanding the cutting-edge technology of the country's enemies. Her team also tested new equipment in the field, providing the designers with feedback. When the Futures Command had run into engineering and manufacturing issues, Wolff suggested Angie's company, and that arrangement had worked well, too. However, St. James wondered if someone had figured out that Angie might have a host of secrets in her pretty blonde head.

"Shall I initiate?" Ace asked.

"Please."

Ace ran through the protocols to get Stryker on the phone. Even with the best encryption money could buy, St. James was all too aware of how comms could be compromised. Her Texan and his Chicago voice print would be rendered unrecognizable and untraceable as part of the process. They would use as few words as possible.

"Shark here."

That was his call sign for this mission.

"Fargo" was hers.

"Was I correct?" he asked once they'd authenticated.

She put her glasses back on the bridge of her nose. Long ago, Wolff had negotiated a strategic alliance with the CIA and their expert team of lip-readers had confirmed Stryker's work, even though the mention of Cleopatra was odd. Shelving that for the moment, she'd run the comment about deepfake propaganda by her tech experts, who had said it was concerning because as of yet there were insufficient mechanisms to detect the false pictures or videos. The right fake at the wrong time could wreak havoc. However, the real kicker was the danger to the US president and/or president-elect. The experts had caught the dual threat that Stryker had missed. "Yes. But could also be the PE." She used the common abbreviation for the president-elect, knowing Stryker would catch on.

"I see."

She'd taken the possible White House elimination to the Secret Service's Counter Assault Team (CAT), who wanted help gathering intel on the assassination attempt because her M2 squad had a reputation for smartly using stealth and discretion. With no location, no timeline, and two possible targets, it was a lot of ground to cover. Especially with the upcoming travel schedules of both the old and new POTUS.

"Yes. Your help is requested with this and what was discussed earlier."

He'd know that she meant finding Angie, as it seemed her disappearance might be related. Even Sam would agree the odds were against two sets of bad actors being in the bar that afternoon. Also, Angie's affiliation with the National Resources division of the CIA and the think tank lent extra credence to using the team on the mission.

"We're in," Stryker replied. "Where's Stingray?"

That was Rey's call sign for this mission.

"He's en route to another party." She had dispatched him to India earlier in the day. Since Senator Browne had been killed four months ago, the NSA had been scouring intercepts for patterns, and they'd discovered there was usually a phone call to someone with the call sign "Cobra" along with a numerical code before each assassination. With the help of deep-learning algorithms, the code had been cracked . . . to an extent. The Saudi kill had been predicted at the nation-state level, but they hadn't known who the target was. The same situation existed now in India. Rey had been sent to help guard the high-profile guru Nanak Das while Jane Parish, a member of British intelligence, would be watching out for the prime minister at the Bikaner Camel Festival. Other Indian politicians were also being guarded.

The lip-reading experts had also caught the word "Cobra" on the video, raising the level of alarm to a fever pitch among the Secret Service. No one knew why these politicians were being targeted.

"Were you able to locate any of my other friends?"

"No," she replied. The images of the men from the bar hadn't found a match in any global intel database.

"Any good birdwatching recently?"

"Nope, sorry. The weather hasn't cooperated." He'd asked for any satellite footage from the night his wife and daughter disappeared, but they hadn't had a bird in the area. That would change now.

"Okay."

They didn't have nearly enough intel. The director didn't like that she was sending her team in blind. She yanked the glasses off her nose again, concerned about Angie, little Harper, and the dangers of the mission, especially for Stryker. "Good hunting."

CHAPTER 14

**Bari, Italy
Day Two**

Feeling like a cat stalking an armed and dangerous mouse, Sam lingered in the lobby of an old castle that had been converted to a museum, waiting for the police captain to leave work. Her hunting blind was located directly across the rain-soaked street from the police station.

The captain's ship, from which Lieutenant Esposito had supposedly fallen, was moored down by the closed-for-the-season Ferris wheel on the esplanade, and Stryker was there checking the boat for evidence. After Ace had located the boat, she had sent Sam a photograph of the captain, and Sam's marching orders were to follow him. If he went to a café or restaurant for dinner, she was to make a move and see what she could learn about how the lieutenant had died. In preparation, she had changed her mask to a Greek goddess look and added a few cup sizes to her bra.

Seduction was one of her favorite games, and keeping busy helped keep her mind off the topic of her missing sister and niece. The odds of them returning home alive became worse by the hour.

Harper always built sandcastles when they went to the beach and would have liked visiting the Castello Normanno-

Svevo, also known as the Swaven Castle. The fortress was first built in 1131, had later been converted to a prison, and now was a mostly empty hulk of prime real estate masquerading as a museum. At least the battlements had allowed Sam to scout the neighborhood between raindrops. She told herself she'd bring Harper for a tour if they got her niece back safe and sound.

Just when she thought her charade of waiting for a ride had worn too thin, the man himself strode out of the tall wooden doors and turned left, into the night. Sam mouthed into her custom molar mic for Stryker's benefit. "Target has left the building."

"Roger that. Inside boat now."

She let the captain get a lengthy head start. He probably had counterintelligence training, and the dimly lit streets weren't busy enough on this bitter winter night to provide much cover.

Squaring her shoulders, she left the cover of the lobby and hit the sidewalk. The distinctive hissing screech of a barn owl sounded behind her. It glided overhead, white belly feathers glowing, and nabbed a small rodent from a curb before its powerful wings launched it skyward again. She hoped it wasn't a sign.

The captain walked into a long stretch of urban park where naked branches almost touched overhead, like longing lovers. She entered the tunnel just as he was reaching the end. Without warning, a figure wearing a black trench coat and wide-brimmed hat slipped into view, bumped into the police captain, and then darted away to the left.

The captain crumpled to the ground.

The familiar feeling of adrenaline shot through her. "Man down. Call an ambulance. Perp on the move."

"Track him. Get what intel you can."

Glad she'd forsaken heels tonight, Sam pulled her service pistol from beneath her fleece jacket and ran through the dark, wet night. She considered disobeying orders and checking in on the captain, but the odds that he was alive were low. Dead men don't speak. She needed a live one.

Cutting through the trees, she sprinted toward the main boulevard that t-boned into the park. When she came to a side street that branched to the right near a gelato shop, she skidded to a halt just in time to see the attacker's dark coat flap around another corner.

Rain fell more heavily, obscuring the sound of her rubber-soled shoes. She approached the next corner with caution and peered around the wall.

Again, he turned a corner. This time to the right.

Her lungs burned as she flew down the narrow corridor, past round, shuttered doors, wrought-iron fencing, a barbeque shop, and a section with nothing but stone walls on both sides. If he'd heard her coming and turned, it would be a Wild West-style shootout. There was nowhere to hide.

She crept up and glanced around the corner. The lane opened to a wider courtyard in front of the Cathedral of San Sabino.

There. He was fifty feet ahead. In front of the wide church steps.

"Stop! *Fermo!*" she yelled.

He pulled a gun. Before he could get a shot off, her reflexes took over and she put two rounds in his center mass. The rain helped drown the pistol's thunder.

He dropped to the wet cobblestones. She swore, realizing what she'd done.

She ran to him, keeping a bead on his head. There was no need. Her shots had hit him in the solar plexus and just below his throat. She'd aimed for his heart but he'd turned at the last instant. The captain's killer lay on his back, legs bent at an unnatural angle, his dislodged black hat on the bottom church step. His build was stocky, and his hair was scraped back into a ponytail. Underneath the body, his dark leather duster fanned out like another pool of blood.

She holstered her weapon, put on gloves, and searched the corpse.

There was no wallet or ID, but there was a knife, wet with fresh blood, in a wrist sheath. Annoyed at both her aim and the fact she'd learned nothing from the two dead men, she pulled aside the killer's shirt to see how far off her shot had been. There was a tattoo where her bullet should have entered.

Intent on photographing the disturbing image of a hooded cobra wrapped around a deep-red apple, she didn't sense the new attacker until cold steel touched the base of her skull.

CHAPTER 15

Eden
Day Two

Angie reached out to grab the metal bars that stood between her and her freedom. They were smooth, not rusted, and cold underneath her fingers. God, what a mess.

Were they all to be kept as sex slaves? Raped? Murdered? Maybe these men were sex-traffickers.

Or was this a ransom setup? A threat to sell the company or else? She considered the work her team did in secret for the Futures Command. Could a foreign government have figured out what her company was up to, even with all the extra layers of security? It had been her fear when she'd agreed to take on that type of additional business. But if an enemy had taken her for those reasons, why abduct everyone else?

She hung her head. Zoe hadn't shown up and was likely at the bottom of the ocean with a slit throat. Her tall, funny, beautiful friend—dead. They had been friends since college, laughing and pulling practical jokes. One time they'd kidnapped Reno's stuffed cat and had cut letters for a ransom note out of magazines. They'd chuckled about that for years.

Was Harper okay? Where was she? What damage would this experience do to her young daughter's psyche?

Tears slipped out of the corners of her eyes.

It had been hours since they'd been dumped in the cells, and dead silence had reigned throughout the cell block. When they first arrived, Angie had tried to engage her cellmate, but when the woman refused to say anything, Angie had been forced to crawl under her dirty blanket and close her eyes.

She'd slept and woken, off and on. When she was awake, she thought about how Tim and Sam might find her, and considered half a dozen ways she could find out more information to plot an escape. Of course, to gather more data, she needed to get out of the cell.

She even thought about work for a time, wondering about the Q4 results Finance was supposed to show her in a few days. Her CTO was on the verge of negotiating a distribution breakthrough, and the CIO was rolling out a new system for lipid and CO_2 data analysis. She also had interviews scheduled for the new HR VP hire. The work that her team was doing for Futures Command in Austin was proving profitable, and was producing insight on how to cross-pollinate the high-tech Army ideas with the production of biofuels. But it looked like she was going to miss the big face-to-face meeting later in the week. Her toes tapped the bed with frustration.

Her sense of time was distorted by the stark lighting and lack of windows, but she guessed it was probably evening. Or maybe even night. She was hungry, but so far the guards had brought only water.

Angie got down off her top bunk and tried once again to talk to her brunette cellmate. She kept her tone low. "Do you speak English?"

The woman looked around with wild eyes and pointed at her back, clearly wanting to make sure it was safe to talk. Seemed she understood the question, though.

Angie took in her surroundings with more care. She'd had some training in spotting cameras and saw no revealing dot or glint. The rear and side walls were limestone, perhaps worn smooth by years of water movement, and would be a hard place to hide electronics. A string of naked bulbs ran between cells, but she saw no sign of a camera there either. Of course, she'd missed the signs back at the bar that they were being drugged, and mentally kicked herself, wanting to be extra careful now.

Could she use any of her other CIA education in this situation? Because her goal was intel, the vast majority of her training had been in the psychology of getting people to help her find information. Over the years, she'd learned a few tricks based on the MICE acronym. Money, ideology, compromise, and ego were the carrots and sticks used to recruit agents. Perhaps it could work on the other captives as well.

A young woman stood in the cell across the hall. Her eyes held a haggard, haunted look, and her may-have-once-been-blonde hair stood on end like she hadn't showered for a week. She had not come in with their group, all of which signaled she was an old-timer. Angie waved at her.

"What's your name?" she whispered.

The woman waved her away with a tired arm and sat down on her bunk.

Angie wanted to shake the bars. Didn't these people want to get out of this place? She wanted a drink. Wanted to see Harper laugh. Wanted to fight with Tim about something. Wanted to hug her sister or run a meeting. Eat a bacon sandwich with fries. Be anywhere but in this cursed cell.

Over the years Tim had tried to teach her to meditate, claiming it had saved his life when he'd learned it in the military. It had helped him get his emotions under control and taught him to stop being such a hothead. She ran her fingers along the bars. He said it would calm her down. Help her deal with the loss.

Screw that.

She whipped her head around and strode the two steps over to Brunette Woman's lower bunk. Angie sat down next to her and pulled her coat tight against the chill.

"I don't see any cameras, but let's talk quietly."

The woman looked at her for a long minute. Her eyes were large and a soft brown. The smudged mascara gave her the look of a street waif. "Luna. My name is Luna." Her accent was thick.

"Angie. Are you Italian?"

Luna nodded.

Maybe she wouldn't even need a trick to get Luna to help. After all, they shared a strong motivation to get out. "Did you overhear any of the men's conversation?"

"Bits. They drowned one of their fellows for not following orders and were upset about it."

"Which orders?"

"I'm not sure. Maybe something about a woman who died?"

Angie swore. Zoe was indeed dead.

"What else?" Angie said, voice tight.

"A mention of Cleopatra. A side comment about helping Lieutenant Antonio find the old queen's treasure."

"Strange."

Luna nodded again.

"Do you know where we are? Who these men are?"

Luna shook her head.

Angie winced. "Why they took us? Or where they took my daughter?"

Another shake.

"Do you speak other languages?"

"A few."

"Please see what you can learn from her." Angie moved her eyes across the hall. "She was here when we arrived."

Luna pursed her lips for a moment and then got to her feet. She walked to the bars, and after looking left and right, started speaking. She tried a few different languages before uttering words Angie recognized as German. The girl looked up. Luna gestured for her to come stand closer. She did and they had a short talk before the girl sat down again.

Luna came back to the bunk and sat next to Angie.

"Well?"

Luna massaged her forehead. "Whoever they are, they bring the women only water. No food. We'll be let out to cook and clean on a rotating schedule. Women are usually here for about a week. Then they disappear. Forever."

CHAPTER 16

Bari, Italy
Day Two

Time seemed to stretch.

It didn't matter how the man had snuck up on Sam in the plaza. The important thing was the cold steel at the base of her skull.

She reacted in a heartbeat.

The instant she felt the unmistakable muzzle press deeper into her hairline, she rolled toward the gunman, wrapping an arm around his gun elbow and forcing the assailant's aim toward the other side of the plaza. But she didn't stop moving.

The pistol exploded. The shock wave of the sound accelerated her action.

She used the base of her right palm, and all her momentum, to clock the attacker under the chin. His face jerked back and the rest of him followed. As his head struck pavement, a loud crack filled the night. His eyes went blank.

Ears still ringing from the firearm's detonation, Sam bent over and checked for a pulse. None. She slapped her palm on the cobblestones. It hadn't been her intention to kill him, or the original attacker whose body was still crumpled by the church's bottom step. She was zero for two.

Standing, she drew her weapon from its waistband holster and scanned the small courtyard. The curved doors and windows of the surrounding houses were all shuttered for the night.

Nothing stirred. The attacker's weapon wasn't silenced, so she expected company soon.

Moving with as much speed as she could, she checked the second attacker's pockets and found them empty. Curious, she pulled aside his shirt and found the same tattoo of a hooded cobra wrapped around an apple.

She stood and left the area, walking fast through shadows down the adjacent narrow lane. "Stryker?"

"Here."

Sam struggled to control her breathing. "Location?"

"Nearing the park."

The narrow lane gave way to a small street. She turned right. "I was attacked. Two men down."

"Dead?"

"Yes." She cringed. "Watch your back."

"You, too. Meet me here."

"Roger."

The small street ran into the thoroughfare where the chase had begun. Sam turned left at the gelato shop and walked briskly toward the park. When she got to the tree-lined tunnel, Stryker was kneeling next to the captain.

"He's gone. Nothing more to gain." Stryker stood. "Follow me."

Alert for additional men, Sam followed at a distance as they headed through the trees for the artery that ran parallel to the sea. It wasn't until they were both in the black Fiat that she allowed herself to truly exhale.

Stryker started the car and drove off, scanning the rearview mirror for a tail. "What happened?"

Now that the adrenaline was wearing off, she felt exhausted. "Let's head out of town and find a spot to decompress," she said, leaning back in the seat. "Get some food."

He drove around several blocks, checking for a tail, and then drove north out of town. She berated herself the entire drive, wishing to have been able to capture at least one of them alive. Killing was her least favorite part of the job.

Fifteen minutes later, Stryker pulled into the parking lot of a restaurant with a view of the sea. A flashing neon sign advertised fresh seafood.

Stryker turned off the Fiat. "Okay, fill me in."

Sipping from a lemonade she'd left in the car, Sam told him about following the captain from the old castle, seeing him fall, chasing the gunman, her return shot to his chest, finding the tattoo, and being surprised by the second attacker.

Stryker listened silently. Her heart pounded as she relived the long three minutes it had taken for the two attackers to die. When she was finished, she said, "I'm sorry we don't have one of them to question about the captain's death."

"That would have been nice, but you're alive, and that's more important."

She cleared her throat. "I didn't figure that the second one would crack his head like that."

"Your training kicked in. It saved your life."

"I know, but . . ."

"Battle is unpredictable, Sam. Not your fault."

She took a deep breath. "Okay, I'll get over it. At least we got a lead. Check out the tattoos."

He took the phone from her and flipped through the pictures. "Send them to Ace."

"Did that while you were driving."

"Good."

She pulled her comfort coin from her pocket and rubbed it between her palms. "Ever seen a tat like that?"

"No. You?"

"No."

Stryker stretched his neck, and a popping sound rippled through the night. "Who the hell are these guys?"

"I have no idea," Sam said. "And I can't help but wonder when the next batch will show up."

CHAPTER 17

Eden
Day Three

The scent of fresh-baked bread and fried eggs was making Angie feel nauseated. Her head throbbed and anxiety thrummed through the rest of her body. Those drugs had a wicked tail.

She stood, waiting for the next stack of breakfast plates. Her task was to deliver the food to the men and children in the dining hall on the other side of a set of swinging double doors. Reno was working with her, and Angie was eager to find a chance to talk.

In the dining room, a large painting of the fall of man in the garden of Eden hung on one wall, reminding her of how strange she'd felt to be a girl when she'd first heard the tale of Adam and Eve in Bible School. The man who had to be the group's leader sat at the head of a table, holding court as jesters watched his every move. His face was handsome enough, but with his widow's peak, receding hairline, and strangely forked beard, he reminded her of the devil.

The industrial-sized kitchen was modern, all stainless steel apart from the large wooden cutting board that dominated the center of the room. A rack of pots hung overhead.

She and her fellow captives cooked and served, free of chains. On the walk to the kitchen building, it had become painfully obvious that they were being held on an island, as sapphire blue ocean surrounded them on every side and there was no other land mass in sight. Why tie them up? There was nowhere to go.

The barren island sported a baker's dozen worth of colorful houses, a courtyard that held a wooden post, and she'd heard there was a garden somewhere. The harbor and cells weren't visible from above. Then there was this community dining hall and kitchen.

Cooking flames rose from two six-burner stove tops and hood fans whirred, pulling some of the scents out. Not enough, though. Her stomach lurched. Would they feed Harper and Layla, wherever they were?

According to cell-block rumor, the raven-haired mistress of the kitchen had no tongue and was named Zola. The woman wielded the only knife in sight and had just four fingers on her right hand. The missing finger reminded Angie of Tim. She'd been so seventh-grade-butterflies-in-the-stomach-head-over-heels-in-love with him. Her husband's straight-arrow honesty and chiseled features had drawn her in at that first Air Force function that Sam had dragged her to, and she'd appreciated his calm strength for years. Where had their relationship gone sour?

She looked down at her own trembling hands. It had to be the roofies. They couldn't be shaking from the lack of alcohol. God, he'd been going on about her drinking for months. Tim was just so judgmental, saying she was ignoring Harper, and him. She understood his concern given his father had killed his mom and sister in a drunken rage, but her drinking wasn't on that level. She usually waited until she got home for her first drink of the day, and paced herself. It helped her deal with the grief. Never was she violent.

A thick-chested young man entered the kitchen. He shared the handsome features, but not the forked beard or nose, of the man she'd heard called the *comandante*. It was probably Antonio, who she'd heard was second in command.

Thunk!

The sound and scream broke Angie out of her reverie. A vibrating knife pinned Reno's palm to the monstrous wooden cutting board. Based on a nearby basket of fruit, it looked like her hungry friend's attempted theft had been interrupted by the weapon-wielding matron. Angie swallowed back the bile that rose in her throat.

Antonio yanked the knife from the cutting board and tossed it into the large steel sink. He shook his head and marched out of the room.

Reno crumpled to the floor, grabbing her hand. Her eyes were shut and Angie wondered if her friend would pass out.

Angie rushed to Reno's aid, applying pressure with a towel as the matriarch grabbed a first aid kit from the pantry and motioned for Angie to deal with the deep wound. Zola's eyes held troubled shadows, maybe a glint of guilt; Angie wondered if the stabbing had been for Antonio's benefit.

She cleaned and bandaged Reno's hand, waiting until Zola was at the other end of the kitchen to whisper, "I'm going to find a way to get us out of here."

Reno sobbed. "Okay."

"Have you heard where our girls are?"

Reno just shook her head.

After hugging her friend a last time, Angie was called back to waitress duty by Zola's arm gestures. Never having worked food service, she felt awkward carrying the plates. If the children worked in the kitchen, she hoped that at some point she and Harper would be on duty together. Angie needed to see her kid's bright blue eyes to know her daughter was okay.

The pine-floored dining hall was full of tables flanked by long benches. Her rough count identified seventy-five men of all ages, and there were at least twenty prepubescent kids. One strawberry-blonde girl looked like an older version of Harper without the braid, and Angie's heart skipped a beat. No, her daughter wasn't there. A handful of male teenagers sat at their own table, but there were no female teenagers about, which added a data point to her new sex-trafficking theory. But it made her stomach even queasier. That knife incident had been horrible.

The men at Antonio's table laughed.

Something about the young lieutenant looked familiar. He was short for a man, about five-seven, with a neatly trimmed mustache and bulging pecs, and wore a long-sleeved T-shirt. Unlike his father, he had an aquiline nose with a bump on the ridge. Every time she was within earshot, Angie tried to focus on his and his cronies' conversation, but she didn't speak Italian.

Over time, she caught a few words that were similar to their English equivalents: Cleopatra. Treasure. That was one group of words. Later, as she cleaned away dirty plates: Camels. India. Prime minister.

What were they planning?

CHAPTER 18

Bikaner, India
Day Three

Jane surveyed the procession that marked the official beginning to the annual Bikaner Camel Festival. If she were prime minister of India, there was no way she'd risk her life by attending an occasion like this in person. Opportunities for an assassin were everywhere.

Fortunately, as a British PSYOPS and counterintelligence officer, Jane was good at her job.

It was more than just her studies in psychology; she naturally saw threats and problems everywhere. That double-edged sense of paranoid perception stemmed from childhood, when her basic need for security hadn't been met. She saw the world as a dangerous place, the glass half-empty, the hike uphill both ways. Those tendencies gave her excellent covert ops skills, but they hadn't worked so well for her home life in Berkshire—her fearful nature had driven her husband into the arms of another woman. He'd left five years ago and she still missed him. She frowned. He'd have enjoyed the wild spectacle occurring in this five-hundred-year-old city.

It was pandemonium. An Indian Mardi Gras. Inside the medieval walls of the old town, the street was a riot of color, sound, and smells. Bearded, turban-wearing men sat on red-cushion saddles atop camels, and led the parade carrying curved swords. Camels either had their fur cut into elaborate bas-relief designs, or they were covered head-to-toe in brightly colored balls, ribbons, and flags. Children ran screaming between the beasts, trailing colorful streamers, while their parents lined the street, some wearing outrageous costumes and grotesque masks. Many adults were getting high, using straws to sip traditional cannabis-infused bhang lassis made from yogurt, nuts, spices, and rose water. Hindi, Rajasthan, and English languages mixed in curious combinations.

Amidst the confusion, her mission was to aid the country's version of a secret service and help protect the PM.

The official motorcade was the last part of the parade. Since the car was enabled with top-of-the-line security features, including bulletproof windows, run-flat tires, and armored doors, she figured the killers would wait to take their shot during the speech that would precede the night's fireworks display.

That was, assuming the PM was the target. Similar teams were in place all over India. The M2 team from America had "Stingray" a hundred miles away in New Delhi, watching a religious guru. What was the officer's real name? The instant attraction she'd felt to him on the video call was disarming and unusual.

Focusing, she was glad she'd drawn the PM. After spending her teenage years in a convent, Jane wasn't keen on religion.

She'd foregone her usual black clothes and dressed to fit in with the crowd. Stationed among them, she made a point to walk near large families so she didn't stick out as a loner. Her tan skin and dark features might have let her pass as a local, but her paranoia meant she rarely left the house without a silicone mask. There was no way she'd be on a mission without one. They were laser custom fitted to her head and completely covered her hair, facial features, chest and shoulders. She could look old, young, or anywhere in between. Today she'd gone for the Asian tourist look. Her aim was to keep a steady distance between herself and the PM's rolling security cage.

Senses alert, she tried to imagine how a team might attack the motorcade. The PM was in a black sedan, which looked out of place in the colorful parade. Although the windows were bulletproof, they were clear so onlookers could see the copious hand waving. The buildings along the route were not high, usually only two stories, and had ornate, carved roof fronts that would make any sniper happy. If he or she could get the PM out of the car.

Jane's boot struck a manhole and the sound made her consider the sewer system. If someone rigged a bomb . . .

The explosion threw her forward, onto her knees. Camels screamed and ran in all directions, nearly crushing her. Clambering back to her feet, she saw that the PM's car was on its side, on fire. Jane pulled her service weapon and scanned the crowd as she sprinted for the sedan, where festival goers were helping dazed security forces pull the PM out of the backseat. Jane had no chance to stop them.

With the adrenaline, everything became slow motion. A telltale puff left the PM's back. Jane swore. She hadn't heard the shot over the crowd noise.

From the exit wound, she calculated the angle and looked up the street toward a corner market. A figure dressed in the red-and-white mask of Japanese theatre tucked a pistol into the folds of his costume. Acting on years of training, Jane fired.

The murderer fell facedown in front of a rampaging camel. If her shot didn't kill him, the camel would.

She just hoped the assassin wasn't affiliated with the Sons of Adam.

CHAPTER 19

Bari, Italy
Day Three

Mulling over the strange tattoos found on last night's attackers, Stryker checked his weaponry from the front seat of Sam's black Fiat. His Glock was loaded and his knife moved freely in its sheath. He patted the extra magazine in the pocket of his leather jacket, and then inspected his clear, tight-fitting latex gloves, which would eliminate fingerprints. Finally, those shielded fingers patted the mask that hid his facial features. All set there, too.

Sam was staking out the front of the bar from the comfort of a café, and he had eyes on the rain-soaked alley just in case yesterday's bartender had given today's a heads-up that they'd been asking around. Better to play it safe.

It was early yet. Nine-ish. Another gray, rainy morning. Stryker wanted to be gone before the place filled up with innocent bystanders. The posted hours said serving began at eleven.

"Sam."

"Yes?"

"Nice work last night."

She had downplayed what happened, and clearly felt embarrassed an attacker had snuck up on her while she was taking pictures, but she'd reacted in a heartbeat. Although he'd reminded her that they were trained to protect themselves, her posture had been slumped throughout their silent breakfast.

"Thanks," she said.

Her tone was still quieter than usual. A quiet Sam was not a happy Sam.

"Any action out front?" he asked.

"No."

Stryker closed the connection. He knew how she felt. He hadn't learned to manage his hot head until the military's mindfulness training. Before that, there had been a string of inappropriate if not lethal fights, all of which left him feeling ashamed and guilty. But Stryker's meditation teacher, a large-as-a-refrigerator bald man, had recognized a fellow anger management problem. The man's name was Thompson and he'd spent time in juvie before joining the military.

Stryker could still remember his teacher telling him, "An angry man has lost the battle before it begins."

Today would be a good test of keeping his cool. The heat was already rising from his chest into his face, a warning sign that he was in danger of no longer thinking straight. But the man he was stalking had to have some knowledge of what happened to his wife and daughter. May have been complicit in their disappearance. Stryker focused on deep breathing exercises and reminded himself that the barkeep would be no use to him dead.

He had additional motivation to stay calm. When he'd spoken with Ace a few hours ago, she said she had found nothing in her databases on men with cobra/apple tattoos. There were a few more databases to search, but for now, this setup was their best chance at finding a lead, especially since no ransom communication had been forthcoming and the police captain was dead.

Deep breath in. Deep breath out.

When it came to emotions, Thompson's instructions said to sit with them and let them pass. Last night, Stryker had done that when sleep failed to come. The anger had sensations to it—heat in the face, tightness in his jaw—and he catalogued them with his eyes closed. Underneath the red-hot anger was a sadness in his gut, a thought that Angie might already be dead. That he'd failed her. That Harper might be dead too. Fear there, too. A dark fear of failure that ran up and down his spinal cord. Subtle. A shadow of grief. He sat with all the feelings until they passed.

Now he was angry again, but it was not the time for additional processing. He needed to focus. He shoved the feelings down, promising to come back to them later. He took a final deep breath to clear his mind, interlaced his fingers, and stretched his arms out in front of him, above the steering wheel. Returning his hands to his lap, he settled in to wait.

Ten minutes later Sam spoke again, using terse mission language.

"I think bartender just drove by," she said. "Late-model Benz. Parking at lot."

They'd scouted the parking lot at the end of the block. Stryker was parked at the other end of the alley so he could see down its length.

"Yep. That's him," Sam added. "Headed your way."

Stryker's heart rate kicked up. "Anyone with him or around?"

"No."

The bartender, a clean-shaven man of medium build wearing a hooded yellow rain jacket, swung his keys around his index finger as he walked down the alley. He skirted a large puddle and moved around a dumpster. It didn't look like he was expecting an ambush.

Stryker had to time it just right.

The guy hit the middle of the block. Stryker got out of the car, locked it, and walked down the alley just as the barkeep turned toward the bar's back entrance. The man pulled open the screen door. Stryker stepped closer. As soon as the man turned the key in the lock, Stryker lunged. He'd been seven feet away, and covered the distance in just over a second. He pulled the man's hands behind his back. The bartender immediately slumped. It wasn't a fair fight.

"Hey, *lasciami andare*!" the bartender said, demanding to be released.

Stryker thought about his missing wife and wanted to dislocate the guy's shoulder. Yanked on it a little. The guy whimpered.

Breathe. He released the extra pressure.

Stryker replied in the man's language, "You scream and I will break your arm before I slit your throat, understand?"

The man nodded. After zip-tying the captive's hands, Stryker pushed open the screen door, turned the knob, and shoved the man inside. Still holding the man's hands, Stryker shut the back door with his foot and turned on a light with an elbow. They were in the narrow bathroom hallway.

Stryker drew his knife and put it to the man's throat. "Tell me what happened to the women you served at the bar day before yesterday."

"Which women? I served a lot of women."

Stryker had the video cued up and sheathed the knife long enough to show it. The rain jacket began to shake.

"Who are you?" The man's voice trembled.

Stryker put the phone in his coat pocket and drew the knife again with a satisfying whisk of the blade. He nicked the man's cheek. Blood trickled. "You cut yourself shaving."

The man began to sob. "Don't kill me."

"Don't make me. Where are the women?"

"I don't know."

"Did the men sitting at the end of the bar take them?'

The smell of urine rose from the already sticky hallway floor.

"I . . . I can't tell you."

"Why?"

"They will kill me."

Stryker made another nick on the opposite cheek. Twin rivulets of crimson tears flowed down the bartender's face.

Stryker put the cold steel of the knife against the carotid and pressed until a thin red line appeared there. He enunciated each word. "I will kill you right now."

"The men may have followed the women to the bathroom."

Grim satisfaction filled Stryker's chest. "Did they come back?"

"No."

"Did you drug the women?"

The man tensed. "I had no choice."

"Will there be a ransom demand?"

"No idea."

"Where did they take the women?"

"I don't know. They've never told me. They just show up, give me drugs to put in the drinks they buy for women, and give me a very large tip on the way out. I have a friend who refused them. His body was never found."

"Is that how you afford the Mercedes?"

"Yes."

"Who are they?"

"I only know the name secretly passed between bartenders."

"Which is what?"

"The Sons of Adam."

"Where can I find them?"

"I do not know."

Stryker gripped the blade's handle until his knuckles turned white. It was a lead, but razor thin at best.

Sensing he'd hit the end of the road, Stryker took the man's phone, gagged him, and locked him in a storage closet. He wanted to be long gone before the bartender made his way out.

He was three feet away from the exterior door when the handle turned.

CHAPTER 20

Bikaner, India
Day Three

Rey left his previous assignment as soon as he'd gotten word that the India hit had occurred in the middle of a camel parade. At first, he thought it a strange place for a kill, but the chaos had worked to the assassin's advantage. At least until Jane took the guy out.

He met her in the parking lot of a tired motel in an urban section of Bikaner not far from the walled old city.

She stepped out of her car, her petite frame short and slight, her muscles taut. A vaguely Asian mask covered the features he'd found so intriguing in their short video call. The air between them instantly felt electric.

Jane held a keycard in the air. "Found it when searching the assassin's body."

The card had a fortress logo, representing a chain of low-end motels called The Castle Hotels.

"Good work. Guess that's why we're here." He sounded stupid again. Maybe he should try being the strong, silent type.

"Yes, I've visited four local hotels in the chain, but none checked out."

"Let's see if we can get the room number from the clerk."

"Hope so. This is the last stop in town."

At the reception desk, the clerk resisted until Rey moved his jacket aside to give the guy a glimpse of the semi-automatic weapon tucked into the back of his waistband. With wide eyes, the clerk relented, giving them a room number.

Rey walked from reception to the second story, alert, Jane at his side. These guys were good enough that it could be a setup. The familiar feeling of walking onto a battlefield made him break out in a cold sweat. He tasted the iron tang of blood on his tongue, and the faces of too many dead airmen and -women passed through his mind's eye. Good friends who'd been cut down in their prime.

Stay present. Focus.

He couldn't afford to be sucked into the past right now.

They stopped in front of Room 208, taking positions on opposing sides of the faded brown doorframe. A hot afternoon wind blew from the desert across the exterior hallway. A single bead of sweat trickled down his temple.

They had synced earpieces. He subvocalized, "On my count."

She nodded. He liked the intelligence in her eyes.

"Three. Two. One."

He could pick the lock if necessary, but would prefer it if the keycard worked. She slid it across the face of the mechanism. Click.

Heart racing, he pushed the door open six inches with his foot, service pistol drawn. Peering around the corner, he took stock.

Twin beds. Both unmade. Sheets and flowered coverlets pulled back. Light on in the tiny bathroom. Dead quiet. No sign of inhabitants.

He pushed open the door all the way and she followed on his heels. Together they cleared the bedroom and tiny bath, which held only a stand-up shower. The sink and floors had been recently cleaned. No hair on the shower floor. No one under the beds.

He went back to the door and closed it with his gloved hand, locking it before returning his weapon to its waistband holster. She also put her pistol away.

He pointed at the two disturbed beds. "Looks like there was more than one."

She nodded before rifling through the drawers of the bureau between the beds while he examined the bathroom more closely.

"I've got nothing."

"Same here." He sniffed the air for any trace of a unique odor. None. "We'll want to get a forensics team in here."

"Yes. The locals can handle that."

"No ID on the body, right?"

"Correct. All I found was the keycard."

"Body is at the morgue now?"

"Yes. Hours ago. They said they'd expedite the autopsy."

Rey liked her cool, efficient manner. That she had the skill to take out the assassin who nailed the PM was a bonus.

They walked out of the room, on the lookout for company. Within two minutes, they were at street level, walking around the building.

"See any security cameras?" she asked.

"No."

Her phone buzzed and she looked down at the screen. "The coroner. He says there's only one interesting tidbit. Photo attached."

"He worked fast."

She swiped at the screen. Her shoulders froze and her scent became acrid. He recognized the smell of fear.

"What is it?" he asked as he moved to stand behind her.

She brought the screen up so he could see it. "Look."

Earlier, Stryker had sent them both a picture of a tattoo taken from the killers Sam had dropped last night in Bari.

"Same tattoo, different tango," he said.

"My conclusion is we have a professional team of hitmen in this town."

"Agreed. And at least one is still alive."

CHAPTER 21

Rome, Italy
Day Three

Angry that someone had taken out one of his men in Bikaner, the *comandante* stalked through Rome's ancient tunnels, his path lit only by the narrow beam of a penlight. He'd entered via a hidden entrance five blocks away from St. Peter's Square, in the basement of a delicatessen close to his favorite gelato shop. One of the new women had been disobedient, causing him to run a little late.

The tunnels that led to the spider-webbed catacombs beneath the Vatican were damp and smelled of rat droppings, stale water, and old earth. It was not his favorite place, but he needed information and the Vatican's spy service was his best option since the arrangement with the Saudis had soured. He would treat himself to a mint-chocolate gelato when the meeting was over.

As he walked, he wondered about how his man had been taken down at the camel festival, and if the recent death of his two fishermen in Bari were related. Could someone have their scent? It was rare for him to lose men.

To take his mind off that worry, he reflected on the current status of finding Cleopatra's treasure. Antonio had experts stationed in digs throughout Egypt and the Mediterranean, and the command hub at Eden monitored online newspapers, newsfeeds, journals, and social media, but the *comandante* wanted more results. Which was why he'd decided on an additional aggressive task force to ferret out clues by more traditional strong-armed means.

One night in his office two months ago, he'd sat his son down over an after-dinner port and discussed the decision. Antonio, uncomfortable with forceful tactics, had pushed back, even questioned the need to find the old queen's journal. The *comandante* appreciated his son was not a "yes man" and had trained him from a young age to think for himself. Some of that training had come with a belt, but the boy had eventually settled. The *comandante* dismissed his son's concerns with a wave of his cigar. Octavian had thought the threat real. Yes, some leaders along the way had figured it all for rumor, a false trail laid by Cleopatra, but the *comandante* didn't give her that much credit.

For him, finding her journal and/or the location of her stash was as important as taking out the targeted world leaders. In this age of computer technology and constant archeological discovery, it was essential that they find whatever she hid before some other party did. He understood all too well the importance of—what did they call it these days?— "controlling the narrative." Perception was everything. Whatever it was, they had to find it first.

He'd check on the latest developments when he returned to the island.

A spider web caught in his hair and he brushed it out, deciding to use his whip to clear the rest of the way. It took a good fifteen minutes to navigate to the agreed location. As he neared the intersecting tunnels where they were to meet, the smooth walls gave way to carved openings where small bodies had once lain. While a few skeletons were still visible, most had been reduced to dust. These catacombs were not open to the public.

At last, his thin ray of light fell on the bent old spymaster he was here to meet. It was said the ancient priest had been born into the family of a humble fisherman. Now one of the world's most powerful men, Cardinal Vinetti wore street clothes but kept a starched white collar to mark the religious aspect of his office. His shock of hair matched the collar's brightness, but his brown eyes held only shadows. The *comandante* regretted that, unlike most powerful men who enjoyed the "candy" he offered, the old priest kept his vow of chastity. Less leverage would make this conversation a challenge.

He reattached the whip to his belt and the men clasped hands. This conversation was going to be a lot like an angling expedition.

The spymaster's voice was raspy with age. "You asked me for the meet. What's on your mind?"

Dangle the bait. "We're working on a project that promises long-term rewards for both of our organizations."

"And?"

"We've run into a snag."

"What sort of snag?"

Who was killing his men? "I'm not sure. That's why I need your help."

The spymaster stood still as death, thinking. "Can I assume your project is related to the recent demise of the Saudi crown prince?"

The *comandante* struggled to keep his face impassive. The old man was smart and well connected, but he shouldn't have been able to finger them as responsible. Did the priest know about their other, recent successes? The *comandante*'s shoulders stiffened. On the other hand, if the spymaster knew their plan and agreed to meet, maybe he already saw the advantages. "What if it was?"

A wry smile passed the dour man's lips. "You should come to confession."

The *comandante* held his breath and said nothing. He knew he was pushing the Vatican's limits with his plan to assassinate so many world leaders.

The spymaster turned. "I must go."

Time for more bait. "Wait."

The old man stopped. The gnarled neck turned, and the spymaster's dark eyes bore into the *comandante*'s soul.

The *comandante* waved his arm. "Look around."

"Why?"

The *comandante* met the old man's stare with a glare of his own. "Before my grandfather and your predecessor worked out a deal, this is where the dwarf-limbed sins of the priests and sisters ended up. Those unwanted children died young because they never saw sunlight. Now, we give their lives purpose."

The old man narrowed his eyes. "Do you wish to discontinue our arrangement?"

"Not at all. It has been mutually beneficial."

"What exactly are you proposing then?"

A nibble on the line. "I believe someone is interfering in my operation. I need to know more."

"And what's in it for us?"

Set the hook, then reel them in.

They spent the next few minutes hashing out the details before the *comandante* left, his steps lighter for having caught the big fish. He looked forward to his mint-chocolate reward.

CHAPTER 22

Bari, Italy
Day Three

Stryker watched the bar's back-alley doorknob turn. It moved too slowly. Someone wanted stealth.

There was nowhere to hide in the narrow hallway. As the back entrance opened, Stryker prepared for a confrontation.

But the white-shirted man who stepped inside was no threat. When he saw Stryker, he dropped his phone and clutched at his heart.

The man's telephone squawked. "Guido? Where'd you go?"

Stryker put a finger to his lips, brushed around the intruder, apparently the cook, and flew out the door.

In the harbor two hours later, Stryker completed his search of the captain's vessel and stepped onto the floating dock. Sam's call last night had interrupted his search of the ship and he'd wanted to finish what he started. She was watching his back from the area of the closed Ferris wheel, from where she could sound an alarm if anyone approached via the harbor or pedestrian walk.

His shoulder ached as he strode down the dock in the half-light of a grim afternoon, passing a variety of fishing boats, sailboats, and pleasure craft. A bright scarf set off his disguise *du jour* and he wrapped it around his mouth to ward off the cold wind.

He'd found nothing on the boat. Not a speck of blood. Not a stray hair. Nada. Zilch. Expected, but still frustrating.

Likewise, the bartender's phone had shown no suspicious calls or contacts.

Bari was dry as a desert well in the scorching heat of summer. All they had were two meager clues. Sons of Adam. A strange tattoo. Ace needed to come through with something, and fast.

He stepped off the pier and onto the concrete jetty, which acted as the marina's parking area. No visible threats, but the empty space between the cars made him feel exposed, as did the seaside sidewalk he needed to walk to reach the black Fiat. He sensed another assailant was out there.

Stryker opened the car door and sat down heavily in the driver's seat. Sam was on the passenger's side, wearing the mask of a charmingly bespectacled African American woman with heavy freckles.

"How'd it go?" she asked.

"Struck out."

"Good thing we didn't bet on it. No evidence at all, huh?"

"No. Not surprising given it was the captain's personal vessel."

"I hear that. Now what?"

He looked down the street at the unmoving carnival ride and the flat gray sea beyond, wondering if his sweet daughter and irascible wife were still alive.

"It's not a good option, but I say we shake down the police station if we don't hear anything from Ace soon," he said.

Sam drank from her lemonade and reached into her pocket, pulling out her silver worry coin. She rolled it between her fingers. "We need to tell my mom."

"No, we don't."

"She's already asking me why she hasn't heard from Angie in two days. I've deflected so far but . . ." Sam's voice trailed off, husky.

"What about security protocols?"

Her voice rose. "Protocols be damned—this is her daughter."

"And my wife. And your sister. I get it. But what good would it do?"

She slammed her fist on her thigh. "It might help me."

He put a hand on her shoulder. Sniffing, she wiped underneath her eyes with her thumb and forefinger.

If he had anything to say that would make her feel better, he would, but it was hard enough for him to keep his own emotions under control.

They sat like that, sharing their loss and fear, and stared out at the frozen Ferris wheel.

Minutes later, Stryker's phone buzzed. He opened the secure email from Ace using the standard voice command to authenticate the encryption.

"From Ace," he said. "She says the only online reference she can find to the Sons of Adam was a Baltimore rock band from the sixties."

"Ha. I don't think they're our guys."

"No." He returned his attention to the email. "But a man was killed recently in Egypt, at a dig about eighteen miles west of Alexandria, near a town called Taposiris Magna. He had the cobra/apple tattoo over his heart. Stingray's en route ASAP." Stryker was glad Rey would be joining them.

Sam nodded, all business again. "I read about that place in one of my history journals. They think Cleopatra's tomb might be there."

"The Cleopatra comment from the bar video just got a lot more interesting."

CHAPTER 23

Bikaner, India
Day Three

Rey and Jane sat at a sturdy wooden table on the back deck of a local Rajasthani-themed restaurant, which overlooked the Junagarh Fort. Nearby, seven musicians in white robes and red turbans played folk music on long-necked string instruments next to a decorative pond. Torches lit the air and portable propane heaters warmed the cool night. The environment felt romantic and the tone of their conversation was comfortable.

"Our flight leaves in three hours?" Jane asked.

Rey checked his phone. "That's right. We arrive in Cairo early to chase the cobra tattoo lead." Wondering about the reaction she'd had to seeing it earlier, he looked at the dessert menu and considered when to ask her about it. "Want to try the *ghevar*?"

"I'd love to." Jane touched his arm. "Hard to resist sugar, saffron, and cardamom."

He was having a hard time resisting *her*, but had no idea if the feeling was mutual. It seemed the light in her eyes was warm, and her smiles genuine. But flirting was hard when you wore a silicone mask over your features. She sure did smell good, though.

They ordered espresso and the round dessert.

Rey sipped from a glass of water. "Nice work nailing the assassin and tracking down the hotel."

"Thank you."

"You're from a PSYOPS unit, right? Will you tell me about it?" he asked. "My background is mechanical engineering and IT."

She gave him a half-smile. "Of course. It's basically using psychology in operations."

He laughed. "I could figure that much out from the name. What's it really about?"

"Persuasion." She shrugged a thin shoulder. "Influencing the opponent."

"Ah. Military propaganda?"

"You could call it that. One man's propaganda is another man's truth."

He'd wondered why she'd been assigned to this mission. Now it made sense. St. James had mentioned the enemy might be using new deepfake technology that could effectively mimic real-life video. He liked to keep up on the latest tech and knew that artificial intelligence was pushing boundaries. Fabricated media was a troublesome turn of events. He already had a distrust of most news. "I suppose."

"It's been a practice since ancient times. Some historians go back to the Romans. Octavian and Mark Antony are said to have waged an impressive campaign against one another."

"Then the idea would have needed to be far older. For them to be successful, I mean."

"I agree," she said eagerly. "An inscription about the rise of Darius I to the Persian throne in 515 BC is one of the first known cases."

"Cool." He was enjoying her enthusiasm. "Any other historical examples?"

"Benjamin Franklin circulated false tales of atrocities done by the Seneca Indians because they were in league with the British."

He loved that she was smart. "I'll never look at a hundred-dollar bill the same way again. What else?"

"Clergymen in India made up stories about the raping of White girls and women."

"Savages."

"Who, the clergymen or the natives?"

He smiled, starting to feel less stupid in her company. "When was the concept militarized, though?"

"French Revolution and the Napoleonic wars. The American Revolution and Civil War. Then the Brits took the concept to a whole new level during World War I with posters, moving pictures, and literature demonizing the enemy. And in World War II, we tried to mobilize public opinion against the Nazis using the same techniques."

"I had no idea."

"It continued through the Cold War, Vietnam, the Afghan War, Iraq."

He studied the fort in the near distance. Part of the red and gold sandstone wall was lit by spotlights. It reminded him of an op in Libya in 2011.

She continued: "Even drug cartels hand out pamphlets and leaflets to threaten rivals and to recruit."

The waitress brought their dessert and coffee. The combination smelled rich.

He took a sip. The fresh brew was hot on his tongue. "It's probably being used in ways we don't even realize." He thought back to the protest he'd witnessed in Saudi Arabia. "Definitely on social media."

"Yes, the Russians, Chinese, and our own governments are very good at sowing discord." She fingered a necklace. "In my professional opinion, social media has inundated everyone to the point that they can't easily tell fact from fiction, so they use their emotions to sort."

"Emotions or intuition?"

"Emotions. Intuition is a warning that has used information from your subconscious, but emotions arise through filters and don't see the whole picture."

He thought about that for a minute. His therapist had said something similar once. "Go on."

"9/11 and the advent of social media created the perfect storm of fear and manipulation. It's fashioned an amazing environment for what I call 'weeds' to flourish. People can't see the truth. And some seeds are planted intentionally."

Rey liked a good conspiracy theory as much as the next guy, but some of the crap he'd seen lately on social media amazed even him. "I see. But we can all choose our thoughts."

"But what if you're scared? Not thinking straight?"

"What do you mean?"

She lowered her voice and leaned forward. "Sometimes, and I'm not saying *we* do this . . . but I've heard the purpose of propaganda can be to make you forget you have the free will even to choose your thoughts. Use fear to confuse, so you'll be more open to lies."

The light caught the gold cross around her neck.

"That's deep. I think we're going to get along." He pointed. "I like your necklace."

She leaned in. "Thanks. You wear a similar one?"

He brought it out from his shirt. "Christopher. My patron saint."

She smiled. "Brilliant."

"Thanks." He wanted to see what else they had in common. "Do you believe in aliens?"

She touched her chest, startled. "No."

"Did Harvey Oswald act alone?"

"Who cares?"

"How about Princess Di and the brakes on her car?"

"Now *that* we can debate."

While eating the sweet *ghevar*, they argued for and against the case of the tampered brakes, who the driver's true paymasters were, why the covert officer testified about MI6 involvement, and why there were no recorded CCTV images. Rey was in his element.

As they finished up their espresso he said, "I saw your shoulders freeze back in the hotel when you saw that tattoo. Did it touch a nerve?"

She looked toward the fort, as if considering her answer.

An instant later, the front window of the restaurant shattered. Jane upended the table and pushed him to the ground behind it. The musicians threw down their instruments and scrambled for safety as chaos and screaming erupted around the patio. Gunshots pierced the solid wood in front of them, pieces flying everywhere.

Impressed by her quick reflexes, Rey ground his teeth against the noise, wishing a missile would take out the entire castle. His pistol wasn't going to do a thing at this distance. They were in trouble.

CHAPTER 24

Eden
Day Three

Angie collapsed onto her bunk. She'd served breakfast, helped wash up, served lunch, and was now exhausted. Her stomach was starting to devour itself, gnawing and gnawing until it felt like it would soon poof away into nothingness.

Worse, she was sweating and had a headache.

A fine Scotch with a bacon, lettuce, and tomato sandwich sounded divine. After a biofuel conference in Scotland two years ago, she'd been treated to a finger of ultra-rare Glenfiddich Janet Sheed Roberts Reserve single-malt whisky. If she focused, she could still recall the pale gold color and heavenly flavor of barley, pear, and heather.

She needed a drink. How was she going to escape from this place?

Tapping her foot irritably, she stared up at the ceiling. Luna snored softly in the bunk below. Angie pulled the dirty blanket close; it sure was cold.

Word had come back from down the cells that Harper and her pal Layla were being kept with the island's other children. So far, she hadn't found any way to communicate, since the youngsters were kept apart.

Red-hot panic had given way to the slow burn of frustration. She wanted to pound her fists on the wall until she punched a way out.

Angie ground her teeth. Who were these bastards, besides people who would keep a four-year-old from her mother? Her kidnappers-for-hire theory had lost traction. They hadn't done any of the usual proof-of-life actions, like take a video with today's newspaper, or have her speak into a phone. And they'd taken so many other women. She was grateful they seemed to have no idea who she was, which was actually the only bright spot in this God-awful situation.

Sex-traffickers then? It seemed a logical, if more distressing choice. Then why the whipping in the courtyard? If the knife to Reno's hand hadn't been punishment enough for attempting to steal the fruit at breakfast, they'd all been forced to watch the *comandante* whip her. He'd had his men tie her to an honest-to-God whipping post and had lashed her with a fury-filled fire in his eyes that made Angie shiver. Eventually, Reno had passed out and the crazed leader had thrust his whip into his belt and walked back to the housing village, a newly lit cigar hanging from his lips. The whole thing had made Angie nauseous.

Why would they damage the merchandise? She was concerned about the wounds. She'd yelled down the line of cages to check on Reno, and it seemed there would be no further medical attention than the lame bandage Angie had applied.

She pressed her lips together and narrowed her eyes. She had to get them all out of here, but so far she'd gathered very little actionable intelligence. If only she spoke Italian.

A loud wheeze came from the bunk below.

An idea blossomed.

Angie jumped off the bed and fought a momentary sense of disorientation. Then she sat on Luna's bed and tapped the snoring woman on the shoulder. "Wake up."

Luna's soft brown eyes fluttered open. She sighed. "I was having a dream about poolside food service. A vegetarian sandwich with avocado delivered by a man with, how do you say, a six-pack of muscles."

Angie held up a hand—the fantasy of a sandwich was almost too much to bear right now. "Stop with the food dreams. I have an idea."

"It had better be good."

"I need your help."

"With what? Laundry?"

"I'm glad you found your sense of humor." Angie paused and lowered her voice. "I don't speak Italian."

"So?"

"You do."

"Yes. But I don't—"

Angie cut her off. "Were you paying attention today while we served?"

Luna pulled herself up to a cross-legged position. "Yes. Those eggs looked amazing."

Angie reminded herself the girl was young. "How old are you?"

"Twenty-two."

"Why were you in Bari?"

"Work. I'm an executive assistant. I wanted to explore the town before heading home."

"Where are you from?"

"Milano."

"Do you want to get back there?"

Luna rubbed her back where the guard had wounded her kidney. "Of course."

"I need your help to understand what the men are talking about." Angie realized she must be feeling stressed. She was drawing out her vowels, sounding like a southern belle.

A suspicious gleam entered Luna's eyes. "I see."

Angie's headache flared. "Can you do that? Listen instead of fantasizing about food?"

"What if they hurt me again?" Luna looked down, pulling her long brown hair over her shoulder.

"What if they sell us off as sex slaves?"

Luna wrinkled her nose. She looked away for a long minute, and then made eye contact. "Do you have a plan?"

"Not yet."

Luna exhaled deeply. "Cleopatra."

"What about her?"

"That's all I heard. They sent a new guy to a dig where her tomb might be. Paolo the archeologist." Luna lay back down on the bed and turned to face the wall. "Can I go back to sleep now?"

"Will you think about my request?"

A noncommittal grunt was the only response. Angie's head throbbed.

Frustrated, she strode over to the black metal bars of her prison and tried to pry them apart, Superman style. They didn't budge.

CHAPTER 25

Bikaner, India
Day Three

As the shooting at the restaurant continued, Rey was transported back to a March night in Libya when he and his team had taken out several enemy vessels. He shook his head. *Stay present.* They couldn't afford the distraction of memory lane.

He wiped the sweat from his eyes.

When a turbaned musician ran by, Rey grabbed the man by the shoulder and pulled him behind the table that he and Jane were using as a shield. "It's us they're after. Go kill the lights."

The man looked at him with blank eyes. Rey swore. The guy didn't speak English.

He tugged on the man's arm and pointed at the electric lights on the outside of the building before making a slashing motion across his throat. Rey had to repeat the charade three times before comprehension dawned.

After the man left, bullets continued to rain down on them. Jane had her service pistol in her hand, as did Rey, but the opponent had a sniper rifle. They needed to even the odds somehow.

Rey looked around the back patio to see what he had to work with. Fallen instruments, a mess of silverware and food, the shallow pond at the back of the property surrounded by torches . . .

He tapped Jane and motioned. She nodded in understanding before helping him push the table toward the water. Once there, he grabbed a bunch of wet and dry water reeds and then ducked back into cover.

The lights finally went out. That would help, but wouldn't be enough.

As they pushed the heavy table back toward the center of the patio, Rey grabbed a torch, only to wince as the long wooden end was ripped out of his hands by a bullet. He quickly picked it up again, fanning the flames to keep it lit as Jane squeezed the excess moisture out of the wet reeds. He held the torch to the dry ones.

The weeds flickered and glowed. Most of the restaurant patrons were gone now, but he could still hear yelling in the restaurant. He needed a screen if they were to make it out of here safely.

Finally, the weeds began to sputter. Once the dry ones were burning brightly, he lit the wetter ones until they caught too. He waved the smoldering mess above the table for a minute or two until a mass of thick, stinking smoke filled the air.

"Now!" he yelled, and they crawled backward toward the side of the building. Once they reached its cover, he dropped the pond grass and they ran back to the car.

"Good thinking," Jane said.

"Thanks." Rey started up the engine and accelerated away. "Fast acting back there. I owe you one."

"No worries."

What an impressive, cool-headed woman, Rey thought.

As they raced into the night to catch their flight, he fought the familiar ringing in his ears while wondering how they'd been tailed to the restaurant. Did the sniper still have the scent of their trail?

CHAPTER 26

Eden
Day Three

Antonio glanced at his watch, seeing that it was almost time for the check-in with Stefano, the sniper. Sensing the hunt for Cleopatra's treasure was under control, his father had asked Antonio for help with an urgent, developing situation. The call would need to be taken above ground. The command center was too far beneath the surface, its single phone line, cabled underwater decades ago, only for emergencies.

He looked out the command center's thick plate-glass window, which held an underwater view of the ocean beyond. It was a mystical tableau of sand-covered shipwrecks, striped angelfish, torpedo-shaped barracuda, and a host of otherworldly creatures. It was also a world he loved exploring, especially the WWII battleship that was sunk not too far off the eastern shore. Sometimes he wondered if he'd come across his mother's body out there, but he didn't even know where she'd committed suicide. He just knew she'd jumped from a vessel. He'd have to schedule a dive soon.

Glad to be done with the chore of reviewing financials, he shut down the computer and the spreadsheets he'd been finessing.

Walking through the lesser-used back door of the command center, he exited into their massive underground cathedral, lit by candles around the clock. There he turned toward the center podium, which sat beneath a painted dome that rivaled the Sistine Chapel's. He had a minute to visit the island's most precious object: *il canone*.

The canon had been written by the founder of their assembly almost four millennia ago, and laid out the precepts by which they lived. He put a hand against the theft-proof plexiglass. Warmth spread through his chest as he looked at the image of the cobra and apple on the otherwise plain brown cover. Although he questioned some of their methods, he'd never been prouder than the day the group's tattoo was inked on his chest.

He was glad to get the original tattoo that matched the canon. Before the age of the internet, everyone got the same illustration, but with the advent of interconnected computers, it had become too dangerous. The men had resisted, but new members were getting variations of the snake and apple theme. And in different body locations as well. Antonio supposed it was for the best.

His watch chimed. It was time.

Under the artificial light of the faux stained-glass windows, he walked further down the aisle, past the curtained confessionals, and out the main door. He ran up three flights of stairs, past the level that led to the women's holding cages, out a door, and up two more flights. While he ran, he recalled an argument he'd had with his father about feeding the women. Starving them for a week just didn't seem right. The whole sex-trade operation made him uncomfortable, but his father argued that it funded their mission, and thus the women needed to be made pliant, like an olive branch. As usual when he butted heads with his father, he lost. At least he hadn't been beaten. Those lessons had stopped when he turned fourteen.

He exited into the harbor cave and then into fresh air. In the brisk dusk breeze, he made his way to the home he and his father shared.

Inside, he shed his coat and went into his office. It was lined with maps of Egypt from Cleopatra's day as well as a few other artifacts from that time period. He sat down at his desk, pulled out a new burner phone, and dialed Stefano's number.

Stefano had the raspy voice of a lifelong smoker, facial hair that required him to shave twice a day, and the intense soul of an avenging archangel. "Cobra here."

Given they'd grown up together, Antonio didn't need to spend time identifying himself. "Hey. My father has read me in and asked me to help."

"Okay."

"What happened after the woman at the festival took out our man?"

Stefano growled, "I traced her and her partner to a restaurant and set up across the way in an old fort. Just as I was about to fire my initial round, a bat swooped down from the ramparts, flew by my head and threw off my aim. Before I could hit the targets, they generated a bunch of smoke and escaped."

"You never were fond of bats. Did you follow the targets?"

"Yes. To the airport."

"Where are they headed?"

"Cairo."

"Are you there now?"

"Yes. I had to take the next flight, though."

"That's fine—you'll catch them." Antonio paused. His dad had filled him in on the Vatican's intel, but the source needed to stay hidden. "We have a new intelligence partner. Can't say who but they have good data."

"Oh?"

"This thorn in our side is a deep-level military team of field operatives." Antonio heard the sound of a lighter. His old friend must be lighting up another cigarette.

"How'd they get on our trail?" Stefano responded after a beat.

"We don't know yet."

Stefano exhaled. "How many?"

"Right now, it appears to be two units. The man and woman you're tracking and another set that took our men out in Bari."

"No problem."

It shouldn't be. Stefano had spent a decade in the Italian Special Forces before coming home.

Antonio glanced at a map on the wall where a green pin marked the possible tomb site. "They are headed to Taposiris Magna."

"Don't we have a man there?"

"Yes, Paolo. But he's in deep cover on our other project."

Stefano snorted. "He's a nerd anyway. Are you assigning Gomez?"

Gomez had been in Bari but was now en route to Alexandria. "Yes. He'll join you and is under your command."

"What about the big job?"

Stefano was the main sniper for the upcoming elimination of the US president-elect. "You have it planned out already, right?"

"Yeah. I just need final wind and temperature measurements."

"Then you should have time to kill these American rats before then."

"I'll get it done."

“You’re our best hunter. Go hunt.”

CHAPTER 27

Eden
Day Three

Angie sat cross-legged on the top of her bunk, bored out of her mind. Luna refused to discuss eavesdropping on their kidnappers—or anything else, for that matter—and the German woman across the hall had withdrawn into herself. Reno had passed word down the cells to say that her hand and back hurt, but that she was hanging in there. Not much else to do.

For pure entertainment, Angie replayed scenes from her favorite musical. She'd seen it so many times she could almost watch the whole love story in her mind's eye. She hummed one of the songs. When her mom lived in LA, she'd been friends with a small-time actress who had later gone missing with her young son. Mom had bemoaned her pal's disappearance, playing the musical that featured her friend's most well-known role over and over again. Angie just enjoyed the music and she often watched it with Harper. Now it was Harper's favorite.

Thinking about the love story reminded her of Peter and Casey's wedding. It was a gorgeous, made-for-TV beachfront ceremony under a white arch covered in red flowers. Bride and groom both had bare feet in the sand under dress and tux, and a handsome young Italian minister had presided. They had all clapped when the couple kissed, and she had been so flooded with emotion that she'd leaned over and kissed Tim for old times' sake. After the nuptials, there had been a banquet, a Euro-dance band, and perhaps a few too many drinks.

The headache still raged, going on two days now. None of the other women complained of an aching head, only hunger, and Angie suspected that she was having alcohol withdrawal.

Had she really been drinking to the point where it had become a physical addiction?

She didn't want to think about that. She wanted to make a plan to get off this godforsaken island. Unfortunately, she'd had to stomp her lovely GPS-enabled sunglasses to smithereens in that back alley. Tim and Sam were likely questioning every soul in Bari about their disappearance, but that didn't mean they'd found any real clues.

None of it boded well for her prospects. Her sex-trafficking theory was gaining traction. From the tidbits of gossip she'd gathered, it seemed most of the women were off the island within a week. Probably sold. The captors wanted their victims hungry and docile. Maybe cleaned the women up before they were sent off in a shipping container, or drugged them again and had the buyer meet them at the docks. The sickos running the show were thorough, and organized. It was clear they'd done this before.

Where might she end up? In the basement of some wealthy man's home? Chained like a dog to a mattress and used over and over again? Or sold to a warrior in Afghanistan who wanted to show off a western woman on the back of his horse? And what did that all mean for the children? That was another line of thought she didn't want to follow.

She dropped her head into her hands, forcing herself to go back over the last two days to see if she had learned anything useful.

The woman in the kitchen, Zola, had a guilty look in her eye after stabbing Reno's hand. Could Angie leverage that?

God, her head hurt. She couldn't concentrate.

Once again, she thought about meditation. Tim insisted that it cured all ills. Maybe she'd try it. Desperate times, measures, and all that. He'd shown her the basics once.

She settled in and straightened her spine. Focused on her breathing. In. Out.

Her mind raced in about fifteen different directions at once. He always said that was normal. To just bring your attention back to your breathing. In. Out.

What about Harper? Was she okay?

In. Out.

Would they kill Angie if they caught her trying to escape? Like they had Zoe?

In. Out.

What was going on at the office right now?

In. Out.

Was Tim right about her drinking?

The argument with him came to mind. It was after the wedding reception. They'd tried to be quiet on the hotel patio, but both of their voices were raised.

"I've been wanting to talk with you," Tim had said. "You're ignoring both me and Harper."

"I am not," she'd replied.

He stood, leaning back against the iron railing. "You are. How often do you work late?"

She pursed her lips. "I run a successful company."

"I know what you do. Answer the question."

"Fine." She crossed her arms. "A few nights a week."

"And you come home after your daughter is asleep."

"Some days I have no choice."

"We all have choices, Angie."

She put her hands on her hips. "What? You want me to quit running the company?"

"No." His blue eyes bored into hers. "I want you to deal with your grief."

"I have."

"Then why are you drinking all the time?"

She looked down at the wine glass in her hand. "I don't drink all the time."

"Every night."

"Not true." But it was. Sometimes she worked late just so she could get a little buzz on at the office in peace, without his judging eyes. "Stop trying to control me."

"Angie—"

God, it irritated her that he remained calm. She was about to blow. "At least I'm dealing with my feelings. You don't seem to have any."

He took a step to the side, as if she'd slapped him. His words came out slowly. "I am trying to help."

She lowered her voice. "It's my business."

"If you feel that way, maybe we should no longer be married."

That was low. "You want a divorce?"

"No, I want you to get your act together. But if you can't, or won't, Harper and I will go."

Her breath caught. "You can't take her."

"You know I can. Your drinking is a problem."

She'd waved him off and had gone to bed in a huff, sleeping with Harper that night. The next morning he'd been gone before she woke, off on an assignment.

She flashed on another memory, seeing their infant son hooked up to every imaginable machine in his small hospital bed.

Grinding her teeth, she straightened her legs and jumped off the bunk. She moved to the bars and paced in front of them for hours.

She couldn't stop thinking about what was next for Harper and Layla.

CHAPTER 28

Mediterranean Airspace
Day Three

As Stryker sat in the back of a nearly empty commercial red-eye flight to Cairo, trying to work a crossword puzzle, his thoughts veered back to Harper. If this wasn't happening, and they were at home, he would be getting ready to start their bedtime ritual. After she squealed about brushing her teeth, he'd tuck her under the lacy pink bedspread and read her a story. She'd listen for a time, her eyes focused on the starry ceiling above the princess bed, before her blue eyes succumbed to gravity. When she fell asleep, he'd brush her hair back off her forehead and kiss the smooth skin. Then he'd go join Angie for a few relaxing hours before bed.

He wished he could sleep now. He closed his eyes, rolled his neck a few times to try to ease the pain in his shoulder, but no matter what he did, he was besieged by memories of his wife and daughter.

The first time he'd kissed Angie, outside a Cuban restaurant in Key West. Their letters, phone calls, passionate visits. The beautiful beach wedding on a humid afternoon. The first, awe-inspiring time he held Harper in the hospital, as Angie passed out from exhaustion. His heart had pounded when his daughter had taken her first steps, and he'd understood why it was such a milestone among new parents.

The stewardess came by and Sam ordered a Scotch. He opened his eyes and went for water.

Sam turned off her reading device. "You can't sleep either?"

"No. Can't even focus on this crossword. I'm keyed up."

"Me too."

They sat in silence for a minute.

Sam pointed at her lap. "I've been trying to figure out why these creeps are fascinated by Cleopatra."

"Think it was her beauty?"

Sam shook her head. "Doubt it. There has to be more."

"What have you found so far?" Maybe learning about Cleopatra would distract him from worries about Harper and Angie. And perhaps he'd learn something useful.

"Not only could you see the famed Lighthouse of Rhodes from her private island palace, Alexandria was the world's most sophisticated city in its day."

"Sophisticated how?"

"Imagine a cultural melting pot like New York, but with an Egyptian flair. Sphinxes lining paths to marble Greek temples, that sort of thing. The Library of Alexandria was also a wonder of the ancient world. Oh! And the city was also kind of techie for its time."

That caught his attention. "Really?"

She turned her e-reader back on and flipped pages. "Yeah. They had coin-operated machines, automatic treadmills, and hydraulic lifts."

His jaw fell open. "You're kidding. Before the time of Christ?"

"No joke. They even had statues with eyes that held flickering lights."

He was getting the picture. "Wow. Didn't think it was that advanced."

"She was pretty educated too. As second eldest in a royal family, she had the best tutors the world could offer. She apparently fell in love with Homer, and besides philosophy and rhetoric, would have studied geometry, music, astronomy."

"And yet now the world focuses on how she seduced two powerful Romans and killed herself."

Sam flipped electronic pages. "Yes. Pathetic. History tells us Cleopatra was charming, eloquent, and the first of her family to learn Egyptian. The rest just spoke Greek. She was also clever. Oh, and this is interesting . . ."

"What's that?"

"She had a grand sense of humor. Was known to be quite witty." Sam paused. "Get this. When Caesar took control of the palace after her father died, Cleopatra snuck into her family home inside a rucksack used for carrying rolls of papyrus."

"I thought it was a carpet."

"Now historians think it was a rucksack. But that's how she seduced him, or how they met anyway. When she was with Antony, rumor has it that one of their favorite activities involved wearing disguises, wandering the streets of Alexandria, and playing pranks on its residents. There's also a story she helped a friend make an escape *inside a coffin*."

"Seems like something you or Angie would do."

Sam turned off the e-reader again and looked at him with concern in her brown eyes. "Do you really think Angie's drinking has gotten that bad?"

That was the downside to working with family. "Wait, how'd we get from Cleopatra to my personal life?"

"It's a long flight."

"I don't want to go there, Sam. Angie could be dead."

"That's a cheery thought."

"Sue me," he growled, upset at having to speak that possibility out loud.

Sam raised an eyebrow. "My, my, the bear is out of his cage today."

He popped his neck. "I'll admit to feeling a little testy."

The stewardess brought their drinks.

"Okay," Sam said. "Why don't you tell me a story then?"

"You sound like Harper. Sorry, I don't have a picture book."

"Let me rephrase my question." Sam sipped her Scotch. "I've just told you some of Cleopatra's life. Tell me your story."

"My life story?"

"No." Sam softened her voice. "The part when you were a kid." She pointed at his left hand, where he was missing the end of his pinkie finger. "You've never told me."

He sat back in his seat and closed his eyes. Other than the police and his aunt and uncle, he hadn't told anyone until Angie. "It's not that big of a deal."

"Tell me then. It's a long flight and your secret's safe with me."

Maybe if he told her, she'd understand why Angie needed to stop drinking. "It was the summer I was seven," he began.

It was hot that summer. Hot and muggy. They lived in a high-rise brick apartment in a part of Chicago that was home to families with all varieties of skin color. His dad always liked a drink when he came home from his work as a janitor for luxury condos. Beer, vodka tonics, Manhattans, and martinis. Sometimes his mom, a paralegal, would join in the fun, or sometimes his dad would go hang out on the stoop with the other guys from the building to talk and laugh long into the night.

There was a lot of arguing that summer. Stryker shared a room with his younger sister, Clarissa, and the two of them would hole up whenever it started, as sometimes things went flying. After stepping on broken glass in his bare feet, he'd learned to wear shoes whenever he left his bedroom after an argument.

Because his sis had been born without hearing, he and his mom had taught her to sign. The two of them would practice when things went crazy with the parents, making fun of other kids or translating comic books.

The power went out on a Tuesday. They called it a blackout. He'd never heard the term before. At first it was fun, like a snow day, but it was August and the apartment got hot. He'd go shoot hoops with his pals during the day, but at night there was nothing to do but toss and turn in sweat-soaked sheets.

The entire city was off work. The men drank to stay cool.

Three or four nights into the blackout, his dad stormed into the candlelit apartment on a wave of alcohol while the rest of them were doing a jigsaw puzzle. "Who was he?"

His mom stood up. "Who was what?"

He pointed at Clarissa. "Her father! You liar! Look at her. It wasn't me!"

His father was a wiry Irish redhead with pale skin. Clarissa had brown hair, but so what? Stryker had no idea what his dad was yelling about, but knew it was time to leave. He grabbed his sister by the hand and headed for their bedroom.

Before his mother could answer the accusation, however, his father pulled out a revolver and shot her in the chest. The sound was so loud in the small apartment that it hurt Stryker's ears. His mom fell to the floor, eyes closed.

Oh no! Was she hurt? Dead?

Heart fluttering wildly, Stryker pulled his sister down the hall to safety, but it was too late. Another boom sounded and Clarissa let go of his hand. There was a wide-eyed and open-mouthed look on her face as she dropped. It haunted his dreams, still.

Stryker turned and put his hands in front of his face, palms out. "Dad, no!"

The next shot took the tip of Stryker's finger off and grazed his hairline. He toppled backward and landed on his shoulder next to his sister.

One final shot echoed, round and round, before Stryker passed out.

After a few long moments, Sam shook her head and tsked. "That's worse than I thought it would be."

"My sister was about Harper's age." Stryker's throat closed up. He took a sip of water. "All three of them died that night."

"He thought he got you, too."

"He did." Stryker shook his head. "But all he got was the tip of my finger and my eternal hatred. This bum shoulder reminds me of him every day. What a bastard."

Sam finished her Scotch. The seat tray in front of her bounced when she put the plastic cup down. "Bastards like the men who took Angie, Reno, and the girls."

"And killed Zoe."

"We're going to get them, Stryker."

"I know. I just hope Angie and Harper are still alive when we do."

CHAPTER 29

Taposiris Magna, Egypt
Day Four

Paolo closed down the phone in disgust. He was just starting to get the lay of the land here at the dig, and now he had to deal with this new command from home. Looking at the yellow ball of sun rising over the desert, he closed his eyes, unsure if he was able or willing to do as Antonio had instructed. When he'd expressed reservations about his preparedness, the boss's son had just snapped, "Then improvise!" and hung up.

As Paolo headed over to his workstation from the day before, he spied a man and a woman walking through the front gate of the former temple complex. They clearly didn't belong, as they wore colorful street clothes instead of the drab tan that he and his coworkers favored. It had to be the American operatives he'd just been warned about. He knew facial features and hair color could be easily camouflaged, but height and weight were harder to conceal.

Swearing the entire time, Paolo walked over to them. It went against his new orders, but as one of the archeologists on site, it was his role to keep trespassers at bay. In Italian, he said, "Excuse me—the site is closed for visitors."

The man responded, "Good morning. I'm Señor Rodríguez and this is Mrs. Pérez. Do you speak English or Spanish?"

Paolo figured them for Timothy Stryker and Samantha Coin. He switched to English. "I do, a bit. But you need to leave."

The woman extended her hand. "We understand it's the middle of the dig season for you and don't want to interrupt, but we're big fans of Mr. Richmond and are interested in donating to his research fund for this site."

"I'm sorry, but—"

Stryker cut him off. "Hullo!" He waved at the head archeologist, a New Zealander named Terrance Richmond, before turning to his partner. "Look, there he is. I'm sure he'll want to chat."

Before Paolo could stop them, the two walked away. Paolo ran after them, wishing Stefano was here to deal with this. But Cobra was running late.

Samantha used both arms to wave down Richmond. "Mr. Richmond! May we speak with you?"

Richmond turned their way and put his hands on his hips. Paolo had already learned the head archeologist was a no-nonsense man. Richmond's salt-and-pepper hair poked out from under his desert cap as he squinted at them, his wrinkles becoming more pronounced.

Paolo said, "I was just telling them no visitors are—"

Stryker stuck his hand out. "We'd like to discuss a donation to help fund your operation."

Richmond gave Stryker a full-body once-over before shaking his hand. "And who might you be?"

The Coin woman also extended her hand and smiled shyly. "We're Spaniards who were in Cairo on business. I've been following your research online and we just had to swing by. I'm completely fascinated by all things Cleopatra."

Richmond shook briefly, seeming to thaw as the thought of a capital infusion sank in. "It's a pleasure."

Paolo hadn't had time to look into the financials here, but money was always in short supply at digs. He could see the archeologist was falling for the Americans' ruse. They had dressed well, expensive jewelry and watches on full display.

He ground his teeth; orders were orders. He thought about how these Americans had been responsible for the death of two of his friends in Bari. Born a church orphan, the Sons of Adam were his family.

"Would you like me to give them a tour?" he asked Richmond.

Richmond gave Paolo a calculating look. "Yes, that's a great idea. That will let me attend to a few things and then we can chat in my tent."

Coin clasped her hands in a pretense of pleasure and Stryker smiled his thanks.

"Please follow me," Paolo said once the head archeologist had wandered away. For this to work, he would need to get them to the northwest part of the enclosure, but first he needed to build trust.

Striding over to near the center of the walled temple area, he stopped in the middle of a rectangular-shaped ruin. "Because of the unfinished exterior walls, experts had written off this temple complex as incomplete." He pointed to the low-lying rocks. "At least until Mr. Richmond discovered foundation deposits here."

"What are those?" Samantha Coin asked.

"They are thin clay tablets about the size of your hand, blessed by a pharaoh. The ones found here had Greek inscriptions that indicated Ptolemy IV sanctified the shrine."

"Neat," Coin said. "Wasn't he the great-great-grandfather of Cleopatra?"

The woman knew her history. "Yes," Paolo said. "This temple was dedicated to Osiris, god of the dead."

Stryker turned in all four directions, as if taking it all in. "Is that why the temple complex is named Taposiris Magna?"

Even the man was playing his part well. "Indeed. The temple's namesake." Paolo turned north and walked a half dozen meters. "We also discovered the complex housed a temple dedicated to Isis, Egypt's most potent mother goddess. It had three rooms, one a sanctuary."

"What did Isis look like to Egyptians?" the man asked.

"In ancient Egypt, her adornments were simple, such as a papyrus staff in one hand and an ankh in the other. By the time of the New Kingdom, she sometimes had wings, or wore royal insignia, and was often represented as half woman, half snake."

"Cleopatra was the physical embodiment of Isis, right?" Samantha Coin asked. "I read you found bronze coins from Cleopatra's reign here. That's part of why we came. I love old coins."

With that last name, this was likely the only thing the woman was telling the truth about. "Yes, the money would have been temple offerings. It was clever of her to use bronze, as rulers usually just minted their visage in silver. All her subjects got to see her image, as opposed to just the wealthy."

"An early public relations move," Stryker commented.

"That's right," Paolo said. "Would you like to see a small shaft?"

"Sure," Coin said.

He walked them to the smallest vertical tunnel at the dig. "This drops only five meters below ground."

Stryker looked down.

Paolo added, "It leads to two carved chambers. No ladder, just hand- and footholds."

He motioned for them to proceed, and the two Americans descended the shaft. As they made the appropriate sounds of discovery at the sight of the painted walls, Paolo mulled over his assignment. He thought of the man who'd recently been dropped into the Midnight Shelf in chains. If he didn't follow through, the *comandante* would not be pleased.

When the Americans climbed back up, the woman's eyes held a fire that showed she was truly passionate about history. It was almost too bad she had to die.

"That was great! Do we have time to look at the deep shaft where you think Cleopatra's tomb might be?"

Paolo couldn't believe his luck, but he needed to play it cool. "Let me go check."

Walking over to the northwest corner where the pit that led to the thirty-meter-deep shaft was situated, he told the workers to take a break. They scattered like ants, happy to rest their backs and hands.

Paolo walked up the stone steps, emerged from the pit, and waved the Americans over. "A private tour. You can take as much time as you like down there. Because royal Egyptian women were often buried in shaft tombs, it's our best lead yet on where she might be buried."

Coin turned to Stryker and touched his arm. "I'm so excited!"

"Here you go." Paolo motioned for them to stand in the metal basket of the portable shaft hoist. "We've recently added a two-person cage. You can go down together." He didn't mention the team had told him the cage was bought at a discount from Scotland because it was past its prime and should be used with only one person at a time.

It was a little tight for the two of them, but they faced each other. Paola handed them hard hats with attached lights. Little good they would do.

"Reach your hands up and onto the grab bars," Paolo said.

After they did, Paolo yanked on the starter rope to fire up the small gas engine and summoned his distaste for enemies of the Sons of Adam. The cage began its slow descent and the cables clacked within their pulleys.

The two occupants dropped out of sight.

It was now or never.

Paolo released the safety brake mechanism and the cage plummeted into the depths.

CHAPTER 30

Taposiris Magna, Egypt
Day Four

Ten feet down the shaft, Stryker felt the hoist shift and the cage began to pick up speed. He made eye contact with Sam. "Trouble." Into his molar mic, he said, "Mayday, mayday."

He tried thrusting his arms out to slow their descent, but the cage was already moving too fast.

Standing just outside the walls of the temple compound, Rey heard the mayday call and sprang into action. He'd been watching the drone feed and thought he'd seen the short archeologist with the thinning hair move a lever on the hoist before high-tailing it a few feet back from the edge of the opening. It looked suspicious, and now Rey knew for certain. He scrambled up the wall and took aim at the archeologist.

Jane got the mayday signal and dropped the rock she'd been moving. Disguised as a worker, she was just meters away from the square pit. She jumped down the stairs and sped toward the hoist.

"Brakes. Get the tango and pull the brake!" Stryker yelled.

Rey pulled the trigger and the archeologist crumpled to the sand.

Jane ran over the dead man and saw a red lever on the hoist marked "brake." She yanked it, hard. The entire iron unit shuddered.

Sam heard the screech of cables and felt the jolt as the cage decelerated. Braced for impact, she held her breath as the cage thudded to a rough stop on the bedrock floor. She put a hand on her pounding heart before moaning with relief.

CHAPTER 31

Eden
Day Four

Angie woke in the dank cell. Again. As habits went, it was *not* one she wanted to get used to.

Staring at the ceiling, she wondered if they were feeding Harper, or if there was a water-only rule for the children. Angie was about ready to gnaw on the disgusting blanket.

She had to learn something today to get them out of this place. While she knew Tim and Sam would be doing their best, her mom always said, "The Lord helps those who help themselves."

Others were stirring in nearby cells. Realizing guards passed through only irregularly and they wouldn't be punished for making noise down here, the women had become louder as time passed. She heard cursing in several languages, banging on cell bars with the tin cups used for their water, and in the distance, screaming.

She sighed and rolled off the top bunk. Luna was still snoring. Angie waved at the German girl across the hall, and finally got a wave in return.

Wanting to take advantage of the momentary friendliness, she nudged Luna with a toe. "Hey, sleepyhead. Wake up."

Luna wriggled and yawned. "Why?"

Angie sat down on the edge of the thin mattress. "I need your help. Heidi over there is in a talkative mood. See what else you can learn."

"Too hungry."

"I'm starving, too. But there's nothing we can do about it now."

Luna pulled the blanket over her head. "Go away," she said in a muffled voice.

As if it were a prayer, Angie recited, "Scrambled eggs. Bacon. Hash browns. Espresso." She had always been a smart-ass when she was stressed out, and this situation definitely qualified.

Luna threw the blanket off her head in mock disgust, rolled her fawn-like eyes, and jabbed Angie in the side. "Get up then."

Angie sprang up, excited by the small success. Luna drank the last of her water, set the cup down with a clink, and then walked to the bars. Looking both ways for a guard, she waved to get the German girl's attention. The young woman across the hall walked to her set of bars and slouched, wrapping her arms around the cold steel.

Luna looked at Angie. "What do you want me to ask her?"

Angie didn't want to voice her suspicions about being sold into sexual slavery. "See if she knows why we're being held here."

Luna translated. The girl shook her head. Strike one.

"Ask her how long she's been here."

"Seven days." The girl spoke again. "She says it's always seven days."

"What is?"

"How long women are held here."

Angie nodded at the confirmation that women left the island within seven days. "Then what?"

"She doesn't know."

Strike two.

Luna pursed her lips and looked at Angie with sad eyes. "She's afraid."

"Tell her we're trying to help."

Luna spoke to the girl, who slumped to the floor, hugging herself and rocking back and forth.

Sensing they were losing her, Angie touched Luna's arm. "See if she knows where their leader lives."

German words were exchanged.

Luna turned to Angie. "It's the biggest blue house. In the village. She cleaned it yesterday."

"And the children?"

"The rose-colored one."

Nice to know where Harper was sleeping. Before she could verbally express her appreciation, a door creaked open and boots *thunked* down the hall. Nodding her thanks instead, Angie stepped away from the bars and retreated to the rear of the cell. Luna followed and sat on the bunk. The German girl scuttled to the back of her cell, where she sat with thin arms around knobby knees, trembling.

Guards dressed in black pants and dark shirts used a keycard to open the girl's prison. They marched the three steps to the back of the cell, yanked her up by the elbows, and carried her out the black metal door.

Her screams echoed through the cages like a church bell sounding a death knell.

CHAPTER 32

**Taposiris Magna, Egypt
Day Four**

Stryker emerged from the damaged metal cage and threw the hard hat to the ground. His head was ringing and his shoulder throbbed from the fall. Finally, his heart rate was back to normal, but he remained furious that they'd been ambushed. He kicked himself, but had felt it necessary to tour the shaft to maintain their ruse. Thank God the team had worked together perfectly, or he and Sam would be pancakes. As they'd ridden back up, all he could think was how he might have never hugged Angie or Harper again.

It looked like he wasn't the only one ticked off.

Richmond stalked down the stairs two at a time, pointing at the dead archeologist. "What in the name of hell happened here?"

In the mood for a fight, Stryker stared Richmond down. "You tell me. Your man just tried to kill us."

"Bullshit. You murdered him. I heard the shot, and look at him."

"Yes, he's dead." Stryker felt control slipping away as Richmond got in his face. "He sabotaged the brake."

Richmond slugged Stryker in the gut.

Before he could return the punch by decking the head archeologist, Rey grabbed Stryker's hands and yanked them behind his back. "Cool it, boss."

Sam did the same thing to Richmond. The two men snarled at each other, chafing against being held.

"Knock it off, both of you," Rey commanded. "I have drone footage that shows what went down. If we hadn't intervened, my pals here would be dead."

As Stryker struggled against his friend's grip, the wild rage began to cool and he visualized it seeping into the desert beneath his feet. Sam turned Richmond away and walked him to the other side of the pit, clearly trying to talk him down. A crowd of workers looked on from the edge of the pit.

After a few deep breaths, the last of Stryker's anger melted away. He hated losing his temper like that. They'd come to wine and dine Richmond in the hopes of learning something about the Sons of Adam. Time for a new approach. Rey must've sensed the shift, because he dropped Stryker's hands.

The animosity in Richmond's eyes dropped by a notch or two when Sam released him, but his eyes remained narrowed as Stryker approached.

Stryker said, "Is there somewhere we can talk? We'll show you the drone footage so you can see what happened."

With a last look at the body of his former colleague, Richmond said, "Fine. Follow me."

"Wait," Stryker said. "Let me see something."

He walked over to the dead man and rolled him onto his back. Peeling back the archeologist's tan shirt, he motioned everyone over. "Take a look."

Stryker could almost hear the hiss of the hooded cobra that leaped off the man's tattoo.

Richmond stepped back as if bitten by the snake. "I suppose we do need to talk."

"Yes, we do. But take your shirt off first."

"I certainly don't have one of those tattoos. I will not."

"You will." He stared the man down. "Or I'll rip it off of you right now."

Richmond did as commanded, glaring throughout the process. No tat.

Twenty minutes later, the assassin's personal belongings had been unsuccessfully checked, and the drone footage reviewed. Richmond eyed them warily from behind his makeshift desk. "You're obviously not wealthy Spaniards here to fund my operation. Why the subterfuge?"

Stryker figured it was time to put the cards on the table. "We work for the US government."

"Do you have identification?"

"No."

"I see."

The two men stared at each other again, dogs circling each other in a fight ring.

Stryker sighed. "What I can tell you is that the dead man belonged to a group called Sons of Adam. We're here because we think they're behind a string of global assassinations. Did you hear about the recent demise of the Saudi prince? Or the PM in India?"

Richmond shifted in his chair. "I did."

"We're trying to figure out why they're on this killing spree. And stop them."

"Why are you here? At my dig?"

"Did you have a security breach recently? We saw a copy of a local police report that mentioned a man who tried to steal some of your artifacts and ended up like his buddy out there."

"What if he did?"

"We want to know the truth about why he was here."

Wind whipped through the tent, ruffling Richmond's hair. "What's in it for me?"

This ass wasn't making it easy. Stryker stared him right in the eye. "You get to live to continue your quest for Cleopatra's tomb."

CHAPTER 33

Taposiris Magna, Egypt
Day Four

Sam had enough of the silverback chest-thumping going on between Stryker and Richmond. It was time to play good cop. Putting her hand on Stryker's arm, she gave her boss a "shut up" glance.

He sat back in his chair and crossed his arms.

"Besides living to see your dreams come true," she said, "there would be some advantages to you helping us out."

"Such as?" Richmond asked.

Sam's mind raced; she hadn't planned on this being a negotiation. "You more or less admitted that your camp was infiltrated by another member of the Sons of Adam group. You have something here they want and until they find it, they'll keep sending more goons."

Richmond grunted.

She took that as progress and carried on. "We can help you keep your site safe. Who knows what else they might destroy? Or who they might kill?"

He narrowed his eyes further until they were mere slits.

Sam added, "You help us and we'll help you."

Richmond leaned his chair back, hands crossed, clearly considering her points. Even if he had security on site, he had to be smart enough to realize she and the team would make far better allies than enemies.

While Richmond shuffled through his options, Stryker stood, finding a sudden interest in a table of bones. Meanwhile, Jane and Rey got up and stepped outside the tent. Sam took note of the pair's body language and wondered if attraction was budding in the midst of the mission. On her end, she pretended to study her phone while she worried about what Angie and Harper might be doing right now. She sure hoped this thin lead would blossom into something more substantial.

After a few minutes, Richmond took a deep breath and sat forward in his seat, putting his hands flat on his desk. "Okay, there was a man here with a tattoo rather like that on his right shoulder."

Sam suppressed a victory smile as the rest of the team retook their places as if drawn to a magnet. "How did you see the tattoo? What happened?"

"In a nutshell, we keep a few locals as security after dark. The tattooed thief came in the dead of night, killed a guard, and started destroying artifacts with a baseball bat. Another sentry heard the commotion and gave chase. In the dark, the stranger fell down a chute."

Belatedly, Sam realized he hadn't wanted to talk about it because that shaft should have been sealed up tight for the night. She let that drop. It would be their dirty little secret. "How did you notice the tattoo?"

"When we retrieved the body, his shirt was ripped. The tattoo was evident."

"What do you think he was after?"

Richmond's eyes shifted from side to side. "No idea, really."

Based on years of poker playing, she could tell this guy knew more than he was letting on. Still, she kept her encouraging smile in place. "Had you seen that tattoo before?"

"I had."

Pay dirt. "Then we've come to the right place. We'd like to eliminate the threat to you and your site. What can you tell us about the tattoo?"

"As you can guess from my work here, my primary field of research is Cleopatra. I've studied her world extensively. Once, I saw a similar apple/cobra image in a report written by one of her temple priests."

"That's promising," Sam said. "What did it say?"

"Not much. The group it belonged to was called Sons of Adam at that time as well. Since the incident, I've done additional research. The group appeared on the scene in 1500 BCE."

"They were old then, even in Cleopatra's time?"

"Yes. Octavian was their leader during his life. They hated anything related to Cleopatra, and their MO was destruction and disinformation. Her temple priest was trying to figure out how to counter their falsehoods. After Octavian died, they fell off the historical record for centuries."

"Until now?" Sam asked.

"Yes." Richardson glanced down at his hands. "It was common practice at the time to destroy evidence of the vanquished. For instance, we believe Octavian demolished much of Cleopatra's legacy. Perhaps they wiped their own footprints."

"What else?"

Richmond looked outside, clearly weighing whether to come clean. "The man who was here smashed some religious figurines, but I think he was searching for something."

"Oh?"

"The materials the attacker was rifling through alluded to the queen's gold journal."

Sam's heart rate ratcheted up. "What gold journal?"

"Good question. I don't know. It was called out in a single line in a letter from one of Cleopatra's servant's descendants to a lover. The letter didn't originate from this site, but as I mentioned, I have a number of her artifacts."

"Could we see a copy?"

"Sure, the thief had it in his pocket when he fell, but didn't manage to destroy it. I'll get you a duplicate before you go."

"Thanks." Sam turned on all her charm, going for broke. "Do you have any theories about the group or the journal? Hints? Rumors?"

Richmond frowned. "I work in facts."

"Yes, but we need more to go on. Do you have any other ideas? Anything at all?"

Richmond drummed his fingers on the desk before answering. "We have an Egyptian archeologist here who claims to trace her lineage back to a man who worked for Cleopatra. She may know more."

CHAPTER 34

Eden
Day Four

Gone was the snarky banter from earlier. After the German girl had been carted away, Angie and her cellmate didn't utter a word. They sat in stony silence until they were called to serve breakfast.

While she delivered plates of mouth-watering French toast to the men, Angie schemed. Upon arrival in the kitchen, she'd made eye contact with the tongueless woman possibly named Zola, and the woman's eyes had held a smudge of emotion. Yet, as certain as Angie was that the speechless woman had regretted what happened with Reno, it would still be dangerous to approach her. Visions of Reno's hand stuck to the wooden cutting board with a vibrating knife made Angie's stomach churn. Her overture might make Zola feel she had no choice but to alert the guards. Like she'd had no option but to squash the fruit theft with a kitchen blade. Reaching out to Zola could be a fatal mistake.

But what choice did Angie have? With no other land mass in sight, she could not simply swim off the island, even if she knew how. Nor had she seen any electronic equipment lying about, waiting to be swiped by nimble fingers. If she had to die, so be it, but she couldn't live with herself if her inaction led her beautiful daughter to be sold to some pervert.

Fortified with that brave thought, Angie spilled syrup on her hands and spent time washing her hands so she'd be last in line to grab plates for the dining room. When everyone else was out of the room, she moved close to Zola.

Angie whispered, "Do you understand English?"

Zola stared at her. Was it a blank stare, or was she deciding whether to acknowledge the advance?

Angie frantically thought through the MICE options. Money? Nope. Ideology? Maybe. Compromise? No way. Ego? . . . Perhaps.

"You run a good kitchen here. But you don't belong."

Zola's eyes narrowed. She did understand English, at least a little.

Angie plowed ahead. "I have skills to get us out of here. But I need your help."

Zola's eyes darted around the kitchen. They were still alone, but not for long.

"There are so many young girls here," Angie said, trying to appeal to the woman's heart. "Can you help me set them free?"

Several women walked through the kitchen door. Angie grabbed her plates and walked out, her heart racing. She set the plates of steaming toast in front of four old men playing checkers at the end of the table. Then she slowly moved back to the kitchen.

The timing was good—again she had a few seconds with the kitchen's mistress. Approaching slowly, Angie realized she'd never felt so nervous during the art of negotiation. But it was all on the line. Her life, Harper's future. For a moment she felt dizzy. She sucked in a breath.

But Zola made no sign of recognition as she handed Angie a plate. She cringed inwardly. What else could she try?

Thinking through everything the woman may have lived through, she had an idea.

"I can help you get *revenge*," Angie said.

Something flickered in the depths of Zola's eyes.

Angie felt a tiny flush of success.

"Just think about it," she murmured before they were interrupted by women bearing dirty dishes. The men served first had finished their breakfast.

Back in the dining room, Angie spied some plates that needed to be washed. If only her direct staff could see her now.

She grabbed the empty plates and realized the light in Zola's eyes was as far as she was going to get today. The idea of revenge had surely struck a chord. But would the temptation of retaliation be enough for the woman to risk everything in an escape attempt?

CHAPTER 35

Taposiris Magna, Egypt
Day Four

After ordering Rey and Jane back to lookout duty, Stryker followed Richmond away from the archeologist's tent to the north door of the temple enclosure. Sam accompanied them—she had done well to take over the conversation when it was clear he wasn't getting anywhere.

Stryker squinted against the brightness of the day. A petite woman wearing a patterned pink headscarf and matching jacket stood to greet them. Professor Saber. Richmond stalked off as soon as he made the introductions.

Saber's eyes were guarded and her arms crossed. She must have heard about the incident in the shaft.

"What are you working on?" Stryker asked to break the ice.

"See this double series of stone plinths?" Saber's Egyptian accent was light and musical.

"Sure."

"It may have been a grand avenue."

Stryker looked at the line of old columns with new eyes. A dust devil whirled down the center before dying out. "I could see that."

"There are fourteen of them, which makes us think there could be a relationship to the fourteen pharaohs in the Ptolemy line."

"Cleopatra was a Ptolemy," Sam blurted.

"That's right," Saber agreed, her shoulders relaxing a notch. "We think she was a frequent visitor. My specialty is ancient religions. This is the most important Isis temple site in northern Egypt, and it was close to Alexandria's power base."

Sam shivered. "We could be standing where she walked."

"We could be, indeed." Saber's face turned serious. "I heard we lost a member of the team this morning."

Stryker nodded in Sam's direction. "It was almost the two of us. The dead man, who worked for a group called the Sons of Adam, sabotaged the lift, trying to kill us."

Saber put a hand to her mouth. "Oh my. I hadn't heard the full story."

"Two sides to every coin. And when we explained to Richmond what happened, he told us about another incident with a thief here at the dig."

"Yes. We were all quite upset."

"That robber belonged to the same group. They have a distinctive tattoo, usually placed over their hearts."

The wind whipped at Saber's headscarf. "I see," she said, pushing it out of her eyes.

"We are seeking the location of this group to stop them from bothering sites like yours. Richmond thought you might be able to help us."

Saber folded her arms over her chest again. "I know nothing of this group."

"He also said you may be a descendant of someone who worked for Cleopatra."

Saber stood up straighter. "That's right. It's been a source of pride through the generations."

"And he thought that you might have some information about a journal said to have belonged to her. That's what the thief was seeking."

"Solid information, no."

"Rumor, speculation, or gossip?" Sam asked with a smile.

Saber's face hardened. "Every family has its tales."

"Will you tell us about your ancestor?" Sam asked.

"There's not much to tell, really. But he gave my great-great-whatever-grandmother this, and another like it, before he left on a last errand for the pharaoh. The other was sold for food during a famine. This one has been passed on through the generations." She pulled a gold coin out of her pocket. Like Sam's, it was encased in heavy plastic.

Sam nabbed the coin before Stryker could get it. He let his hand fall; she was better at interviewing than he was anyway.

Shifting the coin from side to side, Sam's face lit up. "It bears Cleopatra's image. Look."

He took the heavy coin from her. The woman's face had a hooked beak. "Cleopatra had a nose like that?"

"It seems so," Saber replied. "Most of her authentic coins show a similar trait."

Stryker thought about all the tales of her beauty told throughout the years. Well, there were many ways to be beautiful.

Sam pulled her coin out of her pocket. "I have this old Greek coin from my father. It has an image of a horseman on one side and a bull on the other."

The archeologist examined the silver coinage. "Very nice. Yours may be even older than mine."

"It's my lucky charm." Sam retrieved her coin from Saber's palm. "Is yours why you got into archeology?"

Saber tilted her head and looked sideways at Sam. "Yes, actually."

"What's the story that goes along with it?"

"Hmm, I suppose there's no harm in telling it." Saber relaxed, sitting on the stump of one of the old columns that lined the avenue. "Although my mother swore it was accurate, after so many years, I doubt there's much truth to it anyway."

"Do tell," Sam said.

Stryker was used to Sam's ability to charm people into a tell-all mood, but he still gave her a mental pat on the back for breaking this archeologist's reserve so quickly.

"Family legend says that he got the coins from Cleopatra for discovering the location of Octavian's stronghold."

Stryker's internal antennae focused toward Saber. Richmond had said that Octavian was the cult's leader.

Sam made eye contact with him. She'd caught the reference, too.

Saber rolled the coin across her palm and glanced down at the queen's image. "She wrote about the hidden site in her gold journal and was so pleased my ancestor found the location, she let him join her in the afterlife."

Part of Stryker thought that was an interesting perspective. Death as a reward. But most of him was anxious to hear more about this hint of a lead. If the journal held the group's location, it might help them find Angie.

Sam's eyes sparked. "There is a journal then, truly?"

"According to my family, yes." Saber adjusted her headscarf. "It's just nowhere to be found."

"You have no idea where to begin a search for it?"

Saber shook her head. "Sorry, no. That was all he told his wife before he disappeared, and he swore her to secrecy. On her deathbed, she told the children. You know how it goes. And so many generations later, how much of what I've been told was real?"

Stryker's heart sank, disappointment cutting almost as sharply as the wind. Trying to find a two-thousand-year-old journal was almost worse than no lead at all. Where would they even begin?

CHAPTER 36

Taposiris Magna, Egypt
Day Four

Under the shade of the ancient lighthouse, Rey sat next to Jane, their backs against the cool stone wall. They were about ten minutes from the dig, taking shelter from the wind in the shadow of a structure he'd read was similar to the famous Rhodes landmark. They had finished lookout duty and were waiting for their teammates.

Jane still wore a mask, but had swapped out the Asian one for a California surfer look. The long blonde hair whipped around her face in the breeze. It didn't suit her.

He was a little nervous at having pulled Stryker off the head archeologist earlier. Stryker's red hair and corresponding hotheaded personality could get him in trouble, and Rey had wanted to help his boss simmer down. He just hoped the *jefe* wasn't mad at him.

Jane touched his arm. "That was nice shooting from the top of the wall."

His flesh sizzled at the brush of her fingertips. "Thanks. I'll bet Stryker and Sam were glad you moved so fast."

"I'll say. There wasn't much room to spare in that drop."

"No." He sat, in the rare position of being at a loss for words. "Hey, maybe we should use this time to go through the pictures Ace sent."

"Which ones?"

"The men at Saudi airports who might have flown out of Italy."

"Oh right. Trying to find a suspect for the killing in Saudi Arabia."

"Yes. Seems a long shot, but why not."

"Did you play basketball?"

"I did. In college. Why?"

"You're always using these terms. Like long shot."

He smiled. "I didn't make the NBA. I was too short. My knee is glad I quit while I was ahead."

She patted it while he pulled out his phone.

After ten minutes of grinding through camera images of men who had flown into Saudi Arabia on or about the time of the assassination, he checked the horizon, and spied a green sedan approaching.

"That looks like them coming now."

Rey and Jane watched in companionable silence as it drew nearer. He caught another whiff of her perfume; it was sultry, maybe a sandalwood mix. Since the shooting in India, he'd felt that she was flirting with him a little, albeit hesitantly. They were like two wary animals warming to the idea of curling up together in a cold barn.

As the car drew nearer, they walked to the parking area and their own blue sedan.

"What'd you find out?" Rey asked when Stryker got out and headed for the back of his car.

Stryker turned, blue eyes shadowed with what had to be worry for his family. "Sam will fill you in."

They all gathered around Sam, who hardly looked better than Stryker.

"We made friends with an archeologist who descended from one of Cleopatra's 'workers,'" Sam said, using air quotes around the last word. "Based on the archeologist's story, it sounds like her ancestor was a spy. Before he left on a final mission, he gave his wife two gold coins from Cleopatra."

"What about the journal Richmond mentioned?" Rey asked.

"Family rumor says the ancestor hid the journal."

Rey rubbed his hands together with anticipation. "Ooh la la! I love a good family rumor."

"It gets better," Sam added. "The journal supposedly has the location of the cult."

Rey's jaw unhinged. "What?"

Jane put her palms out. "Excuse me, but before we get too excited"—she looked pointedly at Rey—"let's keep in mind the words *rumor* and *supposedly*."

Rey put his hands on his hips. This was a decent lead. If they could find the location of the group, they could get Angie and Harper back and stop future assassinations. Cut off the head of the snake, so to speak.

"Jane's right, but that's all we have," Sam said. "Stryker and I are thinking we should find the journal as our next move."

Jane took a step back. "I don't think that's a good idea."

"Why not?" Sam asked.

"As I mentioned already, it's grasping at air. Speculation only."

"Perhaps, but the trail went cold in Bari. We have two dead tangos there with the tats; men possibly trying to cover up Zoe's murder. Plus, the tat on the assassin who killed the PM in India. They match. That journal is our only lead."

"It's not much of one." The wind lashed Jane's hair into her eyes and she pushed it aside. "What if the group's location has changed in two thousand years? Where would we even begin?"

Sam looked at Stryker, as if for confirmation.

Stryker nodded. "Sam has been studying up on Cleopatra's life so we have that going for us. You two will work Egypt. Start at Cleo's old palace in Alexandria and we'll head to Rome to sniff around the haunts of her lovers."

Jane threw up her hands. "But her palace is underwater!"

"Rent scuba gear," Stryker said, putting his hands on his hips and staring Jane down.

"Whoa!" Rey said. "Let's back up a second. We need a little more background before we do anything."

Sam brought him and Jane up to speed on the queen's early years, and then added, "But really what's important are her final days in Egypt, as that's most likely when she hid the location of the Sons of Adam in her journal."

"I'm all ears."

"Let's start a few years before then. After Caesar was assassinated, his will was read. Cleopatra and their son got nothing, and instead of appointing Mark Antony his successor, Caesar surprised Rome by adopting and giving his name to his eighteen-year-old grandnephew, Octavian."

"Then what?"

"Cleopatra sided with Mark Antony." Sam put her hands in her pockets. "They eventually become lovers and traveled throughout Greece and Turkey." She looked at Stryker. "We'll go there if necessary."

"Didn't Octavian defeat Mark Antony?" Rey asked.

"Yes, there was a naval battle at Actium in late August of 31 BC. Mark Antony and Cleopatra fled back to Alexandria, where they wintered, aware the end was coming."

Rey looked out to sea, imagining the sounds of battle, and the smell of the water, mixed with blood. "How do we know that?"

"She built a fancy mausoleum near the palace and filled it with much of her treasure. Historians also think she was experimenting with toxic poisons that would kill with a minimum of discomfort."

The wind stole the words from his mouth. "I see."

"When Octavian came to Alexandria in the spring of 30 BC, there was little resistance. That's where the Shakespearean drama wraps up."

"Mark Antony killed himself?"

"That's right. Well. He tried. But he botched it and his servants took him to her. Cleopatra and her maids hauled him to the top of the mausoleum where she'd barricaded herself, and he died in her arms."

Rey nodded, remembering he'd seen a movie once with that scene.

"It didn't take long for Octavian's men to get into the mausoleum. Next, *she* tried to kill herself with a belt knife, but they stopped her. Nine days later, not wanting to be paraded in front of Rome in golden chains, she managed to finish the job."

He recalled parts of the story. "With an asp, right?"

"Historians don't think so. She was a painstaking planner, and wouldn't have wanted her fate in the hands of an unreliable animal. Besides, cobra venom causes a lot of distress, including bursts of shuddering."

Rey shuddered himself. "Ew."

"Exactly. By all accounts, she died peacefully on her golden lion-pawed couch, dressed in her pearls and gripping her royal crook and flail." Sam put her hands under her head, like a mock pillow. "A more likely scenario is hemlock and opium. Whatever killed her also killed her two lady servants."

"Hmm," Rey said. "Where did the asp idea come from then?"

Sam idly drew a snake in the dirt with her foot. "Every early account of her death mentioned a snake. Maybe because Octavian called the *psylli*—Libyans who were known to deal with snake poison—when her body was found. They were known to suck at snake wounds and revive those who had died from snake bite."

Rey rubbed his mustache. "It seems they failed."

"They did. It could also be Octavian meant to use the snake imagery to debase her. By that point in history, even though Egyptian pharaohs had used snakes on their foreheads for generations, the serpent was falling out of favor."

He was familiar with the Bible. "Let's not forget the treacherous snake in the Garden of Eden."

"How could I? Especially with the Sons of Adam and their tattoo." She paused. "Still, you should probably check all Cleopatra's old haunts for anything journal related. Besides the underwater palace, the Serapeum is one of the few buildings still around from her time."

"Got it," he said, deciding it was better not to argue. There didn't seem to be a better plan.

Without a word, Stryker got back in the car and closed the door. Sam joined him and the car sped off.

Jane looked at Rey with eyes full of exasperation. "I thought your team was intelligent. This is simply ridiculous."

"What else do you know about Cleopatra's palace?" he asked. Her false hair was whipping around her face. He wanted to kiss her.

"Besides the tidal wave that destroyed it in the fifth century?"

Her mouth looked soft and inviting. "Yes."

Jane put her left hand on her hip. "I saw a documentary about an archeologist who spent ages searching the harbor for the island where it was located. He and his team finally found the site about twenty years ago. Most of the extracted artifacts have been taken to museums around the world."

She didn't seem nearly as distracted by the sexual electricity crackling between them as he was. Did she feel it too? "Are there any in Alexandria?"

"I don't know."

"Guess we'll find out." Movement in the distance caught Rey's eye. "I hope that SUV on Stryker's tail doesn't have evil intentions."

Jane followed his gaze and frowned. "If it does, we'll never catch them in time."

CHAPTER 37

Taposiris Magna, Egypt
Day Four

S am and Stryker hadn't gone far down the eight-lane highway when she said, "I'm glad we at least have a plan now."

"Me too. Good work charming those archeologists."

"Thanks. Seems like a big haystack, though."

"It does, but nice to know one of the possible needles is an old journal."

"Are we taking bets that the journal contains the location of the cult?"

"No. We'll continue to follow all leads." Stryker glanced in the rearview. "Company. Coming up fast."

Life surged through her as she reached for her service weapon. These living-on-the-edge moments were why she loved her job. Time for the ultimate roll of the dice.

She unbuckled her seat belt and moved fast, turning in her seat. A silver SUV was gaining on them. "Shall I notify Rey?"

"Yes, but he's too far back to help."

Sam wondered about the range but activated the radio and mouthed into her mic. "Rey. We have a tail. Looks aggressive."

The line crackled. "Roger that. On our way."

Stryker swerved around a slower-moving vehicle in the right lane.

Sam was thrown into the door. "They're catching up. Got any more you can give it?"

"Top speed already."

Heart racing, she dropped her window. Dry, desert wind stung her eyes as she aimed her pistol. It was too far for a clean shot, and traffic was heavier than she wanted it to be. She hoped no innocents would be caught in the cross fire.

A short-barreled rifle emerged from the passenger window of the silver SUV. Seconds later, their back window shattered.

She ducked. "Stryker!"

"I know!"

He braked hard and yanked the wheel to the right, throwing the car around a corner with a market on one side and a gasoline station on the other. This was a side street. She glanced back as the SUV skidded around the turn and continued the pursuit. A wild shot pinged off a parked car.

Sam popped off a shot through the broken window, but the SUV remained just out of range. Her heart beat double time. Their odds didn't look good.

Sirens became audible in the distance. Local police must've gotten a call.

Stryker stomped on the gas pedal, and the car rocketed down the residential street, which soon turned into a dirt path. Thick clouds of dust spewed from the back of their vehicle. He made a quick turn and they were flying down rows of some kind of orchard. Another right, another quick left, and then they were back on paved road.

The dust cleared and shots came at them again. Stryker swung the car back and forth, jerking her around. A bullet hit the trunk, and another hit a rear brake light. Glass shattered into the street.

Her breath came in fast jerks. She wished for a rifle. Or an RPG.

Making do, she wasted another round targeting the enemy driver.

Stryker turned right, running a red light and passing a mall. Cars honked their displeasure as the race continued across a causeway. Blue water gleamed on both sides of the road. It looked like they were crossing a river, or wide irrigation canal.

Sam heard a loud pop and their car fishtailed, squealed, and broke the railing. They sailed through the air before the car dove, nose-first, into the water.

Upon impact, she was thrown out the broken rear window, tumbling like a gymnast through cold water for what seemed like forever. Eventually, she slowed enough to surface and get her bearings. The temperature of the water was shocking! Her teeth began to chatter. The cold would probably kill them if they didn't get out soon. Of course, for a sniper, having them here in the water would be like hunting frozen rabbits.

She searched for the SUV. No sight of it on the bridge. It was their lucky day.

Coming up for air, Stryker swam toward her. "You okay?"

"Got banged up a bit, but I'll live. You?"

"I'm fine." He nodded his head toward the causeway above. "Our company left."

"Yeah, but we have a new problem."

She pointed at the three dark-blue police cruisers that squatted near the broken railing, lights flashing.

CHAPTER 38

Alexandria, Egypt
Day Four

On the way to Alexandria, Jane feigned a nap in the car. After helping Stryker and Sam talk their way out of police custody, she and Rey had dropped them at Cairo West Air Base, an Egyptian base utilized by the US military. Per Stryker's command, she and Rey had jumped back in the car and headed to Cleopatra's underwater palace.

As they drove, she fantasized again about kissing Rey. The energy between them while they'd waited for the others at the lighthouse had nearly made her lose her senses. It was palpable, the electricity she felt when he was near. She'd wanted to kiss him then. Instead, she'd forced herself back to business.

Rolling her head into the window, she bit her lip. What the hell was she thinking? Truth be told, she wasn't. From the instant she'd met Rey in Bikaner, she'd been drawn to him. The air felt charged between them, and she'd seen his eyes as he watched her, knowing he felt it, too. But it was crazy on so many levels, she didn't even know where to begin.

Since her husband had left her for another woman, she'd been closed to offers of romantic entanglement. Too loyal, she had stayed with the bastard for years after she'd realized the affair. When he finally left, she'd written the whole love thing off as a waste of bloody time, and had refused her friends' attempts to introduce her to new men. She'd closed the sidewalk to her heart, put up yellow caution tape, and installed a large pit to catch any who trespassed. That had left her alone. And she liked it that way.

She deepened her breathing to further the ruse. Rey drove in silence, but she could feel his eyes on her when she occasionally shifted.

Rey was trouble. Not only for her sealed-off heart, but also for the debt she owed.

She had suspected the Sons of Adam ever since the assassination of Britain's PM. Their fingerprints were all over the killing spree, and when she'd seen the first tattoo, she'd been certain. She'd grown up an orphan on their island, where the men showed off their tattoos and talked frequently about kidnapping women. Her cousin, Antonio, belonged to the group, which was why she had volunteered for this mission. No, he wasn't just a member—she'd found out the last time he was in London that he and his father led the cult now.

When she'd been about to be sold to a wealthy "husband" in Russia at the ripe old age of twelve, Antonio had helped her escape to a nunnery in Florence. There, the sisters had pretended to believe their claims that she was eighteen. She spent years behind those Catholic walls, genuflecting and praying to ensure the hunt for her grew cold. After leaving the cloistered sisterhood, she made a career in propaganda because she was fascinated by the success of the group's lies. Truly impressive. Thousands of years in the making. Global reach. And so subtle, no one realized it was happening right under their noses.

Using the sex trade to keep men in ideological line was clever. Not like the overly obvious Russian propaganda campaign during the 2016 US election. Even the Brits were only playing a short game when it came to social media. The west could learn some lessons from the Sons of Adam. And if the cult had developed good deepfake tech, manipulating public opinion would be as easy as breathing.

Now, she felt torn in half as she tossed in the stiff seat. Rey was sweet. He was the first man she'd even had the potential to care about for years. But she was still loyal to Antonio. Owed him her life, actually. She couldn't let Rey and the M2 team find the location of Antonio's island stronghold.

CHAPTER 39

Eden
Day Four

It was another freezing cold day on Eden. Weathermen were calling for sleet, but the *comandante* enjoyed being outside in the brisk air. After lighting a fresh cigar, he pulled a new burner phone from his pocket. While he walked past the garden to a spot on the island's leeward side where he could watch the surf pound the shore, he called his man.

"Cobra here."

"Did you take them out?"

"They had two cars," Stefano rasped. "We chased one until it landed in the water. But I think they lived. Police arrived before we could finish the job."

The *comandante* pulled his peacoat tight and puffed thoughtfully. The pesky American team was still buzzing around like flies. "What about the others?"

"Couldn't follow both cars at once. Was hoping our friends were watching with a bird and can tell us where they went."

The *comandante* wasn't sure where the old Vatican spy was getting his intel. Maybe the Russians. He knew better than to ask, but guessed the old spymaster had access to satellite footage or some signals intelligence, and maybe some eyes and ears on the ground around the world. "I'll find out. What details can you give me?"

"The car that didn't go for a swim was a dark-blue rental, parked at that lighthouse outside Taposiris Magna less than two hours ago."

"Okay. I'll find out where your party went after their swim. Let's put two other men on the blue car and you take the swimmers. I'll send Michael to join you once I know where you're headed."

Michael was one of their best. Like most of the other boys, he'd grown up with a fire in his belly for the work they did.

"Thank you."

Today's cigar was especially fine. "Before you go, update me on your work in the States."

"In conjunction with Antonio's computer experts, I have men in twenty major metropolitan areas, stirring up dissent. It's been easy for them to find local groups who share versions of our beliefs. Massive inflation, the huge right/left political chasm, and social media disinformation are playing right into our hand."

"They're ready to go then?"

"They are. If it's civil war you want, it'll only take a spark to light the fire."

"Excellent. Good work."

The *comandante* rang off and threw the phone onto the rocks below.

Walking back toward the village, he stepped on his electronic keycard. It must have fallen out when he'd pulled the burner phone from his pocket. Now it had a large scratch down the front side. No matter, he'd get a new one. He put it back into his coat and then paused, considering his next move.

Earlier, Antonio and his men had shown the *comandante* their latest deepfake video. In it, the US president-elect stood in a control room full of computer equipment, ordering workers to hack into electronic voting systems and change votes. Of course, if it had been that simple, the president-elect wouldn't have won in the first place. But he also knew technology-wary Americans would fall for the ruse. When he'd complimented the realistic nature of the video, his men had gone on at length about how they had been training the artificial intelligence behind it. The how-to lecture was boring, but the results! Incredible!

He finished his cigar and threw the still-glowing butt into the sea. Pulling his knife from its sheath, he began to clean his fingernails. He'd initially planned civil war in the United States as a wonderful Plan B in case the mission to kill the president-elect was thwarted. But the more he thought about it, the more it made sense as an integral part of his plans.

CHAPTER 40

Palatine Hill, Rome, Italy
Day Four

Stryker stopped tapping his foot. It was Angie's habit, not his. But he did feel impatient. They'd lost so much time already. First, while he and Sam shivered in wet clothes, Ace and the director took hours to convince the Egyptian authorities that they weren't any sort of threat. Then, the flight to Rome had been delayed, followed by another painful hour spent waiting to rent a car, and now they were last in line to enter the remains of the home that had once belonged to Caesar Augustus, first known as Octavian. Cleopatra's mortal enemy had outlived her by over forty years, and most of that time had been spent here on Palatine Hill.

When an icy rain began to fall, Stryker sighed and opened the black umbrella they'd acquired on the way here from a local market. Italian winters were not made for seaside picnics.

He leaned over and spoke in low tones to Sam. "You sure we're not wasting our time with this?"

She tilted her head and whispered back. "The journal is our only clue to Angie's location."

"I know, but why would it be here?"

"I want to get in Cleopatra's head. It was great to learn more about her on the flight. She spent time here in Rome."

"But this is the home of her archenemy."

"I'm glad you've been following along. I know history isn't your thing."

He clenched his jaw. He hated being criticized, and although that's not what she meant, that's how it felt. "Please just summarize what you learned about the time after Julius Caesar met her in Egypt. What happened after the rucksack incident?"

"Sure. They enjoyed each other's company for around eight months. Two weeks after he left, she gave birth to their son, Caesarion. Even though they knew how to end a pregnancy in her day, she decided having the baby would be a good move."

He could see the political advantages. "Sure, it gave her an heir, and her brother became window dressing."

"Exactly. And Caesar took her younger sister with him when he left, setting Cleopatra up to rule."

Stryker glanced around, on the lookout for anyone who might want them dead. "Okay, when did she visit Rome then?"

"Once she had Egypt under control, she made the trip. It took two months by ship."

"That's a trek. Was she welcomed here?"

Sam shook her head. "Probably only by Caesar. Rome had been dealing with a decade of civil war, and they didn't think fondly of Africans. Even those of Greek background."

"Hmm."

"It must have been a shock for her—the two countries' cultures were quite different. Romans killed their second daughters while women flourished in Egypt, owning property in their own name, running businesses, marrying who they wished and divorcing if they chose."

He frowned, thinking of Harper. "Romans killed their daughters?"

"Often all but their firstborn."

He furrowed his brow. "That's gruesome."

"Yes. Now imagine Cleopatra comes to Rome. She displays her won-the-lotto-times-ten wealth, and Caesar sets her up with a house."

"Why aren't we at her place?"

Sam put her hands in her pockets. "It no longer exists. It was on Janiculum Hill."

"I see. Was Rome as nice as Alexandria?"

"Not even close. If Alexandria was New York, Rome was a Wild West town with mud streets and a swinging-door saloon. Caesar and Octavian turned it into a metropolis using Alexandria as an example."

He shivered, tired of waiting in the cold rain. It made his shoulder ache. "Interesting."

"It surprised me too. For instance, the Roman calendar was all messed up. Caesar imported the Egyptian calendar, adding new names to the months, of course."

"Like August?"

"Yes." She smiled. "But back to the love story. They weren't together long. Cleopatra was here when Caesar was stabbed to death on the Ides of March."

He looked over his shoulder, still on the lookout. "Was she a suspect?"

"Not from what I can tell. The culprits were pretty clear. Their togas and shoes were covered in blood as they ran through the Roman streets shouting that they'd killed a tyrant."

That seemed *crystal* clear to Stryker. "And Mark Antony rose from those ashes?"

"Right," Sam agreed. "Until he and Octavian, Caesar's great-nephew and heir, began to fight for power."

"When did he switch from Octavian to what was his new name, Augustus Caesar?"

"He got the Caesar title when Julius Caesar died and named him heir, and then was named Augustus by the Roman Senate after winning the civil war with Mark Antony."

"I see. How did Cleopatra get together with Mark Antony?"

"He summoned her to Tarsus, in Turkey. After ignoring his requests for months, she showed up in full Egyptian splendor. Then she wowed him with a party so extravagant that the rose petals were knee-deep."

Stryker's jaw dropped, thinking of the expense. "You're kidding."

"No."

"Guess we all have different tastes. I'm not really one for walking through rose petals. They come back to Rome at some point?"

"First Mark Antony married Octavian's sister," Sam answered. "But that attempt at political solidarity didn't go well. Later, after Cleopatra gave birth to Antony's twins, it sounds like they spent more time in Athens."

"Such a royal soap opera."

"You see why poets had a heyday."

"I do now." Stryker looked at the ruins of Palatine Hill ahead. "Sounds like we're here because there's no better place to start."

At that moment, the line moved and they were given access to the house. As they toured the ruins, Stryker learned that after eliminating Mark Antony and Cleopatra, Octavian bought up several pieces of property and had this mansion built close to the forum and next to the house of the Vestal Virgins.

Stryker didn't know what to look for as they walked through. Most of the place was a wreck, with only a few reddish paintings remaining on the walls. He had no idea where one might hide a journal. Assuming Octavian had found it and hidden it at all, which wasn't likely. It felt like they were wasting precious time. Stryker yearned to find his daughter and wife.

The tour ended and they walked to their new rental car. The rain had turned into sleet, making the sidewalks slick. Sam grabbed his arm for stability as they walked past remains that were built on the ruins of Nero's palace. Through the frozen rain, they got a glimpse of the Colosseum in the distance.

"Did that spark anything for you?" Stryker asked.

Sam seemed deep in thought. "No. It's all percolating, though. Thanks for entertaining my need to get a feel for Cleopatra's time."

"Sure."

They got in the car and headed down Via Celio Vibenna to find a hotel and dinner. He wanted to check in with Ace. It was slow going on the icy streets, and accidents had piled up in several intersections as they drove by the old gladiator stadium.

He'd noticed the black SUV behind them a few minutes after the drive began, and took several turns down narrow streets to see if it was a tail. When it pulled closer and a gun appeared out the passenger window, his question was definitively answered.

"Sam, grab your weapon. Our friends are back."

CHAPTER 41

Eden
Day Four

Antonio sat in the dining room with a group of men he'd grown up with on the island, finishing a savory lunch of mushroom risotto. Their new chef knew how to put together a meal. How had she lost her tongue? His father had mentioned a Russian customer, but Antonio hadn't paid much attention. Still, it was unusual. But not his worry.

It was too bad she wouldn't be here long—because the men used the cooks for sex, the women usually killed themselves after a few months. Most threw themselves off the cliffs, one had used a knife, and another had tried to swim for it. Her body had washed up on shore a few days later.

Antonio had argued with his father about the practice, and, as usual, had lost. All Antonio could do about it now was plug his ears when he heard the screams. The men made fun of him for it, but he was used to their derision.

Pity his mother was dead. He'd learned that in other times, the mate of the *comandante* ran the kitchen. His grandmother had, but she'd died in the same accident that took his cousin Jane's parents, and brought his father back to the island with him and his mother in tow. Once his mother killed herself, his father had usually chosen cooks from the women snagged during group fishing expeditions.

Lunch had been tasty, but he was in a foul mood at having to sit across from Michael, a slow eater and prematurely graying-at-the-temples bully. There'd been no other place to sit.

Michael finally finished and put down his fork. "Sounds like I'm going to join the current mission. How did those Americans give Stefano the slip in Egypt?"

"They ran their car into a body of water," Antonio answered. "But we've tracked the groups."

"To where?"

He hoped they weren't on Cleopatra's trail. It would surely set his father off, and when the *comandante* was in a foul mood, the island quickly became an extremely small place. "Alexandria and Rome."

"Sounds good. How about the next target?" Michael asked as a brunette woman came to take their dishes.

"You mean the US president-elect?"

Michael's eyes held enthusiasm. Hunger. "Yes. Is that kill still on?"

"We're on track, yes."

"You sure, momma's boy? Wasn't she from America?"

Antonio cringed. Not this again. "What if she was?"

"You probably don't have the guts. That's why Stefano has been working that angle."

"I'm just too busy."

The last dishes were removed from the table.

"Right." Michael sneered. "You're just too soft. Probably still don't even know your own mother's name, do you?"

"Screw you."

Antonio shoved his chair back and stood abruptly. Eyes turned at the sound of wood screeching across the tile floor.

The conversation was over.

Antonio stormed down the dining hall and out the door. Michael had been cruel to him when they were kids, and the hard look in his eyes had reminded Antonio of a particular incident.

One night in the dining hall when he was seven or eight, he'd gotten into an argument with his father over the name of his mother. He'd recently stolen the picture he kept in his wallet and decided he wanted to know her name. Innocently, he'd asked his father about it and had gotten yelled at during dinner. Michael, and the entire island, had heard the whole thing.

The next day Michael had called him effeminate names. When Antonio had tried to run, Michael tackled Antonio and kicked him. He pulled into himself, trying to protect his head while he was beaten.

A teacher had finally pulled Michael off and Antonio had run home, where he sobbed for hours, missing his mother and feeling sorry for himself. When his father came home, he asked what the problem was; Antonio told him the story. Instead of being angry at the bully, his father's face had clouded with anger before taking the heavy leather belt off his trousers. Antonio had to pull his pants down and endure a long, painful spanking. It was the first of many. Thank God that had been before his father discovered a penchant for the whip.

Eventually Antonio had learned not to ask about his mother. But he still wanted to know more about her. She had loved him. Who were her people? Did he have grandparents or cousins on her side of the family?

A few times, when he'd been out in the world on business, he'd attempted research on his mother from the anonymity of an internet café, but without a name, he'd hit a brick wall. Perhaps that was his father's intention.

With the abuse, he'd considered leaving the group and finding an out-of-the-way place to live out his life in peace, like Jane had in England. He enjoyed visiting her when he was near London. There were challenges to a move, though. He had no marketable skills and would miss the men who were his friends. But the worst was that the group tracked down those who left. And killed them.

Antonio grunted as he entered the command center and sat down in front of his monitor. It was time to get back to work. They had some American rats to track down.

CHAPTER 42

Eden
Day Four

Although she felt anxious about the overture she'd made to Zola that morning, Angie's body felt lighter than it had in years. As she did a few pushups in the dim light of her cell—anything to keep her mind off Harper and Tim— she realized that she felt hungry only when surrounded by the scents of food. Who knew, she might even come out of this having lost a few pounds. Unless she died here. She chuckled at the thought of leaving a good-looking corpse. Cry or laugh, those were her choices.

Her respite from the galley was short-lived, as it was also her day to help out with dinner. The usual expressionless guards came and walked her and several other women down the hall and up flights of stairs. As they were climbing, Antonio came barreling down, pushing guards and women out of the way. He stopped in front of a simple gray door that had avoided Angie's notice before now.

He swiped his keycard to enter and quickly descended a plain-looking stairwell. As the solid metal door slammed behind him, Angie wondered what could be hidden in the island's depths.

The guards shuffled her group up the remaining stairs and out into the cold evening. She had been allowed to keep her down jacket and she huddled inside it on the short walk to the community dining hall. It reminded her of better times, when evening meant a hot shower and a simple meal with her family. Her eyes sought the shadows where the children's rose-colored building lay clumped together with the men's houses a few hundred feet away. She needed to get inside the *comandante*'s blue abode.

Depositing the women in the kitchen, the men went to sit in the dining room, laughing now that their chores were finished. With a small jerk of her head, Zola motioned for Angie to approach. Torn between excitement and worry, she felt as if she was being called to the front of a classroom without any answers.

As she drew near, Zola pointed to a set of wine glasses on a tray, and then to a door on one wall of the kitchen. Zola held up all nine of her fingers and pointed downstairs. It must lead to a wine cellar. Angie's conjecture was confirmed when she stepped down the stairwell and saw a dim space lit by a single overhead bulb. Dry goods lined the shelves, and one entire wall was dedicated to bottles of wine.

Angie moved closer to the wine shelf and stared at the variety of dust-covered bottles. Which ones was she to take back up?

The sound of light feet on the stairs caused Angie to turn. It was the blonde girl who reminded her of a slightly older version of Harper, wearing an azure jumper that set off light blue eyes.

"Zola sent me down here to help with the wine."

"You speak English?"

"Yes, Antonio teaches some of us."

Angie was flabbergasted. Was this Zola's way of assisting? Could she get a message to Harper?

"I was hoping you spoke English so I could practice," the girl continued. "But we can't be seen talking."

"Okay," Angie said slowly. "Our secret. Why do you want to practice?"

She brightened, giving a little twirl that made her skirt fan out. "I'm to be married in a day or so."

If Angie's mouth had held any liquid, she would have done an honest-to-God spit spray across the room. The girl was a child. Barely pubescent. "Married? Aren't you young for that?"

"No, I'm eleven. They were waiting to find the right husband for me."

The right husband? Dear God. What rubbish had they used to brainwash this child? "Are the girls usually younger?"

"Oh yes."

The girl's tone was so matter-of-fact that Angie lost her voice at the horror of it.

The child continued: "My husband is from, how do you say it, Al-a-bam-a?"

While her mind whirred, Angie defaulted to polite. "Yes, Alabama. You speak English very well."

"Thanks." The girl's smile beamed with pride. "We need ten bottles of this red over here." She pointed to an upper level of the wine rack, far-right side. "Zola only has nine fingers, but usually means ten."

Angie handed the girl five bottles and grabbed the other half herself. As she did, gruff voices came from upstairs.

She lowered her voice. "What's your name?"

"Rebecca."

The men's voices grew louder.

"How long have you lived here?" Angie asked.

"Forever."

Interesting. Rebecca hadn't been kidnapped. "Were you born here?"

"No. We sometimes get babies and raise them. I help."

Babies? From where?

The men's voices drifted off, but it didn't matter—Angie's heart continued to pound, her mouth as dry as the dust coating the wine bottles. "The girls that are brought here. Are they married also?"

"Of course," Rebecca said with a grin that turned Angie's heart to lead. "You too. In another three days."

CHAPTER 43

Alexandria, Egypt
Day Four

Although Rey appreciated Sam's data dump about Cleopatra's final days, he still felt overwhelmed. Finding a two-thousand-year-old journal containing the location of the Sons of Adam seemed an impossible goal.

Nevertheless, after arriving in Alexandria, they'd found a travel company willing to take them diving, even though it was a windy afternoon and visibility promised to be poor. Currently, he and Jane stood in the bow of a small vessel as it motored toward the underwater site of Cleopatra's royal palace. Even with the wind, the boat and water smelled of fish.

Considering that Stryker and Sam had been attacked on the Egyptian causeway, Rey remained on high alert. A satellite could have tracked them here.

Jane's faux blonde hair was tossed by the wind. "I still think this a waste of time."

He wondered if he could talk her into sharing a hotel room with him later. The mission might be a wild goose chase, but they could still have some fun. With a background in psychology, she might not freak out about his PTSD. "You're probably right, but we need to go see for ourselves."

Alexandria's distant shore was lined with white buildings that gave the harbor the look and feel of a modern city. Rey tried to determine their location compared to the ancient map he had studied.

He pointed west. "I think the lighthouse would have been over there."

She nodded, seemingly unimpressed.

As a mechanical engineer, he thought it remarkable. Built in the third century BC, the structure had been the world's first lighthouse, and the second tallest building in human history for centuries after—only the Great Pyramid at Giza had been taller. Its construction took twelve years to complete, and used mirrors and a furnace at the top to warn ships they were close to shore.

The motor stopped its putting and the boat drifted. From the stern, a voice hailed them to come to the back of the boat. They were the only passengers. He was grateful the man spoke English. Rey's other language, Spanish, didn't get much play in this part of the world.

The man's voice was heavily accented. "Please. It is time for you to dive. We are over the palace ruins."

The captain pointed to a rack of wetsuits and Rey picked one out, suiting up quickly before checking his tanks and respirator. The equipment was older but had the sheen of being well maintained. He checked the seal on the bag that would keep their cash and papers safe and dry. When he finished, Jane was ready as well.

They both spit in their masks to prevent fogging. "Ready?" he asked.

"Let's hope the pollution doesn't kill us."

With a last look around for danger, Rey fell backward into the water. Jane splashed down next to him.

He got his bearings. Jane was to his right. They dove into the murky water.

The captain had unfortunately been correct. Visibility was horrendous. This was no crystal-clear Caribbean dive.

Luckily, the water was shallow and they reached the bottom with only a few flipper kicks. At least it would be hard for a team of assassins to bother them down here.

Shapes began to appear in the gloom. He reached out and touched Jane's arm, pointing at several broken columns that lay on their sides like a giant's forgotten game of pickup sticks. He put his arm out as a gauge. The pillars were at least four feet in diameter.

Swimming on, schools of tiny white-and-black fish nibbled at the ubiquitous crust that covered everything manmade. It seemed the only artifacts the archeologists had left were those too large to easily recover. A pointed roof appeared in front of him and Jane traced its ridge before they moved on. He wanted to see a sphinx, a lion, or other artwork, but as they swam, trying to keep inside the boundary of the palace area, he saw very little.

Just as he was about to give up, a massive bowl, probably carved from granite, appeared out of the gloom. Joking around with Jane, he stood in it as though using it for a photo shoot. Her eyes crinkled in a smile as she played along, taking a picture with only her hands.

Frustrated by the waves of silt obscuring everything, he was about to suggest they head back to the boat when he heard the unmistakable sound of a vessel. Perhaps their hired captain was trying to keep from drifting. But no—the sound was growing louder. Someone else was approaching.

He pointed up, but when Jane put her hands to her lips, signaling silence, he agreed.

Surfacing toward the late afternoon twilight with caution, Rey motioned for Jane to stay submerged as he poked his head above water.

Only fifty feet away, a second boat was moored to theirs. A man with a rifle stood in the stern. When he spotted Rey, he aimed and fired.

Rey swore and ducked back under the waves.

The bullet streamed through the water six inches from his right arm. Rey pointed left and down. Jane took the hint and dove, swimming hard. Once they hit the bottom, they kept going; they'd have to parallel the shore for a while before they could swim safely to land.

Up above, the boat was zigzagging, trying to locate them. He touched his lucky St. Christopher medallion and prayed the boat wasn't equipped with some new tech that would ID them like a school of fish.

He checked the oxygen level in his tank. Not enough. It was a long way back.

CHAPTER 44

Rome, Italy
Day Four

Stryker barreled down the one-way street as fast as he dared on the icy Roman roads, trying to lose their pursuers. These guys must have great intel to have found them so fast.

He came to an intersection and hustled through, only too late realizing that the street had become unidirectional in the other direction. Three men standing on the sidewalk jeered and hooted, letting him know his mistake.

"I hope nobody heads our way," Sam said, pulling her weapon.

He didn't have time to agree with the obvious. "Pull up a map on your phone," he said. "See if you can find a way to lose them."

Five-story buildings sat cheek-by-jowl here in the heart of Rome, and the roads were thick with motorbikes and pedestrians as everyone headed home for the day. Sleet was falling faster than the wiper blades could handle, and ice coated the car's windshield. Horrible conditions to evade the SUV hot on their tail.

A shot pinged off the back bumper. Sam returned fire.

The street ended at an old brick building with a circular tower. To the right was a set of stairs, topped by a series of balustrades. He turned left, the back wheels of the car spinning a little as he rounded the corner. A motorcycle whizzed by on his left, the driver honking and waving his fist. At the next intersection, Stryker turned right, passing a small corner restaurant.

Sam looked over her shoulder. "They spun out on that corner. See if you can take the next left."

It was another narrow one-way street. He gunned it, but the black SUV recovered from the spinout and began to gain on them. The one-story wall on his left side lasted at least a half-mile. The enemy's car crowded his rearview.

"Where is that turn?" he growled.

Ahead was a strange intersection where the right turn was at only fifteen degrees, which meant they'd be headed almost exactly back the way they'd come.

Sam pointed to it. "Take that."

As he did, another shot rang out, breaking the back-passenger window. Stryker felt a sting across the top of his left shoulder.

He ground his teeth and tried to ignore the pain as he headed down the straightaway.

The next shot went through the back window and clean through the front windshield, creating a dime-sized hole. Sleet immediately began to ooze through it, like blood from his shoulder wound.

When they came to a "Y" split, he waited as long as he could before veering left. Sam let a volley of bullets fly. In his rearview, the SUV yanked on the wheel too hard, and spun the rear of their car into a white van parked by a wrought-iron fence. The wrenching sound of the metal-on-metal crash was impressive.

"Nice shooting." He cracked a small, satisfied smile. "Let's see if that helps."

The narrow road had a stone wall to the right and a walkway to the left. It was another long stretch.

"C'mon, give me a turn," he said, fingers violently tapping the wheel.

Finally, they came to an open gate. The sign to the left said it was a morgue. He wryly noted the irony and pulled the car through the entry.

Sam turned in her seat. "They aren't behind us. Can you get around the building?"

"Yes."

He navigated around and out the other side, past a church built in a circular style. From there, he was able to make a few quick turns in succession, until he finally took a deep breath. "I think we lost them."

"Whew." Sam exhaled. "Nice driving."

"Thanks. I think we need to dump the car and get on the underground."

"Agreed. The shattered glass is like a neon sign."

An hour later they were warm and dry inside a family-run *pensione* that had taken cash with no questions. They had a plain room with two queen beds and a narrow view.

Stryker checked the courtyard below. "Let's call Ace before we get food."

Sam brought out her phone and initiated the call before sitting down at a small table.

After dealing with the encryption, Ace came on the voice-only call. "How goes it?"

"Other than getting chased twice today, we're fine," Sam answered. "Well, Stryker has a flesh wound across the top of his shoulder."

Stryker sat down on the couch, and then shrugged. They'd grabbed some butterfly bandages on the way and cleaned it up with peroxide. It hurt, but he'd had worse.

Ace ignored his gun wound. "I've been looking into the string of recent assassinations, and there are more than we realized."

Stryker was starting to think of Ace as a cold fish. But she hadn't been with the team long, so he told himself to cut her some slack.

"Oh?" Sam asked.

"Some killings were initially ruled as accidents. For instance, a senior member of the New Zealand cabinet died in a supposed gas leak. I've asked for the case to be reopened. These guys are good and have worldwide reach."

Sam shook her head. "Crazy."

"It gets even more interesting. A banker in Rio had a heart attack two years ago. A priest in England had a car accident last month. Autopsies on both mention a cobra tattoo, although on the younger man it was on his thigh. Both files were later deleted. I had to get creative to find them."

"What's their goal?" Sam said. "Why these victims?"

"We don't know. Seems like more than terror. And in these last two cases it looks like they might be killing their own."

Stryker raised an eyebrow. That was a new wrinkle.

"What else have you found?" Sam asked.

"I've had an analyst looking at possible sites for a clean rifle shot for all the president and president-elect visits in the coming weeks. There are way too many."

Sam made eye contact with Stryker, her concern plain. "What's next on their agendas?"

"The president has an upcoming talk in Sweden and one in Saudi Arabia. The president-elect will be in Rome after a stop in Paris."

"Hope the protests from Saudi Arabia don't spread. Rey told us about those."

"Yes, most cities in Saudi Arabia are experiencing some form of uprising."

Stryker interrupted. "When will the PE be in Rome, and for what?"

"In three days. For a public appearance with the pope in Vatican City."

He wondered about the political climate back home. With inflation and unemployment spiking, climate-related disasters wreaking havoc, and social media fanning the flames of every type of conspiracy theory imaginable, it felt like the entire country was on the verge of taking up arms against each other. "Why are they still doing appearances like this?"

"They refuse to cancel," Ace said. "Say they'll wear a vest and they've got extra Secret Service on duty. If you're available in three days, they'd actually like your help there in Rome."

"That's fine. But right now, we're still dealing with what happened in Bari. With the group planning an assassination, and no ransom demand, this is far beyond a normal kidnapping."

"You thinking a sex-trade-type pickup?" Ace asked.

Those words had been rambling around in his skull and every time he even thought about them, ice filled his stomach. "It's my working theory." The syllables seemed to catch in his throat. "Why else nab Zoe and Reno?"

"That's my conclusion on the kidnapping, too, and I'll dig into it more. Nothing else fits."

He wasn't sure if he was relieved Ace shared his theory or if her confirmation threw more wood on the fire of his fear. "Thanks for looking into it."

Ace continued, "But we still don't know their motive for the assassinations. What's the connection?"

Stryker frowned. "Don't know."

"Well, why don't I send you the top five sniper nests in Rome according to our researchers, and you can check them out if you have time?"

"Sure," he said, glad to change the subject. "But have the Secret Service scope them out as well."

"Agreed," Ace said. "Meanwhile, you guys need to double-down and find the journal with the location. That'll lead you to Angie, and hopefully you can stop whatever assassination attempt these sickos have planned."

Stryker was all in, but it was hard to go on offense when he wasn't even sure the journal existed or if they could find it with the hitmen so hot on their trail.

Sam disconnected the call.

He sat back on the cheap couch, considering if Ace could be working the other side. "Sam, how do you think we were made? Twice in one day."

"Lots of possibilities. Satellites, foreign operatives, compromised comms."

"Think Ace could be a mole?"

"She was well vetted and is a Navy squid." Sam shrugged from a nearby chair. "I like her pearls and purple blouses, but sure don't know her well."

"Money can be a powerful motivator."

"It can. But I think we need to focus more on the motive of the kidnappers."

He nodded. "I suppose. Whatever the motive, we need to get to the bottom of it. Maybe Rey is having more luck than we are."

CHAPTER 45

**Alexandria, Egypt
Day Four**

It was full dark by the time Rey and Jane pulled themselves onto shore in front of a well-lit seaside hotel. Exhausted, he took his flippers off and managed the seven steps to a lounge chair where he plopped on his back and tried to catch his breath.

The opposition clearly had great intel, but the killers had not been able to follow them underwater. At some point, the oxygen in their tanks had run out and they'd dropped the depleted bottles, joining them with the shipwrecks of millennia. They'd been forced to surface to breathe, but the swells and fall of night had hidden them from view. The enemy vessel had likewise slipped off and was nowhere to be seen.

"You okay?" he coughed out.

She perched on the edge of the chair next to him, still alert for trouble. He liked that about her. "I'm fine. Nice evening swim. A bit chilly out here in the wind, though."

The cool air felt good to him. "Dodged a bullet back there." He touched the medal on his chest.

She patted the roll-top waterproof bag on her belt. "I'm glad we brought our money and papers in the dry sack."

"Me too. And the car keys, though they've probably made the vehicle by now."

She pursed her lips. "Too bad. Our weapons are in the boot."

His breathing was starting to return to normal. He was hungry and tired. "What do you think about a cab, clothes, hotel, and food?"

"I like it. We can circle back to the car later."

The street behind the hotel was busy and they had no trouble hailing a taxi, although the driver did get out of the car to look them up and down before spreading a blanket from the "boot" onto the backseat and motioning for them to enter. They tipped the driver well for his trouble and walked a dozen blocks in case he remembered dropping them off.

An hour later, they were in a three-star hotel in East Alexandria, waiting on room service. He'd been pleasantly surprised when she'd agreed to one room.

They took turns showering. When she emerged, her damp, long black hair and striking face took his breath away.

He touched her cheek with tenderness. "You look good."

She backed away, but slowly, her eyes lingering on his. It gave him hope.

They sat on the couch and ate a delicious, seven-cheese fondue meal. He enjoyed heavenly smelling beef with caramelized onions and peppers, and she dipped shrimp and crab sticks into the boiling pot.

When a loud noise came from the hallway, he jumped up, grabbed a fondue fork, and ran to the door. Jane was beside him in a flash, but instead of jerry-rigging a weapon like he had, she put a hand on his arm.

"Whoa," she said. "I think it was a door shutting a few rooms down."

He blinked. "We're not under attack?"

"I don't think so. But let me check."

She stepped in front of him and opened the door, peering both ways. "Not this time," she said, closing it again. "You have great reflexes."

Should he tell her? Why not? She'd figure it out when he had nightmares later. "I have PTSD."

His post-traumatic stress disorder had been a huge turnoff in the past. The few other times he'd broached the topic with women, he'd gotten blank looks or eyes narrowing with caution.

Instead, Jane's eyes held understanding and compassion. "I'm sorry to hear that. How does it affect you?"

His shoulders relaxed. "Other than being easily startled, I have nightmares almost every night," he said as they retook their seats.

"You did well when we stormed the hotel room."

Normally, he didn't like talking about it, but she was in PSYOPS, and had covert experience. That's why she was on the mission. He sensed she understood. "I break out in a sweat every time."

She nodded.

"And I really have to fight to stay present," he added. "Shootouts are my least favorite part of the job."

"Have you tried drugs or therapy?"

"Both. Not for me."

"Yes, it's tricky business getting over trauma."

He nodded, pausing to take a sip of tea. It was not a night for alcohol, although he'd have loved a pale ale. Even though that noise had been nothing, he needed to stay alert. "What do you think about the propaganda war between Octavian and Mark Antony? You mentioned it briefly the last time we had a chance to talk."

She looked at Rey sideways, clearly noting the change of subject, but she didn't push a further PTSD discussion. "I think it's more interesting to consider what probably happened after Octavian won their war, and Cleopatra and Mark Antony were dead."

Rey finished the last of his beef and wiped his mouth with a napkin. "Oh?"

"Sam's understanding of Cleopatra's life was impressive, given how little Octavian left of the queen's reign."

"You think he removed traces of her time in power."

Jane finished her last shrimp. "Absolutely. He ruled for another forty-four years. Think about that for a minute."

"That's a long time."

"Indeed. Plenty of time to make Mark Antony and Cleopatra look bad, or tear down statues of her throughout Egypt."

Rey nodded. "Tough mission we have here."

"It is. I think we should be in Bari, following the police trail."

"Sounded like that lead went cold."

"You think this one is hot?"

He leaned in and whispered, "No, but I think you're the hottest woman I've ever seen."

Her dark eyes held a veil of secrets he couldn't read, but then she kissed him, and he stopped wondering what she was holding back.

But when she silently sobbed after they made love, his interest returned. "Hey, are you okay?"

She curled up in his arms and cried for another minute. He stroked her hair and murmured soft words in her ear. He hoped he hadn't been a lousy lover; with the way she'd groaned with pleasure, it sure hadn't seemed that way at the time.

"I'm all right," she said at last. "It's just . . . been a while since I've let my guard down."

"No worries. I sure understand that."

She rolled over and nestled into him. "Let's sleep now."

Since she hadn't pried into his PTSD, he returned the favor, but his curiosity about her meltdown remained.

CHAPTER 46

Eden
Day Four

While Angie and her cellmate cleaned the upstairs bedrooms in the yellow stucco house, she wondered if Rebecca, the child bride from the wine cellar, had been able to get a message to Harper. After the shock had worn off, Angie had told the girl to tell her daughter that she loved her.

What she really wanted was to take her baby in her arms and hug her.

In the house she was cleaning, two guards lounged downstairs at the kitchen table, playing cards. While Luna ran the vacuum, Angie used the noise to cover the sound of washing her face in the single bath between the two upstairs bedrooms. The warm water on her skin felt divine. She also stole some toothpaste and used her finger to run the minty gel around her teeth. When the vacuuming continued, she tore her shirt off and splashed water on her armpits, longing to shampoo her disgusting, disheveled hair. She made an unhappy face at herself in the mirror; she looked ten years older than she had when they'd been snatched.

She furiously scrubbed the sink, toilet and shower, frantic for any way out of this nightmare. The short chat she'd had with the poor girl in the wine cellar still haunted her. Who were their captors? Her best guess was Mafia. Were they doing all this for money?

The vacuum finally stopped and Angie broke herself out of the self-pitying reverie. She made eye contact with Luna, but they knew better than to speak here. The memory of Reno being whipped for trying to steal fruit sealed their mouths shut.

As they used a feather duster to clean the plain bedrooms, Angie looked for anything she could use in an escape attempt. But there were no phones, computers, keycards, or even bags of chips lying around.

The men's laughter floated up the stairwell like a lazy cloud. If she strained, she could almost make out their words. Angie stopped dusting and walked over to her cellmate. She put a hand on the brunette's arm and pantomimed for Luna to listen by cupping a hand behind one ear.

Luna huffed but stopped work and focused on the conversation. To make it sound like they were still working, Angie continued dusting, eyes glued to Luna.

Minutes passed. Soon they'd have to head back downstairs. As Angie walked toward Luna, the woman's eyes grew wide, her face blanched, and she put her hand to her mouth.

Angie's heart rate kicked up. What had Luna learned?

Three hours later, they were finally done cleaning houses and back in their cold, damp cell. They sat on the bottom bunk like schoolgirls, knees pulled up to their chests, both blankets wrapped around them. The suspense had been gnawing at Angie's gut all afternoon.

"Tell me what they said," Angie demanded softly.

"These men are not just kidnappers."

"What did they say?"

"They spoke of someone named Cobra."

"Cobra? Strange name." Could it be a call sign?

"Yes. They said he was on the hunt for a black ops team from America."

Angie clenched her fists under the blanket, emotions at war. Her sister and husband had to be on her trail, but these kidnappers were trying to stop them. "What else?"

"This Cobra. He's a sniper."

Angie grimaced. "Is there more?"

"Yes, I thought I heard this tidbit while serving lunch, and now I'm sure. He's going to kill the new US president in Rome in just a few days. The one who was recently voted in."

Angie put a hand to her heart. "That's horrible."

Her thoughts raced. Last fall's election had been the most contentious she'd ever seen. The campaign had been ugly, and violent confrontations at protests had rocked major cities across the country. Unemployment was at an all-time high, food banks were busier than they had been since the Great Depression, and both sides of the aisle were using hyperbole to fire up their respective bases. Talk of civil war raged on social media, probably fueled by Russian and Chinese bots, and Angie had been glad to escape the charged, partisan environment during their holiday. What would happen to her country if the president-elect were taken out before the inauguration?

"Are you okay?" Luna asked.

"That would be really bad for my country."

Luna nodded.

"Who are these guys? Mafia?" But as Angie spoke the words, she wondered why the Mafia would want to assassinate the president-elect.

Luna just shrugged.

As Angie huddled in the cold, a new resolve stiffened her spine. Dealing with the economic fallout from the latest pandemic had left her country brittle and dry, and the president-elect's death would spark a war that would make the US's original civil war look like a Sunday picnic. With modern weapons, it would be a bloodbath.

"Did you hear anything else at lunch?"

"I forgot to tell you. The leader's son got into a fight with the man across the table."

"A fistfight?"

"No, with words."

"What did they argue about?"

"The other man harassed the son, telling him he was soft on the plan because his mom was from America."

"Hmm. Anything else?"

"It sounded like the son didn't know the name of his mother. Isn't that strange?"

"Yes. It is."

The conversation lulled. "Thank you," Angie said, patting her new friend on the arm as she climbed out of the lower bunk. "You're a great help. I don't know how yet, but I am going to find a way to get us out of here."

And then I'll stop the plot.

CHAPTER 47

**Temple of Isis, Pompeii, Italy
Day Five**

Sam's gaze was fixed on the dark-blue mountains in the distance, their tops covered in a layer of lazy morning clouds.

The taxi had dropped them in the heart of the Pompeii tourist zone and now they were walking past the Great Theatre on their way to the temple. Sam marveled to herself at the daunting work that had been done to excavate this town, most of which had been buried under mounds of ash when Vesuvius erupted in AD 79.

She said, "The picture I have in my head of Cleopatra is becoming clearer all the time."

"You said that about Rome yesterday," Stryker said. "So why are we here?"

"It's all about Isis."

"My wife and daughter have been kidnapped by a crazy cult that wants to kill either the old or new POTUS and our best lead is a two-thousand-year-old goddess?" Stryker sighed, shaking his head.

"Let's look at the facts. We know that Cleopatra was highly intelligent and ruthless, a prankster, and, most importantly, marketed herself as the actual embodiment of Isis."

"Why is that important?"

"Put yourself in her shoes. You want to hide something, and suspect that your palace may be overrun by bloodthirsty Romans at any moment."

"Okay, then I'd want to hide it outside my stronghold."

"Me too. But where? While I own quite a bit of the area around the Mediterranean, it's hard for me to go anywhere unnoticed. I could disguise myself for a short period of time, but any significant absence from the palace would be keenly felt."

He smirked. "You are quite popular."

"I am." Sam liked this game. "But I have spies and priests or priestesses at my disposal."

"That you do."

"Therefore, if I can trust any of them, like the great-ancestor of that archeologist we met, I might have them hide something at an Isis temple."

"Why's that?"

"The temples are my home away from home given I'm the incarnation of Isis. And Pompeii here would have been an easy trip for one of my sleek and sexy Egyptian ships."

"What about Homer?"

"I love his work, but it doesn't give me a good hiding place."

"Is this your famous women's intuition?" he joked.

Her instincts had saved her bacon more times than even Stryker knew. "Don't discount the subconscious."

His tone turned serious. "I meditate, remember?"

"Good thing, too. Or you'd be impossible to hang out with."

He scowled, and she wondered if she'd gone too far. Always touchy, he had been in an understandable funk lately. Not that she'd been exactly peppy, but she felt they were on the right track. He clearly wasn't so sure.

They turned a corner and entered a courtyard. "This is it," she said. "Keep your eyes peeled."

"For what?"

"I hope we'll know it when we see it."

"That's encouraging."

She ignored that last comment.

The temple area was not large, but she was impressed by how well preserved it was, especially compared to Caesar's house in Rome yesterday. A small building about the size of a she-shed still had visible paintings of the goddess on both sides of the doorway. Roped-off stone steps led to a raised area full of columns that had once been the actual temple. Several walls were still standing. The architecture was a bastardized combination of Greek, Roman, and Egyptian styles. It looked promising.

She turned to Stryker. Today he wore an African American mask and mahogany-colored contacts. She was also Black, but with features other than her own. It was both annoying and nice that in Black disguises she got fewer suspicious looks here in Europe than she did back home in America. In low tones, she said, "I'm going to sneak up those stairs and look around as soon as there's a break in the tourist flood."

"Okay. In the meantime, tell me about this goddess."

"Isis arrived in Italy at least fifty years before Cleopatra, and was quite the popular deity. Paintings of the temple were found all over town on dining room walls. Experts think this building was rebuilt in 62 AD after an earthquake, so if anything is to be found, it'll be below ground."

"Unless there's a clue rebuilt into the temple. What's Isis's claim to fame?"

"Remember the saying from that cartoon, 'Oh mighty Isis?'" At his blank stare, she continued. "Motherhood and apple pie?" He still didn't blink. "Wow, okay. Just kidding. Fertility, nature, and knowledge. She was also a healer."

"Funny." He glanced around, always on the lookout. He stiffened slightly. "Was she worshiped for the same reasons everywhere?"

She followed his gaze and saw a bulky man turn the corner. Had he been looking for them? "No," she replied, grateful for her disguise. "I was reading this morning that in Greece, Isis became patron goddess of the sea, and in Rome, she and Venus duked it out for citizens' favor. As a linguist, you'll like this bit: the Egyptian word for 'throne' translates to 'Isis' in Greek."

"I do like it. And I think now's your chance. Go."

She took a quick glance around to confirm his assessment, then scampered up the stairs and snuck inside. He could handle himself if it came to that.

The two elaborately painted rooms of the interior had numerous recesses for statuary, although all were empty. On the southern wall, a painting had survived the ravages of time. It held an image of a woman in white robes, holding a snake in one hand and reaching toward a draped figure with the other. A crocodile lay at her feet.

Sam crossed the black mosaic floor and entered through the reddish-brown archway and into the next room, which had a mural of snakes guarding a wicker basket and several benches lining the stone walls. But no clue. The final room in the corner was a small place of purification, one that she'd read originally used the waters of the Nile. Cleopatra would've appreciated that.

Sam went back to the mosaic and tried pressing different tiles in various combinations, but nothing happened. There was no place else to search.

Tears threatened. She had been so *sure* that this was the key to finding Angie and Harper.

The dark-and-light alternating tile pattern reminded her of a mandala, albeit one merged with one of those made-for-the-internet images that caused your eyes to cross. Depending on how she looked at it, the patterns were either circular or crisscrossing lines. It was mesmerizing. Hypnotic.

Sam took a deep breath and allowed her mind to drift, thinking over the other Isis temples she'd researched. The one in Hungary was too far north, and Rey was covering the ones in Egypt. The temple in Rome had been destroyed. But there was one in Greece, on the island of Delos.

Stryker would not be pleased.

CHAPTER 48

Eden
Day Five

Inside the cave near the far wall of the harbor, Antonio stared at the piles of boxes. When his great-grandfather had led their group during World War II, he had offered up their island to the Italian military, who had jumped at the chance to have an unmapped munitions refueling station. In return, his great-grandfather had secured favors from Mussolini to operate unimpeded in Italy for decades. Yet for some reason, after the war had ended, his ancestor had never dealt with the physical remnants of his wheeling and dealing, not even to sell it on the black market.

Bombs, artillery shells, land mines, and grenades. There was even one round naval mine that looked like an alien head due to its horny protuberances. The entire cache had enough firepower to blow the island to bits. And his father had assigned him the task of figuring out how to get rid of it all.

At least this cave had been a fun escape when he was a child. He was generally forbidden to play with girls, except he'd somehow managed to sneak off with Jane once in a while. They'd play jacks in this storeroom, or sneak down to empty boats at night to laugh together.

He crossed his arms, wondering how he was going to deal with this mess. Most of the old naval mines had been placed strategically around the island, but the majority of the munitions were a dangerous, outdated pile of scrap.

Could he sell it now? Dump it in the ocean? He would need to hire an expert, but that presented its own set of issues.

Another problem was the planned celebration after the assassination of the US president-elect. Once a year, the men were allowed sex with all the women in captivity. With no set schedule, the event was meant to be a reward for hard work—the rest of the time the men made do with female staff, like the tongueless cook. Every year, he managed to find some excuse to be off the island. This year, however, there was too much going on for him to make a sudden visit to Rome.

There was so much on his plate. One of the girls was about to be "married" to a senator from Alabama, and there were delivery tactics to finalize. He ground his teeth. Of all the things he had to do, selling the children was the worst. The truth was, there was no wedding for any of the women or children. These were transactions to men who wanted sex slaves. He knew this girl would be locked up in the senator's basement, but he had no choice. He did enjoy the hunt for Cleopatra's lost journal, and overseeing his staff of computer experts, but right now that wasn't making up for headaches like the American black ops team.

While he thought, he began to pace the length of the cave. He'd been on edge all day.

After opening his email last night, he had a new problem on his hands. Jane. To be more precise, Cleopatra's journal and Jane. She'd sent him a short message using an email address he didn't recognize, signing it with a nickname only the two of them knew. All it said was "The Americans are on the trail of the journal, which may hold the location of the island. I am trying to stop them. Shorty."

Exclamation points still jumped in front of his eyes. Their hideout was in jeopardy! And Jane was putting herself in danger to stop the Americans.

Of course, his father didn't know he'd helped Jane to escape to the convent years ago, so he couldn't reveal the source of the information. Nor would his father be open to moving anyway. He thought back to the last time they had discussed moving to a different location.

It was a warm night, shortly after his grandfather had died and his father assumed the mantle of the *comandante*. Sitting on the front porch, sipping a Greek retsina, they'd argued about moving from the island.

His father lit a cigar. "No, we don't need to relocate."

"But we live in a new world. You've seen what satellite imagery can do."

"We are disguised from above. No one has a reason to look here. We are a speck in the middle of the ocean."

"I understand that, but we've been here too long."

"We've been safe here. I was in charge of security for your grandfather and have protections around the island. It's fortified against attack."

Antonio took a sip of the smooth wine. "Yes, and I know the men are sworn to secrecy."

"It's more than that. You know any visitors come here blindfolded and we take care of those who flap their mouths. Like that banker in Rio."

"That's a great precaution." Antonio had actually thought the killing of the banker overzealous, but one issue at a time. "They still know it's an island."

His father put him off with a wave of his cigar. "It would be too much trouble to move. Where would we go that's safer than here?"

"I don't know, but could do some research if you like. Perhaps a cave in the Alps."

"No. This is our place. It's been in our family for thousands of years. I was born here. You grew up here."

Antonio's mother had died near here, too. "But—"

His father put out a hand, signaling the discussion was over. "Enough. Let's talk of more pleasant things."

Antonio stopped pacing, and looked out to the harbor. He was in a bind. If he told his father about the message, the *comandante* would insist on learning the source of the intel. That road led to ruin, his and Jane's.

But if he were able to stop the Americans with Jane's help, he'd be a hero and she could skip back to London with no one the wiser.

He frowned. It wouldn't be easy. He'd tried responding to her message, but the note had bounced due to an invalid email address. Further communication would have to come on her terms.

Stefano had missed the two in Rome. Again. And before Antonio had known one of the operatives was Jane, she and the man had slipped through the trap they'd laid in Alexandria. Probably by swimming to shore.

He clenched his fists. How hard was it to kill these people?

CHAPTER 49

Eden
Day Five

The day after Angie had learned of the plot to kill the president-elect, she was back in the kitchen. Zola was making bread, and the mouth-watering smell revived Angie's dormant hunger. The urge to eat passed when she saw the trace of the bloodstain on the wooden cutting board and recalled Reno's public whipping. Angie clasped her hands together every time she passed the stain.

While she worked, she chewed over the information she had so far, waiting for an opportunity to approach Zola and wondering why these men would want to kill the president-elect. A sex-trafficking ring Angie could almost understand—not the exploitation, but the drive for money. But when you threw in an assassination attempt on the US president-elect, the motives became murkier. It was like she was staring into a pond, and a few times she saw glimpses of bright gold answers, but most of the time, the water was cloudy. Today, the evidence she needed was flashing in the weeds, just out of sight. There were no answers, only questions.

Her chance with Zola came early, while the mistress of the kitchen was kneading dough on a white cutting board atop a stainless-steel countertop. Everyone else was in the dining room.

Heart pounding fast, Angie briskly walked to Zola's side. The baker didn't look up from her task.

"I want to clean the leader's house this afternoon," Angie whispered.

Zola's eyes stayed locked on the dough. Maybe the woman was afraid. Angie sure was; her heart was beating double time.

Angie touched Zola's shoulder. "Please. Can you make that happen?"

Zola pushed the bread aside and put more flour on the cutting board. In the flour, she used her finger to write:

Y E S.

Angie quickly drew a heart in the flour before grabbing plates heaped with eggs and bacon. Saliva flooded her mouth, but she reined her appetite, and her emotions, back in. Getting inside the leader's house was just the start of what she had in mind.

CHAPTER 50

Delos, Greece
Day Five

Even though the sea breeze held the bite of winter's chill, Stryker would have enjoyed the scenic boat ride across the aquamarine water had he not been convinced that Sam was leading him on a useless tour. He wished there was any other set of clues to follow, but Ace had come up empty-handed. Although she was following the sex-trade idea, all she could report at the moment was that it was an absolutely sickening worldwide mess with no single person or group leading the criminal enterprise. Nor was there a related trail to explore in Bari.

Sam swore the island of Delos contained an Isis temple they *had* to see. Out of the corner of his eye, he glanced at her. She was practically bouncing with excitement, or nervous energy. Such a history geek. He wished Angie and Harper were with them, that this boat ride from Mykonos was a festive family holiday, like the wedding in Bari was supposed to be.

What if he found Harper, but Angie was dead? How would he raise their daughter alone? Or what if Angie was alive, but not Harper? He quivered in the wind for an instant before steeling himself. Their daughter's demise would make it even harder to get Angie's spirit back. Until they'd lost Malachi, she'd been his heart and soul. He'd searched for years to find a mate and still loved her dearly. He really missed her right now.

Then there was the drinking.

He knew Sam thought he could have done better when it came to approaching Angie's drinking problem. But could he? In quiet moments, he recognized that he was afraid she would ruin Harper like his parents had damaged him.

Turning to Sam, he asked, "What do you think I could do differently? You know. With Angie?" He swallowed. "If . . ." His voice broke. "*When* we get her and Harper back."

Sam tore her gaze from the island and looked him in the eye. "I'm glad you're planning to get her back. What do *you* think you could do better?"

He had a tendency toward being a judgmental bastard. It went hand in hand with his OCD. If something wasn't perfect, it called out to him to be fixed. But he'd never been able to really fix people. "I've tried to support her, but have probably judged her, too."

"Maybe you could talk to her about that. Let her know you're working on it, and ask her what she needs."

Sparing him further self-reflection, the boat bumped up to the pier, which was lined with old tires. The deckhands lashed the ropes tight and began to help tourists off the boat. He and Sam joined the line, and were soon walking toward a low-slung building.

Several men and women held cardboard signs that offered guide services. Most ignored them. Figured. They were still in their Black disguises. Every time he wore his, he got ticked off about how men of color were treated. The first couple of times he couldn't believe it. White women crossed the street and wouldn't make eye contact. White men puffed up or went stiff instead of giving him a casual nod. It was ridiculous, and had given him an entirely new perspective. Today, though, it was keeping the Sons of Adam off their trail.

One of the guides looked to be in his seventies, with a worn face and white, bushy eyebrows. But his wiry body was fit and his eyes held a sparkle of intelligence that drew Stryker in. None of the other tourists seemed to be interested in the elder guide's services, and Stryker felt a little sorry that he was having to work at his age.

When the man smiled at him, Stryker asked Sam, "What do you think about using a guide while we're here?"

"That's a good idea," she replied. "The temple itself is not much to look at. Maybe we can pick his brain."

They walked over and provided aliases as a form of introduction, and the guide gave his name as Dimitri. Although Stryker was proficient in Greek, Dimitri spoke capable English with a thick accent.

"We're interested in a tour of the Isis temple," Stryker said. "Can you take us there?"

"I'd be happy to," Dimitri answered. He had a slow and relaxed way of speaking.

After they settled on a fee, Dimitri nodded his head in the direction of the hill and then set off at a surprising clip. They walked past what looked like the ruins of a town, its flagstone floors surrounded by bone-white columns bleached by millennia of sun and wind.

Dimitri waved his arms but kept walking. "To the right was the residential area and to the left the commercial. Delos was an important port town and had a lot of commerce; many people from around the world visited."

On the way, they stopped once to look out over the port and Dimitri flirted with Sam by quoting Homer to them in his slow voice. He said it was a poem about shipwrecked Odysseus, who had just pulled himself from the sea and spied the beautiful daughter of the unfamiliar land's king.

"I have never with these eyes seen anything like you, neither man nor woman. Wonder takes me as I look on you. Yet in Delos once I saw such a thing, by Apollo's altar."

When Sam perked up, Stryker recalled that Cleopatra was a big fan of Homer.

As they continued to climb, Sam and Dimitri discussed the importance of Delos in its heyday. Stryker was more interested in what they would find today.

After twenty minutes of stone paths and stairs, they stopped at a view that took Stryker's breath away. Or maybe that was the climb. Since Dimitri didn't seem winded, nor did Sam, Stryker decided it was the amazing vista. The sea seemed darker from this vantage point. Brown islands dotted the distant horizon, and low rock walls declared how busy the town must've been thousands of years ago.

"This is it," Dimitri said, eyes full of mischief. "The statue inside is a replica. I used to help restore the temples. Shall I rest while you explore?"

As Dimitri found an upended column to use as a bench, they walked the rest of the way to the temple. The façade was held aloft by two Doric columns, and multicolored rock walls lined both sides and the back. The latter were put together higgledy-piggledy, using local stone in a variety of shapes and sizes.

Sam stopped under the classic Greek façade and frowned. "Not much to look at."

"No," Stryker agreed.

Weeds covered the front part of the floor, and the rock sign declaring the old stones as the Temple of Isis was broken in half. White blocks rested in front of the headless statue of a white-robed woman. The air smelled fresh, but the temple gave off an aura of neglect. He'd been afraid of this.

They were alone at the temple site, most other tourists having opted out of climbing the hill.

"Might as well look around while we're here," he said.

Sam nodded and they both began an inspection of the sculpture and surrounding walls.

There was nothing noteworthy. Nothing at all.

He gave up after ten minutes. "I'm going to go chat with Dimitri."

"Okay." Sam's voice sounded dejected. "Just give me five minutes more."

Stryker found a rock to sit on next to the thin old man.

"Did you find what you came for?" Dimitri asked.

"How do you know we were seeking something?"

"You don't act like most tourists. Not a single picture in front of the temple."

Stryker grimaced. Busted. "You're right. We're trying to find something to help my wife and daughter."

Dimitri nodded. "I lost my wife and daughter three years ago."

"I'm sorry. What happened?"

"They were buying food from the market. A car hit them as they crossed a street. My wife was killed instantly. My daughter lived for a week—then she died too."

Stryker nodded, at a loss for words. They had found nothing here and had no other leads. Would he end up like this old man, telling tales of his wife and daughter and how they died?

CHAPTER 51

Eden
Day Five

As she walked through the cold wind to the leader's house, Angie mentally tried to prepare, but with no food or whisky in days, she wasn't sure if she was thinking straight. Her mind felt clear, but there was a lot that could go wrong given what she was about to attempt. If she were caught, she'd be killed. Probably whipped to death. Harper would be without a mother.

A few houses away from the *comandante* and Antonio's blue home sat the rose-colored structure where the children lived, along with two female teachers. Angie yearned to bust down the door and take her daughter in her arms. She wondered briefly about the instructors. Were they kidnapping victims? Children of the group roped into brainwashing the next generation?

Beside her was a fresh-faced woman Angie had not interacted with before. The clean-looking woman had yet to get the grimy, unkempt look Angie knew was descending on her like a fog. The woman's eyes held wariness and fear; Angie didn't trust where this new captive's loyalties might lie.

They stepped into the blue house together, behind a set of baby-faced guards who immediately went out onto its wide deck to smoke.

While the other woman headed for the kitchen, Angie grabbed a feather duster and moved from room to room until she found the office. It was upstairs and had the best view of the house. Dark rainclouds blanketed the horizon and the sea was a heavy slate gray. Wind whipped against the window, shaking the panes.

Angie closed the door most of the way, but left a crack to hear when the men came back in from the deck. It could also be trouble for her if the other woman turned her in.

First, she searched the old wooden desk, seeking anything that would help her escape or facilitate communication with the mainland. The computer was on, but password protected. The surface of the desk was bare save for a luxury glass-topped humidor full of cigars. None of the drawers revealed anything of use.

A yellow sticky note on the monitor held names, many inked out with a thick pen. She recognized several recent assassination victims, including a US senator and the German chancellor.

In the wastebasket, she spied a keycard and nabbed it. The card had a jagged scratch down the front, but the black magnetic strip appeared unharmed. Would it still work? It *was* in the trash. She shoved the card deep into a latex-lined, interior pocket of her black jacket.

A file cabinet revealed pages of names, dates, and figures. After studying the report for a minute, and seeing a few politicians with zeros next to their names, her best guess was these were lists of the women and girls who had been sold or given away for political advantage. Bile rose in her throat. Just before she put it away, she saw Rebecca's name next to that of a well-known senator from Alabama. Memorizing the politician's name, she clenched her jaw in anger and disgust.

Another page looked to be a list of donors. The king of Saudi Arabia was at the top of the list, and one name may have been Japan's prime minister, but she wasn't sure. She committed those to memory, too.

But she needed more.

Scores of books lined the wall behind the desk. Machiavelli. Hitler. Sun Tzu. There was a book on the Salem witch trials, a booklet of Chinese poems with a small-footed woman on the cover, and a copy of the *Malleus Maleficarum*. From a college history class, she knew the latter to be one of the most blood-soaked works in history, as it was the medieval witchcraft handbook which led to the persecution of tens of thousands of innocents. The shelves also held books on propaganda, both old and new, histories and how-to manuals.

A Roman bust labeled "Augustus" stood on a pedestal, while two framed maps hung on the wall opposite the heavy desk, one labeled "Egypt in the time of Cleopatra." There was that Cleo reference again. Glancing around, Angie saw a locked case that held bronze coins, one clearly a woman with a hooked nose. Sam would dig those. Piles of books littered the window seat, all about Cleopatra. Curious.

Movement in the grassy area near the small village caught Angie's eye. Rebecca was walking away from the rose-colored house, a bounce in her step. Other children, including Harper, threw confetti as the bride-to-be twirled, her white dress billowing like a young Marilyn Monroe. Was this her supposed-marriage procession? Angie took a breath and held it, biting her lip and holding back tears.

A noise, like a chair scraping on the deck, broke Angie out of despair. If she could get out of this place, she vowed to track Rebecca down and rescue her from the evil creature in Al-a-bam-a who had *purchased* the child. Angie tightened her fists. At least she'd had a Harper sighting, and her daughter looked healthy. Angie had to hold herself back from yelling out the window or running down to scoop Harper up.

Knowing time was short, Angie returned her attention to the desk. There were no safes in the room, so she felt around the desk for false bottoms or hidden chambers. The first five drawers were solid, but she hit pay dirt upon knocking the lower-left. It had a fake partition that she pried open with a ruler from the middle drawer.

Expecting something explosive, she was surprised to find some letters tied with twine, along with a newspaper clipping of an American actress who had disappeared in her late twenties. Looking more closely, she realized the actress was Mary Vanelli, the friend of her mother's who had a small part in the musical they'd always watched together. Why was the clipping hidden here?

Angie scanned the love letters between Mary and a man named Salvatore, grateful they were written in English. It made sense, though—the actress was American. About to put them away, the last one caught Angie's attention. It was more of a note. It read, "I'm leaving. This place is insane and I won't raise my boy here." Alarm bells went off in her head. Before she could make sense of what she'd found, she heard the patio door open and boots tapping on kitchen tile.

Hastily, she folded the "I'm leaving" note with the clipping and placed them into her pocket with the keycard before putting the remaining paperwork back in order. She finished dusting the office with sweat on her brow.

As she and the other woman wrapped up their work, she doubted the keycard would work. Her mind raced, trying to fit all the pieces together.

CHAPTER 52

Delos, Greece
Day Five

On her hands and knees, Samantha pushed away the dirt around the base of the white rocks that lined the sides of the Isis temple so she could sit out of the wind. She felt stupid and her heart ached with a raw fierceness as she thought of the time they'd wasted. The online images had accurately portrayed the desolation of the site, but she'd been hoping to find some sort of hidden clue.

Since Stryker and Dimitri seemed to be having a good conversation, she might as well sit down and think for a minute. Plus, she didn't want to go out and see the disappointment in his eyes.

She leaned back against the stone, brought her knees to her chest, and put her chin in her hands. There'd been a lot of serpent imagery at the temple site earlier that morning in Pompeii. And she could have sworn she saw something snakelike here on her first pass.

Cleopatra's suicide by asp had been bothering her. Most historians didn't think it was actually a cobra that killed her, as it would have been too painful, taken too long. Yet every early account of her death included a snake. Octavian even called in the *psylli*—he thought she died of a snake bite, even showing off a model of her with an asp as he did his victory lap around the Mediterranean.

Why?

Sam closed her eyes.

The queen *was* a prankster.

What if the asp was Cleopatra's final ruse?

Or a clue?

Back on her feet, Sam examined the statue, the white carved rocks, the temple façade, and then turned her attention to the rock walls. Along the back wall, near the right corner, she spied a fist-sized rock. Dark gray in color, it had a vein on it that curved like a snake. Yes, that's what she'd seen earlier.

Kneeling and tracing it with her fingers, she realized it was actually a thin carving. She'd have never seen it if she hadn't been on the lookout for snake symbology. Although the late afternoon was chilly, sweat broke out under the wig part of her silicone mask. She tried pushing on the rock. Nothing happened. Did it point to something else?

The rocks around it were a mix of sizes, shapes, and colors, but none moved when she poked and prodded them. Maybe she should try just pulling the stone out of the bloody wall.

After checking to make sure Stryker and Dimitri were still talking, faces turned toward the harbor, she attempted to do just that, shoving the twinge of guilt at disturbing a temple aside. It didn't budge—which made sense given it had probably been here for more than two thousand years. She tried again, this time with more force.

It wiggled.

Heart in her throat, she grabbed a stone from the ground and pried at the snake rock until it finally gave way in her hand.

Inside was a bronze coin.

Gently, Sam pulled it out and used extreme care to brush the dirt off of it with her shirt. It held the visage of Cleopatra.

All hesitation gone, Sam ran out of the temple. As she shoved the coin and the rock under Stryker's nose, she belatedly realized she'd forgotten about Dimitri, the guide who might be angry to find his charge had desecrated a temple. But too late now.

"Look," she said, breathless. "Hidden beneath this rock."

They each took an artifact, and then traded. Dimitri raised a bushy eyebrow. Stryker nodded his appreciation, not yet getting that the coin was a clue.

She wanted to tell Stryker her theory about the snake carving, but held her tongue.

Dimitri spoke first. "The rumors are true."

"What rumors?" Stryker asked.

"Never mind. I shall take you to the living temple now."

Stryker and Sam exchanged a look.

"What living temple?" Sam asked.

"It's not my place to tell you. But I'll deliver you to the shrine."

CHAPTER 53

Delos, Greece
Day Five

Progress at last. Standing in the shadow of the Isis temple on Delos, Sam's grin was as wide as the horizon as she thought about Cleopatra and her snakes. The echo of their guide's announcement that he would take them to a shrine echoed in her ears.

Stryker shrugged and stood, going along with Dimitri's plan to take them to a place he'd called the living temple. Perhaps Stryker had found a level of trust in the old guide and she wasn't going to argue.

As Dimitri led them behind the ruined temple and away from the harbor, Sam was glad she'd worn sturdy shoes as the path soon became no more than a rough goat trail. The landscape was rocky, and there weren't many trees. The sun was heading toward the horizon, and she wondered if they'd make the last boat back to Mykonos. They'd been warned it left at sunset.

She had to temper her enthusiasm, reminding herself that the coin she'd found was just that. Not a journal with an indication to her sister's whereabouts.

After about ten minutes, they approached the zenith of the hill and a small olive orchard. Between the trees, she could see the other side of the island and its glittering turquoise coast.

On the far side of the orchard, Dimitri took a sharp turn off the path and walked along the rocky crag. In less than a minute, he disappeared between a narrow gap in the rocks. She slipped inside, feeling claustrophobic, as she had to go in sideways.

Stryker said, "Too thin for me. I'll have to wait for you here."

"Okay." She hoped they really could trust their guide.

After twenty feet of uncomfortable squeezing and crab-like walking, she emerged into a small grotto. A spring bubbled up in the center and a dark cave stood off to the right, a soft glow coming from within.

Dimitri's eyes sparkled. "Here you go."

"Now what?"

"No idea. I'll be with your friend."

Sam could only nod, unsure of what to do next. When Dimitri left, Sam knelt beside the pool. She splashed water on her face and washed the coin off in the cool water. It was a find, but at the end of the day, it wasn't the journal with the location of the cult.

Straightening, Sam studied her surroundings, looking for snakes, real *or* carved. This would be great habitat for the former.

When she found nothing around the perimeter of the pool, she headed to the cave. Only ten feet deep, it was lined with simple white stone shelves that held votive candles. On the back wall, an eight-by-ten framed picture of a goddess in flowing white robes, her arms wrapped in snakes, stood with a defiant gaze. Was this an Isis temple? Maintained by locals?

Or a particular priest or priestess? How had Dimitri known about it?

The sanctuary smelled of beeswax, dampness, and a hint of flowers—thanks to the dried offerings in front of the picture. The floor was a mosaic, the center of which was a coiled snake. *Now we're talking.*

Sam ran her hands over the tile, seeking any sort of opening, but it all felt the same. *Wait, this one has an edge.*

Using a fingernail, she pried the tile up, exposing a finger-sized hole. Hoping it wasn't a snake den, she put her finger in and then pulled up. The tile groaned and a hairline crack formed around the edge of a square, but the sides had been shut with mortar. She'd need a tool. Walking back to the small pool, she found a sharp stone and went back inside.

The rock helped to remove the old grout, and within a few minutes she had pried the hatch open. Inside was a dusty stone box.

Gripping the sides of the rough treasure, she pulled it out, then grabbed one of the votive candles and brought the old box to the ground so she could get a better look. This was it. The moment where she learned if she'd brought Stryker on yet another wild goose chase. The goofy part of her played a dramatic drumroll in her head.

Her heart pounded as she lifted the lid to reveal a thin book, wrapped in linen. The front and back were made of shiny gold, and an image of a woman with snakes winding around her forearms had been stamped on the cover, surrounded by a delicate dual band of tiny embossed dots. The back cover had no border and bore only the likeness of a coiled snake. An ornate gold clasp bound the handful of thin pages.

Holding her breath, she opened the gold cover.

Their luck had run out. She couldn't read a word written inside.

CHAPTER 54

**Alexandria, Egypt
Day Five**

With its dual staircase and curved-top windows, the Alexandria National Museum reminded Rey of an Italian villa. He'd read that the place was built by a timber merchant and sold to the US embassy. The white building had undoubtedly been a hub of espionage activity during that time, but now it was a sprawling museum, one that he hoped would provide a clue to finding Cleopatra's journal and the cult's hidden location.

As he and Jane waited in line to buy tickets, he wished for a chew. Instead, he sipped at the strong coffee he'd picked up from a street vendor and kept an eye out for the men who had tried to kill them yesterday in the harbor. No one looked suspicious.

He checked his phone. Reception was spotty here in Alexandria.

Jane stroked the blue collar of his new shirt. "Sure you don't want to spend the day in bed?"

He and Jane had made love again this morning without her breaking into tears. After, he'd asked her what was bothering her, and she'd deflected. He hoped she'd worked through whatever it was. Later, in the shower, she'd told him she liked his eyes, and that endeared her to him, given kids back home had always made fun of them.

He grinned at her. "Of course you and the bed sound fantastic. But duty calls."

"All right. Let's play tourists then."

After a cat nap last night, they'd left the hotel and worked their way back to their parked car by taking three different taxis and a brisk walk around the diving business's neighborhood. Without a weapon, he felt exposed. Naked. Which was why they had risked returning to the rental.

The night had remained quiet as they'd checked for explosives, pulled their service pistols from the trunk, put on their holsters, strapped in their weapons, and grabbed their small bags of luggage. He wished for a scanner to check for GPS trackers. After, they'd decided to abandon the vehicle—it had clearly been used to follow them. Back at the hotel, they manually checked everything they'd brought back for a tracker, but found nothing.

Today they were in new disguises, but he doubted it would throw off their pursuers. Jane looked better au naturel; his baseball cap, white hair, and cane was likely not his best look either. He was even wearing socks. He hated the things; they made his feet feel caged.

A plaque on the wall noted that there were nearly two thousand artifacts on display. "Looks like we need to narrow our hunt to the timeframe of Cleopatra and her family."

"Agreed."

After walking through tiled hallways, shiny with wax, they came to a currency hall, where row after row of coins were displayed in locked glass cases. Sam would have dug it here.

"Have you seen any update on those protests in Saudi Arabia?" Rey asked when a woman in a burqa passed by.

"Last I saw, the streets were still full in all the major cities."

He shook his head, hoping the stubborn government would relax its attitude. "Speaking of . . . here's the hall for the Islamic era."

As they passed that hall and another for the modern era, he continued to watch for company. The building was wired with security, and facial recognition software was still a threat given the custom-fit masks didn't change their facial structure. He motioned to the cameras with his eyes and Jane tilted her head down.

When they arrived at a darkened hall of sunken relics, Rey gestured for Jane to follow him inside. Life-size pictures of ocean-bound artifacts stood behind the recovered versions.

"Looks like they had better visibility than we did yesterday," Rey said.

Jane murmured her assent. She pointed to a sculpted head and read the bronze plaque out loud. "Alexander the Great."

"Popular fellow."

"Probably not for the folk he conquered."

"True," he agreed. "Look at this one." He inclined his head toward a black granite statue of Isis. The leaning goddess stood with pointed breasts and arms at her sides. "She's missing her head."

"That's too bad. It's a nice piece."

He moved on. "Now we're talking."

In front of him, a basalt figurine was labeled as Cleopatra. The sculpture was also nude, and carried what looked like a large block hammer in her left hand.

"Not sure it helps us much," Jane said.

Privately, he agreed, but took a photograph anyway. "Back at HQ, they're gathering all the Cleopatra-related images they can find."

"Why?"

"To see if they can detect any patterns. We'll help."

They continued to wander through the museum, him capturing the many versions of Cleopatra: with two snake heads, in the form of a white bust, on a golden throne, wearing a royal headdress, and with arms wrapped by snakes. Each face looked different.

Items marked from her palace included hieroglyphic-adorned plaques, several ankhs, more sculptures, a sphinx, and a ten-foot-tall obelisk. He photographed it all, annoyed that nothing obvious was leaping out at him.

Leaving the museum for the Serapeum, they held hands in a taxi that smelled of pine air freshener. He began to fantasize about a life with her. What would it be like to have a family, like Stryker and Angie did? To have someone to enjoy life's ups and downs with? To share one's hopes and dreams with? He was tired of the single life. Ready to settle down.

He leaned over and kissed her lightly. Her eyes crinkled ever so slightly when she kissed him back. It was adorable.

They arrived at the Serapeum. Although it had been the largest place of worship in the Greek quarter during the queen's reign, the remains were disappointing. No structure remained above ground. It reminded him of the hollowed-out shell that they'd seen in Taposiris Magna.

"Not much to see here," Jane said.

"No." He sighed, tired. "That giant Corinthian victory column is cool, but everything else looks burned to the ground and plundered."

"Shall we go then?"

"I suppose we should look at the catacombs. While we're here."

They found a set of stone stairs that led to excavated halls filled with boxy chambers for bones on either side.

The crypts dampened his previous mood. Angie had been gone for days, an assassination was imminent, and they'd found nothing that would help them with either.

Jane looked around. "Did you know the Catholic Church used to keep the offspring of the priests and nuns underground?"

He touched the medal at his neck. "What offspring?"

"The ones they weren't supposed to have. That's why they hid them away. The children died, malformed from lack of sunlight, and were buried in crypts like this."

When he caught her eye, shadows stirred again in the depths of her gaze.

CHAPTER 55

Eden
Day Five

When Angie finished her cleaning shift, she was escorted back to her cell. She'd gotten no more glimpses of her daughter from the window.

With only water for an evening meal, she and Luna sat on the bottom bunk under their blankets and compared notes. Working all day without food made Angie feel exhausted.

"Learn anything in the kitchen today?" Angie asked.

"Maybe. The leader and his son weren't at lunch and the men seemed more talkative."

Angie squashed a sliver of hope. It was probably nothing. "Oh?"

"They use something called the dark web to locate buyers for us and get paid in bitcoin. Have you heard of those things?"

Angie nodded. The dark web was the modern equivalent of a dark alley, utilized to remain anonymous. Bitcoin was an electronic form of cash, often used by criminals who haunted the virtual backstreets for nefarious purposes. "I have—go on."

"One of them commented that hungry females are much more cooperative with the clients."

Angie had suspected as much. "I don't feel very cooperative, do you?"

"No," Luna said. "Just hungry enough to eat a bear."

"Me too. I'd eat almost anything right about now. Any other tidbits?"

"They have a team that produces propaganda about archeological finds."

"Archeology? I don't get it."

"Me neither, but they also have an assassination squad—"

Angie interrupted. "Like that Cobra guy?"

"Yes, and a team to steal Cleopatra-related artifacts and destroy them. It sounded like many of the men are archeologists."

"That's all super weird. Why would they do any of that?"

Luna just shrugged.

Angie debated whether to tell her new friend about the keycard, and decided it would be safer to not mention it, or the other things she'd found. "I really appreciate you keeping your ears open. Thank you."

"No problem. Can I sleep now?"

"Sure," Angie said, and climbed to her upper bunk, where her brain churned. Propaganda. Love notes. An assassination squad. Cleopatra and destroyed artifacts. What was the common thread?

She stared at the ceiling for at least a half hour, but her brain remained a jumbled mess.

Tim was her sounding board. She tried having a fake conversation with him in her head and all he told her was to meditate. She'd try anything.

She assumed the straight-backed posture Tim always used and began to focus on her breathing. The last time she'd attempted this it hadn't panned out so well.

Deep breath in. Deep breath out.

Sounds in the nearby cells became clearer. Luna's rhythmic sleeping breath. The tossing and turning of the new prisoner across the hall. Reno's voice yelling something unintelligible in a nightmare. Angie's mind slowed as she continued the breathing exercise.

Again, she saw the argument with Tim. This time she saw the scene from Tim's perspective. He knew she'd lied about drinking every night and was doing his best not to judge her for it. With his past, he was worried about the impact on Harper. Understandable. Geez, she hadn't even known blue was now her own daughter's favorite color.

Breathe in. Breathe out.

There was a dark pit in her stomach. She breathed into it and had a vision of herself in the *comandante*'s office, getting caught by the guards and shot. Dead like Zoe. Angie's body lay on the floor, near the desk, and she breathed out the possibility of her demise. She'd be able to join her baby.

In a flash, she was back in the hospital room, her heart broken. She hated to admit it, but Tim was right. She'd been avoiding this pain, and had been using the drinking to stuff down her feelings about the baby's death. Baby Malachi. Tears rolled down her face as her mind's eye saw her red-haired child take his last breath. The monitor red-lined and the nurse came in to turn off the alarm before giving them both a sympathetic look. No heroics would save Malachi from the invasive brain cancer. *My baby. He can't be dead. Can't be.* Tim had tried to hold her then and she'd fought him off, pounding on his chest, screaming. She'd eventually needed to be sedated.

Her heart wrenched. Tired of pushing the pain away, she let herself fall into the murky pit of grief and sobbed silently. *My baby. He's gone. He's really gone.*

At some point, sleep claimed her.

CHAPTER 56

Alexandria, Egypt
Day Five

As Rey and Jane walked up the ancient stone stairs of the catacombs, his knee ached from the prior night's swim. It didn't take much play-acting to stick with his disguise by limping up the staircase. The air smelled faintly of the sea.

In the light of the cool afternoon, the ruins held few people. With surprise, he noted Terrance Richmond's short frame and salt-and-pepper hair. The man was bent over next to a headless sphinx.

He nudged Jane. "Hey. That's the archeologist from Taposiris Magna."

"You're right."

"Think he followed us here?" But as he spoke the words, he considered their disguises. How would Richmond know it was them? Rey reconsidered. If the man was an operative, he wouldn't be fooled.

"Let's go find out."

Before he could stop her, Jane marched toward the columns that stood next to the sphinx. Rey followed a half-step behind, limping, all senses on high alert.

Jane touched the archeologist's shoulder and Richmond straightened, his eyes indicating surprise.

His voice sounded an octave higher than usual. "Why, what on earth?" He shook his head and took a breath. "You startled me." Richmond glanced at Rey. "Who are you?"

Rey hoped their disguises were good, but wanted to be sure. "You don't know?"

"I've never seen you in my life!"

Was the man lying?

"We met out at your dig. Had a chat in your tent."

The archeologist squinted and looked them up and down. "Your voice is familiar," he told Rey. "You're the bloke who killed my new archeologist. In disguise."

Rey frowned. "I'm the guy who saved my team from getting killed."

"Are you following me?"

"Actually, we wondered if you were tailing us."

Richmond's expression grew pinched. "I think not. I'd be happy to never see you all again. That death at the camp. Then Professor Saber was nearly killed. That's why I'm in town. Still answering questions."

"What happened to the professor?" Jane asked.

Richmond shook his head. "We found her slumped over the wheel of her car, beaten and left for dead."

Rey and Jane exchanged a look. The Sons of Adam? Who else would it be?

Jane scowled. "Is she okay?"

"At the hospital now, still unconscious."

Rey interjected. "Sorry about that."

"You should be," the archeologist shot back. "Two lives ruined since you came sniffing around."

"I am sorry."

Richmond shook off the apology. "Have you ever had to deal with Egyptian red tape? They've threatened to shut us down. We've worked for *years* trying to find Cleopatra's tomb there. And we're close. I can feel it."

Rey had some cash in his wallet and dug it out. "Would this help you grease some wheels?"

The archeologist looked at the money as if it were contaminated, and then seemed to have second thoughts. "It might," he said, snatching it out of Rey's hand.

"Find anything interesting here?" Rey asked smoothly.

Richmond waved his hand at the remains of the once-proud temple. "No." His voice softened. "But I like to visit here whenever I come into town for supplies. She walked here, you know. This is sacred ground."

He tapped a foot on the old brown stone.

The comment gave Rey an idea. "Where else would Cleopatra have walked? We visited her underwater palace yesterday, but not much to see there."

Jane was watching the two of them, a strange look on her face. She clearly regretted saying hello.

"Well, she ruled for twenty-two years, you know," Richmond said. "That's a long time."

"It is a stretch of time, but I imagine there were some places she visited more frequently than others. Perhaps temples, like this one?" Rey asked.

The archeologist looked up, as if accessing a mental map. "Memphis is an obvious choice. She would have been crowned there after her father died."

Rey pulled his phone out and spoke into it. "Memphis."

"Philae is one of the more famous Isis temples," Richmond added. "It's down near the Nile's first cataract. They relocated the entire thing to an island when they built the Aswan dam."

"Philae." After taking an audio note, Rey looked at Richmond. "Great. Where else?"

"Buto, near the small village of Kom Butu, is a Wadjet temple site closer to home. Not as much to see. Some tunnels have been excavated. However, she definitely would have gone there, as Wadjet was the patron deity of Lower Egypt."

"Haven't heard of her."

"Snake goddess."

"Ah." Rey spoke the name into his phone. He'd never recall these places if he didn't. "Any other ideas?"

"Deir el Shelwit, down near Luxor, is another small Isis temple. It's been recently renovated."

Rey started to repeat the words into his phone when the archeologist grabbed his hand, face suddenly crestfallen.

"No, wait. I remember now. That temple was built by the Romans after she was gone."

"Well, this is marvelous." Rey nodded. "Thank you."

"You're welcome. Good luck, and do let me know if you discover anything interesting."

They said their goodbyes, and the archeologist walked off.

When he turned back to Jane, her arms were tightly crossed.

"Don't tell me you want to head to Philae," she said.

CHAPTER 57

Eden
Day Five

Angie woke with a start, hands clutching her chest.

Her baby. He was dead.

She lay on the thin mattress for a minute, and let reality settle in. She didn't like it. But it was the truth.

The therapist she'd had for three short weeks told her she needed to accept that Malachi was gone, but that acceptance had eluded her—until now. Maybe it was the threat of her own demise, but she finally felt she could live, even without him.

And she needed to quit drinking. It hadn't helped. Had only masked the pain and she'd almost lost the rest of her family because of it. Truth be told, the whole reason she was in this mess was because she just *had* to have a drink after lunch. Alcohol was no longer her friend.

This fresh outlook reminded her that she had to get out of here, and warn the Secret Service about the danger to the president-elect's life. They had two, maybe three more days before she and Reno would become human trafficking victims and Harper would be left here alone. Angie couldn't let her daughter be brainwashed and "married" off.

Plunging her hand in her pocket, she felt the treasure from the *comandante*'s office. The keycard was cold and smooth in her hand.

She listened to the sounds in the cells. All was quiet. It was probably the middle of the night. A perfect time to see if what she had in her jacket was a late gift from Santa or coal in her stocking.

Her heart began to hammer like a caged bird trying to get out. This would be the most dangerous thing she'd ever attempted. But she had to try.

She slipped off the bunk and moved to the front of the cell. Nothing but the snores of her fellow inmates greeted her.

Blood pounded in her ears. She pulled the scratched card from its nest in her pocket and slid it across the face of the electronic keypad.

Silence.

The scrape had probably damaged the magnetic strip. Angie swore like a sailor under her breath.

Again, she moved the card across the face of the keypad, but more slowly.

Click.

Angie froze, swallowing hard. Would it trigger an alarm? Did any of the women hear it?

Panicked, she waited, wondering if she should lock herself back in.

Breathe in. Breathe out.

Time slowed to a crawl. She stood still as a statue for at least five full minutes.

Nothing happened. No alarms. No group of baby-faced guards thundering through the cells. None of the women seemed to notice.

Time to explore.

She pushed the door open, glided out, shut the door, and locked it again, pocketing the card. Now what?

Biting her lip, she walked down a few cells until she found Reno. Her friend was curled up on the lower bunk, strands of her red hair just visible above the gray blanket. A freshly bandaged hand was draped down from the mattress. Angie sighed, glad her friend was at least warm and perhaps even getting medical care. Her fingers floated toward the keypad of their own accord, but she yanked them back. Now was not the time. She needed to explore and the women would make a ruckus. If one of the boats had a key in the ignition, she'd come back for Reno, Harper, and the others.

Sticking to the shadows, she walked down the tunnel that led to the harbor. The sense of danger made her tremble.

Peeking around the corner, she saw through the dim light that tonight there was only one boat. A rowboat.

Frustrated, she pounded her fists into her thighs and then slunk back the way she'd come. Outside her cell, she paused for a beat, and walked on, up the stairwell, until she came to the door that she'd seen Antonio enter. Was that today? Yesterday? God, she needed food. It didn't matter.

The keycard worked and she opened the door quickly, stepping inside and heading down like she'd seen Antonio do. There was no light in the space, so she kept her fingertips on the wall, feeling her way, imagining this was what it would be like to be blind.

The steps ended at another door, again guarded by a keypad that read her card. It was dark inside, but not as completely black as the stairwell had been, due to a few monitors with active screensavers.

Most of the space held desks with side-by-side computer monitors. The wall to the right was made of floor-to-ceiling glass. She moved closer and put her hand on the cool surface.

Realizing the other side was *water*, she jumped back. That must be the sea. What if that glass burst? She gently knocked on the slick surface. Thick. Still, it made her heart race even faster. She needed to explore quickly, and then get out of here.

Turning her attention to the desks, her eyes grew wide.

A candy bar! She rushed to the workstation and stared at the wrapped delight someone had carelessly left on a pile of papers next to an empty bottle of chinotto Italian soda. Snatching it up, she ripped the paper off with her teeth and bit into it. Chocolate. Peanut butter. Sugary, heavenly goodness. She savored the taste, chewing until it was a nougat pulp, and swallowed. God, it was good. No, beyond good. It was the most delicious thing she'd ever tasted.

Taking another bite, she sifted through the papers by the light of the monitor, not daring to turn anything on. One stood out.

Assassinio had to mean assassination.

Especially with the name of the US president-elect heading the top of the list. She also recognized names of a US Supreme Court justice and three senators. There were a few she didn't recognize. Pat O'Brien. Alice Wanderer. Chris Smythe. Maybe one was the prime minister of Finland. She couldn't recall. Was there a common thread? She chewed thoughtfully.

Footsteps thudded down the stairwell. Was it morning already?

She frantically scanned the room. There, on the other side, was a plain door. Crouching low, she ran for it.

CHAPTER 58

Mykonos, Greece
Day Five

Stryker put his pad and pencil down on the patio table. With care, he closed the ancient journal.

"What's it say?!" Sam demanded. "C'mon, you've been at it a while."

They sat on the concrete deck of a Mykonos hotel, the water lapping at their feet. Although it was full dark and well after midnight, the town's famous windmills were lit up and dotted the horizon to their left, just beyond the boat-filled harbor. The thump-thump of a dance club resounded in the distance.

They'd had to hustle to catch the last ship off Delos. While Sam had searched for the journal, Dimitri had told Stryker that the temple had been moved up the mountain generations ago, and was tended by a few old priests and priestesses. The guide hadn't known the journal existed, only that if anyone found a bronze coin bearing the likeness of Cleopatra, he was to bring them to the new sanctuary. All the island guides were under the same set of instructions.

Sam had wanted Stryker to review the journal as they chugged back to port, but he'd played it safe, insisting they get to the hotel before cracking it open. With its shiny gold cover, it surely would have drawn a crowd. It wasn't until they had checked in and deemed there were no immediate threats in the area that he had settled in to see what Sam had found—*after* sending backup photos to Ace.

"I wanted to check through the entire document to make sure I wasn't missing anything. There are some pieces that I'll need an expert to translate, but I think I got the gist of the parts that mention the hidden location." He paused, stroking the edge of the polished gold. He also wanted them to double-check his translation. His modern Greek was passable but he was no expert with the version Cleopatra had used. "Want me to summarize that section, or read the best pieces?"

Sam had showered while he worked, and now she sat in front of him mask-free. Her dark curly locks fell wet around her shoulders. "Oh, read it for sure."

"Okay. Sorry for the blank words."

Dear One,

Like Theseus taking on the Minotaur in the labyrinth, you've followed my thread and found this journal. Perhaps you're one of my . . . children, or you're a devotee of the goddess. Either way, I want to tell you about the Sons of Adam and how you can . . . my last wish and destroy them.

My grandmother had warned me of a cult that was thousands of years old, even in her time. They were originally known as Aryans and became Levites, who influenced the Hebrews. They also invaded India with . . . falsehoods and fabrications. Today, the same ancient sect continues to spread lies like a never-ending pool of blood.

Now known as the Sons of Adam, they are a group with no regard for history, who want to rewrite the past in the image of their frightening future.

I have been at war with them throughout my entire reign.

They supported my brother and later Octavian, in the hopes of marching me through the streets . . . in golden chains. I will not have that. It's hard to say what you will know of me by the time you find this, as I'm sure my statues will have been felled, the noses cut off my sculptures, and my many . . . denied. But know this: Egypt during my time knew peace and prosperity for all her citizens.

The war Octavian waged was a war of opinion in the . . . of Rome, and I can see now that my beloved and I underestimated our enemy's resourcefulness. At every turn, he slandered Mark Antony and me, using all means at his disposal to defame us. By the time we . . . his tactics, which were to win the hearts of Romans through deceit, it was too late, his army and navy too large.

At the time I write this, I suspect his stronghold to be an island fortress somewhere in Greece. My best spy is trailing one who will be forced to tell the exact . . . and I hope the spy returns the locale before Octavian takes Alexandria. I dare not hide this journal and the location in the same place. But if you found these . . . your same cunning will lead you to my storeroom, where I will secrete the cult's location and have stashed a treasure trove of truth, so that history may know the facts. Find the . . . guarded by the snake goddess and you shall be able to strike a knife across the throat of Octavian, as I wished to do with my own hand.

Make it so.

Stryker looked up. The eastern sky showed a glimmer of light. He yawned. Sam's eyes were closed and stayed that way for a few beats after he finished. The backstory had stunned him, too, and he wondered what ancient history the group was trying to cover up.

"A letter from Cleopatra. What a gift." She hummed in appreciation, and then her brown eyes popped open. "But wait. That's it? A Greek island?"

He stretched his shoulders. They both hurt. "Yes. Other than a small note if we succeed, that's all. I reread it several times."

The light left her eyes. "There must be hundreds of them. That doesn't help us at all."

"It might." He aligned the pencil with the journal. "We can let Rey know what to look for in Egypt regarding the storeroom the letter mentions. And we'll have Ace get the computer guys analyzing Greek islands for unusual traffic, satellite dishes, that sort of thing."

"But that could take weeks." Sam's chest slumped and she put her chin in her hands. "Angie and little Harper could be . . ."

Stryker reached out and grabbed Sam's hand. "All we can do is our best."

CHAPTER 59

Eden
Day Five

Angie made it out just in time. The door had been closed only a second when she heard men filing into the room and taking seats at their desks.

She leaned against the doorframe, breathing fast. That had been close. Too close. And she still had to find her way back.

One bite was left of the candy bar. As she put the morsel in her mouth, she realized she'd need to find a place to discard the wrapper. Hopefully, the owner of the candy bar would never notice, but with her luck, they'd probably search every cell for someone with chocolate breath.

She sighed, walking down a short hallway to see where she'd ended up. On the other side of a wooden door was a cavernous area with pews. Much to her surprise, she was standing near an altar glowing with candles. Behind her, Christ hung on a life-sized cross.

Curious. An underground church.

Shoulders tense at the thought of being caught, Angie hustled down the steps, heading down the center aisle for the shadowed back wall. Most churches had their main door opposite the altar, so that was a good place to start looking for an exit. If men were already out and about, she needed to get back to her cell. Pronto.

She came up short when she realized there was a plexiglass case in her way on top of a podium. Pausing, she studied it, but there wasn't enough light. She squinted. Was it a book of some sort? With a brown leather cover? Must be important. Wishing for a flashlight, she tried to pry the top off the case, but it failed to budge.

A burst of laughter from the adjoining room reminded her she didn't have much time. Crouching low, she ran for the back of the church, where curtained confessionals lined the back wall. She caught her breath before risking a look around the corner.

There was the sought-after door, but no trash can. What to do with the candy wrapper? She couldn't be found with it. The thought of swallowing it made her gag.

Walking back to the pews, she found they had hymnals. Flattening the wrapper, she placed it inside one of the songbooks, but not before taking one last whiff. She longed for three more bars, or, better yet, a grilled chicken breast with a baked potato smothered in butter and sour cream, topped with salt and pepper.

Returning to the door, every sense on overdrive, she opened it into pitch blackness. Feeling a sense of déjà vu, she felt her way up several flights of stairs until she came to another door. She cracked it open. The harbor with its tiny rowboat lay in front of her, only now she was on its other side. She'd have to hug the wall to get back to her tunnel. Outside, the gray light of dawn was just starting to push away the night's darkest hour. It was enough for her to spot the camera halfway between this church door and the tunnel, pointed at the boats. Its red eye blinked in time with the blood in her temple.

She swore a silent curse. There was no way she could go back the way she'd come, through the church. The camera had a cord, but unplugging it might call in the cavalry. That's if it hadn't already picked up her movement.

With no better option, she hunched over to hide her face and scurried along the wall, pausing beneath the camera just for a moment to study it. A plain black security camera. At least it didn't have a swivel option.

It seemed to take forever to reach the tunnel. Once she did, she turned the corner and raced back to her cell. The other women remained asleep. Using the card, she slipped inside and locked the door behind her. Jumping onto her top bunk, she willed her breath to slow as she hunkered under the old blanket. Luna rolled over but kept snoring.

Angie had gotten the lay of the land, and seen the list of assassination victims. But how was that going to help her get off this cursed island?

The door creaked open and a security guard walked slowly down the hall, boots slapping against the floor. Had the camera seen her?

CHAPTER 60

Mykonos, Greece
Day Six

Waking a few hours after dawn, Stryker got up and tried to calm his nerves with green tea and a meditation on the patio. When the meditation failed, he went for the crossword puzzle from last Sunday's paper, which he'd been unable to complete during their recent plane trips. Fishing boats dotted the calm sea and the air smelled salty, fresh, and clean. Sam was still asleep in the bed closest to the wall, having taken first watch.

He was glad they'd made a little progress yesterday by finding the journal, but his hopes still felt dashed. Instead of revealing the location of the cult, the gold-bound notes had sent them on a further hunt, this time for Cleopatra's storeroom and the promised locale. True, they'd learned the queen suspected the Sons of Adam were on a Greek island, but there were over six thousand of those scattered like stars across the expanse of the Aegean and Ionian Seas.

If Angie and Harper had been taken by sex-traffickers, it was only a matter of time before they were shipped elsewhere. Thinking about them sold off to some creep made the tea taste bitter in his mouth.

Back inside, Sam started to stir, then yawned and sat up. For some reason he'd never been able to figure out, Sam was obsessed with the Peanuts character, Snoopy, and wore a nightshirt that sported an image of the beagle sleeping on top of his dog house.

Sam stretched. "Did Ace send us anything before she cut out for the night?"

Stryker set the crossword puzzle and erasable-ink pen down on the table. "She's still searching for a Greek island that might house a group of fanatics."

"Nothing, huh?"

"She found a trail of ancient tombs destroyed, and museum pieces related to Cleopatra stolen, but came up empty-handed on any local island that would fit the profile."

Sam made a face. "Where are they? And what is this group trying so hard to hide?"

Without waiting for an answer, she jumped out of bed and went into the bathroom. Ten minutes later, she returned, alert and wearing an Asian mask. "Shall we call Rey?" she asked, joining Stryker on a metal patio chair. "Wonder why he didn't answer last night."

Stryker twirled his pen. "Yes, please. Give him a ring."

Today Rey picked up.

"That's great detective work," he said once they'd filled him in.

Sam's chest puffed out a little at Rey's praise. "Thank you. But we still need to find the storeroom she mentioned. Sounds like you're also thinking about Isis temples?"

"More like places Cleopatra would have frequented. We ran into the archeologist from Taposiris Magna and he mentioned Memphis, Buto, and Philae as fitting that bill. We were going to start at Philae."

Sam looked out to sea. "Memphis is not an Isis temple, but Buto and Philae sound promising. Wait, isn't Buto associated with the goddess Wadjet?"

"You're the history expert," Rey said.

"Give me a second." Sam placed the call on hold and ran her fingers across her phone screen for a short time. "I thought so."

"What?" Stryker said, aligning the pen and newspaper.

She removed the hold from the call. "Buto was Wadjet's temple. The goddess Wadjet was often represented as a cobra and Cleopatra mentioned the 'snake goddess' in her journal when she referred to the storeroom that contains the cult's location. Definitely start in Buto."

Sam looked at Stryker for confirmation, and he nodded approval. It fit with what Sam had told him of her theory about Cleopatra and the snake ruse.

"Will do," Rey said. "Philae was also moved brick by brick to a new location when they built that big dam."

"That's right," Sam said. "Forgot about that. Not ideal for the purpose of finding a treasure trove."

"Since we're zeroing in, what about putting a SEAL team on alert?" Rey asked. "We may need some backup."

Stryker had been thinking along those lines as well. With no paramilitary division, the think tank often called on the Navy SEALs when they needed extra firepower. "Good idea. I'll call St. James to see if she wants to run it by Wolff."

With that, they ended the call. As Sam put her phone down on the patio table, it knocked the pen to the floor. When Stryker bent to pick up the ballpoint, the glass window behind him exploded.

He grabbed at Sam's arm but she was already diving over him for the inside of the room. Rolling after her, he came up with his pistol in his hand, kicking the door to the patio shut as another bullet struck, leaving a quarter-sized bulge. "Let's go."

He shoved his phone in his pocket and decided they'd leave their other disguises here. Time to travel light.

Moving swiftly to the hallway door, he opened it and peered in both directions. Fifty feet down the hall, a man in slacks and a white dress shirt fired a semi-automatic. A bullet whizzed by Stryker's face and hit the doorframe. Wood splintered, one sharp piece catching his cheek.

He winced and pulled back. "They have us boxed in."

Sam's eyes darted about, clearly assessing the situation as well. They'd be too exposed to leave by water. There were no nearby boats. What could they use as protection in the hallway?

He tapped on the bathroom door. Wood. But the exterior door had given off a *clink*. It was metal, like the patio door that had stopped the sniper bullet. Still, he'd have to access the screws that held the hinge plates to the door from the hall side.

"Sam, I need a screwdriver." She dug in her backpack and yanked out a multi-use pocket tool. "Great. Cover me."

Inching the door open, Sam sent a volley down the hall. Once quiet descended, he yanked it open . . . then swore. This wouldn't work. He couldn't get his arm around the wide door without being exposed. Unless they could pull the door from the frame. He snuck a glance at the screws. Wait. They were nails. Even better. He'd rip it out of the frame.

"Keep up the cover fire," he said.

Another bullet slammed into the bathroom wall. Adrenaline surged through Stryker and he pulled on the doorknob. It didn't budge. Good nails.

Leverage, he needed a lever.

Sam let off another shot and had the favor returned, while he smashed the coffee table and stuck one of its sturdy wooden legs in the opening between the door and the top of the frame. Pushing the wood, he displaced two nails. Again, he levered the door away. In seconds, he'd succeeded in ripping it away from the frame.

As he moved it, he grunted, surprised at the weight.

Next to him, Sam looked like an avenging Amazon. Her nostrils were flared and her breathing rapid.

"I'm behind you," she said.

With that, he rushed into the hallway, using the hefty metal door as a shield. Bullets thumped into it but he bulldozed down the hall. The hail of fire stopped, and Stryker slowed, unable to see where he was going.

As he pushed past a hallway, he heard the sound of feet slapping concrete, and then a splash.

By the time he'd turned, Sam was already around the corner and in hot pursuit. Letting the heavy door drop, he followed.

They pulled up short at the archway that led to the water's edge. Their opponent was swimming arm over arm toward his rifle-toting buddy in the fishing boat.

Sam had a bead on him, but Stryker pushed her arms down. "You'll open yourself up to a sniper shot. Let's get out of here."

CHAPTER 61

Kom Butu, Egypt
Day Six

After Rey hung up the phone with Stryker he turned to Jane. "Sounds like there's hope for Angie and Harper yet. If we can find Cleopatra's storeroom, we can learn where they're being held."

For an instant, an unreadable emotion crossed her eyes.

"You okay?" he asked.

"Yes. Let's go after I touch up my mask." She turned her back on him and headed to the bathroom.

An hour later, halfway to the small town of Kom Butu with Jane navigating, he was still wondering what haunted her.

He reached out and held her hand. "You sure everything's all right?"

She looked out the window for a minute at the verdant green Nile delta landscape. "Yes." She squeezed his fingers. "Sometimes the past haunts me is all."

"Do you want to talk about it?"

"No. Why don't you tell me some stories of growing up in Minnesota?"

Accepting defeat for now, he told her a story about running a lawnmower into a tree, even affecting a Minnesotan accent. She laughed.

He learned that she liked poetry and had learned to play the piano as an adult. When he asked about her childhood, however, she dissembled, saying only that she was an orphan before trying to pry into his time in the Air Force and the underlying cause of his PTSD. Instead, he decided they probably both had pasts better off left alone, and he changed the subject to movies and books.

Although he kept watch, they weren't followed. Eventually they pulled into a dirt parking lot delineated by a few small boulders.

"You sure this is it?" he asked. It was another less-than-impressive ruin, this time in a wide, open space surrounded by a few modern buildings. There were three mounds and a brick-strewn area that looked like it may have once been a building.

"I'm sure."

He parked and they exited the rental car. Sounds of everyday life came to him on the breeze. Children laughing. Arabic music playing. The smell of barbequed meat made him hungry.

"Not a popular tourist destination," he noted, and grinned when she gave him her shy half-smile. "And nice that HQ was able to convince the archeologists to take the day off. Let's explore."

They walked around the mounds, but found only excavated piles of dirt, black pipe, and wind-scoured plants. Next, they cautiously approached a central pit.

A wooden ladder with rope rungs led down to an excavated six-by-six-foot area. A silent pump stood in one corner, probably used in the wet season to push water up the side through the attached black ABS pipe.

"Ladies first," he offered.

She laughed and climbed down. He tossed her one of the flashlights they'd purchased during a pit stop. Powering it on, she lit up a wide-mouthed tunnel.

He scampered down the rungs and turned his light on as well.

"Let's see how much work they've done for us."

The tunnel began with smooth walls. No electric lights had been strung, so the flashlight beams were the sole source of illumination.

Even though there'd been no cars up top, this was the perfect place for an ambush. Rey took the lead and cleared each corner with his weapon, ready to fire.

They walked like that for about five minutes before the walls began to change to old brickwork, occasionally enhanced with a carved image. They came to a "T" and he turned right. Within twenty feet, the tunnel stopped at a cave-in.

"Retreat," he said.

"Roger that."

They turned and headed back. "Let's stop if we see snakes on the wall." After hearing of Sam's finding yesterday, he was eager to make his own discovery.

"Okay."

Rey was no expert, but the wall sculptures were clearly of ancient Egyptian origin. They passed a bull, an ankh, a flail, a cat, an eye, and then a half-woman, half-snake image.

"Hold up," he said, examining the carving more closely.

The woman had a human head, but a short snake's tail. He pushed all aspects of it. When nothing happened, they moved on. Before they made it back to the "T," they also found an etching of a rearing cobra. He probed it, again failing to find anything remarkable.

Back at the "T," he put his arm on hers. "I'd like to clear the hall before we examine it."

"All right."

The new hallway was narrower, allowing only two people abreast. It curved gently and sloped upward, eventually bringing them out in an egg-shaped chamber with colorful friezes on the walls. The scenes illustrated daily life. Flooding fields, planting, harvesting, fishing. The ceiling held bright yellow stars.

"What do you think?" he asked. "For ceremonies?"

"Seems a good guess."

"But no snakes. Let's go back down the hall."

"We might end up in Philae yet."

"Might," he said, just as his light caught on an image of a woman—or goddess—with upraised arms, snakes coiled around both wrists. "Wait. This looks promising."

With a moderate amount of force, he pushed the goddess's head, each foot, each snake, and her chest. He sighed, as he didn't recall seeing any other serpents on the way down the hall. This carved figure was about a foot tall. What if he tried pushing both snakes at once?

With both thumbs, he pressed the stone. In the floor next to Jane, he heard a small pop, and a trap door flopped open.

CHAPTER 62

Kom Butu, Egypt
Day Six

Clever, Jane thought. But the trap door was a problem.

"My turn. Let me go scout while you guard," she said, drawing her pistol.

"Okay."

As she started to descend the long set of stone stairs, her mind raced. The Sons of Adam had been searching for Cleopatra's journal for millennia, with no success, and yet Sam and Stryker had found it in a matter of days. She had to give Sam credit: digging into Cleopatra's history enough to understand the woman was a prankster had been key. Having an asp in the room but not using it to die was the ultimate ploy.

Jane took a deep breath, sad and disappointed. Rey was the first man in ages to have nabbed a piece of her heart. She'd enjoyed sleeping next to him, wrapped in his strong arms, and had felt an unfamiliar tenderness when he'd cried out in his sleep during his PTSD nightmares. Was this really the end of the line?

When she reached the bottom of the steep stone stairs, her last threads of hope disintegrated. The space mirrored the oval chamber above, but was filled with relics. Shelves upon shelves were lined with scrolls, statues, and jewelry. Water pooled at her feet, but the high-water mark was dry, now that the flooding season was past. It had to be Cleopatra's hidden treasure.

A pillar in the center of the room drew her. Atop the dais was a map carved in onyx, clearly marking an island off the west coast of Italy. It was *the* island. Eden. She swore. Cleopatra's spy had found the location of the Sons of Adam and the group had stupidly stayed put for thousands of years. Well, was it really stupid? They didn't know the queen had found their location, and until the fairly recent advent of technology it was a decent hideout.

Stop the mental gymnastics. You've been avoiding this for days. Face the truth.

Rey couldn't live to tell anyone about this. It was time to pay her life debt to Antonio.

She backed away from the map, fighting tears. At least they'd had a few wonderful days. It was a shame, but her conscience gave her no choice. She was loyal to her core.

That's why she'd emailed Antonio from the privacy of the bathroom, telling him the journal had been found and requesting that he send help to Kom Butu. He'd be thrilled they'd found this cache at last and desperate to keep it quiet. Jane would need his goons, who were to await her signal, to dispose of Rey's body. She could slip back to her life near London. Perhaps now that Rey had cracked open her heart, she'd find someone else to share life with.

She bit her lip, squeezed her pistol tight, and walked back up the stairwell. "It's amazing," she said, modulating her tone. "Come take a look."

"Coast seems clear," Rey said. "Find something good?"

She tried to sound convincing. "You won't believe it."

He motioned for her to precede him. She turned and walked back down the stairs. He followed close behind.

The instant her foot hit the bottom stair, she whirled, raised her pistol, and fired at his beautiful face. And yet somehow his hands were on hers, twisting, the muzzle turning.

There was a flash, a boom.

Her last thought was the realization she'd been shot in the head.

CHAPTER 63

Rome, Italy
Day Six

Sam turned to Stryker. "How do you think Rey and Jane are doing tracking down that Greek island?"

"Hope to hear from them soon."

They were alone on the top of Castel Sant'Angelo, looking for all the world like two Hispanic tourists. Maybe they could get a chicken enchilada later. It sounded good. "Let's get a selfie with the basilica in the background."

Stryker put his arm around her and gave a forced smile.

She snapped the photo, pulling away and studying the picture for effect in case anyone was watching them. Not bad, but she needed to lose a few pounds. Maybe not an enchilada then.

The sun neared the western horizon. Rome was spread out before them, a shadowed banquet for history-loving eyes. She wished they could rest and enjoy it all. Or take some time to study that journal.

She showed him her phone. "Look at those bags under my eyes. I'm tired from our near-death experience this morning at the hotel."

"Me too, but we need to stay alert." He slowly swiveled his head. "They probably picked us up flying out of Mykonos. They seem to have good intel."

"They do, but it's not perfect. Took them a day to find us in Greece."

"Shouldn't have been able to find us at all."

"That's the truth." Sam reached for lip gloss but the tube was empty. "Glad Ace was able to leave some new masks for us at that dead drop near the Arch of Constantine."

"Me too. Should buy us a little time. But I'm still wondering if she's a mole."

"If she was, it wouldn't have taken them that long to find us in Greece."

"Unless the delay was to throw us off that scent."

Liking Ace's demeanor and sense of humor, Sam waved Stryker's concerns away.

After getting their new disguises and some pizza that didn't live up to its reputation, they'd walked the streets of Rome. After several hours, they'd ended up here. Per the earlier request, she and Stryker were scouting sniper nests while Rey and Jane worked the goddess/snake angle in Egypt. Now they stood below the statue of Saint Michael on the castle's viewing platform.

She glanced around. "What do you think about the enemy's game plan?"

Stryker put his hands on the stone railing and pointed. "The pope and president-elect will be down there in the basilica. Because they'll be on a balcony, a sniper only has so many angles. But the skyline here is open, the buildings short. Up here he'd have a clear shot, but it's a little on the long side. Depends how good he is."

Sam smirked. "Or she."

"Sure, or she." He pointed to the west. "That church over there . . . the upper dome has a clear view, but tricky footing. Both have nice river access for a quick getaway."

"Where else?"

"Nearer the Vatican you've got a number of bookstore-type buildings with windows that face the square. The attacker could infiltrate the basilica itself, but that's a whole other level of planning."

"What about the roofs of those columned structures that encircle St. Peter's Square like arms?"

"They're close, but no easy roof access. And federal and local security like the Swiss Guards will be crawling all over them."

"Crowd?"

He shook his head. "Tough shot, and way too many people."

"What would you do?"

"If I had a nice rifle and a few guys for backup, I'd set up back here. Tourists will be gone for the day, and it's a lot of space to cover in terms of security. You'd only need to take out a few guards to have a clear shot."

"I don't know," Sam argued. "This seems too obvious."

"Oh? Where would you set up?"

"I'd try to do something creative. Rent a dirigible and shoot an RPG into the balcony before parachuting to a waiting backup vehicle. Or sneak into the basilica as a maid and poison the water."

He nodded, seeming to assess her ideas. "It's always best to expect the unexpected."

CHAPTER 64

Kom Butu, Egypt
Day Six

Rey stepped back and let Jane's body fall to the cold, stone floor, the familiar buzz of battle adrenaline pumping through him. The bullet had gone through her skull, but he grabbed the flashlight he'd dropped and checked for a pulse anyway.

None.

His shaking hand went to his St. Christopher medal and he stroked it twice. He thought back over their short time together. The tears after sex. The veiled look in her eyes. And the reaction she'd had to seeing the Sons of Adam cobra/apple tattoo. Had they sent her? No. She wouldn't have had a response to seeing the tat if they had.

He swore and shook his head again, lips clenched tight.

Thank God for his training. When she'd whipped around, his hands had instinctively flown up to protect his face. Then he'd lunged to the right as the gun had gone off, reaching for her weapon and dropping the flashlight. She'd fought him and the gun went off again. It had happened so fast.

He touched his ear. Blood.

The pungent smell of spent gunpowder filled the small space.

Sadness filled him and he sat down next to her body, wishing she hadn't attacked him. His dream of a family was shattered again. A sob wracked his chest and before he knew it, he was crying, for himself, for her, for the family she'd never had, and for whatever had driven her to this extreme and final action.

For once he didn't fight the tears, and they poured out, a flood of emotion. He tucked his knees up to his chest and dropped his arms and head onto them while he rode out the storm.

When the rawness left, he wiped his cheeks. His former therapist would be proud of him, even though he doubted a few tears would go far toward healing his PTSD. He'd simply seen too much over the years in the Air Force. This was just another rock on the pile of good lives wasted for bad reasons.

Feeling anger warm his face, he stood, grabbed the flashlight, and focused on taking a good look so he could report back. Given the fuss over the place, he'd expected to see gold furniture and piled-to-the-ceiling sacks of gold coins. Instead, there was only a few pieces of jewelry and a single pile of old money. He picked one coin from the stack and pocketed it for Sam.

The rest of the space was filled with statuary and scrolls, except for a pillar in the center of the room that must hold something important.

Atop the place of honor was a dark chunk of polished onyx. Chiseled into the stone was a map. There was Egypt. Alexandria. Greece. Italy. An "X" marked an island off the west coast of Italy, about even with Rome, maybe a little north. Bingo.

Yanking his phone out of his pocket, he took pictures of the stone map, and grabbed a quick video of the remaining items.

Stryker needed to see this ASAP, but Rey's SAT phone had no reception down here.

As he headed toward the exit, he stopped by Jane's body. Full retrieval would have to wait, but he could at least leave it at the top of the stairs.

After pocketing her flashlight and adding her firearm to his waistband holster, he scooped her up and began the ascent. From this angle, he could see the gear mechanism that powered the trap door.

After he laid her gently on the stone a dozen feet to the side of the opening, he returned to study the gears more closely. Those Egyptians were clever. He could reset the door by pulling the lever.

He did, and used his foot to move dust and dirt around to obscure the opening. Moving off down the hall, he held his weapon at the ready on the off chance that Jane had called in the troops.

CHAPTER 65

Kom Butu, Egypt
Day Six

The coast was clear until Rey climbed the ladder. Two men dressed in black stood between the cars.

Rey hesitated.

The men stared at him, seeming to wait for something. Or someone. Like Jane.

Rey held his ground. Only his head was above ground level.

Long seconds passed.

One man turned to the other.

In unison, they aimed over the hood of the rental car and fired.

Swearing, Rey ducked as a bullet pinged off the wall behind him.

Sweat soaked his back and forehead. His hands gripped the sides of the ladder as he fought to keep his head clear. *Just stay present. I'm not back in Libya.* And yet part of his mind heard the explosion of Tomahawks and the continual roar of 30mm Avenger seven-barrel cannon rounds.

Focus.

He ran through his options.

The tunnels held no way out, and the assailants held the high ground and a superior position between the two vehicles.

There was no cover between the pit and the cars.

He had no backup.

Wait. Maybe his phone had service now.

He leaned as far as he could to the right and took a shot at the car. A satisfying ping greeted his ears.

Moving with speed, he jumped down the ladder and hustled back into the shadows of the dark tunnel. With his left hand, he reached into his pocket and dialed Stryker.

"Rey."

"Hey. Before I get killed, I found a map that shows an island a few clicks off the coast of Italy, a little north of Rome."

"Okay, but what's up?"

"I'm holed up at the dig in Buto. Twin tangos have me pinned down inside a pit. Tunnels lead to the find, but no way out."

"Where's Jane?"

"Dead. She tried to take me down. We may be compromised."

"Roger that."

"I'll text you the pics if I can. How about some reinforcements?"

"Locals?"

"Sure. Sirens off. Maybe we can catch them off guard."

"On it."

Stryker hung up.

Rey took a deep breath. With his fat fingers, he'd need both hands to send the pictures and video. But he didn't want to be exposed. With two weapons and help on the way, maybe he could risk it.

He sprinted to the top of the ladder and leaned left to make them think he was still in position. The attackers were in the same spot, and one let off another round, shattering the top of the ladder. Ducking, Rey fired another shot and jumped back down, moving to the safety of darkness.

He put his weapon under his arm while he operated the phone. As fast as he could, he sent the pictures and video to Stryker as well as Ace at HQ. Then he put his pistol back in his hand and exhaled.

He recalled only villages nearby. Bigger towns were a few miles out, and the nearest city was probably fifteen minutes away. If the attackers had also called for help, who would arrive first?

As he bounded back up the ladder, shots were fired over his head. He returned fire over the top of the pit, making his bullets last.

He was surprised that it didn't take long for the sound of screeching brakes to reach his ears. Or maybe he was still zoned out from Jane's attack. Risking a glance, he saw three unmarked cars had surrounded the area. Good guys then. The assailants had nowhere to go.

Without warning, the men burst from their spots and ran toward the police in a suicidal charge, firing. The authorities responded in kind, and the attackers dropped to the ground.

Rey took a deep breath, and then shuddered.

It would take him some time to get out of this mess, especially with Jane's body to explain. But more than that—given the fanaticism he'd just witnessed, it was not going to be easy to take their island stronghold.

CHAPTER 66

Eden
Day Six

After returning from her predawn scouting trip, Angie had to use extreme self-control to maintain a semblance of sleep as the guard walked toward her cell. She nearly passed out from relief when he kept moving. Eventually her heart rate slowed down enough to nod off. At first, she dreamed of the luscious candy bar, but that soon turned into nightmares of being chased through the underground church by priests in red robes that dripped blood.

When she woke up, it was to news that one of the new women brought in hours earlier had thrown herself off a cliff on the way to serving breakfast, and died on the rocks below. The mood in the cells became more somber than usual.

On Angie's walk to the village to clean houses, she replayed what she'd learned of the computer room and church, all the while feeling as if she had a crimson, traitorous X on her forehead. It was the camera that was most troubling. Throughout the vacuuming, scrubbing, and polishing, the memory of its red eye taunted her, threatening to ruin every plan she considered.

The long day finally turned to night. She waited a good three hours after the snoring began before venturing out of her cell.

Walking on quiet feet past the rows of incarcerated women, she didn't pause until she reached the tunnel mouth.

There. She finally had something to smile about. The boat the new women had arrived on was moored in the harbor. To board it, she'd need to get to the other side of the port.

Scurrying along the wall, she stopped beneath the camera. It was mounted on the wall, just out of reach, no ladder in sight. Would she be better off to cover the lens with her shirt or just make a run for it? The harbor's lone light was high enough on a pole that taking it out wasn't an option. She could cut the camera's cord, but that would leave a trail.

Considering her options for the umpteenth time, her breath grew shallow and her heart beat a rapid rhythm in her chest.

Decision made, she pulled her shirt over her head and flung it up in the air. It missed. Picking it up off the floor, she tried again. This time it hung askew from the mounting, not over the lens at all. She jumped as high as she could and yanked it down. With all her might, she went for try number three. Finally, the shirt landed perfectly over the lens of the camera.

She immediately sprinted for the boat. If someone was watching the camera right now, she'd be dead.

Hustling down the pier, she slipped into the boat. Inside, she found the wheel and the ignition, but no key. She exhaled sharply. Plan B.

She jumped down the stairs and opened the white cupboard. Just as remembered, there was a sack of pills. She grabbed two handfuls and stuffed them into her pants pockets. After one more for good measure, she shut the door and ran up the stairs.

After checking the murky night for intruders, she left the shelter of the boat, ran back to the camera, leaped up, grabbed her shirt, and then continued to the tunnel's edge. Slipping around the corner into the shadows, she caught her breath.

A slapping sound echoed through the night, one she recognized as a guard's boots on the stone walkway as he patrolled the cells. She'd bunched up her jacket under the blanket to resemble her sleeping form if one looked quickly, but she couldn't be caught here.

She raced out of the tunnel and toward the little nook she'd seen about fifty feet away, on the opposite side of the cavern from the church door. Sprinting, she did her best to hug the wall and move quietly. Heaving a breath, she ducked inside.

Light barely illuminated the fifty-by-fifty-foot space. It was mostly filled with boxes, although there was one octopus-like metal object along the back wall that looked like a picture of a naval mine she'd seen once. The boxes were labeled *cartucce* and *bomba*. She wished Tim was here to confirm her suspicion that this was an old armory, but the five-letter word was close enough to *bomb* that it seemed like a good bet.

She lingered just inside the mouth of the cave. The guard sauntered out of the tunnel and toward the boat. He didn't look like he'd noticed anything amiss in his patrol of the cells, but he was headed in her direction.

The guard moseyed onto the boat and reappeared about thirty seconds later. As if strolling in a park, he meandered back down the dock and onto shore, heading directly toward her.

There was a space behind the octopus mine but it wasn't large. She held her breath as she slid between it and the wall, hoping like hell the thing wasn't sensitive to touch. Hunkering down behind it, she waited, heart pounding so hard it might ignite the mine just from its frantic electrical signal.

She ducked as low as she could, trying to think of some kind of weapon she could use if he came inside. *Nothing.*

From his shadow, she could tell he walked to the edge of the munitions depot, dragging his flashlight's beam against the plain rock walls.

This was it. She imagined wrestling with him for his flashlight and knocking him out cold, or him getting the upper hand and taking her to the *comandante*.

He walked away.

She exhaled, saying a prayer of thanks. Then she counted to a hundred before leaving her hiding place. Sticking to the shadows, she finally dared to look around the corner.

The guard remained on patrol, but he was headed toward the door to the church.

Eventually, he ducked inside and she took a lungful of air. It was time to head back to her cell.

However, she needed to tell Reno to be ready for tomorrow night.

Angie shivered. The most dangerous part of her plan was yet to come.

CHAPTER 67

Rome, Italy
Day Seven

Tonight was the night. The pope and president-elect would make a historic joint address from a balcony above St. Peter's Square. Sam also hoped that Ace would be able to confirm the location that Rey had discovered and they could rescue Angie and Harper.

As Stryker and Rey took a food break, Sam stared out the window, twin emotions of excitement and fear running through her veins.

They were still in Rome. Below their hotel room balcony was Piazza Navona, a two-thousand-year-old baroque square filled with fountains and a tall obelisk. If she'd flung the window wide, she could have heard the splash of the Fontana del Moro. Despite everything, Sam loved this city. She wondered if Angie would want to finish her vacation here in Italy, or if she'd be ready to get back to work. Probably home and work.

Maybe I'll stick around for a few days anyway. So many sights to see. If Angie was still alive.

Earlier, Rey had spent an hour filling her and Stryker in on Jane's betrayal and everything he'd found in Buto. The bodies of the two suicidal attackers sported combinations of cobra and apple tattoos, so they were working under the hypothesis that either Jane had warned them, or the Sons of Adam had some excellent, state-level intel. Sam still didn't believe Ace was a mole, although Rey, Mr. Conspiracy, had jumped at Stryker's suggestion.

Sam pulled out her phone and mulled over the images Rey had sent from Buto while he was under attack. Cleopatra had made the storehouse sound like a treasure trove, but the pictures illustrated no piles of gold, just the one sack of currency. She reached in her pocket and fingered the special gold coin he'd brought for her. She was convinced it was authentic. It had Cleopatra's face on the "heads" side and Mark Antony's on the other, so was likely minted in Egypt. The queen wore her diadem over hair braided into the usual sections. A magnificent pearl necklace graced her neck. Sam considered all the fuss about Cleopatra's beauty and wondered if it was all a smoke screen to detract from her intelligence, wit, and cunning.

Turning her attention back to the photographs, Sam remained puzzled that the remaining contents of the treasure trove appeared to be mostly statuary, paintings, and scrolls. What was the big deal?

She looked over at the men. "Hey, Rey, will you come look at this with me for a sec?"

"Sure."

Sam pointed. "Why do you think Cleopatra hid this statue of a goddess?"

"No clue," Rey said. "Is that what it is? She looks fat."

Sam laughed. "Maybe she's pregnant. I think this is one of those really old ones. No face, just breasts, and a big belly."

"I wonder where her arms and feet are. How old?"

"We'll need to date it, of course," Sam said. "But I remember reading archeologists found a palm-sized figurine just like this carved from a mammoth's tusk. It's called a Venus figurine, and can be dated to at least thirty-five thousand years ago."

Rey's eyes grew wide. "Wow."

"You think that's old," Sam said. She flipped through a few more pictures. "This looks like a female rock carving. See the breasts and hips?"

"Sort of. Older, you think?"

"Two others like it from at least 230,000 BC may be stones modified into female forms. Scholars are arguing about the timeline."

Rey's face scrunched up. "Even thirty-five thousand years ago is a *long* time. But why is that relevant?"

"I'm not sure why Cleopatra thought it important," Sam mused. "But historians think the goddess, in various forms, was worshiped as the primary deity for that entire stretch of time."

"Wait. What? God wasn't always male?" Rey asked.

"Hello?" she teased. "Did you miss all those Isis temples?"

"But those were pagan temples," Rey said.

"To those people at the time, their worship was as valid as yours in the church."

Rey put his hand on his necklace, thinking. "What about male gods? When were they added into the mix?"

"Many historians believe that the earliest Israelites, before the seventh century BC, were polytheistic, and some of those gods were male."

"Poly, huh? Many gods. When did the 'one god' idea start?"

"They trace the idea of a singular male deity to around 1350 BC, when the pharaoh Akhenaten, these days known as King Tut's father, made the sun god the sole focus of official worship. That's about the time monotheism really took root."

A light bulb went off in Rey's eyes. "Isn't that about the time of Moses?"

Stryker was stretching at the table, a sure sign he was getting impatient.

"Yes."

Rey shook his head, amazement coloring his tone. "I had no idea."

"I still have no inkling why Cleopatra hid this stuff." Frustrated, Sam looked back at the phone. "Will you show me the map again before we get on the call?"

Rey scrolled through pictures until they were looking at the four-foot-tall dais. "Here's the map. Check it out."

Stryker initiated a video call to the director on one of the laptops Ace had provided. "Enough, you guys. Time to find out if the map is the real deal."

Rey pulled a chair up behind Stryker.

Was the location Rey found accurate? Sam hustled over to sit next to Rey. Blood had soaked through his ear bandage. She felt a rush of sadness that Jane had betrayed him and put her hand on his shoulder.

Ace and St. James were on the video call, but in two different windows. Ace's wheelchair would make it hard to sit near the assistant director.

In a trademark move, St. James ripped the glasses off her eyes. "We can't claim victory yet, but this is amazing work. Sam, kudos to finding that journal. Rey, good job surviving Jane's attack and getting out of there with the location of the island."

Rey gave an unenthusiastic thumbs-up. "Thank you. Were you able to locate the island?"

"Ace, fill them in," St. James ordered.

Ace wore a pretty purple blouse with pearls so large they had to be fake. Still, they looked good. Just not as fine as Cleopatra's. "I'm going to share my screen."

A map of Italy and the surrounding ocean came into view.

"As you recall, earlier we'd been seeking a Greek island with the capacity to house a few hundred militants," her disembodied voice continued.

"Maybe that was a red herring," Sam suggested.

"Perhaps, or Cleopatra didn't know the true location at the time she hid the journal. Either way, there are a number of islands in the area noted on the onyx map Rey found. But look at this one. It caught my eye immediately."

The image panned and then zoomed into a small island due west and slightly north of Rome.

Rey tugged his narrow mustache. "What tipped you off?"

"A few things. Besides being in the right location, the island has been privately held for as far back as there are records. It also has no public ferry traffic."

Sam exchanged glances with Stryker, whose face mirrored her emotions. Excitement and fear. What if they were too late?

Ace went on. "But there are frequent boat trips. And sat feeds show two hidden radar dishes and a personal cell phone tower. Take a look at these images."

The screen flashed to a high-res image of the island. It had a small fishing village at one end, and a large garden plot near the other. The radar dishes were hidden in the wind-whipped trees. Next, using a time lapse, a few unremarkable fishing boats came and went on the computer monitor.

"Have you been able to backtrack feeds and see if there was any traffic between the island and Bari last week when Angie and Harper went missing?" Stryker asked.

"Yes and no. That night we had no bird watching Bari, but since then we have. The island gets a lot of night traffic. Only men are on deck, and when the boats return, they disappear into an underground harbor of some sort."

Sam held her breath.

Ace continued. "Finally, we did catch a partial image of a man. Our analysts say there's an eighty percent chance it was one of the attackers in the shootout with Rey yesterday. Based on all that, our conclusion is it's the Sons of Adam stronghold."

Sam slowly released her breath. Stryker slumped, seeming to grow ten years younger.

St. James continued before any of them could react further. "We have full authorization to take the island tonight. Stryker, you and Sam will work with SEAL Team Nine and will liaise with Rey, who will stay in Rome helping the Secret Service."

Stryker jumped out of his seat. "We're on it."

"Be careful. Especially since there's a chance they may be expecting you."

CHAPTER 68

Eden
Day Seven

On the way to the kitchen for evening serving duty, Angie stuck her hand in her jeans and felt the stolen pills. Did her pockets bulge? After careful counting, she believed she had enough to make an impact on the island's manpower, but she'd never been able to get a full count of the men.

The sunset was a glorious mix of purple, orange, and gray hues. She took a deep breath of the crisp sea air and tried to calm her nerves.

She hadn't felt this anxious since her wedding, although of course that was a different kind of nervous. Tim. She missed him. These last few days had taught her a lot about herself. What she was willing to die for, and how she wanted to live her life if she survived. Her husband had been right: she'd been drowning her feelings in a vat of alcohol, neglecting him and Harper while she worked and drank, rinsed and repeated, avoiding the circle of life because she couldn't deal with the inevitability of death.

She'd miss whisky, but she missed their family life far more.

Given her lies, there would be some atoning to do if she made it out of here alive.

She straightened her spine. Her internal pep talk wrapped up, she strode in the door. It was game time.

The kitchen was a hub of activity. As Zola directed traffic—pointing here, grabbing an arm there—pots of soup boiled on the stove. Women were carrying fresh-baked bread and bottles of red wine into the dining room, which was more boisterous than usual. No sign of Luna or Reno, however. The women Angie was working with tonight were all new.

The cook was her only potential ally; the others were unknowns and thus had to be considered likely traitors. Angie had to find a way to make this work.

Pouring the wine wouldn't do.

The bread was already made.

A whiff of the tomato soup caught her nostrils. She walked over to Zola. "May I dish up the soup tonight?"

The mistress of the kitchen eyed her up and down, glancing once to the dining room.

Going for broke, Angie pulled a capsule out of her pocket and showed the older woman, while patting her pocket to show she had more.

Zola raised an eyebrow, smiled ever so slightly, and nodded once.

Angie said a silent prayer of thanks and walked to the six-burner stove, where two huge pots of soup bubbled. To minimize any chemical change to the drugs, they needed to cook as little as possible. Looking around, she spotted a stack of cheerful yellow pottery and brought it over. As she filled each bowl, she dropped in a pill and then set it on the counter to be delivered to the hungry crowd.

Soon, she got lost in the rhythm of it, surreptitiously drugging bowl after bowl until a loud burst of laughter from the dining room caused her to drop one of the pills. Breath catching in her throat, she watched it roll along the floor into the path of the serving women.

Zola made a fuss and walked away from the cutting board. As she stepped on the pill and crushed it, she shooed the women to their next task, ignoring the panicked look that must have been plastered on Angie's face.

Breathe.

Angie turned back to the soup, crisis averted. Her hand trembled as she poured the next ladleful into the bowl.

When she ran out of soup and pills, she joined the other women in serving. To her dismay, neither the *comandante* nor his son had joined the rest of the men for dinner. Angie's mind raced. Those two were the most important to get out of the way.

An hour later, it was time to clean up the dishes, and there was still no sign of them. When the men began to yawn and file out, the bow-legged *comandante* walked into the kitchen with one hand resting on his whip. He spoke gruff Italian to his son, who trailed behind.

Antonio scowled and made an equally sharp retort as they sat down in the deserted dining hall.

Where had they been?

Outside, a heavy fog was rolling in.

Zola rushed to make them a meal, but the soup and the drugs were gone. Angie looked back and forth, from father to son. Her entire plan would collapse if they weren't taken out. Today, Antonio wore a V-neck sweatshirt and a gold pendant. His father sported a green cable sweater and smoked a cigar. Their facial structure was not similar, as they had different nose and eye features. Recalling the love note and news clipping, she realized why Antonio looked familiar.

There was only one card left to play.

When the *comandante* got up from the table to use the restroom, she took a fresh wine glass to Antonio.

Bending close to his ear, hoping the girl had been right about his ability to speak English, she whispered, "I know a secret your father has kept from you. Come to my cell in an hour and I will tell you."

CHAPTER 69

Near Eden
Day Seven

As their vessel whipped through the waves of the rough sea, Stryker kept his eyes on the horizon. He had no idea when the sun had set, because the ocean was covered in thick fog. He was only aware that the gray, dim light was slowly replaced by a darkness that seemed beyond black.

Sam sat next to him in the heavily reinforced fifteen-foot Zodiac rubber boat, officially called a Combat Rubber Raiding Craft (CRRC). The other seats were filled with men ready to die for the mission ahead. Stryker couldn't recall all their names, but felt like he was surrounded by brothers.

A beefy SEAL code-named Matte killed the craft's engine. His New Jersey accent was strong when he spoke. "With the radar they have on the island, we'll want to put in here. Do you both have your supplies?"

They were already in wetsuits and scuba gear, knives strapped to their belts. Stryker patted the dry bag that contained his service pistol and phone, and then the other that held a few blocks of carefully wrapped C4 explosive, blasting caps, detonation cord, and a lighter. He nodded.

"I'm ready," Sam said.

Matte cut the engine. "Okay. Get in the water and check your comms."

Stryker put on the special-issue diving mask and fell backward into the water. Earlier, Matte had shown them how the comms housing was sealed by a hydrophobic membrane that prevented water from passing through the electronics. Somehow, the permeability of the membrane kept internal pressure equalized with external pressure, enabling the microphone to be used at almost any depth. Stryker was just glad they could talk underwater. The unit had a range of a thousand feet.

With no light from above, and the sea floor far below, it felt like he'd descended into a dark hell. All he could see were bubbles floating toward the surface and the black underbelly of the CRRC.

He turned on the special microphone. It beeped. As instructed, he waited two seconds. "Testing, testing."

A beep sounded in his ear, and Sam said, "Snoopy here, ready to take on the Red Baron."

Stryker smiled, glad Sam was feeling spunky. "Sounds like we're on walkie-talkies."

"Better than hand signals."

Matte broke in. "Good work. You've got the hang of it. Grab your propellers and cut the chatter to save batteries."

Stryker surfaced near the boat and one of the other SEALs handed him a camo-painted device that looked like a Frankenstein-esque union of missile and fan. He'd used these devices before, but this one was probably more powerful.

"Turn it on," Matte ordered.

Stryker did and tested it out by zooming around the boat. All he had to do was hang on, and the device pulled him along far faster than he could swim. Nice. It would spare his shoulder. Sam took his idea and went the other direction, the headlight on the propeller leading the way, thankfully lighting the gloom.

"We have a few miles to go," Matte said. "Daniel will stay with the boat, and we have twenty other SEALs already en route. Let's go."

Suddenly feeling pre-battle butterflies, Stryker nodded.

Matte added, "Be extra careful. Sonar has picked up a lot of naval mines and we don't have a sweeper in the area."

CHAPTER 70

Rome, Italy
Day Seven

Rey was stationed on the roof of the souvenir store just outside of St. Peter's Square, where he had a view of the busy throng that had gathered in the light fog around the tall obelisk that dominated the center of the square. The crowd waited for the pope and president-elect's speech. The Secret Service had claimed ownership of the columned buildings that hugged the square, and there were other men and women stationed throughout the area. Some Swiss Guards. But as far as he was concerned, it was a skeleton crew. Most assets were in Stockholm, guarding the current POTUS.

Rey could tell from the radio chatter that few thought the threat here was real. In the pre-mission brief at the safe house down the street, they'd either ignored Rey or took turns sneering at him, clearly resenting his presence.

He'd just shrugged it off—it was nothing he wasn't used to.

Still, he wished for a sniper rifle of his own to go with the service pistol at the small of his back, just in case he spied a problem.

He checked his watch. Stryker and Sam should almost be in position. Their goal was to take the island before the joint address, in case they could find something that could stop an assassination.

The crowd below were huffing and rubbing their hands together. Some stomped their feet, moving in place to stay warm. Many wore hats and scarves, which made finding anyone suspicious more difficult. The fog lent a damp smell to the air. He wished this address wasn't at night, but then again, Lord only knew what conversations had gone back and forth between the various secretaries to arrange it.

Moving a few feet so he could see the thoroughfare leading away from the square, he spied a woman whose long black hair reminded him of Jane. Since she'd attacked him beneath the dig in Buto, he'd rehashed every moment they'd spent together, wondering when she'd decided to kill him. What an actress. Although in retrospect, her voice had sounded strained when she'd told him to come below to check out the unbelievable find. "You won't believe it," she had said. He still didn't.

The tip of his ear ached, though.

He brought his mind back to the present. When planning where to station himself, he'd researched the longest recorded sniper kill. It was from a distance of 3,871 yards, but half of the longest ten kills in history were from less than 2,500 yards. He'd tried to position himself about halfway in the kill zone. Assuming it was a sniper. Someone could have infiltrated the Vatican with the intent to take out the president-elect with a handgun or knife. That would be a lot harder to pull off, though, and didn't seem to be the MO of the Sons of Adam.

As he scanned the crowd once again, another thought struck him. Maybe they'd infiltrated the Secret Service. He wouldn't put anything past this group.

CHAPTER 71

Eden

Day Seven

Sam shivered in the cold water. Maybe she didn't need to lose a few pounds; perhaps she should pack an extra five on. Some blubber would be handy right now. The propeller had been useful when it came to getting them to the island quickly, but it also meant she wasn't expending any energy to stay warm.

They'd passed several round sea mines and given them a wide berth. Each was about the size of one of those plastic exercise balls she hated and had creepy-looking antennae. Based on her training, she knew they were called contact mines, but had always thought of them as "alien-heads."

The comms unit beeped in her ear, signaling a call. Matte had told them that when they heard the beep, they were to hold their breath and be as silent as possible since bubbles and breathing could sometimes interfere with sound clarity. Matte was cute. He'd winked at her and told her she resembled Halle Berry. Not that she was looking for a date.

Matte's voice came over the line. "Island a few clicks ahead. You two stick together and try to find the underground harbor. We're setting some depth charges in case we need a distraction and will storm the other side."

Stryker swam on her right. She gave him two thumbs-up while keeping her hands on the propeller.

Most of the swim here had been through deep water. She was looking forward to finally seeing sandy bottom filled with plant life and colorful fish.

Sam slowed. Was that a—

She pushed the comms button and waited two seconds. "Stryker, is that an old battleship?"

"Let's take a quick look on our way to shore."

The huge ship was tilted on its side and covered in algae. They swam alongside it for a while, until Sam guessed it to be at least five hundred feet long. Twin turrets loomed out of the darkness, sporting what looked like machine guns.

"Hope all the sailors survived."

He pointed. "There's another old mine."

A round metal alien-head with protruding antennae appeared on their left. "They are all over this place."

"Let's keep moving."

They were coming at the island from its east side because that's where they suspected the harbor was hidden. With tonight's fog, even cloud-penetrating radar would have a tough time seeing what was going on up top.

While they swam, Sam's mind flashed on memories of Angie. Dad cooking hamburgers and hot dogs on the grill. Mom making them chore lists, and the two of them quibbling about who did what. Christmas stockings. Sam protecting Angie from the bully down the street, and Angie sticking up for her when kids made fun of the white streak in her hair, or treated her differently because of her skin tone.

The water grew shallower. It looked only fifteen to twenty feet deep based on the distance between the reefs and the surface. They had to be getting close. Sam's stomach did flip-flops and her teeth chattered.

The battleship reminded her of World War II, when so many Jews perished in gas chambers for Hitler's mad idea of a perfect Aryan race. In her journal, Cleopatra had mentioned the Sons of Adam were Aryans, too, from northern Europe. But they didn't seem to be anti-Jew. Instead, they'd kidnapped women and children. Then it hit her.

"Stryker."

"What?"

"I figured it out."

"Figured what out?"

"The cult's motive."

"Do tell."

"Cleopatra talked about a group spreading lies and rewriting history. The battleship we just passed reminded me of the same ploy by the Nazis, but our guys aren't anti-Semitic. They kidnap *women*."

"I'm not following."

"Well, the group's name is Sons of Adam, which matches their snake tattoos. Eve was sure the villain of that story."

"I still don't get it."

"Remember how we talked about Egyptian women owning property and how they could divorce their husbands?"

"And Romans killed their daughters. Yes."

"In humanity's earliest days, not only could women own property, it was passed from mother to daughter."

"Not father to son?" Stryker asked.

"No, that came later. After the time of Moses and the advent of monotheism."

A rock wall appeared in front of them. The island. Left or right?

Stryker motioned left and they swam that way along the rocks. "What's your point, Sam?"

"Cleopatra hid a bunch of goddess statues. The kidnappers destroy ancient artifacts related to powerful *women*. We think they run a sex-trafficking ring. It all adds up."

Frustration colored his voice. "What does?"

"In the war between the sexes, these guys are five-star generals. They hate women."

The blackness of a yawning limestone cave appeared in front of them.

CHAPTER 72

Eden

Day Seven

An hour after Angie whispered in Antonio's ear, she was back in her cell, pacing back and forth. Would he come with a weapon and shoot her? Would he kill Harper for spite? Her daughter looked enough like her that it would be easy to guess they were related.

Luna sat cross-legged on her lower bunk. "What are you so anxious about?"

Should Angie give the younger woman the keycard? She'd been thinking about it all day. It was her best option, especially now that she was on Antonio's radar.

She pulled the scratched magnetic card from the depths of her pocket and gave it to Luna. "You can hide this in a crack in the bricks on the floor. Be ready to take everyone to the boats."

"Why?" Luna's russet eyes narrowed. "What are you planning?"

Before Angie could answer, the door at the end of the hall creaked open and footsteps pounded the stone. Luna glared at Angie, but pocketed the card.

In a flash, Antonio stood in front of their cell, his brown eyes narrowed. He growled for her to come closer. When she

310

did, he grabbed her jacket and pulled her near. His breath smelled of espresso.

"Tell me," he growled.

She met his stare with the steel she'd used in acrimonious board meetings. "Here?"

His eyes darted around the cells, landing back on hers. Finally, he pulled his keycard from his pocket and swiped the keypad. Grabbing her by the arm, he roughly pulled her out and locked the door behind her.

They marched down the hall, and then down the stairs that led to the glass-walled room with all the computer equipment. He flipped on the lights. No one occupied the space. For a second, her mouth watered as she glanced at the desk that had held the tasty candy bar, and then she turned to face Antonio.

"What do you know?" he demanded.

"The name of your mother," she said.

CHAPTER 73

Rome, Italy
Day Seven

As Stefano straightened his uniform, he thought, not for the first time, that it should have been him running the operation instead of the *comandante*'s son. The boy had always been too soft. Nor had Antonio helped at all when it came to figuring out a way to masquerade as a member of the Rome police department. Stefano had to call in his own favor from a childhood friend.

Now, the outfit helped him blend in as he walked through the shadows of Vatican City.

Earlier, he'd established two escape routes, one on either side of the castle. This American team he'd been hunting was good, and he lamented the loss of his men in Buto. Nevertheless, the foreign operatives would fail today in protecting their newly elected leader, one way or the other. Thanks to his training with the Italian Special Forces, he had learned to lay out multiple contingency plans.

The night was young, the area around St. Peter's alive with tourists and lovers. He strolled through the square and around the Egyptian obelisk he and his brothers would tear down someday. The twin buildings that encircled the square like outstretched arms had rooftops that would be perfect sniper's nests. But they had to be crawling with federal agents and Swiss Guards.

Parting the throng, he headed past a souvenir shop, and moved down Via della Conciliazione, which was flanked by rows of three-story tan buildings. There would be agents and guards stationed at intervals atop these buildings as well. Passing between streetlights, which were also shaped like obelisks, he kept his eyes trained up, but saw no one.

His thoughts circled back to Antonio. It wasn't right that he was second in command. Stefano knew he'd make a better lieutenant. He was more ruthless, and more passionate for the cause. Antonio had questioned their role in the world, even arguing against selling women.

Stefano, on the other hand, saw the need for what they did, and how they managed it by swiftly targeting enemies like the United States. His face glowed with pride. If all went according to plan tonight, that country was about to fall into civil war.

He increased his speed. His favorite rifle was waiting for him at Castel Sant'Angelo.

CHAPTER 74

Eden
Day Seven

Dressed like a black-caped version of Death, Zola crept from the kitchen to the nearest house of men. With the amount of drugs the American woman had doled out, her rapists should be sleeping like hibernating Russian bears, but she needed to be cautious, just in case one of the rats hadn't finished his soup.

She'd been on this cursed island for a month, ever since she'd gotten on the wrong side of Baron Sokolov. The malicious white-haired man had removed her from her post as the Russian ambassador to India, and cut off her finger and tongue, before sending her here. Hoping her son, Pyotr, a gifted covert operations warrior, would find her, she'd held onto hope like a life preserver, fantasizing about rescue every time the men had raped her.

The men had a rule against sex with the merchandise, so she and the teachers had been their only outlet. More than once she'd looked to the cliffs while picking greens in the winter garden, considering taking her own life.

Antonio was the only one who hadn't touched her. Was it out of respect? Or something else?

Then the American had shown up. It had taken Zola some time to agree to help; her body was sore from the repeated abuse, and were she to be caught, she didn't think she could handle much more pain without breaking. But now, she could almost taste their blood.

The first house loomed in front of her, and she worked the door open silently. She crept in, and up the stairs, keeping to the side to minimize noise. At the first bedroom, she turned the knob ever-so-slowly. Inside, a man snored. It was Patrick, who liked to punch her stomach a single time after he raped her.

His pistol was on the nightstand next to the bed. Silent as a cat, she moved the two strides to the bedside and released the firearm from its holster. For a moment, she flashed back to weapons practice in a Moscow gun range, and then released the safety and fired the loaded sidearm once into the dead center of Patrick's forehead.

Hoping the noise wouldn't raise an alarm, she searched the nightstand and found a silencer. Moving to the next room, she repeated her retribution. As the bullet left her gun, she imagined light returning to the eyes of an endless line of women and children. So many had been brutalized by these men over the last two thousand years.

House after house, she extracted vengeance, but when she came to the *comandante*'s abode, no one was home.

She knew he hadn't eaten the drugged soup, but was willing to take him on anyway.

Where was he, with his evil whip?

CHAPTER 75

Eden
Day Seven

Antonio wasn't sure he'd heard the woman correctly. He was proficient in English but her words didn't make sense. "What do you mean? The name of my mother?"

"Yes, she was Mary Vanelli."

His heart skipped a beat. "How do you know this?"

"You look like her. She was a friend of my mother when they both lived in Los Angeles."

He did resemble her. The picture he had, and what he saw in the mirror when he shaved, both showed a similar aquiline nose. "I'm sure I look like a lot of people."

The woman glanced around, clearly uncomfortable. "I also think I know how she died."

"She killed herself."

"Perhaps. I found some papers while cleaning your father's study."

He slapped her across the face. "You're lying."

She slowly pushed the dirty blonde hair out of her blue eyes and shot him a look of pity. Then she reached into her black jacket and pulled out a yellowed news clipping and a note, handing them to him.

He took the mini-package like it was a live viper.

The note was curious. It read, "I'm leaving. This place is insane and I won't raise my boy here."

The article held a picture of an actress who looked like his mother. The woman, named Mary Vanelli, had disappeared twenty years ago at sea. Her husband, Salvatore Umbeco, had been on the family boat at the time and claimed she'd jumped overboard. He was questioned by the authorities and released. The body had never been found.

Like a wall cracking in an earthquake, Antonio's certainty began to crumble. That was his father's name.

"Sit down," he commanded.

She dropped into a chair.

Antonio sat at a computer and pulled up an internet browser. His fingers danced across the keyboard. He retrieved several archived news articles about the death of an up-and-coming actress named Mary Vanelli. It had been a scandal. She'd moved to Italy with her husband and died a month later. The Americans had accused the Italians of a cover-up, saying she was a happy-go-lucky soul who would have never taken her own life.

A dread began to gnaw at his insides, like a rat chewing an apple in the storeroom. He'd been taught that women were disgusting, filthy liars. It was why his father and the group exploited them, sold them as sex slaves.

Her name was Mary.

In a flash, he remembered the night they left the island, being awakened in the dark, the furtive walk to the boat, his mother's nervous laughter. Then the other boat catching them, his father yelling, "Mary! Mary!" before climbing aboard and slapping her. He'd told Antonio to head below to the cabin on the other boat. When his father came back to the island, he'd told Antonio that she'd jumped overboard and killed herself.

His head dropped into his hands, emotions ricocheting from disbelief to anger before finally settling on certainty.

It explained everything. And his father had kept this from him his entire life.

The door from the church banged open and the *comandante* strode into the room, smoking a cigar and carrying *il canone*. The woman beside him tensed.

Eyes darting to the two of them, the man who had raised him stopped short and pointed at her with a cigar. "What is she doing here?"

Antonio stood up and gestured at the computer. "Is this my mother? Mary Vanelli?"

His father waved this idea away. "We've discussed this." The baritone deepened to a warning tone. "You don't need to know about her."

Antonio's mouth felt dry. He waved the newspaper and note. "It looks like I do know about her."

His father came closer and looked at the note, face reddening. He gestured to the woman in the chair with *il canone*. "Has that creature been filling your head with lies?"

"She gave me information and I researched it." Antonio stared his father down. "Tell me the truth. Is that her?"

The *comandante* took a drag of his cigar, looking back and forth between the computer and his son. The light in his eyes darkened and he threw his hands in the air. "Yes, fine," he growled. "That's her."

Heat crept into Antonio's face. This was all too much. "They didn't think she killed herself."

"Women are weak," the *comandante* spat.

"Why? Because she thought this place crazy?"

His father's laugh chilled him to the bone.

"Yes, you little punk," the *comandante* replied.

The conclusion was inescapable. "You did it! You killed her!"

"When she left me, Stefano and I tracked her ship down. He brought you back here and I slit her throat." His father strode over and shoved him in the chest with a finger. "Her body was dumped off the Midnight Shelf."

Through the disagreement, the blonde woman had slowly inched away.

Antonio sat down on the nearest desk, feeling sucker-punched. All he had of his mother was one dog-eared picture that he kept in his wallet. Every day he missed her. "You bastard."

"Should I have dragged her back by the hair?" The *comandante* stubbed his cigar out in an ashtray on a desk.

"Why couldn't you just let us go?"

The *comandante* pointed at the book in his hand. "No. Our canon warns against women and their powers."

"How can I trust that? You've lied about everything else."

His father hit him with the ancient book.

Antonio took the blow across the side of the head. Always before, he'd taken the abuse, but disgust for his father filled him and he threw a punch to his father's gut. Doubling over in pain for only a moment, his father responded with a jab to Antonio's jaw. His chin snapped back, white-hot pain rocketing through his head.

In a desperate search for a weapon, his eyes fell on the computer monitor. Picking it up, he slammed it over his father's head just as the older man came in for another blow. His father stumbled to his knees, pushing him into a desk and knocking its contents—pens, keyboards, a chinotto bottle—to the floor. Antonio tumbled with them. Glass shattered.

He shook his head. Blood ran down his cheek from his temple.

His father kicked him in the calf, and he heard something
crack. Sudden pain took his breath away and he closed his eyes
tight. When he opened them again, his father had drawn a
fishing knife and was lunging toward him, blade outstretched.

CHAPTER 76

Eden
Day Seven

Stryker's limbs twitched with the anticipation of holding Angie and Harper in his arms once again. If he needed to blow the island apart to find them, he was ready to do that.

They were close.

The underwater propellers had gotten them here quickly. He wasn't sure what to make of Sam's theory about the kidnapper's motives, and he cared more about what they'd done than why they'd done it, so he set it aside for the time being. The island's roots were to his right, pockmarked with limestone caves. He hoped the SEALs would hold off on using explosives until they were needed. That had been the deal.

A large opening appeared to his right. Wishing the ocean was calm tonight, he powered down the light on his propeller and popped his head above the waves. Yep, it looked like a harbor all right. There were two boats moored on the left side, and dark tunnels extended further into the shadows. That was the way to his girls.

He ducked back underwater and turned on the comms. "Sam, Matte. We have ID'd the harbor. No sign of life. Going in."

He waved to Sam and used his propeller to swim inside the cave toward the boats. If anyone was aboard, he wanted to take them out first. Finding an underwater shelf and some rocks for weight, they stashed their propellers and fins in case they'd need them later. Then they swam to the stern of the nearest boat and used the attached ladder to climb aboard, knives out. All was quiet, so he took off the mask, drew his weapon out of the dry sack and checked it. Looked good.

Making as little noise as possible, he put on a pair of rubber-soled shoes. They were wet, but serviceable. Sam readied herself, too.

Making haste, they cleared the boat. No enemy combatants, but he did find a cupboard full of white pills. Roofies. Bile rose in his throat, replaced by a deep anger.

Every swearword he'd ever learned came out in a torrent. Where were the conniving, blasted kidnappers?

They moved on and cleared the other boat. With the fog and a single light, the entire harbor felt eerie, like the ghosts of the dead might rise from the mist at any moment.

On the run, he unplugged a security camera and they sprinted to the first opening that led off the huge cave. He'd brought a penlight and swung it around. It was a fifty-by-fifty makeshift storeroom filled with boxes. The Italian markings indicated the crates were filled with WWII ammunition and explosives. Not what they needed.

Moving to the next opening, he paused at the sound of hushed whispers. He motioned for Sam to take the other side of the tunnel mouth and he waited, gun raised.

There were shushing sounds and hushed whispers. No heavy boots. Still, he waited until a ragtag group of women burst forth. When he saw Harper, he rushed in and picked her up, crushing her in an embrace. Relief flooded him.

"Daddy!"

He patted her back and her hair. "I'm here, baby. I'm here."

She wiggled away so she could look at him. Her face was clean, and her strawberry-blonde hair held no rat's nest. That was a good sign.

"Where's Mommy?" he asked. "Do you know?"

Behind him, Sam had found Reno and was talking with her. At the redhead's side was Layla, but without her glasses. A dark-haired woman carrying a pistol ushered the children toward one of the boats.

Harper replied, "I think she's hunting the bad guys."

Stryker exhaled. "Okay, good. I'm going to do that, too. Let's get you set up with Auntie Reno. I want you to go get on that boat, all right?"

Her head bobbed. "Sure."

He stroked her hair. "I love you, princess."

She kissed her fingers and put them on his lips. He smiled.

Carrying her over to Reno and Sam, he interrupted. "Reno, can you watch Harper?"

"Yes. Do you have any food? Haven't eaten in a week." Reno leaned forward to whisper in his ear. "This has to be a sex-trafficking setup. They starved us to make us more cooperative."

The confirmation burned in Stryker's gut and he set his jaw. "We'll get you all something to eat soon. The SEALs are here, too. What else do you know?"

Reno pointed to the raven-haired woman. "Zola can't speak, but I think she was trying to tell us another boat will be arriving soon."

"Get out of here then, pronto. Do you know where Angie is?"

Reno shook her head.

Frustrated, he clenched his fist. Where was his wife?

CHAPTER 77

Eden
Day Seven

Seeing the knife headed for Antonio, Angie grabbed a laptop and hit the *comandante*'s forearm. With Antonio writhing in pain, she'd been forced to jump into action, hoping to save her skin. And Antonio's.

The knife skittered away.

While the two men had argued in Italian, Angie's mind had gone into overdrive, trying to figure out what was happening. From body language and English's helpful relationship to Romance languages, she'd deduced that Antonio had confronted his father, who had admitted killing his mother. What was in that book the older man had used to whack Antonio over the head? Something about their Cleopatra obsession?

Those thoughts took a backseat as she scooped the blade from the floor. Her victory was short-lived, however, as the *comandante* grabbed her left foot. She landed with a thud on her ribs, but held onto the knife. When he tried to regain his footing, she whipped her feet at his face and connected with his cheek, drawing blood.

As he fell back, she scrambled to her feet, knife in hand, ready to attack. But the *comandante* was already in motion, lunging at her legs again. He caught her across the shins, causing her to fall forward, but she turned it into a roll over his shoulders. Coming up behind him, she turned and put the edge of the knife under his left shoulder blade, behind his heart.

"*Fermare!*" It was one of the few Italian words she knew.

As commanded, he stopped and put his hands up.

Her mind raced through options. Before she got far, the *comandante* swung around and tried to knock the knife from her hand with his whip. She absorbed the blow, letting the whip wrap around her arm and then she grabbed the leather, causing him to lose his balance. She was going to have to hurt him to make him stop.

Before he could pull the whip free to strike again, she tugged him forward and kicked him in the head. He toppled sideways, crashing to the ground. One malevolent eye stared at her so she slammed her foot into his temple. The eye finally shut.

Several feet away, Antonio still clutched his lower leg. With that much pain, it was probably broken.

"Is there any rope? We need to tie him up."

"No," Antonio replied.

Angie looked around. "While we figure that out, I need your help to stop the assassination attempt."

CHAPTER 78

Eden
Day Seven

Sam and Stryker ran into the tunnel mouth that had produced the escaping women and children. Where was her sister? Had Angie's luck run out?

This couldn't be good.

It didn't take them long to reach a prison. Stinking cells, their doors open, stood on both sides of the hall. Bile rose in Sam's throat as she imagined Angie here for an entire week. And according to Reno, the men hadn't even fed them. That made her mad. Fighting mad.

They came to a door that led to a stairwell. They ran up a few flights, where the exit spit them outside. In front of them was a large building, while off to the left, the village was barely visible through the fog. Other than the whisper of the wind, the island was eerily silent.

Stryker motioned and they ran for the center structure. Out of breath, she took one side of the door, and Stryker the other. After clearing it, they entered a dark kitchen. Using a penlight, they moved into what seemed to be a large dining room. Another beam of light was moving around the opposite end of the space.

"Captain Matte?" Stryker yelled. "Is that you?"

"Stryker." Matte's accent cut through the darkness. "All clear?"

"Yes. There?"

"Clear."

They ran, joining groups in the middle of the dark hall.

"What have you found?" Stryker asked.

"The entire village is full of dead men in their beds. Killed execution style."

Sam recalled the woman they'd called Zola herding children with her pistol. Was this her work? Sam would bet on it, and wondered about the woman's backstory. It took a lot of anger or anguish to do a deed like that.

"Saved us a firefight," she said.

Matte nodded. "True."

"There are women and children in the harbor, including my daughter, taking shelter in a boat," Stryker said. "They should have put out to sea by now. Can we bring in a rescue ship?"

"Yes. We have a couple waiting in the wings. We can bring one to either the harbor or down by the village."

"Not the harbor. There are a ton of old naval mines guarding it. Also sounds like the enemy may have an incoming ship."

"They do. Was going to warn you. Wanted to clear the island first."

Sam interrupted. "Anything we can do to help the women's ship clear the mines?"

Matte glumly shook his head. "Don't think so, but we'll try."

"OK." She turned to Stryker. "We need to go check out that stairwell. Maybe Angie is down there."

CHAPTER 79

Eden
Day Seven

Angie helped Antonio struggle to his feet. He hadn't responded to her statement about stopping the assassination attempt.

"I really need your help to stop the assassination," she repeated.

Wincing, he leaned on a desk. "How do you know about that?"

"That doesn't matter now. What can we tie your father up with?"

She looked around, but the plain office offered nothing in the way of rope or zip ties. They'd have to make do.

Walking over broken glass to the *comandante*, she yanked the whip from his unmoving hands and used his fishing knife to cut it into strips. "While I do this, can you call off your men?"

He didn't move. He had to be in shock.

She decided to start with a smaller request. "What about a member roster? Can you print out a list of your men?"

He nodded. "Give me a minute."

Sitting at an undamaged workstation, he logged in and typed in some commands. Soon, a nearby printer began to spit out pages.

Once she finished binding the *comandante*'s wrists and feet, she stood and rubbed her hands together. For an instant, she felt dizzy, likely from lack of food. Shaking it off, she grabbed the pages, looked at them briefly, and folded them into her jacket pocket.

"Is there any food here?"

"I don't think so." He looked up at her. "You're going to take down the entire organization?"

"Yes."

He blinked a few times, as if to clear his thoughts. "Okay." He nodded once, then several times with more vigor. "What's been going on here is wrong."

She looked him in the eye to see if he really had a change of heart. His gaze told her he'd indeed changed sides. Not surprising. In many ways, he was a victim too.

"If you cooperate, I'll do my best to see that they go easy on you." She meant it.

He nodded.

Angie picked up the book. "Is this important? Should we bring it?"

His eyes lit up as he reached out to pull it from her hands with care. "It explains everything."

"Good. Now what about the president-elect?"

Antonio reached for the desk phone, dialed a number from memory, and spoke into it. While he talked, he clutched at his injured calf. As the conversation went on, his voice rose, and color entered his cheeks. After several tense moments, he slammed the phone down on the receiver. "Stefano won't stop. He thinks I've been compromised."

"That's not good."

"No. And worse, it's only part of the plan."

Her stomach dropped. "What else?"

"A false attack on the president in Stockholm." He looked away. "And my computer guys. They've been working on a deepfake video in case the president-elect somehow survives."

She'd never heard the term. "What's a deepfake?"

"In this case a video that was created using artificial intelligence. Extremely hard to detect that it isn't real."

Great. As if fake news wasn't bad enough. "What's the video going to show?"

"The president-elect talking in detail about cheating to win the election."

Her heart skipped a beat. "That will throw the country into civil war!"

"That was the plan. We tried to influence the election and when that didn't work, we came up with a new plan. We didn't want the president-elect to take power."

"Wow." She shook her head, disgust turning her mouth sour.

He reached for the phone. "Let me tell them to stop it."

"I don't think you can. They should all be asleep. Drugged at dinner."

He raised both eyebrows. "I see."

"Can you stop it?"

He turned to the computer. "I don't think so."

Out of the corner of her eye, she saw a flash of movement, and then the main door to the command center closed. The *comandante*'s leather bonds lay in a heap on the floor, near a large shard of broken glass.

She'd been so focused on stopping the assassination attempt that she hadn't turned around to keep an eye on him. And he hadn't made a sound. She clenched a fist. His escape was going to cause trouble.

CHAPTER 80

Eden
Day Seven

The *comandante* slipped up the stairs. He felt like a coward, but he needed more firepower if he was going to take on that woman. She had his knife, his whip was torn apart, and the broken glass he'd used to cut his bonds was not a good weapon.

What had she done to his son? After all he'd done for the boy, she'd somehow figured out his old secret and had used it to turn Antonio into a traitor. The *comandante* put his hand to his heart, wondering if the pain he felt there meant he was having a heart attack. Should he have told the boy about how his mother had died? Of course not. Antonio would come to his senses once the *comandante* got the evil succubus out of the way.

In the stairwell, he paused to catch his breath and look at his phone. A boat full of young men, all eighteen-year-old descendants of his men stationed in France, was expected into the harbor this evening. He'd been on his way to meet the crew and potential members when he'd stopped in the command center to see if there were any new secure messages from his friends in the Vatican. Those Americans had proven challenging to eliminate.

On the phone in his map app, a dot blinked, indicating the ship was entering the harbor now. He'd cut through the cells.

When he burst through the door, however, he put his hand to his mouth. Where were the women? Every single cell was empty. Had that woman somehow let them out? Angry, he slammed his palm against a flat keycard reader.

No matter—he would personally track each woman down and teach her a lesson she'd never forget.

He ran down the cell hallway and into the harbor. One boat was tied up, but where was the other vessel? There were supposed to be two docked here.

Ah, there. His ship was just pulling up on the opposite side of the cavern. As it slipped through the dense fog, it looked like an apparition. The men aboard would help him set this all straight.

CHAPTER 81

Rome, Italy
Day Seven

Stefano hung up the phone and shook his head. Antonio had clearly been compromised. Call off the mission? Hell no!

How long had the *comandante*'s son been working against their plans? The attack on his men in Buto came to mind. What had gone down there?

Still, this current situation was a complication for which he hadn't planned. From his spot near the top of Castel Sant'Angelo, he looked down the Via della Conciliazione toward the basilica, thinking.

He and his favorite rifle were in an alcove of the arched passageway that circumnavigated the round castle while Michael was nearby, scouting. The fortress was closed for the night and Michael's job was to ensure it stayed that way. The four security guards who'd been on duty had been picked off without incident. Now, they had a clear view of the pope's balcony, even with the light fog. But it was a long-range shot because he knew the buildings near the Vatican would be crawling with Secret Service agents and Swiss Guards. Unless . . .

Perhaps he could modify one of his backup plans. He'd stashed another rifle closer to the action.

Yes. The more he considered the idea, the more he liked it.

With Antonio gone to the devil, the enemy might find him here.

His phone vibrated. The team in Stockholm reported they'd successfully staged a false attempt on the president's life. One of his men had detonated a small grenade in a trash can near the president's car as the leader walked to his limousine. That should cause the crew here to relax, thinking the day's havoc complete.

And he had a man in the Swiss Guard, running interference on communications.

The mission would get done, even without Antonio.

CHAPTER 82

Eden
Day Seven

Stryker ran back down the several flights of stairs, past the door to the cells, and down several more sets until he pulled up short in front of a metal door, propped slightly ajar with a length of brown leather. His heart pounded wildly. What if she was dead? Were they too late?

Sam gave him a look that said whatever happened, they were in this together.

They entered.

His wife was standing next to a man typing at one of the computers, a long knife in her hand. Stryker let out a strangled cry and she turned, her face lighting up like it had when he'd asked her to marry him.

The next thing he knew, she was in his arms.

Angie heard a shoe scrape on the floor and turned, expecting to see the *comandante*, back with a pistol to kill her. Instead, it was Tim and Sam. Sam's face held a look of relief, and Tim's eyes told her how much he loved her. She was crying before he even put his sturdy arms around her.

God, she'd missed him.

Sam wiped a tear from her eye and sidestepped around the lovebirds. Sam hoped the time apart had helped them figure things out. They'd been really good together once, and perhaps would be again.

She focused on the short, thick-chested man with an aquiline nose and neat mustache. "I'm Sam. What are you working on?"

He looked at her briefly and turned his eyes back to the screen. "I'm trying to stop a civil war from breaking out in your country."

That was a surprise. "Good. Please continue. Do you know where the sniper is located in Rome?"

"Yes. Castel Sant'Angelo. On the river side."

CHAPTER 83

Vatican City, Rome
Day Seven

As soon as the Secret Service radio plug in Rey's ear reported that POTUS had been attacked in Stockholm, a ripple went through the agents stationed in Rome. Chatter reached a fever pitch. Most agents thought the odds of attacks in two places on the same night highly unlikely.

Rey wasn't so sure. An IED placed in a trash can didn't seem like the Sons of Adam's usual style.

The Secret Service channel became full of static and they switched to a frequency they hadn't briefed him on. He tried to contact their leader with a backup phone number. No answer.

His phone vibrated.

After authenticating, he joined with his alias. "Stingray."

"The tango is on top of Castel Sant'Angelo," Sam said. "The side near the river. Go stop him."

"Good work. We'll get him."

Rey hung up, and again tried to raise the Secret Service on the backup number. This time he got through and quickly relayed the message. Then he ran down the stairs of the souvenir shop. There was no time to waste.

Rey bolted into the street, pushing through the large crowd that had gathered to watch the joint address, until he reached the Via della Conciliazione. His knee ached as he ran, but he ignored the pain, pushing on through wisps of fog.

In his earpiece, he heard two members of the Secret Service switch back to his channel and express frustration that they couldn't get through to the Swiss Guard to stop the address. Maybe there was a Sons of Adam mole in the guard. Or perhaps they were jamming comms.

Several men he recognized as feds from the pre-mission brief ran alongside him and then sprinted past him. At regular intervals along the dark avenue, he passed streetlights with bone-white obelisk bases, which gave the night an otherworldly glow.

By the time he was halfway to the old, circular castle, the back of his throat burned and his lungs felt raw, reminding him of high-school basketball practice. The pain in his knee was approaching unbearable, but he knew the stakes and kept moving.

Throngs of tourists passed him, headed toward the square, as did a policeman in desperate need of a shave.

Something about the man with the heavy stubble looked familiar, but where would he have seen a Roman cop? He brushed it off and kept running, but the farther he got, the more his gut told him to stop.

He halted to catch his breath, hands on his hips. His knee was screaming. The Secret Service agents had outpaced him and were closing in on their quarry atop the castle. At this point, there would be no harm in following the cop.

Rey spun on his heel and joined the crowd. The officer was a little taller than average so Rey tracked him easily. The man's pants bore the uniform's distinctive crimson slash down the sides, and as he moved with the tide, the red flashed. Not wanting to alert the watchman, Rey kept to a walk, but made it brisk. He flexed his facial features briefly, glad to have his own face disguised in case the modern-day member of the *Vigiles Urbani* somehow turned out to be part of the cult.

Rey wracked his brain. Why'd the guy look familiar?

The cop approached the edge of the square, keeping to the left of the street. Suddenly, the man disappeared. Had he turned or gone inside the building on the corner? A religious bookstore, from the looks of it.

By the time Rey reached the same corner, the man's shadowed mug was nowhere to be seen.

Which meant he'd gone inside the bookstore. Only a nightlight illuminated the holy books in the window. Rey tried the doors. Locked.

This was a conundrum.

Reaching inside his wallet, he pulled out a pick set. The locks were old and the tumbler released freely. Putting the picks and his wallet back, he palmed his service pistol, released the safety, and entered the shop. It smelled of old paper and beeswax. Cards, bibles, and religious iconography lined the shelves. Toward the back of the store, a hallway led to another room.

Hearing nothing, he moved with stealth through the hall, and then to a door at the back of the next room. This one was unlocked, which meant the cop could have found a way in. Was he an officer? Or was it a disguise?

The door opened with a small creak, and Rey paused, waiting until he was sure there was no sound from above. If it was the sniper up there, he'd be setting up his weapon and checking windage, distance, and such. The windows had a perfect view of the basilica. The Secret Service had cleared the similar rooms across the avenue under the pharmacy, and he assumed they'd cleared these as well. But right now, they were all down at the castle.

Rey snuck up the stairs, and then peered around the corner to see a long, dark hallway with three closed doors. Perhaps this was office space? He'd not seen any workplace downstairs.

The pope and president-elect had to be on any moment.

He paused, wondering if Stryker had found Angie. This mission was coming full circle.

That's when Rey remembered where he'd seen the policeman before. It was from those pics that Ace had sent from the Saudi airport of the men who had flown from Italy. He and Jane had reviewed the photographs under the lighthouse in Taposiris Magna. One of the guys had heavy stubble and a wide mouth, just like the cop.

The fake cop.

Rey had to give it to him. The guy had pulled a double-fake, and then gone for the layup instead of a three-point shot from the castle. A shot from here, for a sniper, would be a slam dunk.

Rey touched his medallion. Which door?

If it were him, he'd go for the farthest so as to better hear anyone coming. Rey pulled a penlight from his pocket to search the floor for traps. Sure enough, a few jingly bells were strewn across the hall.

As Rey always did when he was in deep trouble, he broke out in a sweat. *Stay present. Focus. One step at a time.*

He inched down the hallway just as the crowd roared. Out of time.

Turning the knob, he threw open the last door. Office. Empty.

"Hey. I'm coming for you!" he yelled.

Who cared if the sniper spoke English? The goal now was distraction. Fueled only by the last dregs of adrenaline, Rey sprang back into the hallway just as bullets strafed the office he'd just left. He dove to the floor as more shots slammed into the wall behind him. The volley was coming from the middle room.

With his heel, he kicked open the offending door and then rolled for cover on one side of the doorway.

He'd always played better offense than defense. Peeking around the bottom corner, he saw the fake cop near the window, behind a sniper's tripod. He let off a round and ducked back. The sound of breaking glass shattered the night.

When he scrambled to his feet and looked again, the room was empty. He ran to the window. A metal grappling hook dug into the frame, attached to a rope that dangled toward the street.

A bullet whizzed by, narrowly missing his wounded ear.

The shooter was on the ground. And the plaza was packed with people.

The sniper turned and ran through the tall Roman columns that hugged the square. Rey used the claw and rope to lower himself and took off in hot pursuit. The assassin pushed a woman aside and she fell, screaming.

The crowd was leaping out of the sniper's way, but not fast enough. Rey used the open path and gained on his opponent, lungs and knee again on fire. The killer weaved back and forth, heading for the front of the crowd. Was the enemy going to try to kill the president-elect from down here?

Finding a new burst of energy, Rey sprinted toward the assailant. As they neared a three-tier fountain, the false cop turned and fired at him. The bullet struck him in the chest, but the assassin's movement had allowed him to get a clear shot off first.

As Rey pitched backward, the assassin's head exploded, right before the body fell into the lowest pool of the fountain with a huge, bloody splash.

CHAPTER 84

Eden
Day Seven

Too soon, Stryker pulled away from his wife. Unlike Harper, Angie looked a mess. Her blonde hair was disheveled, her face dirty, and she smelled pretty ripe too. But her eyes were clear.

"Let's wrap this up and check on our kid," he said.

"Have you found her yet?" Angie asked.

"All the women and children are on one of the boats. We told them to get out of the harbor."

Angie nodded. "Good idea."

Stryker turned to Sam, not wanting to mention all the buried naval mines. "How goes stopping the assassination?"

"Rey has been warned about the sniper on top of the castle. You were right about it as a nest."

"Great." Stryker pointed to the man at the computer. "What's he working on?"

"Stopping the video that will launch a civil war if the shooting fails."

Stryker winced. *A civil war?* It was always something.

Walking over to the man who sat at a computer station, he put a hand on the fellow's shoulder. "Are you making progress?"

The man had a thick Italian accent. "I didn't set up the deepfake video. I don't know how to stop it."

Stryker replied in Italian. "What's its purpose?"

The man kept typing. "We figured it would ignite the divide that we've helped create in your country. We have men waiting for the signal."

Why was this man helping? He exchanged a glance with Angie, asking with a raised eyebrow if he could trust the fellow. She nodded and began to talk to Sam.

While his wife was occupied, Stryker quietly asked the man, "Is there a way through those naval mines that surround the island?"

The man turned in his seat and looked up at Stryker, making eye contact. "I heard you mention your daughter. I'm sorry, but our captains are trained to avoid the mines in the narrow channel. With an unfamiliar pilot . . . well, I will pray for them."

The tension in Stryker's gut ratcheted up. "Okay. Thank you."

The man nodded, and turned back to his monitor.

Stryker returned to thinking about the level of resources and planning necessary to generate a convincing deepfake. "I'll want to know more about the video later. Are your computer servers here or in the cloud?"

"They're here. We don't trust the cloud."

"Excellent. Where are they?"

The man pointed to a tall metal cabinet that held a lot of computer equipment. Lights were blinking on and off like a demented Christmas tree. For a minute he considered trying to save the servers for later analysis, but the immediate threat to law and order was too great.

"Then I'll take care of it. Wait outside for me with the women."

The Italian hesitated a beat, then stood and hopped away on one foot, a pained look on his face.

Stryker turned to Angie and Sam. "Wait on the next landing."

They all left the room and he removed the olive Mylar C4 packages from his pack, along with their attached blasting caps. He set the two-by-eleven-inch blocks near the server rack, and unwound the detonating cord as he backed toward the door. After lighting the fuse, he hustled out the doorway.

"Go!"

He pounded up the stairs, pushing the three others ahead of him toward the door of the cell block. They rushed through it just as the C4 detonated with a deep boom.

Stryker lost his balance and caught himself on a cell door. "Keep moving!"

Smoke billowed up from below. Angie fell to her knees, but picked herself up and kept scrambling forward. Sam flanked his wife, and he put an arm around the waist of the hobbled Italian.

"Careful when we get to the harbor!" Antonio yelled.

They ran through the fumes, along the cell block and into the tunnel. Nearing the end, they slowed to a stop.

Huddling in the mouth of the tunnel, Stryker's stomach sank. As he'd suspected, the ship that had been there before was gone, carrying his daughter into the mine-infested water.

Another, crawling with men, stood in the mist.

CHAPTER 85

Eden
Day Seven

Angie felt Antonio tugging at her arm.

"That's a ship full of potential new members," he said. "We need to go back, through the cells."

"I agree," Tim said. "We're seriously outnumbered. We can rendezvous with the SEALs from up there."

Angie was so ready for this nightmare to be over. The adrenaline had ebbed and she was beyond tired. But they had to get off the cursed island and find Harper.

As they backtracked down the cell blocks, Angie gave her rank prison the middle finger, hoping to never see it again.

The smoke from the earlier explosion had cleared. They approached the stairwell and heard a rumble from below, followed by a large crack.

"The glass window," Angie cried. "Run!"

Tim threw open the stairwell door. Water was rising rapidly, heading for them. He pushed her, Sam, and Antonio ahead of him up the stairs. Angie ran as fast as she could, taking the treads two at a time.

They sprinted up the stairs and out into the fog-bound night.

Tim turned back. "I think the water just drowned those cells."

"Good riddance." Angie put her hands on her knees, lungs burning.

Sam put her arm around Angie's waist, but turned to Tim. "With the harbor compromised, shall we head to the village?"

He nodded, putting an arm around Antonio's waist again for support, and they set off at a brisk walk. The silence was strange. Angie was used to this area bustling with men and children.

"Where is everyone?" she asked Sam. Angie wanted more of the story than she'd gotten from Tim earlier.

"Do you know the dark-haired woman named Zola?"

"Of course."

"When we arrived, she was toting a gun. The SEALs said that when they began to take the island, the men here were dead in their beds, execution style."

Angie whistled softly. "An avenging angel. I wonder what they did to her."

"I don't want to think about it."

"Me neither."

When they moved through the village, Antonio stopped and turned toward his blue house. Angie just now realized he was still carrying that old leather-bound book. Geez, she was exhausted.

"I need to get a few things," he said nervously.

Tim shook his head. "Sorry, you don't."

Antonio looked at her, pleading. "But if there is more information about my mother—"

Angie jumped in. "You know her name now. And what happened."

"I've wanted to leave the island but . . ." He trailed off, looking at the village.

Angie nodded toward the pier. "C'mon. There's nothing for you here anymore."

He dragged his feet, but after a few paces, turned his face toward the water and picked up steam.

By the time they got to the jetty, an eighty-foot boat sailed out of the mist and glided to a stop. It was sleek, covered in steel-gray armor, and had a small tower over the cabin.

A man with a Jersey accent shook her hand as they boarded and introduced himself as Matte.

"Matte, do you have any food? Bacon, peanut butter, steak, chips, shit-on-a-stick. I'll eat pretty much anything at this point."

He seemed startled, but waved over a young man. "Take her inside. Give her whatever she wants."

Even though Angie drooled in anticipation of a tasty bite to eat, she had the presence of mind to realize that this hell wasn't over yet. The *comandante* was still out there with a boatload of hitmen, and they had yet to find their daughter.

CHAPTER 86

Eden
Day Seven

Stryker turned to Matte, glad Angie was going to get some food in her. "Thanks, she's my wife."

"No problem. Sorry it took us a while. Naval mines everywhere. What did you find?"

"We need to finish this," Stryker said. "I'll fill you in."

They spoke for a minute and the boat pulled back from the dock and headed for the underground harbor.

Stryker looked the ship over. It was about the same size as the fishing vessel he'd seen parked in the harbor, but this craft was built for war. It had a V-hull, twin engines, and two types of mounted machine guns: a .50 caliber and a 7.62mm Gatling gun. Matte had called the boat a MAKO, redesigned from the earlier MK V, which Stryker had seen once in a port in Iraq.

He settled in the rear, behind the .50 caliber. One of Matte's guys manned the Gatling gun. Stryker set his weapon to rapid-fire mode, which would give him about forty rounds a minute.

Then he put on ear protection and waited.

Due to the mines, it took forever for the ship to make it around the island. Finally, it inched close enough to see the mouth of the harbor. In his mind's eye, the enemy's boats were straight ahead, one behind the other.

Matte spoke over a bullhorn. "This is the US Navy. Surrender now."

A burst of machine-gun fire met his request, pinging off the bow of the armored boat. That answered Stryker's questions about how the enemy ships were outfitted.

An underwater explosion shot a plume of water up into the air forty feet to starboard. Were some of those naval mines remote-controlled?

Stryker aimed the heavy weapon and let loose. His arms soaked up the recoil and he cycled a few bursts, with pauses in between to aim into the fog.

The Sons of Adam returned fire, but the MAKO's hull sloughed their bullets off like drops of rain.

There were more bursts of sound; water splashed high around them. One blast was so close it rocked the ship. Matte ordered Stryker and Sam to stay put even as the SEALs kept gesticulating from their sonar to the water and yelling. Chaos reigned as the explosions continued.

Stryker tried to focus, to see into the cavern, but the dense mist obstructed his view. His shoulders, which had ached all day, began to burn.

They needed some wind. Or . . .

He yelled his idea to Matte, who nodded. Ten seconds later, the ring of explosives they'd set around the island detonated with a thunderous boom.

The firing stopped for about twenty seconds, and then picked up where it left off. Stryker's temples pounded. The SEALs' explosives must have been set on the back of the island, far enough away from the harbor that they'd had minimal impact.

Earlier, he'd asked if they had any rocket launchers on board and the answer had come back negative.

Angie poked her head out of the cabin, a banana in her hand. "Aim high. Try to hit the old ammunition!"

He nodded his thanks. That might work. The munitions storeroom was directly behind the enemy ship. If it was still dry. But he guessed the water from the command center's broken window had drained directly into the harbor.

He looked at the gunner on the other side of the boat, who confirmed that he had heard her suggestion. Together they adjusted their aim for the back of the cavern. Stryker let off a stream of machine-gun fire. Then one more.

Another explosion rocked the sea fifty feet to their left.

A stray bullet whizzed through his hair, burning his scalp and ripping off his ear protection. Close. Too close.

He ignored the pain and sent several other loud bursts to the back of the harbor. The strategy wasn't working.

Walking over to Matte, Stryker explained his latest brainstorm.

"You want to do what?" Matte asked.

"We're firing blind."

"But it'll get you killed."

"We're sitting ducks out here. If it's my time to go, get my wife and kid home safe." Was it his day to join Malachi in the ocean beyond all sea?

Matte shook his head, clearly not comfortable with the plan.

Stryker knew it was their best shot. "We can't give them time to regroup or escape. Do you have what I need?"

"Yes."

"All right then. Let me get suited up."

Another SEAL took over the .50 caliber machine gun while Stryker donned a new wetsuit and fins.

Angie came over, concern in her pale blue eyes. "Really?"

"It was your idea."

"Not like this."

"It has to be done."

She crossed her arms. Gave him that intense look of hers, and then kissed him. Another underwater blast pushed them together and he held her tight.

Eventually, he let her go.

She gave him a mock salute. "Look for a mid-fifties man with a receding hairline and forked beard."

After winking at her, he secured the scuba mask and stepped backward into the cool water.

Diving deep, he got his bearings. He didn't want to use a lighted propeller to enter the harbor, as men on the fishing boats might see him coming. It was all about stealth.

Passing a slime-covered mine, he held his breath, hoping it wouldn't explode while he was nearby. He swam around that one and immediately dropped his legs and back-pedaled with his arms. Another, larger mine reared up right in front of him. If the current shifted, he'd smack right into it and be blown to bits. His heart hammered in his ears as he swam backward and to the side.

He didn't drop his guard until he reached the wide mouth of the harbor a few minutes later. Swimming forward, he stayed deep, figuring the fog and water to be his best defense.

When the keel of the first boat reared overhead, he continued swimming directly underneath the ship's backbone. He guessed the cult's leader would be on this boat, as it was nearest the mouth of the harbor. The women had taken one vessel, but he and Sam had cleared two when they'd arrived. Heart racing, now that he was at the most dangerous part of the mission, he swam halfway down the length of that second ship. It would make good cover.

He got everything ready, and then surfaced into the shadows.

Angie had told him what the cult leader looked like. That forked beard was a dead giveaway. The *comandante* was yelling orders on the back of the first boat. Stryker couldn't resist.

"Hey!" he yelled.

The man turned, eyes narrowed.

"This is for my wife and daughter."

With that, Stryker lobbed a grenade onto the boat. The *comandante*'s eyes grew wide and he dove for the deck just as Stryker turned and threw a second device into the munitions storeroom. Putting his mouthpiece back in his mouth, Stryker dove for the propeller he'd left on the shelf when he and Sam had initially stormed the harbor. It would take him precious seconds to get there.

KABOOM.

Bye bye, you evil bastard, Stryker thought.

A secondary detonation rocked the night. Then another. The old ammunition had taken out the other boat. Even ten feet underwater, he heard the roar. A fireball whooshed overhead and he dove deeper, ears attuned for the one thing that might complicate his getaway.

Crack.

There it was.

Rumbling vibrations disturbed the water, even this deep. The limestone island was falling apart.

He made it to the shelf, grabbed the camouflaged propeller, and sped away as flaming wreckage began to hit the water above him.

A rapidly sinking rock hit his lower calf, torquing his ankle. He swore and kept moving. Other debris fell from the roof. He dove deeper. Then he was out of the harbor and zooming toward the boat, careful to avoid the mines.

Mission accomplished, he thought, with satisfaction.

Then he heard another explosion. The sound came not from the direction he'd just left. No, it came from up ahead.

Angie!

CHAPTER 87

Eden
Day Seven

Ninety seconds earlier, Angie was watching the mouth of the harbor from the relative safety of the boat's interior. Stryker had disappeared overboard several long minutes ago. Explosions continued to spew spouts of water high in the air all around them. She'd never learned to swim, and his being in the water made her nervous.

"Do you think he'll be okay?" she asked Sam.

"I'm sure he will."

Angie took another bite of delicious banana. "But what if . . ."

A commotion near the back of the boat distracted her. Several men were huddled around one of the outboard motors, gesticulating at a black rubber line and swearing. Behind the wheel, a wounded SEAL was slumped over.

She gathered that the motor wasn't working. "Think a stray bullet damaged that fuel line?"

"Looks that way. One got our pilot, too," Sam said.

An explosion sounded from deep inside the belly of the harbor cavern, almost immediately followed by two others. Several large swells rushed out of the cave mouth, rocking the boat.

"Hold on!" Sam yelled.

Angie grabbed a metal support as the vessel was tossed about.

Nearby, Matte pushed the hurt SEAL aside and frantically tried to regain control of the bucking ship.

The boat continued to move in the rough water. Matte swore. "We're headed for a mine. Jump!"

Matte pulled a cord and a siren began to blare.

Sam grabbed Angie's arm and rushed her to the side of the ship. Frozen by the sight of the bucking sea, Angie resisted jumping, but her sister pushed her overboard as fireworks rocked the night. She let go of her snack as she fell.

The ship blew apart, forcing her through the cold water in an awkward somersault. When Angie finally stopped moving, her ears rang, and she was underwater. *Which way is up?*

She panicked and thrashed about, sure she was going to drown.

CHAPTER 88

Eden
Day Seven

The underwater explosion reverberated through Stryker's chest. His ankle hurt like hell and it took two long seconds to pilot the propeller upward so he could get his head above water. Fearing the worst, his stomach churned.

A stone's throw away, the boat was on fire in the fog, a ghastly flaming hulk. Heat burned his face. Men splashed and yelled. Dark water was everywhere. Stryker paused the propeller and turned in a circle, squinting to see through the mist. There, a woman's hand. Twelve feet away, and groping for air. Angie couldn't swim.

Stryker dove the submersible, and kicked hard. Within a few seconds he'd covered the distance, only to see Angie stop struggling and start to sink.

He swam up behind his wife and put his hands under her armpits Then he drove toward the surface. After breaking through the waves, Stryker pulled away from the fiery boat. The island was crumbling, so he couldn't head there. He shouted for help.

"Hang on!" a disembodied voice responded. "A rescue ship is coming."

A long fifteen seconds later, Sam's face appeared out of the fog. She swam over to him.

"Naval mine?" he asked.

"Yeah, they lost control of the boat when a bullet hit the pilot and the fuel line."

He put his face near Angie's nose. "She's breathing at least."

"That's good, but we need to get her out of the water," Sam chattered.

His sister-in-law needed to get out, too, or both women would freeze to death.

"Are you okay?" he asked.

"Yeah. I had to push her overboard as the explosion ripped the boat. I tried to grab her hand. Missed and belly flopped. Just cold now."

Together they kept Angie's unresponsive head above water until another SEAL vessel arrived.

Stryker yelled, "Medic! We need a medic."

As soon as the SEALs aboard got them on deck, they laid Angie flat on her back. Stryker felt her neck, and found a weak pulse.

A bald SEAL rushed over. "What happened?"

"Blown off the boat," Stryker answered. "She almost drowned."

The serviceman checked Angie's eyes and rolled her onto her side. He slapped her back, gently at first, and then a little harder. Angie coughed, spit out some water, and began to breathe a little deeper.

"Bring me oxygen," he ordered.

Another SEAL hustled into the cabin and reappeared with an oxygen tank, mask, and a space blanket. As the medic placed the plastic oxygen mask over Angie's mouth, inspiring only a few weak breaths, Stryker and Sam exchanged a look of concern.

The SEAL tucked the blanket around Angie. "If she doesn't respond soon, we'll need to cut her clothes off to get her warm."

Stryker held one of Angie's hands, Sam grabbed the other. Sam mumbled a host of fervent prayers.

He thought about all the things he wanted to do with Angie. The things he wanted to say. The life he wanted to live with her.

Just when he was about to give up hope, Angie's eyelids fluttered open. She yanked the mask off her face, and then jerked up, coughing and pounding on her chest. "What are y'all looking at?" she wheezed. "Can't kill me off that easily."

Stryker smiled and they helped Angie to her feet and into the cabin.

The medic shouted after them. "Get her some antibiotics when she gets to shore. It'll keep her from getting pneumonia."

They sat Angie down on a bench next to the wet cult member who'd helped them try to call off the assassination attempt. Stryker put an arm around his wife.

Matte ordered the SEALs to power up the twin engines. Someone brought them all cups of hot coffee and promised Angie dry clothes.

As the boat sped up and away, Stryker hoped that Harper, and that other fishing vessel, had managed to avoid the other mines.

CHAPTER 89

Eden
Day Seven

When Angie could finally stand, a SEAL gave her some dry clothes, and she changed, and then hugged both Sam and Tim for a long minute. After the lovefest, she was given some more food, as her earlier banana snack had been interrupted.

She had never been a big fan of blueberries, but the medic had insisted she break her enforced fast with mild food. The yogurt delight she devoured was almost as heavenly as the kiss she'd shared with Tim before they'd taken down the *comandante* and his men.

She turned to her husband. "Guess your crazy plan worked out okay."

"We need to teach you to swim," he replied with a twinkle in his eye.

"Maybe someday." She shooed him away.

On the back deck, Tim went to talk with Sam and Matte about the possibility of survivors on the island, but Angie doubted there would be anything left other than bodies. What Zola hadn't taken down, the explosions had.

Now that her sister and husband were done mother-henning her, she sat down at a tiny table across from Antonio and handed him a fresh cup of coffee. He looked like an angry wet cat huddled in a blanket. Maybe she could get some answers out of him. "You okay?"

"My calf aches, even with painkillers from the medic. And I think I'm in shock."

She chose her next words carefully. "Your father caused a lot of pain and misery, but I'm sure you'll miss him on a personal level."

"I . . . can't believe he's gone."

"I'm in a little shock myself. It was a helluva week."

"What were you doing . . . before?"

Angie wrapped her hands around the coffee cup, grateful for the warmth. "Before your men kidnapped me and my daughter, and killed one of my best friends?" The words came out stronger than she'd intended, but she didn't care. She felt ticked off.

His eyes turned shadowed and he looked away. "Uh, yeah. Before all that."

"I was at a wedding. Some friends of mine."

He looked at her with sad eyes. "I'm sorry."

"For what, exactly?"

He pulled the soggy old book from under his blanket and put it on the table, staring at it. "For my role in all of it. All the women we kidnapped and killed. The children we sold. Your pain. Your friend's death. I've done much that requires atonement."

Angie was surprised at the apology, but an angry pulse still beat in her temple. "What's in that book of yours anyway? What was behind all this?"

Antonio opened the damp leather binding and fanned through the pages. Rivulets of black water ran off the shiny surface of the table and onto the floor. The writing was an unintelligible swirl of dark smudges. He looked away, then met her eye. "Our oral tradition was first written on stone, and then put on paper by Octavian."

"What did it say?"

"It was pretty simple. Women lie. Their sole purpose should be to serve men and make babies. Their bodies should be hidden to stop temptation, and all effort should be made to erase the history of early goddess worship and promote a singular male god."

"You lied about history because women lie?" Angie asked, frustrated.

"Right," Antonio said, turning his eyes from hers. "Women subjugated men and cannot be trusted with power. Therefore, we used early forms of propaganda to make women, and particularly queens and goddesses, look bad." He took a drink of coffee. "At the same time, we vilified the snake, which had always been a symbol of sovereignty, royalty, and divine authority. Using the Hebrew people, we even tried to destroy all the old temples."

She should have known. That painting of the Garden of Eden in the dining hall. The books in the *comandante*'s office: Machiavelli. Hitler. Foot binding and witches. And all those books about propaganda. Topping it off was their obvious hatred of women. "Your group used *religion* as a weapon?"

He nodded.

Angie took a deep breath to control her tone. "What was in it for your cult?"

"Control the gender of the deity and you have the power."

"The power to do what?"

"Everything. Religious ideology lays the foundation for ethics, values, and most cultural behavior. It's been that way since the beginning of time and remains true today."

Angie grimaced. "You mean like the women in Saudi Arabia who can't drive a little red moped without a body covering?"

"Uh, yes." He cast his eyes down for a moment. "Religious myths teach us right from wrong, especially when we're young. In western culture, we have waged campaigns so that Eve's original sin is repeated in commercials, Sunday comics, and social media memes."

"This is hard for me to get my head around," Angie said. "The cult drove all that?"

"Fish don't understand that they're swimming in water. There was a point in history where the entire balance of the war between the sexes shifted."

Angie nodded, wishing Sam were part of the conversation. "Go on."

Antonio added, "We, the Sons of Adam, known earlier as the Aryans, were behind that shift. Our founder and his tribe came from the north and joined the early Israelites. We selectively promoted the 'women are bad' part of Genesis and have been repeating that refrain ever since."

Angie smiled cynically. "So, with your massive effort to destroy artifacts and temples, combined with your propaganda campaigns, you basically wanted to hide any traces of goddess worship to keep women under the male thumb."

"Yes, that's it in a nutshell."

She took a sip of coffee. It tasted like ash on her tongue. "You manipulated spiritual faith to gain political and personal power. And the implications are everywhere, even today."

"I suppose." He picked up the smudged pages. "I think I'd like to be alone for a bit. Would you mind?"

She wanted to punch him. "Not at all."

He limped out of the cabin and threw the book in the ocean before ducking around a corner. Maybe he truly did feel some remorse.

She took a few deep breaths to get her equilibrium back and thought about how hard she'd had to fight to become CEO. How, in many parts of the world, she still had to travel with a male VP to be taken seriously. And if they ever got her back, how her daughter's choices in life would be so different than Angie's grandmother's opportunities.

Idly, she rubbed at a splotch of ink on the table, which caused her to think about the printout she'd had Antonio get her before Tim had shown up. *What if the member roster got wet?* She jumped up and found her black down jacket, which was a dripping mess on the floor of the boat. Panicked, she reached inside the pocket. She slumped with relief, realizing the interior pocket of the jacket was waterproof. The printed list of cult members would be quite the prize for law enforcement.

When her blood pressure dropped back to normal, Angie popped her head out of the cabin. Most of the crew was on the back deck.

Tim's phone rang and he spoke for a minute before hanging up and pumping his fist. "We did it! Rey stopped the assassination attempt."

All the SEALs roared their approval with arms held high. Men gave each other high-fives and let out war whoops. Tim hooted along with them, obviously savoring the sweet taste of victory.

Sam and Tim put their heads together for a minute, talking, and then they both smiled.

Her sister came over and gave her a hug. "Sounds like Rey's vest saved his life. Thanks for the intel you gathered.

The president-elect's life wouldn't have been saved otherwise."

"Team effort. I'm looking forward to hearing how you found me."

A boat appeared in the fog.

"Later," Sam said.

"Yes."

Their armored military boat pulled alongside the fishing vessel and Angie searched anxiously for Harper's face. There was Reno. Angie waved, a moment of missing Zoe stabbing her heart. Then she saw her daughter, hair held back in a messy braid. Harper was waving wildly and calling out for her and Tim.

SEALs lashed the two boats together and Tim reached over and grabbed Harper, pulling her tight to him. Angie joined him in the hug, feeling safe and whole for the first time since Malachi had died.

She kissed her daughter's cute little head and smiled up at Tim. His eyes sparkled back, full of all the good things she'd missed and had found anew. The last threads of her anger dissipated.

They were going to be okay.

CHAPTER 90

Washington, DC
Post-inauguration

Angie was impressed by the Oval Office and the newly-sworn-in person who sat at the broad desk in front of the presidential seal.

President Aurora was a tall woman with long white hair and piercing blue eyes. Her outfit was simple, but elegant.

"I'm pleased you could join me so that I could thank you all in person," she said, her eagle-eyed gaze moving from Angie to Tim, then onto Director Wolff, Assistant Director St. James, and the rest of the M2 team.

With a gaze like that, Aurora was going to get things done.

Angie's stomach growled. She wondered if she'd ever feel full again. At least she didn't miss the alcohol. Sure, she'd gotten stressed a few times and thought about a drink, but now that she knew it didn't help, she was finding other ways to deal with all the challenges of being a CEO, wife, and mother.

"We appreciate the opportunity to serve you and our country," Wolff said.

The president nodded. "You've served us well. Tell me all about how you found the location of this cult."

Wolff deferred to Tim, who took about ten minutes to share the highlights. During his recap, Angie learned a few new details, as they'd been busy catching up on a personal level and making sure Harper was fine after the ordeal. Most of the prior assassination victims had been female, except the Saudi prince and Sir Wallace, the forward-thinking British PM, which threw them off the trail. The biggest nugget of information for Angie was that her sister had figured out the trickster-type personality of Cleopatra and had used that to find the journal, which led to the map. Clever.

The president turned to Angie. "It sounds like you worked to take the cabal down from inside. Was that planned?"

Angie laughed. "I wish. I'd have stocked up on food like a chipmunk."

"They didn't feed you the entire time?"

"No, ma'am."

The president shook her head. "I'm glad it ended well for you and your daughter." She fussed with some papers on her desk. "You remember the young girl that was sold off while you were there?"

Angie's heart rate ticked up. "Rebecca?"

"Yes. Thanks to your description, we found her in the senator's basement in Alabama. He's being arrested . . ." She looked at her watch. "Right about now. We'll use DNA to reunite her with her mother."

Angie swallowed the emotion that choked her voice. "That's wonderful! What about all the other children, and women?"

"Even though most of the records on the island were destroyed, Antonio has been very useful in helping us, and Interpol, track down the victims and the Mafia bosses who enabled many of the horrible transactions. He knew all the players." Aurora looked at Angie. "The list you brought out was invaluable as well." The president glanced around the room. "You have brought down the world's largest sex-trafficking ring, and I'm impressed."

"What about that deepfake video?" Angie asked.

The president nodded. "Yes, we're taking that very seriously. Deepfake is a new technology, and it sounds like this cult had recruited some of the best minds to work on it. They were a little further along than our cyber teams, but we're focusing additional resources on detecting those types of propaganda." She turned to Wolff and St. James. "Good work. Nice to see Futures Command take care of that threat."

The directors bowed their heads, accepting the compliment.

The president grabbed a pen from her desk and twirled it. "Still, the possibility of civil war is all too real given how polarized this country has become. One of the goals of my administration is to make sure that the information our citizens are getting is not from Russian bots or other bad actors, like this cult you took down. There's been a huge effort from our enemies to undermine facts and we want to reestablish trust. I think the internet giants are with us on this, too."

"What about Saudi Arabia?" Rey asked. "I saw the protests."

"We have an update that has yet to hit the news channels, so please keep it to yourselves. Saudi Arabia has just decided to allow women to stop wearing the burqa, get divorced if they choose, and they can ride on motorbikes without a body covering."

Recalling the incriminating ledger she'd seen in the *comandante*'s office, Angie wondered if Antonio and his memory had anything to do with "encouraging" that progress.

Rey tugged his mustache. "That's a good start."

"It is."

Silence descended on the group for a moment.

Sam raised her hand. Cute. "What about all the artifacts we found in Cleopatra's vault?"

"We're working with Egyptian authorities to help them construct a world-class museum on the site. I have a few friends who are donating large sums of money to the cause. The goal is to establish a place that highlights the breadth of religious history, with the aim of fostering a culture of equality. I've also arranged for you to have a private tour before the find goes public."

"That's wonderful," Sam said.

Angie silently agreed.

The president smiled. "Cleopatra will be remembered now as not simply a beautiful woman who seduced two Romans, but as an intelligent, powerful queen who took down the world's oldest conspiracy."

CHAPTER 91

Kom Butu, Egypt
Two Days Later

As soon as Sam slipped through the line of reporters and ducked down the trap door at the site in Buto, she felt like she'd entered a special new world. She was grateful the Egyptian administration had granted them a few minutes alone with the treasure, before the TV reporters and government archeologists gained entrance.

Stryker, Rey, and Angie began setting up LED lights, and the two archeologists from Taposiris Magna had tagged along for the discovery event. Watching Terrance Richmond and Professor Saber's mouths drop open, Sam knew exactly how they felt: she was tingling like a wide-eyed sixteen-year-old holding the keys of a brand-spanking-new sports car.

The shelves of the storeroom were stacked high with sculptures and scrolls, paintings and that single sack of gold coins. She tsked and exhaled loudly, shaking her head. Those photos had *not* done this place justice.

Rey tugged her elbow and walked over to the four-foot-tall dais. "This is the map. Check it out."

Sam traced the onyx tablet with her finger until Richmond playfully smacked her hand and gave her a set of latex gloves. She put them on, wondering about how the cult's location had originally been found. "Do you think Cleopatra's spy captured one of Octavian's men?"

"Probably," Rey answered. "It would have been tough to follow them to the island unseen."

Angie and Stryker were checking out some of the scrolls. Sam decided to leave Richmond and Saber at the dais.

"Let's look at the sculpture," she told Rey.

They didn't get far before Rey stopped and bent down in front of an exquisite black-granite bust of Cleopatra that sat on a middle shelf, surrounded by gold, marble, and stone statuary. "That Antonio dude sure sung like a canary once we had him behind bars."

"Sounds like he had a come-to-Jesus moment. At least he cleared Ace of any involvement."

"True. But talk about seriously brainwashed. How awful that his father killed his mother."

"I know."

"And can you believe the extent of their organization?"

"Worldwide reach." Sam paused. "Raising the Vatican's unwanted babies. And what about all the hooks they had into political parties, churches, and royal kingdoms around the globe?"

Rey made a sour face. "I knew there was something fishy about that Saudi killing. The prince was pushing hard for change."

They moved to a life-sized statue of Isis, snakes entwined around her arms.

Sam traced the snakes with her gloved finger. "I figured their organization was big. But they had fingers in pies I hadn't even imagined."

"The medieval witch hunts were obvious, once I thought about it. But foot binding, genital mutilation, a war on contraception, and even that weird new incel movement?"

She teased him. "You don't identify as involuntarily celibate?"

"Ha. No, I just haven't found the right babe." His face grew long. "I thought for a minute that Jane and I . . ."

Sam mentally kicked herself. "I shouldn't have brought it up."

"No, that's okay. I'd been wondering what would have made her do it. Try to kill me." He pointed to the base of the stairs. "Right over there."

"Sorry."

He gave his head a quick shake. "Anyway, Antonio told the investigators that he'd helped Jane get off the island when she was young."

"Oh?"

"Yes. She was about to be sold off and Antonio helped her escape to a convent."

"That would inspire some loyalty," Sam said. "And, I mean, can you imagine growing up in that group?"

"No." His face flushed red. "It really ticks me off that Jane lived there for years. And to think Harper almost got sucked in."

Sam was relieved about Harper, too, and felt sorry for all the generations of women whose lives had been touched by the toxic cult. "Antonio should write a book."

As Rey nodded in agreement, Stryker, Angie, and the archeologists joined their conversation.

"How'd you figure it out, Sam?" Angie asked.

"You mean the cult's motive?"

All the heads nodded, wanting to hear.

Sam basked in the limelight. "I figured out they hated women on the swim to the island."

"What clued you in?" Rey asked.

"In the note we found, Cleopatra mentioned a group spreading lies and attempting to rewrite history. The old battleship Stryker and I swam over reminded me that Hitler and his Nazis had also tried to rewrite the past, but the Sons of Adam weren't anti-Jew. They captured *women*."

Rey shook his head. "Sure, but that wouldn't have helped me connect the dots."

"I just put it all together. Cleopatra's snake signs and the comments in her letter. The cult's likely sex-trafficking, and their snake tattoos." She waved her arms and continued. "The type of goods she left behind. These statues and paintings all show God as female."

Rey put his hand on his necklace, thinking. Stryker's eyes were at half-mast, like he was taking it all in. A smile traced the corners of Angie's mouth.

Sam put her hand to her chest. "I'm glad Antonio corroborated my theory, but I'm downright thrilled that the earlier side of religious history will get more exposure." Sam pointed to another lifelike goddess statue, this one in gold. "Like this one. Look at this stunning example that Cleopatra hid away for us to see."

Professor Saber nodded. The woman's face still held eggplant-colored bruises, but there was a light in her eyes. "I can't wait to check the age of these treasures."

Sam turned to the scrolls. They smelled old. Not too much dust, but she was sure she couldn't read a word. "Back at HQ, they were able to decipher more of Cleopatra's journal. Sounds like some of these scrolls may be from the Library of Alexandria."

Rey tilted his head. "The lost library?"

"The very one," Sam answered. "I think this extensive and undeniable religious history is what the Sons of Adam were really afraid existed."

"Because the material will rewrite the history books and potentially change our cultural norms?" Angie asked.

"Exactly."

Rey stepped forward, tilted his head, and squinted at a scroll. "I just don't get all the fuss. These men spent significant time and effort hiding this. What's the big deal? Who cares if people thousands of years ago worshiped female gods?"

"Think about it," Sam replied. "What better way to profit from half the population? Keep them under control and stop them from owning property, voting, or even being able to file for divorce. Make billions from selling their bodies. Just associate your biological sex with the big guy upstairs."

Rey put a hand to his chin and slowly nodded twice.

"Still," Angie said, pointing to the scrolls. "Nothing's going to change overnight."

The others moved over to look at the pile of gold coins, and Sam and Rey were left alone.

"Is their plan starting to make sense?" Sam asked.

He shook his head slowly, eyes wide, arms crossed. "Maybe. My head's still spinning at their audacity." His voice lowered. "It was the ultimate conspiracy."

Sam turned a full circle, looking at the entire cache before putting her hands on her hips. "Quite the salvo in the war between the sexes. It was audacious, all right. But they misjudged the old queen. Then they started losing ground in the first great war, and things really started to shift in the seventies. Technology has helped accelerate change and make things more balanced." With a challenging gaze, she caught Rey's eye. "But I'd wager you still make more money than I do."

He gave his head a fast shake and grinned. "Oh hell no. I'm not taking that bet."

EPILOGUE

Key West, Florida, US

A day after the visit to Cleopatra's vault, Stryker was back home in Key West, relaxing in bed next to his beautiful wife. It was nighttime, and the lamp on the bedside table gave her face a soft glow. He took a deep, contented breath.

Pulling his hand out from the sheet, he dangled a gold necklace in front of Angie. "I got you a souvenir."

She reached up and took it from him, bringing it close to her face to study the fine gold chain and intricately carved amulet. "It's gorgeous. An ankh!"

"Yes. Saber mentioned it's an Egyptian symbol for balance between the masculine and feminine. Thought you might like it."

"I love it!"

Angie held it out, silently asking for help.

He clasped it around her thin neck, pleased his olive branch was a success. "Good. You deserve something lovely out of our failed holiday."

Angie set her Scotch on the table and snuggled into him. "The president made it sound like Antonio was cooperating."

He put his arm around her. "Maybe they won't be too hard on him."

"I was pretty mad at him, but I've been thinking it would've been tough to grow up in that world. It's amazing he helped us out at all."

He stroked her hair. "I saw you talking with him on the boat. Getting to know a strong woman probably helped him realize the cult was morally corrupt."

"Perhaps. I think they *woefully* underestimated Cleopatra."

"Me too. They were victims of their own propaganda. That's why we were able to find the journal instead of Antonio and his gang."

"Exactly. Speaking of old books . . . what'd you think about the origin story from *il canone*?"

"About why the cult started?" Stryker asked. They'd been given some of the prison interview transcripts and that piece stood out.

"Yes," Angie replied.

"Well, if some queen castrated me," Stryker said, feeling squeamish, "I'd be pretty ticked off."

"Did you forget the raping the princess part?"

Stryker held up his hands in a show of mock defense. "Innocent until proven guilty."

Angie smiled. "But even if you were innocent, making *all* women out to be evil? And then creating an elaborate system to punish half the species for thousands of years?"

"Quite the impressive grudge," Stryker noted.

"Speaking of grudges," she murmured, and then pulled away, looking him in the eye. "I'm done drinking. You were right, about all of it."

This was unexpected. He studied her face. Her gaze held the steely determination of a CEO.

Pointing at her bedside drink, he asked, "What about that?"

She handed him the smoky liquid, clinking the ice cubes. "Try it."

"I'm not much of a drinker."

"Try it anyway."

He took a sip. Salt? What he didn't swallow, he spit back into the glass. "Yikes! Is that how it's supposed to taste?"

She chuckled. "Oh hell no. Just screwing with you. Since I hate sea water so much, I added a few tablespoons of salt to the bottle. It's less tempting that way."

He laughed. "I'm glad."

She kissed him then. And what a sweet kiss it was, igniting a passion that he had deeply missed.

The next morning, he still felt the warm glow from connecting with Angie. Harper hadn't let them sleep in, of course, but he'd enjoyed the rest in his own bed.

Angie had gotten up with their daughter and given him thirty minutes to meditate. He felt something delicate shift in his heart, and had relished having a quiet mind and feeling the subtle flow of energy throughout his spine and up through his crown. It was the best meditation he'd had in a year.

After showering, he joined his family at their dining room table, and enjoyed the view of the sapphire ocean outside the wall-length windows. It was a gorgeous Florida winter day. Angie was happily scarfing down a huge plate of eggs, hash browns, and bacon, and Harper was back to wearing a brand-new pair of her favorite jeans with the cat faces on the knees. He tossed their German shepherd, Sierra, a few scraps and could tell from the wildly wagging tail that the dog was just as excited as the rest of them that everyone was home.

"What do you think about making it a beach day?" he asked.

Harper dropped her fork. "Beach day?" she squealed, starting to bounce in her seat.

They both looked at Angie.

"I have some work to catch up on . . ." She trailed off. "But by the look on both of your faces, I think that can wait until tomorrow. Sure, let's go."

While Angie packed a lunch, he loaded up their bikes. Harper helped. He turned to his daughter, who was clean and smelled of strawberry shampoo. "Do you want to take your bike with the training wheels or ride on the back of mine?"

She jumped up and down. "The back of yours!"

"Okay, you got it."

He finished getting the gear ready and Angie joined them, handing him a small cooler, which he strapped onto his bike.

They took off and rode through their quiet neighborhood. The weight he was able to put on his ankle made him feel grateful it was nearly recovered, as was the scalp wound. He reached out and grabbed Angie's hand and they rode like that for a while down the street.

It was a perfect moment.

The beach was close, and a little busy for his taste, but they found a spot on the edge of the crowd and set up a large Snoopy beach towel in honor of Sam, and a few others near their red and white cooler. It took an effort, but he let his towel be messy. Harper got tools to make a sandcastle and went to work in the wet sand about twenty feet away.

Angie squinted. He'd have to ask his engineering buddies at Futures Command for a new pair of GPS-enabled sunglasses.

"Any silver linings for you from this mission?" she asked.

He thought about it for a minute, and stretched his shoulders. Both felt better. "I told Sam about what happened when I was a kid. You know, with my dad."

"You don't like to talk about that."

"I don't. Between remembering all that and missing you both, I realized I'd been pretty hard on you. I can be kind of an ass sometimes, and I'm sorry."

"Accepted. Anything else?"

He felt a wave of sadness wash over him. "I never really let myself grieve for Malachi either. It's tough for me to do sadness. Anger is way easier."

"I understand that. You should try drinking." She laughed.

He laughed too. "I'm glad you've quit. It's nice to have you back. All of you, even the sad parts."

"It's nice to be back." She nodded in the direction of Harper. "I already feel more bonded with you both."

He leaned over the distance between the chairs and kissed her.

"I need your assistance with one thing, though," she said.

"Sure, what can I do?"

Angie grinned. "Help me make another baby."

He chuckled. "With pleasure."

After their conversation drifted into comfortable silence, he decided to go play in the sand with Harper.

She was by the edge of the surf, and he sat down and put his legs in the water. "Looks like a nice castle," he said.

She'd built a circular fortress, which reminded him of Castel Sant'Angelo. Rey had done a great job stopping that assassin.

"It is." She put a moat around it and water rushed in. "It's like my T-shirt."

"I'm glad you like your shirt."

She had a small pink horse in the beach-toy set and set it to galloping around the castle. "Can I be a knight when I grow up?"

Malachi would've liked playing knights and swords. Maybe even pink horses.

"Sure," he said.

"What about a princess?"

"Yes."

"How about a cook in the castle?"

He looked out to sea and saw some kids on a jet ski riding the waves. Malachi would never get to do that. "Yep."

"A doctor?"

"Of course."

"My doctors are boys."

It was a female oncologist who'd told them there was no hope left for their son. "There are women doctors too."

She picked up boy and girl toy figurines and marched them around the castle. Together, the figures filed up to the top of the castle, and then fell into the moat. Harper made the appropriate scream and gurgling noises, killing them off. "A boy at school said when you die, you go visit God, a man up in heaven who has a big gray beard."

Was Malachi in heaven? "What do you think?"

She fixed him with a look as though he were a particularly dull student. "That boy is silly. God doesn't have any parts."

He laughed. "I think you're right."

She wiggled down next to him in the sand, and he put his arm around her tiny shoulders. Looking out over the turquoise sea, he felt his heart grow big and warm. Yet, a single tear ran down his face.

Angie joined them, and they sat like that, arms around each other, joined as a family in grief and joy.

Savoring the moment, Stryker was reminded of the last note in Cleopatra's gold journal. She'd said:

The Sons of Adam have caused generations of suffering. I weep for their destruction of the past, as I cry out against the inevitable invasion of my beautiful Alexandria, with her golden Isis temples and her red-tiled-roof houses. I openly sob for what they will do to the women, and the weak. Your odds are long. Yet, if you somehow succeed in destroying their nest and balancing the scales, know that at long last, as Homer wrote, I am smiling through my tears.

AUTHOR'S NOTE

Dear reader,

This was a fascinating story to research.

Cleopatra had sparkling eyes, a commanding presence, and a rich voice. Her beauty has been debated, but it's clear she had a host of responsibilities as empress of Egypt, including commanding the army and navy, dispensing justice, setting prices, distributing grain, collecting taxes, dealing with foreign powers, building temples, and acting as high priestess. Everyone answered to her. She was the first to introduce coins of different denominations to her populace and was known to be a prankster with a cunning wit.

She was also smart. According to Plutarch, she spoke nine languages, including Greek, Latin, Hebrew, and Troglodyte (Ethiopian), and she was the first Ptolemaic ruler to learn the Egyptian language.

Her city, Alexandria, was ahead of its time. It had automatic doors and hydraulic lifts, hidden treadmills, and even some coin-operated machines. Magnets, wires, pulleys, and other mechanical innovations delighted its citizens.

The party where Cleopatra wowed Mark Antony with knee-deep rose petals was well documented.

Egyptian women of Cleopatra's time were highly educated and legally autonomous. They married and divorced at will. Female workers were often represented in art, or in tombs, selling wares, making offerings, running barges, loaning money, and trapping birds. They owned property and businesses, such as wineries, perfumeries, mills, camels, and slaves. A third of Egyptian property in Cleopatra's time may have belonged to women.

Their female Roman counterparts, however, were supposed to be inconspicuous. They had no legal rights, and carried their father's name while they walked about in public with their eyes cast down. Historians believe Romans were allowed to kill female children, except the firstborn.

An earthquake in the fifth century caused Cleopatra's palace to slip into the Mediterranean Sea. Some of the most famous landmarks of her time have vanished, including the lighthouse, the Library of Alexandria, and the museum. Even the Nile has changed course in the two millennia since she ruled.

Historians continue to disagree over whether Cleopatra's death involved an asp. The cobra, a symbol of power in Egypt that adorned the headdresses of her ancestors for thousands of years, can still be seen on figures of Isis. When Octavian found Cleopatra dead, he called upon a group of *psylli* who were said to be able to remove venom from a snake bite. Historians, however, believe she experimented with deadly poison for some time before her suicide. How she smuggled the poison into the mausoleum remains a mystery. The invention of her spy and the story that followed is from my imagination.

Octavian ruled for forty-four years, twice as long as Cleopatra. He died at the age of seventy-six, having had plenty of time to destroy her statues and rewrite history.

Taposiris Magna is much as described, and at the time of this writing, archeologists are still hoping to find Cleopatra's tomb there. The double portable shaft hoist is fiction.

Scholars believe they have a letter written by Cleopatra that she has signed with "Make it so." The rest of the journal contents in this novel are fictional.

Cleopatra, A Life, by Stacey Schiff, is a wonderful biography if you'd like to read more about the queen. If you're interested in learning more about goddess religions and Isis, I recommend *When God Was a Woman*, written by Merlin Stone.

While the Sons of Adam cult is my creation, I would not be surprised to find a group like it hiding in the shadows.

The history of propaganda, including the war Octavian and Mark Antony waged, is accurate, as are the rendering of Benjamin Franklin's false tales of atrocities and the lies of clergymen in India.

Genital mutilation and sex-trafficking remain massive worldwide problems. According to UNICEF in 2016, two hundred million women have been subjected to genital mutilation, mostly in Africa. Statistics on sex-trafficking are difficult to define due to the nature of the illegal activities, but the International Labor Organization estimates global profit to be over $99 billion. Yes, that's a "B," as in billion. Per year.

The catacombs of the Vatican's unwanted children were based on those that I once saw in Guatemala that were said to have housed the unwanted offspring of the priests and nuns. Like in this novel, those children were kept below ground and died young and deformed from lack of Vitamin D.

I'd take Sam's side of the bet about making less money than Rey. Federal statistics show that women make less than their male counterparts in most professions. In 2021, the median pay for full-time female workers was about 83 percent of that made by their male peers.

Artificial intelligence deepfakes are all too real. According to whichfaceisreal.com (check it out for an eye-opening experience), in early 2019, a graphics hardware manufacturer released open-source code for their face generation software called StyleGAN. The photorealistic software uses an approach in which two neural networks train each other to create images that are indistinguishable from real photographs. State actors and other espionage groups are already using this technology to produce fake photographs and videos.

In August of 2018, the *MIT Technology Review* ran an article with the headline "Defense Department Has Produced the First Tools for Catching Deepfakes," which notes this may be the beginning of a new type of arms race.

A number of military think tanks exist. The Army recently created the US Futures Command in Austin, Texas, and the Air Force has a geopolitical and technological Global Futures Report. They may indeed have a field team to help ferret out threats, but these characters and their mission are my invention.

To add authenticity to the M2 team, I leaned on several memoirs, such as *The Art of Intelligence* by Henry A. Crumpton. In it, he describes the CIA's lack of military firepower and how they worked with the Navy SEALs on missions in Afghanistan, such as Operation Anaconda.

Until next time, I'll leave you with a final quote by Euripides, a Greek dramatist who wrote plays a few hundred years before Cleopatra's time. "Man's most valuable trait is a judicious sense of what not to believe."

Thanks for reading *Cleopatra's Vendetta*.

Lastly, are you curious about my other thrillers? To stay informed about my new releases, and get a behind-the-scenes look at my writing process, email me at Avanti@VanOps.net.

I have several other books available, including the international bestselling VanOps thriller series. All of my novels can be read separately, and each is written in a similar way, with short chapters, global threats, and award-winning style.

Thank you for your kind reviews.

Avanti

ACKNOWLEDGMENTS

This book wouldn't have been possible without my father's influence. He was a proud Marine who enjoyed action-adventure novels and James Bond movies. Amongst other lessons, he taught me to water ski, skateboard, and to shoot a BB gun. I remember him smoking cigars and watching the fragrant smoke curl into the air. Unfortunately, he died too young. I miss him. This book is dedicated to his memory.

As always, Michelle Ocken helped shape the earliest outline, brainstormed along the way, and is the unwavering president of my fan club. She deserves boatloads of appreciation.

The fingerprints of world-class editor Andrea Robinson are all over this book; she took the rough story and spun it into gold. Marianne Fox provided top-notch copyediting, polishing the manuscript to a fine sheen. Talented cover artist David Ter-Avanesyan patiently illustrated the story with a beautiful cover. My publishing house, Thunder Creek Press, does a wonderful job with formatting and distribution.

A special shout-out to my fantastic beta readers: M. Cambridge, Richard Davis, Silvia Pascale, Ruth Thompson, M. Wilcox, K. Mitchell, K. Tunney, Joseph Harrison, J.Z., M. LaRoche, A. Schwietz, C. Thibeault, and C. Hoffman. Each of you helped make this story shine, and I appreciate your contributions.

The generosity of my fellow authors amazes me, and I'm deeply grateful for their kindness and support.

Finally, thanks to all the fans who encourage me to shoot for the moon. You're the best!

ABOUT THE AUTHOR

International bestselling and multi-award-winning author who blends intrigue, history, science, and mystery into nonstop action thrillers

Avanti Centrae is honored to have won nine literary awards.

She finds inspiration from her father, who served as a US marine corporal in Okinawa, gathering military intelligence. Avanti graduated from Purdue University and has spent time in a spectrum of professions, from raft guide to Silicon Valley IT executive. When not traveling the world or hiking in the Sierra mountains, she's writing her next thriller in Northern California, helped by her family and distracted by her German shepherds.

If you'd like to hear about specials for her fans, such as giveaways and deleted scenes, you can visit her web page (http://www.avanticentrae.com). Drop her a line, or sign up for her quarterly-ish newsletter.

For more frequent updates, follow her on Facebook (www.facebook.com/avanticentrae), Twitter (@avanticentrae), or Instagram (www.instagram.com/avanti.centrae.author). Either way, let her know what you loved about *Cleopatra's Vendetta* and what you want more of in the books to come.